POMEGRANATE

POMEGRANATE

A NOVEL

Helen Elaine Lee

ATRIA BOOKS

New York   London   Toronto   Sydney   New Delhi

An imprint of Simon & Schuster, Inc.
1230 Avenue of the Americas
New York, NY 10020

First Atria Books hardcover edition April 2023

ATRIA B O O K S and colophon are trademarks of Simon & Schuster, Inc.

For information about special discounts for bulk purchases, please contact Simon & Schuster Special Sales at 1-866-506-1949 or business@simonandschuster.com.

The Simon & Schuster Speakers Bureau can bring authors to your live event. For more information or to book an event, contact the Simon & Schuster Speakers Bureau at 1-866-248-3049 or visit our website at www.simonspeakers.com.

Interior design by Dana Sloan

Manufactured in the United States of America

1 3 5 7 9 10 8 6 4 2

Library of Congress Cataloging-in-Publication Data
Names: Lee, Helen Elaine, author.
Title: Pomegranate : a novel / Helen Elaine Lee.
Description: First Atria Books hardcover edition. | New York : Atria Books, 2023.
Identifiers: LCCN 2021062146 (print) | LCCN 2021062147 (ebook)
ISBN 9781982171896 (hardcover) | ISBN 9781982171902 (paperback) |
ISBN 9781982171919 (ebook)
Classification: LCC PS3562.E3535 P66 2023 (print) | LCC PS3562.E3535
(ebook) | DDC 813/.54--dc23
LC record available at https://lccn.loc.gov/2021062146
LC ebook record available at https://lccn.loc.gov/2021062147

ISBN 978-1-9821-7189-6
ISBN 978-1-9821-7191-9 (ebook)

For Jordan

For my part, I prefer my heart to be broken.

It is so lovely, dawn-kaleidoscopic within the crack.

FROM "POMEGRANATE"
BY D. H. LAWRENCE

Mama was gone and not gone.

She had disappeared into the hospital while Ranita was at school, getting tamed and stuffed with facts and equations, and there she lay, immobilized by tubes and wires. Ranita had stood beside her hospital bed, watching the blue ventilator bag fill and empty, trying to understand how Geneva Atwater had been felled by something as tiny as a blood clot.

She had seen her dying.

And after the mourners filed past Ranita at the wake, grateful for the phrase that helped them navigate the sudden woe, *sorry, so sorry, so sorry for your loss,* she had stood beside the coffin and stared at her mother, lying in its white satin folds like a parody of a fancy gift box display. The shiny wig Daddy knew she would have wanted, low on her forehead like a helmet. Skin waxy and mouth pressed shut. Eyes closed to her, for good now.

She had seen her dead.

But she heard her mother's voice in the back door alcove, at the table, in the basement. And now she would never please her. Never tell her what she was keeping inside. Never love her more than she feared her.

A month after the funeral, she sat across from Auntie Jessie, picking at one of the casseroles the church ladies kept bringing. She'd brought a book to the table, which had never been allowed, but there were fewer *shalts* and *shalt nots*, now that Jessie had joined Daddy at the house until things eased up. He stretched out work as long as possible and escaped to go fishing on the weekends, and both he and Jessie tried to stave off the bloated gloom with food, encyclopedia facts, artificial cheer. Neither one talked about Geneva. Neither one asked Ranita about her sadness. That was the family way, and what hurt kept haunting like a hungry ghost.

She heard the front door open and close, and there was Daddy in the archway, smiling like a moonlighting jester. Chuckling from his belly like he was launching a magic trick, he pulled a dented orb from a brown paper bag, and Ranita told herself to smile.

She'd seen photos and drawings of pomegranates, but not a real one. "Where'd you get that?" she asked, more edgy than she intended, and his smile wobbled.

"Your birthday getting lost in the shuffle and whatnot, I thought . . . ," he began. She looked away. "Eclipsed" was more like it.

He put the fruit in her hands. "There's no making up for what's past, but this here . . . it's got some surprising and wonderful news buried just inside."

Expecting a whole lot of nothing, her fingers studied the scratched and ordinary skin. He said they should wait to open it; sometimes waiting made things better.

"You hungry, Lennox?" Auntie Jessie asked, getting him a plate and listening as he told about the engine repairs and paint restorations that had filled his day. She kept him chattering while Ranita muted their voices in her head, turning the pomegranate to take in its flat and faded spots, pressing on the sharp crown at the top. And when she was about to get up and wait on something else, he said, "Let's open it."

Ranita peeled back the rind and pried the bloodshot gems from the spongy membrane that held the whole thing together. She was struck silent. Awed by the wild design of it, and by the little bursts of sour-sweet juice from the seeds that turned her fingers red.

There was a whole world, strange and crazy-beautiful, underneath the skin. Layer on crooked layer of ruby crystals. And chambers, like inside a heart.

ONE

February 2019

I live my life forward and backward.

Seems like my body remembers what I can't afford to forget.

I'll be carrying on, trying to choose right, and then the past comes for me, rumbling from my chest into my shoulders, pushing through my neck and up into my head. I try and answer its call, own where all I've been.

Remember, even when forgetting feels like the only mercy.

Four years of captivity, and here I sit on this hard plastic chair, surrounded by cinder block, about to leave Oak Hills. Waiting to be thrown back to the world. And I cannot get still. My knees jackhammer; my feet tap. They've got wills of their own. My interlocking fingers steeple and flatten and steeple.

I try and empty my mind, but my Oak Hills life thunders to the surface and flashes before me, like those shifting pieces of colored glass in the tin kaleidoscope I had when I was six. Damn, really? On my out day, which is stressful enough. I choose a pomegranate and try to see myself holding it, broken open, in my hands. Leathery skin. Pointy stalk. Jeweled seeds.

And I can just about feel the shape and weight of it again when I hear the shout, "Did I say you're free to go?" and I'm surprised to find myself standing up. I look the overseer in the eye . . . why give him a name when all I am is *inmate*? . . . and rein in my anger as I sit my ass back down.

It's true what they say about time slowing down the shorter you get. These last few days have inched by, me hoping and praying I've got it in me to keep doing right. I wait to get back the belongings I came in with, wondering what my stuff will look like to me now. Clothes that no longer fit. Cheap pleather purse full of what? Lip gloss. Suspended license. Empty wallet. Two keys that no longer open anything.

Dear God . . . dear Power Greater Than Me (whoever . . . whatever you are) . . . let me prove I deserve to be a mother to Amara and Theo. Let me handle my business, work my program, stay on track. Keep away from temptation, avoid the people who can pull me down. In here, meetings give you the fellowship that gets you through, and a place to say . . . to remember . . . you're a human with a story that's got a next chapter. Even if the confessing *is* excruciating, I'll find a meeting and go every day if I have to.

Own being powerless and powerful.

Choose right.

Behind the walls, in this concrete desert, everything's regulated and decided for you. All the everyday stuff, the whats and the whens. Wake up and go to chow. Get your meds. Go outside and come back in. Take a shower. Go to sleep. Line up for this. Sit down and wait for that. And all those things that on the outside you do and pay no attention? Behind the walls they're the high points of your day. Makes me feel like that German shepherd of Jasper's. He named him King and kept him in a chain-link corridor. Nobody ever played with him or loved on him. He lived to eat.

Buff that floor. Scrape those plates. Sew labels into these T-shirts, one after another and then some more, and sew American flags for the folks who hate your kind to jab you with. Improve yourself with classes and groups.

All day long you're told what and when and how, and the cost of defiance, too. And you hear the echoes of ancestors, whispering that though the best chance of survival may be submission, that could also be the death of you. And love . . . affection . . . touch . . . the stuff that makes your heart keep beating? Contraband. Now who, I ask, can keep alive that way?

Nothing much grows in here unless you go hard against the script. To keep alive, you've got to choose what you can, small though it may seem. Imagine yourself past the razor wire. Notice those trees and birds way in the distance. Look at the sky and picture it whole. You've got to see yourself free from the demon that rides you, believing something new, something clean, can happen, after all. Behind the walls, nothing's small. And choosing, it's something precious, and it means life just might have some mystery in store for you.

I choose you, Maxine once told me, *and you're against the rules.*

Yesterday, at the end of my little leaving party, I stood there as she left the dayroom before me. All of my well-wishers were there. Gwen and her latest boo. Avis, crocheting her endless blanket. Eldora and the family she builds and mothers in here. Even my new cellie Keisha came, though she still thinks she can do her time solo. We ate the makeshift treats and canteen snacks they all chipped in, and everyone said what they'd do if it was them getting out. And when it was over, I watched Maxine's proud, upright back fade away.

Tender-tough Maxine. Along with her free-world walk and the way she breaks down the politics of just about everything 24/7, her ink and her no-nonsense way and her legal know-how, there's a world of other stuff inside. She can talk up pomegranates and make me taste them. She can conjure grass or clouds or cornfields, tell Chesapeake riverbanks and make me feel the current and the muddy floor.

I wanted to run after her, call out to her, touch her. *I love that back*, that's what I was thinking. *Its moles and scars. Its tats. Its defiant pride, no matter what she's been through.* Like most of us in here, the only sleep she knows is broken.

Last night, I sat in my cell with the card everyone signed and the little in-spite-of gifts from the leaving party, so sweet and painful, and started counting down the last bit of time I owed.

I could feel Keisha's crying shake the bunk above me. Mostly we look away to give a little privacy. This time I stood and asked, "You alright?" Like usual, she didn't answer. I'd seen her with a letter earlier and figured it must have been the kind that tells you something bad, maybe the kind that says you've been foreclosed.

I made my voice as gentle as possible. "Word from home?"

She sat up, pulled the envelope from the covers, and ripped it up. Then she threw the pieces to the floor, oozing angry and bitter, and said, "Where the fuck is home?"

I didn't even know what to say to that. Maybe it's a good question for most of us in here, but I couldn't answer and I couldn't just go back to my bunk, so I stood there looking at the photos she'd stuck up on the wall with toothpaste. And I knew it was risky, but there's one sure way to get a woman to open up.

"That your baby girl?"

She nodded, wiping her eyes with her sleeve. "Tyeisha. She's almost three."

I was relieved. Pained, too, I'll admit it, when she said, "She's with my moms." Some folks have mothers beside them through their thick and thin. Then I asked about her girl. Keisha kept her answers short, but

I saw a light in her eyes come on. "She knows her letters and numbers. Her favorite color's green."

She jumped down from the top bunk and walked across the torn pieces of her letter to get to the stingy window where she likes to stand, looking out at the sky. Something in me wanted to make her face reality, tell her even if she could find the drinking gourd up there, she wouldn't be following it to freedom. And part of me wanted to hug her to me like she's one of mine. *But I'm out of here tomorrow*, I reminded myself, getting my feelings in check as I turned away.

Trying to ignore her, I got ready to rise up and go, come morning. Took my hair out of the cornrows I've been wearing these last few years, thinking on how I tripped when I first got here. No relaxers. No extensions. Barely any hair products at all. Easiest thing to do is either learn to braid or figure out something you can trade to someone who knows how, turn in your weapons, and forget about cute. I sat on the edge of my bunk, picking out my braids with the end of my comb, and it felt good as I freed up my hair, though when it was all loose I couldn't help thinking how Mama would have shut her eyes to the sight of me either way, cornrows or my wild kinks, and did my best to smooth it back into an Afro puff.

I gathered up my worldly possessions, starting a pile on my bunk. Laid out my second-string beater sneakers, T-shirts, socks, two of the unsexiest bras you ever saw, and a week's worth of high-waisted gray cotton underwear you can't really call panties. Comb and hair grease. Wounded dictionary. I unfolded the loose-leaf paper Eldora pushed into my hand today and my eyes teared up as I looked at what she'd shared with me from last summer's garden plot, though she had so little to spare: pale discs from her bell peppers and zucchini seeds, smooth and eye shaped.

I'd already returned everything I'd borrowed from the donated library that made up the one cubic foot of reading and writing material allowed, and passed on my flip-top tuna and ramen noodles. Traded envelopes and paper for extra socks. Put aside my extra toilet paper for Keisha, along with the little bars of soap that made me itchy and ashy. Tossed my shower flip-flops. And that was it, what I had to show for my Oak Hills life. I was already wearing my good sneakers, my thermals, and the windbreaker that passes for a winter coat.

Looking at my list of Boston-area NA meetings before adding them to the pile, I tried not to be cynical about the names: Freedom Express . . . Clean and Proud . . . The Solution . . . South End Miracles. I read through the affirmations I'd put on index cards, remembering how embarrassed I was at first by their corniness, certain that Jasper was having a good laugh at them, at me, from the afterlife. The cards and letters and artwork from Amara and Theo. The program from Daddy's funeral service. And the kites Maxine's left for me over the last two and a half years. I keep that cache inside the Bible a missionary prison volunteer gave me. The little paper messages that gave me and Maxine another way of touching, and added some mystery and discovery to a world of regulations and taboos.

No sacred space in here except the ones we create, we made do and left them behind the dayroom microwave, where even if they were found, they could not be tied to us. Milagros. To be added to the free things list we make out loud, and the one I keep on my own.

Maxine got me plugged into recognizing and naming the things that cost nothing and don't depend on permission, the things available to everyone, present and past tense. Future, too, one hopes. The smell of new-cut grass. Skipping stones. A curl of white birch bark. Eyelash kisses. Reading. Looking. Walking, even if it's only round and round the Yard.

Next I added my notebook log of everything I did to keep in contact with my kids. Once I got my balance, I started putting it all down: every phone call; every card and letter; every visit Daddy, Auntie Jessie, and

Auntie Val made here with them; every call to the caseworker, whether it got answered or not; every paper filed with DCF.

Then I pulled their photos off the wall, trying not to be vexed by the curled, worn edges, and spent some time with each one. The baby pictures, school photos, backyard snaps, and the one we posed for during visitation one year in, with the tropical beach background. Amara's 13 now and Theo just turned 8, and it's six months since I've seen them. Like always, I saw how much Amara looks like me, and wondered how hard that's been. People used to say, *Girl, you spit her out*, and I'd smile, like it was some kind of trick or spell I'd managed, while hoping things would turn out different for her. Same wide nose. Same full lips I got from Mama, who told me I could learn to hold them in and "minimize" them, like she had. They got me teased when I was little and cruised before I was even grown. Same freckles and eyes that shift from green to brown, depending on who knows what . . . my contrary mood, that's what Mama said . . . mud with a bit of algae, in my opinion, though I've heard them called by fancier names.

Black folks, we're still obsessed with eyes and skin color and hair, and all my life people have either praised my eyes or decided I think I'm the shit for having them. Whatever. It's not like I went to Walmart and picked them out. We all know what they come from: Ownership. Possession. Rape. Anyway, I hope Amara uses hers for seeing.

In Theo's face, like always, I saw Jasper. He's got his father's sharp nose, which people love to focus on . . . *dark, but keen featured*, Mama would say . . . and his deep plum skin, instead of the russet brown of mine and Amara's. Like Daddy's, his eyes are dark and sparkly. But sometimes when I look at my boy I feel like his father's still among the living, and I work at recalling what drew me to him, the pluses, instead of the minuses.

Wondering just who my kids are now, and what it'll take for them to forgive me, my heart started banging around, and I laced my fingers together to stop them from shaking, then fished my cards from the pile to play some solitaire and thought some love over to my kids across the miles.

I pictured my boy, tender and easy to cry, asking his nonstop questions. *What are dogs feeling when they bark? Why aren't the double o's in "look" and "loon" pronounced the same? Why are leaves green?* And Amara, asking whether thinking you can do something makes you better at it, why her teachers talk down to the students in her class, whether a family is something you're born into or something that's decided. I hope Val and Jessie at least try and answer the questions about facts. *How far away are the planets? What do you call a dolphin's tail?* I know the harder ones are the problem. *What does "mother" mean? Which fights are worth it? How can you tell where you belong?*

Keisha left her post at the window and climbed back up. She went still, slipping under, and I closed my eyes. Sleep would be hard to come by, and I prayed to get through one last night and morning without a shakedown storm.

Heartsick at losing Maxine as I gained my freedom, I tried to focus on the blessing of having been with her at all. And then I named what I was grateful for, moving from macro to micro. I had someone who'd loved me right. People on the outside who'd never stopped showing up. Children I could still earn back. One thousand one hundred and fifty-nine clean days, but who's counting? A novel I'd just finished that was echoing through me. Trees that would soon be in reach. And the photo of Amara, torn down the middle by a shakedown boot heel, had survived. I had mended it, and here it was, on the pile right beside me.

Out loud, I said, "I don't know their favorite colors," speaking to I-don't-know-who, just trying to get a sounding in the big, wide dark. I expected no answer from Keisha and got none, but I could hear her breathing and it was a comfort, that thread of body music just above my head.

Then morning came. The sky faded to stubborn gray. The lights came on and the morning noise kicked off, and when they hadn't come to set me free I went to chow and couldn't eat a bite. Looked for Maxine, but she didn't show.

Two COs came for me soon after, barking orders to get my things and come with them. Like usual, they looked at me like I'm trash, even though the places they come from were at least as shitty and broken as the ones that grew most of us in here, even though they and theirs know the same rung where we've bottomed, turnkey being the other path out of the basement so many of us know.

And now I'm waiting to be told I'm free to go.

I stop trying to call up my pomegranate. It's gone, for now. So I start my silent chant: *Get to Auntie Jessie's. Meetings. Job. My own place. My kids.* I can do it. I'm never coming back.

My two aces are my aunties. Daddy's baby sister, Val, she got a job in Boston and moved here to help. Since he died she's been carrying the whole thing by herself. The house, the kids, they're off-limits to me. And she's in charge.

And big sis Jessie, she's letting me crash with her for a couple months, even though she just got out of the rehab from her stroke. I can stay until my cousin Gil gets back from Afghanistan, where the warring never seems to end. Jessie, she stood by me when I screwed up, disappeared, relapsed. Until she didn't.

She drew a hard line with me, but she kept on showing up for Amara and Theo. And once I had 30 days clean, she came to visit, along with Daddy and the kids. Sent me cards and photos and novels from Amazon. Put money on my books, adding to my 72-cents-an-hour "job" doing laundry, cleaning, flag sewing, kitchen work, minus the half taken out for forced savings and the deductions for medical fees, account activity fees, disciplinary violations. Jessie said she'll give me shelter, and I know the deal. Long as I'm working my program, I can stay.

Soon as they say so, I'll be walking through the gate, a year since they let me out to say good-bye to Daddy. Wake or funeral, I had to choose and picked the former, unsure I could keep my shit together for the funeral, arriving in church with escorts, everyone's eyes on me. At least I had a few quiet, private minutes with Daddy during the viewing at the funeral home. Soon, when I can bear it, I'll visit his grave.

Looking at him lying in his coffin, I thought he seemed peaceful, unburdened. Unlike Mama, who seemed to still be raging, still saying no to me. Now I've lost Daddy, who said yes even when he shouldn't have.

I was swamped by sadness as I stood beside his body, and by anger, too, the general kind, at all the things: the world, the way things work, the "carceral state," my lot. And at Daddy, too, I admit it, for leaving me. Before I walked away from his casket I closed my eyes and imagined slipping my two-year sobriety chip into the pocket of his suit.

Jessie and Val were standing at the door to the viewing room, exhausted. Wrecked. Greeting the neighbors and friends from work and church who filed in, and at least I was spared making small talk about what felt like the end of the world. Amara and Theo sat together in the corner, looking numb and out of reach, blaming me, no doubt, for taxing Daddy till he broke. I hugged them, but their arms hung limp. They were going through the motions with me. Daddy, the backbone, he was the hard loss.

The aftershocks still hit, and the sadness body-slams me again and again, just when I think my mourning is done. Feels like a part of me now, like the rainy-weather ache of a mended bone. We're all still standing, but I can't help worrying about the TPR law. Termination of Parental Rights, if you can believe that, and if that ever does go down, I'll be thinking on joining Daddy, and I know ways, fast and slow, to do that.

I get $75 gate money in cash and a check for the $264.57 in my account, and peek in the bag they give me, the stuff I came in with four

years ago. I keep the keys and throw the purse in the trash. It's winter
in America, I'm making a new start, and along with the windbreaker
they let me keep, my lightweight sweats and T-shirt will have to get me
home. They show me where to change and I force my expanding hips
into them, then return my DOC scrubs, grab the bag with my belongings, and hold on tight to my release sheet, my hands shaking so bad the
papers flap like white flags: *Okay, I still surrender. Whatever you say still goes.*

I try and imagine myself singing, but seems like that's over. Lost in
the crash that landed me here.

I try and see myself down the road in my own cozy apartment, but
the hallway's as far as I usually get. I try to forget the room where I last
holed up, tornadoed with covers and clothes, unwashed dishes and pizza
boxes and the bitter, vinegar smell of cooked-up drugs. And if I'm not
careful with my imagining, my before blocks out everything that might
could happen, pushing it all together into a shakedown pile, and I'm in
the middle, yelling, *Remember me? There's a sista in here, trying to breathe her
way into tomorrow. Remember me?*

I stand up, like I'm told. And as I approach the gates, the CO who's
opening them up gives me a last bit of scorn: "Hasta luego; see you back
here soon." I throw some shade his way and walk through. And here it
is, what I've been wanting and fearing. Freedom.

TWO

Waiting for the taxi that'll take me to the bus, I stand here shivering in the February cold, looking at the walls and razor wire from the other side now, blinded by the sunlight. One hand shielding my eyes from the glare, I whisper: "Good-bye."

Good-bye to the funk of captivity and fear. Good-bye to my little tomb. Good-bye to everyone who's still fighting to keep alive in there. Good-bye to Maxine. A sudden wind blows sandy grit in my face. I close my eyes and look away.

I keep checking my cheap plastic watch and here's the taxi, pulling up. I climb in, and the ride's a blur of barren trees, frozen ground and tire tracks, grass, and plants that are sleeping or dead.

When the taxi lets me out, I run to catch the bus, and after the door unseals with a big air-freshener-on-body-funk exhale, I step up and say hello to the brotha in the driver's seat, like I was taught. I find a window seat in the back and settle in, remembering all at once how much I hate February in Massachusetts, though it's all I know. Me and my cousin Judy used to call it the tunnel month, when it's hard to even imagine the light of March and April up ahead. Gray, everywhere you look. Strip malls rush by and then there's concrete highway all around, and I lean against the window and try to slow down everything that's rushing through my head and breathe.

Finally, I see Boston, coming into view. The paint-dripped gas tank and choppy harbor, South Bay, where Jasper landed twice. And now we're in the Big Dig tunnel, where I always panic over what'll happen if there's a crash down here in the wall-to-wall traffic and help can't reach us.

When we resurface, my heart's knocking like an old radiator. Traces of dirty snow line the streets and people hurry to wherever they're going, scowling, hunched against the cold in their puffer coats. We pull onto a dark South Station bus ramp, winding around to the gate, and soon as I get off I'm drowning. Voices and phones ringing and music blaring. The crush of people pulling bags that bump and clack across the tiles. Disembodied announcements of arrivals and departures. The smells of exhaust, burnt coffee, perfume, piss, and food. The colors, swamping me. I look for the emptiest spot I can find and sit for a minute to collect myself.

While I'm watching people going in and out of the bathrooms, I see a woman leaning on the wall as she tips out, and I feel the edge of a muddy memory. Thank God I can't recall exactly what went down, but I can smell the grime and misery, I can feel the tiled floor and see stalls tagged with tributes and insults, and I suspect I did some time in there on my knees.

I turn away and try to keep my head above my before. Fuck. I'ma have to start crocheting again, or take up knitting . . . something that'll keep my hands busy and my mind quiet. A hobby where you end up with something lovely you can hold and feel, that you actually created. Right now, though, I'm looking, looking, looking at everything swirling around me, wondering is everyone looking at me, or past me. Either way, I'm a musty smell, a stubborn stain. Down-and-out, pitiful, on the verge of doing wrong or about to burst into angry protest that our lives matter.

Most folks look unhappy, hostile, checked out, even though they're walking around free, and man, that brings me down. I haven't figured out how Maxine keeps her eyes open without being flattened by what she sees.

It takes me 15 minutes, but I get up and take the escalator down, seeing myself through the eyes of the people riding up, and Lord, if I don't stop this train of thought, I'll never make it to Jessie's; I'll just hit the corner and opt out before I even try, settling on the sidewalk like a torn balloon.

At a meeting last week, someone raised her hand and shared that tale. Soon as she was gated out, she rode back to the city and went directly . . . didn't pass go, didn't collect a cent . . . to Mass & Cass. Never even made it home. And Aquila, she OD'd before she even found a place to stay. And just last week I saw Caprice Johnson, back inside after six months. "Hey, Cherry," she said, using the name I've tried to leave behind, and asked me where she could get her high on.

I climb onto the city bus, where the heat's blasting and folks are packed in tight and trying to lose themselves on the Facebook and Instagram scroll, or listening to music, earbuds in. Me? I've gotta use pure mental power to refuse the smells of perfume and shampoo, sweat and sour breath and wet wool, the humming and sniffling and coughing, the bouncing legs and nervous finger tapping, the cleavage and armpits and unfamiliar patches of skin all up in my personal space. I try and shut down my senses, and here I am, taking a ride through my before.

Even with a blindfold I could get to Jessie's. The streets are talking to me, and it's a good thing the bus is noisy enough to muffle what they're saying, since most of it is not good. I wish I could get lost, but I swear, I'm circling the drain of my past.

And then, thank God, I remember something good. I pass a stretch of elms and see myself at 13, riding free on the black BMX bike Daddy got me, Lori Watson beside me on her aqua-blue cruiser for a minute, and then solo. I said I was going to the library and took off, feeling like motion itself, trying to see what was out there beyond the world I knew. Broke my curfew and ignored the fact that some parts of the city had become war zones, crack claiming some folks and bullets, others. And rode on, knowing I'd have to take my punishment later, in keeping with the talent for trouble Mama said I had. Underfed, punished, silenced, I lied and defied Mama to get outside. She was clueless, anyway. She had no idea where was safe and where wasn't.

The bus chugs on, and finally, a seat opens up. I sit, balancing my sorry little bag of stuff on my lap, and turn away from the crotches in my line of sight while I try to conjure something good. Leaning back against the cloudy window, I think of Daddy doing his favorite thing: fishing at Blue Hills in the pre-dawn dark. I went with him twice. The first time, after Mama died, was grim, but placid. The second was a full-on disaster.

Can I get there, from this landlocked state of mind? I focus in and try to bring him close, but instead of the fishing trip redo I'm after, I get the one I've tried to forget. There I am next to Daddy at the water's edge. Unfree, Black, and 21. No prospects. No direction. No occupation, besides Jasper. Just bent on wildness and aimless resistance, while Daddy tries to break down his fishing code.

The smell of Popeyes pulls me back to the present, praise God, but I turn to see a teenage couple wrist deep in chicken, which brings on other memories. Too many workdays and late-night runs after too many things I'm trying to leave behind.

The body, it remembers.

I never did go to Blue Hills with him after that second failure, but Daddy kept on fishing, and he took the kids. "I'll be there till the day I die," he said once when I called from Oak Hills. "And if you ever put me in a home, I'll just escape and drag my heart monitor *and* my oxygen tank to the water's edge, need be."

"That would drive the fish away." I laughed, but I could picture the green blip of his monitor in the morning darkness. His heart, seen by all the living things as they wakened.

I'll take them fishing, Daddy. And soon as I can, I'll buy a pomegranate in your name. And instead of tearing into it, I'll try and wait. Then open it real slow, catching my breath at the seeds before I close my eyes and go back with you to the reservoir, where everything's quiet and I'm awake enough to hear the good news beating underneath our ordinary Black skin.

I get off and walk the last couple blocks to Auntie Jessie's, cursing the cutthroat wind that tears through my flimsy jacket, then wait till she buzzes me in. And here I am at her door, mustering up the strength to knock. I take a deep meditation inhale to ground me in the here and now, and do it. "Coming, just you hold on!" she calls out, and I wait, so nervous I'm trembling, until she gets the door open. And here she is, standing with one hand on her walker and holding out the other to welcome me.

I haven't seen her since before her stroke eight months ago, and I can't believe its toll. She's bent and thin, and her freckled face has been hollowed out and pulled south. The short 'fro she's always worn is mostly gray. But she's got on her reddish-plum lipstick. Never leaves the house without it, says it "livens up" her face. And I can still see the pride and grit in her eyes that always did make me respect her, even . . . maybe especially . . . when I was messing up.

Soon as I step through the door, I lean over the walker to hug her, careful not to make her unsteady. And here's the Auntie Jessie smell of cocoa butter lotion that I didn't even realize I've missed.

"Ranita," she says, with the slight slur I've noticed in phone calls. It is so good to hear my name in her mouth, however it comes out.

"Come," she says, shuffling into the living room, "put your things down. There's a towel in the bathroom for you, if you need to freshen up." I thank her, go in, and shut the door, grateful beyond belief to be using a private bathroom. The powder-blue tiles I remember are a comfort, but it pains me to see the shower chair and safety bars and commode. I hope I look and smell okay. I did wash up this morning, but I check my pits just in case, and think about spraying myself with her cologne. No. Not unless it's been offered. My hair, rough and scraped back into its ponytail puff, does not look good. My clothes are dingy, but I know they're clean. I wash my hands and face, reminding myself that Auntie Jessie's is one place where maybe I don't need to pretend.

When I come out, most of what I notice is familiar. I smell Gonesh No. 6, the incense she's always liked, and see the blue microsuede couch where I've crashed over the years, grateful that it can't talk. The wood and glass coffee table whose corners she cushioned with foam, so the kids wouldn't hurt themselves. The brass shelves with her African violets and framed family photos, and her collection of elephants made from glass, pottery, stone, wood, that she let the kids line up and march across the room. And like always, she's got a jigsaw puzzle set up on a card table. This one's a coral reef full of divers and fish.

The TV's new, and so's the navy velour La-Z-Boy. There's the framed portrait of Daddy, who's always been her fontanel. And a small cracked, faded one I don't recall seeing, where he's eight or nine, sitting on a porch swing, arm around a shaggy dog. Looking closer at his soft face, I'm slammed by a wave of loss.

Jessie's watching me from the kitchen doorway. Her face always has announced her feelings and it's filled with love as she says, "I found that over at the house, in a shoe box with his boyhood trinkets. Rabbit's foot, fishhooks, Cracker Jack prizes, and whatnot."

I turn away and wait for the grief tide to go out, and she shifts the subject to Gil painting one wall periwinkle blue when he was home on his last leave. "You know that's my color, and even if I had to settle for white everywhere else, the landlord let me paint one wall, long as I promised to make it white again when I move out. We do what we can, right?"

"Right."

"You hungry?"

Black folks always ask this right up front. If we can't do anything else for you, we will try and feed you. And for me, that's been double-edged.

Jessie and Daddy always were focused on food . . . what we'd just eaten, what we should cook next, what was on sale, the best way to season chops and make gravy and keep a baked ham juicy, what sauce to make, what fruit was at peak season, whether the corn was sweeter that June or the year before. They couldn't seem to let up on cooking and eating, or on feeding me. It was a comfort you could count on to soothe, and a way to change the channel. Listening to Jessie chatter on now about what she thought about making and did make, I wonder, not for the first time, what she and Daddy and Val missed out on, growing up.

I am hungry, in more ways than she would ever let me tell her.

The kitchen table's loaded with roast chicken and dressing, greens, real mashed potatoes, and iceberg lettuce salad. And I see her famous 7-Up pound cake on the counter. It smells like home in here, and soon as I sit down I realize we're using Mama's precious china plates. The years I spent staring at these plates during long, painful dinners come back to me. After she died, they stayed safe in her glass-front showpiece cabinet, and Val must have given them to Jessie when Daddy passed.

Jessie takes my hand and it's time to say grace. Head bowed, I work to be here, and feel the current of her blessing move through me. I'm grateful. For breathing free air. For this custom. For this woman, known and unknown to me, who's been there across the years.

I put a mountain of food on my plate, and then I can't seem to get started. I put a forkful in my mouth and have to force myself to chew. She's watching me, wondering what's up, worried there's something wrong with the food, and I want to tell her what it is, but I'm not sure how to sort it out enough to say it. Picturing the cost and effort it took to get this meal made, I feel awful, and tears are ready to spill. I put my fork down and say, "I'm sorry, Jessie. . . . All this . . . it smells and tastes delicious; it's just that . . ."

Her face is a closing door. "It's okay. No need to say another word."

"It's me, not the food, Auntie Jessie, I promise. . . . The thing is . . ."

"It's okay," she says, going hard at her potatoes. "Not everything needs explaining."

"But . . ." It's all I manage to get out. The past, this day, this crossroads, it's just too many things. I jump up to make some tea and turn away from her hunched back as I busy myself with filling the kettle and getting out the mugs and tea bags, waiting for the water to boil.

I didn't starve at Oak Hills. My tight jeans tell that truth. But even though chow amounted to the three main events of the day, it was joyless, except for the fellowship you sometimes got while trying to fill the stomach hole. The food was stank. And like everyone else, I ate from the canteen as much as possible.

Inside, folks talk endlessly about the meals and treats they had when they were free, the barbecue, the rice and beans, the banana pudding and red velvet cake that are lost to them. Their faces glow as they remember out loud how food means gathering. Food means family. Food means celebration and being close and pleasure. And I remembered right along with them, telling about strawberry preserves and buttery corn bread and stewed chicken that fell off the bone. But food is complicated. If Daddy and Jessie were bent on feeding me, Mama was in charge of keeping all bodily appetites in check. Have a taste, but not too much. Keep your liking small. Food may be abundance and kinship, but it also means a world of other things.

By the time I sit back down, I've decided to press past Auntie Jessie's uneasiness and try to tell her something about going from captive to free in the space of a couple hours.

"Appreciate you," I say. "I'm thankful to be here and I'm thankful for the love you put into this meal, and for what all it took to plan it and buy it and make it."

She looks up from her plate and nods.

"But. And. For the last four years, the chow line has served up a stretch of tasteless, processed grub. Fried and greasy everything . . . veggies canned and boiled down to mush and wounded fruit . . . meat you can barely identify . . . carbs to fill us up. What passed for food at Oak Hills had next to no flavor or nutrition. And it was made and served with zero love." I decide not to mention the roaches and rodents that ate alongside us.

She's looking at me, and her eyes are reflecting my trouble, even without those truths. Damn. I didn't want my homecoming to start off like this. I pause for a minute and then try and sum it up in a way she'll find bearable. "Jessie, it's hard to go . . . in what feels like a minute . . . from so little to so much."

"Nita. I just wanted the meal to be a bright spot, a good thing."

"It is. It is good. . . . It's just that . . . sometimes it's hard to receive when you've been poor."

Her back looks a little more bent, thanks to me, and she struggles to her feet to get the pound cake, I feel shitty, and she waves away my offer of help. And as I watch her shuffle on her walker, my eyes go to her feet. Jessie's always been plump . . . pleasingly so, her second husband, Cedric, used to say . . . whether on a diet and at war with food, or in full surrender to it. I don't think I've ever known a woman, especially a Black one, who was happy with her looks. And she was right there with the rest of us, no matter that she was sexy and got plenty of attention from men. The only part of her body she didn't find fault with was her legs. They were toned and shapely, and she showed them off with short skirts and dresses, and fabulous kicks.

Daddy used to call her Imelda, and tell me about the latest ones she'd bought when he came to visit. She had high heels, wedges, mules, boots, and usually in colors that matched her outfits to a T. I remember putting them on and trying to walk in my favorites, red patent leather strappy sandals, when I was little. And looking at the shoes she's got on now, sensible, boxy, black orthopedic flats with rubber soles and Velcro straps, makes me sadder than I could say, if saying were allowed.

I take a forkful of chicken, and before I know it I'm shoveling it in, until I notice that Jessie's back at the table, looking more worried than she did before. That's me, good old all-or-nothing Ranita, no medium setting, just on or off. *Slow down*, I tell myself. *This is not a contest at the Topsfield Fair.* I try and take my time, savoring this plenty.

After we have pound cake I clean up the kitchen and she goes to the living room and puts on the TV. "I need to see what those Republicans are up to," she says, and while I try and tune out the loop of awfulness, Jessie tunes into every detail, even the third time she hears it. Every day tops the last one in crazy and terrible, and it seems like this is the bad news she can stand.

I'm focused on the framed school pictures on her shelf. I've got the same ones, but something about the way they're up there, in order, makes me feel like I'm watching my babies get older, photo by photo, and seeing what I've missed. I want to ask about them, but today of all days I'm trying to keep my balance.

I stretch out on the couch and Jessie hands me the throw I made for her that's just like the one I've got. After getting clean, I made one for everyone I knew. I was a crocheting fool, until I got fed up with the sameness of the stitches and the yarn no one on the outside wanted that they had in spades. Burnt orange, the color in the crayon box that's always sharp. With knitting, you can do cable and popcorn stitches, fancy patterns and whatnot, and make sweaters and mittens and hats, but the needles, ready-made weapons, are not allowed inside. I drift off, picturing myself knitting a gorgeous purple sweater, and wake up panicked that I've missed my out date and I'm back behind the walls.

I wish I could tell someone what this moment I've planned and waited for feels like, but I'm not sure why I should get to, seeing how everyone else has suffered behind my bad.

Jessie pushes down her La-Z-Boy footrest and says, "I'm ready to turn in. First, though, I want to go over the house rules. You're welcome here until Gil gets back, which could be as soon as two months from now, but might be longer. You're welcome to what all I've got, including food, until you get some money coming in and can contribute. You do your part with the cooking and cleaning. You work your program and take care of your business and don't take me through any drama. No smoking. No company. No partying. Zero tolerance for drinking or drugging. You got me?"

"Jessie, I . . ."

"Don't talk. Just do. Actions speak louder . . ."

"I know, I know. Than words."

"We don't have to solve everything tonight. You go on and fix the sofa bed so you can get yourself a good night's sleep."

I try and help her get up from the chair, but she refuses, telling me she's got to be able to do for herself, and then shows me the sheets and blankets and pulls a parka from the closet.

"You'll need something warmer than that windbreaker to get through the rest of February and March. And maybe you can use this," she says, showing me a backpack. "Tomorrow we'll see about getting you more clothes, see if some of the things I can't get into any longer will fit you."

"Jessie, before you go . . ."

She stops and bumps her walker around to face me, and I can see how beat she is. She probably expects me to try and hustle her.

"Nothing. Just sleep tight."

She nods, turns around, and before I know it she's in her room.

The sudden emptiness and longing remind me of those times inside when you've just been broken open. Maybe you had no choice in the matter. Or maybe you cracked your own chest and took your heart out, hoping to get it seen or hand it over to another human for a minute. And then, for one reason or another, that's over. And you've got to return it to the shelter of your rib cage and put yourself back together so you can resume acting fierce.

I don't have to be fierce for anyone tonight. I fold up the crocheted throw. It's ugly as hell, I might as well own it, but my auntie's nothing if not loyal. I pull out the bed and bury my face in the soft sheets she set out for me, inhaling the clean, powdery smell, and strip down to my thermals, wishing I could retire them for some real pajamas, soft flannel with pictures of something lighthearted on them, bunnies or flowers or clouds. Things take on the smell of where they've been, and these long johns are giving off cut-rate industrial detergent and the common wash load. They smell of fear and longing, mine and everyone else's who's trying to survive Oak Hills.

When I drape my clothes over Aunt Jessie's recliner, the keys I got back this morning tumble out. The brass one I wish to God I didn't recognize, and the silver one that stands for something I'm praying to get back. I grip them, feeling the notched edges dig into my hand, and put them in the inside pocket of my new backpack.

The full-sized mattress feels huge. And unmoored. No, I'm not missing the hard, slim bunk that's bolted to the wall, but I feel uneasy out here in the middle of the room. Looking at my bag, way over there in the corner, I decide to bring my few belongings close, and I can't help going through the contents, though I know there's no surprises, no mysteries inside.

I take each item out, and the last one is the folded paper holding the seeds from Eldora. I picture her out there working her plot, waist deep in green and looking free. And as I return my things to the bag, I count my blessings. Making it to Auntie Jessie's. Having a belly full of home-cooked food and a warm, safe place to lay my head. A real coat and a backpack. A handful of garden seeds.

I lie here, wide-awake sober, looking at Auntie Jessie's bedroom door. I'm grateful. I'm free. And I know the code.

THREE

Oak Hills
2015

When morning broke, Ranita heard fitful stirring from the bunk below. Along with all the women down the tier, she roused beneath the scratchy wool blanket that had covered countless other bodies, and faced the real: another day of human debt. Still, mornings were beginnings, weren't they?

The nights began with limbo, as darkness briefly tempered and then amplified the sounds of grief and fear and rage. And before things quieted to a low rumble of pain, she and everyone else at Oak Hills tried to refuse the noise and imagine a way out of no way.

Just before sleep, most everything they'd depended on, outside and in, was burned away. Their threads and bling and cribs and rides. Their weaves and manicures, their thick hips and cleavage and supple skin. Their reputations and posturing and excuses. Their legal analyses. The stories they spun and told about themselves. Their charms in bed and service as adornments on someone's arm. Their game, their talents for conversating and living large and staying alpha. Or beta. The jobs and comfort and respectability they might have known. The kids and kin who carried on a world apart. Gone. And it was down to their gods and what was buried in their hearts to see them through to morning.

All day they hungered, and prayed the night would bring them peace. But for most, safety was a mere concept and the night offered neither asylum nor forgiveness. In the dark lurked those who'd stolen innocence and trust. In the dark, past became present.

Some things they tried to remember. The sudden light of fireflies. Daylilies. Hopscotch. Trees. And the things that remembered them uncoiled like ferns, elbowing out of winter mounds to unfurl their serrated blades.

They went over their If onlys.

If only I'd been born on a different block. If only I'd said no. Or yes. If only I'd never met him. If only I'd been stronger, braver, better, cleaner. If only I'd stayed home. If only home had been different than it was.

If only. If only.

If only I'd been more. And less.

For some, sleep finally came, and for those who were nightmare-free, there was temporary freedom. Either way, morning followed, and they woke to find that they were still captive.

The first thing Ranita thought on waking was that she'd been inside for over three months. Spring was lost to her. March, April, and May, gone. In one way, it seemed like each empty and lonely minute had passed at a slow crawl. And at the same time, she'd been through enough for a lifetime. Before taking on the fluorescent light of day, she spent a moment picturing herself up high in the spokes of the pine tree back home that she'd named Avery.

Opening her eyes, she could tell by the striated light that it was nearly six, and she could feel it coming, the morning count, when her body would stand and present itself. *The heart keeps beating*, that's what her father had always said.

She thought how they ought to give out chips for surviving prison. For 90 days in NA you got a green one, and she tried to imagine how it would feel to collect little bits of color just for keeping alive at Oak Hills, where everything except their skins was gray.

On the van trip there, she'd squinted through window grating to see dormant orchards and pondside cabins and rolling hills slide by. Pastel ranch houses and colonials with gazebos and jungle gyms. Red-white-and-blue on porch-front flagpoles. Children playing in the snow and running free. The van drove past all of that, to where people either couldn't fight living with a prison or needed the jobs it would bring, far away until the houses got smaller and smaller, and the cars older and older, and everything man-made was rusted and weathered against a backdrop of majestic hills and woods, until it reached Oak Hills. Far away from family. In the midst of all those evergreens they couldn't touch.

The van had made its way through concentric walls and fences topped with coiled razor wire, and she'd stumbled off in ankle chains, surrounded by COs who couldn't have been less interested in her struggle to right herself, as winter blew through her orange jumpsuit and a cluster of geese looked on in wary curiosity.

On floor-buffing detail in an office three stories up, Naomi had chuckled as she watched her stumble, though she'd nearly fallen herself, stepping from the van a year before. She watched the door swallow Ranita.

A young poet coming in to lead a workshop saw the empty van drive away. Another sista down. The Chaplain saw her coming in as he was going out. Another soul in need of sustenance. And CO Stewart pointed the way into Reception and Departure. Another offender to be corrected.

"Welcome to Oak Hills," he barked, "your home away from home." Ranita heard the unspoken *bitch* in his tone and tried for the pride that had been sown into her, or for contempt as big as his. But dignity was hard to come by when you shuffled forward in chains. She held her head up and tried to look straight ahead, but on the inside she was starting to unravel. Riding the tail end of the high she'd managed to score before leaving the downtown jail, she knew she'd have to either find a source and fix, or surrender to the agonies.

Like others before her, she tried to leave behind her body as she parted and lifted and bent and spread and squatted and opened herself. She tried to disappear as her skin burned from the delousing soap and she shivered from the icy shower. By the time her name was replaced with a number and she was dressed down and photographed, she had started shaking. And then she was marched to the holding cell where the fresh catch waited to join the general population.

Back at the jail, she'd known some faces from around the way, but here she was on her own. Some in the tank looked menacing. Some looked scared. Some looked too stoned or strung out to be threats, and she knew she was headed in one of those two directions.

"What they say you did?" one asked with a smile that might be sisterly or not. Ranita was inside the walls, where the future had been settled and she'd be getting retribution instead of help, where everyone was in the process of surrender to some one or some thing.

That night she gripped the tiny bar of soap and the stunted, flaccid toothbrush she'd been given, hurtful reminders of the daily, and mourned the sweet release of dope. Lying curled and fetal above Naomi, she surrendered to darkness and memory, and began to kick. Jerking like a tangled marionette, no methadone, no Suboxone to be had, she gave in to the vomiting, the shitting, the hot and cold flashes, the shaking and cursing and begging for deliverance. She kept picturing the busted *Bud eise Ki g of Beers* sign at Mario's Paradise Lounge. Just like that, strung together with neon tubing, sections blown and sputtering, she flashed the news: *H lp me. I am broke way d wn.*

She survived the bone-deep ache and the crawling skin. The incan-

descent pain from just brushing her hair. The bottomless misery, as the
beast crawled out of her and she came around the turn. And when the
haze began to lift, she felt each aching muscle, each joint, and each remembered sin. Coming out of the blind, stumbling fog to the truth of
where she'd been, of what she'd done and not done, she saw herself and
tried to bear the shame.

She worked on shrinking her yearning and containing the cry that
rose each time the cell door locked. She tried to choose sight when the
real came back with a focus so clear and sharp that even the beautiful
things hurt. She saw a red-tailed hawk from the window and had to
close her eyes.

Eyes open or shut, she could smell the burn and feel the lift-off as
the dope entered her bloodstream, could imagine her joints loosening
and the rhythm of her body slowing, smoothing out as she slid into the
warm, mind-body-soul womb-hug from the universe that she'd never
be able to forget.

God, how she wanted relief, and she knew where to get it. She'd
seen the packets kicked under cell doors and she knew which ones, the
imprisoned and their guards, had access to the greatest escape of all.

Still, here she was, a 90-day double survivor, and that was something.

And there it was, the loudspeaker command. She stood and stepped
forward, saying: "Here. Present. 51673 Atwater." Counted. Checked.
Verified.

Afterward, all down the tier, women dressed while waiting for
their cellies to finish up at the contraption that was toilet on the bottom, sink on top, and all one piece. By silent arrangement, while one
relieved herself, the other turned to face the wall. Then came the order
for Movement, and they went to chow.

Eight hours later, after breakfast and work detail and another standing count and lunch, it was recreation time. And following the order to
relax and socialize, they filed into the dayroom and tried to make this

hour matter or at least to help it pass, under the steady gaze of their keepers.

Some walked laps around the yard and some drifted like flotsam, disconnected, unclaimed.

Some waited to use the phone that cost so much it bled their families even poorer, trying to unsee how the one at the head of the line looked even more heartsick when she hung up than before she'd dialed.

Folks were gathered by the TV, tuning into *The Young and the Restless* or *Days of Our Lives*. One woman got so worked up about the story line she yelled at the top of her voice about who was honest, who was faithful, who was about to get betrayed. Now and again, war broke out over what story to follow, whether some character or another was dead for real, or someone argued for a switch-up to the drama of an up-close-at-a-distance talk show feast of lives turned inside out. But today things were placid in TV Land.

Someone was writing a letter.

Someone was drawing a picture.

Someone was writing a poem.

The spades players were assembled around a table and Ranita stood and looked on, eager to watch the contest unfold and hear the trash talking, the camaraderie, the everyday humor and antics.

Today they were stuck on the coming election. "A brotha's voted into the White House, twice, and here comes this orange clown. He'll never win, even white folks aren't that crazy, but I just wish I could figure them out."

"You don't gotta figure out a vampire. You just protect yourself with garlic and a stake."

Everyone laughed, but it had a sober chill.

"But how you gonna protect yourself from something unless you understand it?"

"First off, you think he can't win? This country's changing . . ."

"And not."

"Amen to that. It's browning up, though, and far as I can tell, some folks'll do anything to keep their place. Second, your answer's right there in your question, sis. *We're* the key. The thing they can come together on is being above us."

Someone laughed, but it was sorrow tinged.

"Want in on this next round?" one turned to Ranita and asked. She shook her head. Today's discussion was heavy, and she barely had her balance back. And what was a game of spades without Hennessy?

She drifted over to the corner where Eldora and her family were braiding hair, defying the rule against outside-of-the-cell grooming that even the COs overlooked. Eldora was dropping some plant world knowledge. Mothering. Binding them together with a story about how trees have to bend to survive. She had reached out to Ranita when she first got there to try and bring her into the fold, and belonging was tempting, but it cut at least two ways, and she hadn't yet decided on her path. She sat with them for a minute, hoping for a bit of company, a little laughter, a new story of some kind.

"No give at all, and a tree won't make it," Eldora said, using her hands and her deep, throaty voice for emphasis. And then she paused to welcome Ranita with a nod and a *Hey, baby* before going on.

"Strong winds and ice will weigh it down and do it in. But too much give, and a sapling gets a 'set' to it that it just might not recover from." *I used to know that*, Ranita thought.

"And if it can't stand straight," Eldora continued, "it's uprooted easier. Trees, they've got to do some bending, up to a point. And here's the good news: In the forest they don't need to stand up tall on their own. They've got the other trees around them for support."

A couple held hands on the sly behind their chairs, until a CO shouted, "Get some space!" and hands separated. Bodies moved apart. For now.

And Gwen was over there doing her thing, promising with stud swagger to make the locked up and lonely forget their fantasies of men, promising love and satisfaction that would last the forever of their latest bid, or at least the night. Sweet-talking a fish who'd just arrived that week.

Can't blame me for trying, she'd said to Ranita two months before, when she'd informed Gwen that she was not, as yet, inclined that way. It wasn't that she couldn't imagine loving on a woman. She'd had a crush on Lori Watson back in middle school, and had spent many a lonely seventh-grade night wondering what her kiss and skin would feel like. And she'd done the deed with a few, but that was commerce. If she did go gay-for-the-stay, it would have to be about a connection, a summons, or a spark.

She heard the banter of the spades players heating up and tuned back in from across the room. Who was the king of the jungle, the lion, who chilled while the females did the hunting, or the tiger, who rolled solo? "Those are the choices?" someone asked. "None of the Above."

As people called out other answers—elephants . . . they were smart and tribal; gazelles . . . graceful and fast; bonobos . . . they mated face-to-face and girl-on-girl—the announcement came for Movement. The fun was over, time to go back to their cells.

With their bodies, they said compliance does not equal respect. They said, *I am not your slave. You are not my king.* "Uncle Tom overseer," Ranita muttered to herself, tasting the bitter pleasure of her small defiance as she took her sweet time getting to her feet.

Back in the cell, stretched out on her bunk, she was feeling a smidgen better. The tree story had lifted her mood, and the sass and humor in the dayroom, dark though it was, reminded her how Black women carried on. Until they didn't. She knew both truths.

She opened the sci-fi novel she'd gotten from the Oak Hills library, trying to get lost in a different apocalypse than the one where she was caught, and felt sudden movement beneath her. Naomi, expert at the ear hustle, sprang into action, and then Ranita noticed toilets flushing and heard the code talking. Makeshift percussion on desktops, bed frames, metal doors and walls: *shakedown, house in order, shakedown coming, shakedown*. Naomi grabbed her three colored pencils and her drawing of the woods that could be seen from their window and started stuffing them into the gap between bed frame and wall.

"Shakedown," she said, "mind your valuables."

Unsure of what they would come for, Ranita glanced from the books on the window ledge to the photos of Amara and Theo that she'd stuck to the wall, and then pushed the homemade card they'd just sent her into the middle pages of her borrowed book and prayed it would be spared.

And then it came, a sudden raging storm. Brogans hit the tier. Cells got cracked. And there were the raiders, snapping on their rubber gloves.

The invasion had one voice, one shout, though it was three headed: "Mouth open, tongue up! Don't make me have to use my hand! Arms up! Fingers spread! Part your hair and shake it out! Lift those feet!"

Standing side by side in the narrow space they thought of as their house, Naomi and Ranita opened their mouths and hands in outward surrender. They fumbled with their combination locks, unfastened their footlockers, and stood against the cinder block, looking away from the little plastic mirror where they usually struggled to see themselves, as their possessions were thrown to the floor. Fighting the shame of so little mattering so much.

Stone-faced COs checked behind the toilet. Pulled the mattresses from their frames. Emptied the desktop. And Ranita watched as the delicate Bible pages of her dictionary were crumpled and torn, and tried to stand like a tree, tall and immovable, improbable in that wasteland and bending just enough to survive.

There went Naomi's notebook of contacts with her kids. There went

Ranita's letters and cards from home. She tried to think of something good: water in the desert, a handful of sweets, a kiss. It was no use. She turned to the Serenity Prayer she knew from years before, wincing as she saw her books land on the pile, looking on as the marauders turned and sifted, like it was a mound of rotting trash or compost, kicking and stepping back as though roaches might skitter out.

It had almost run its course when Naomi's colored pencils, yellow, red, and blue, fell to the floor with the small clinking of a striker playing a metal triangle.

"Awww, we got us a artist here," one head of the Oak Hills Cerberus sneered, "and I know you know this is contraband. You think this is your house? This house is mine."

Silent against the wall, shaking on the inside, Ranita wondered was it art, or hope, or pencils that were against the rules, while they waited to see if Naomi's hubris would cost her a trip to the hole.

She got a D Report instead, and before the storm troopers rolled on, one of them stepped on a photo of Amara that had slid from the pile. Ranita suppressed a cry and stood watching, wondering couldn't he feel it beneath the heel of his boot, as he peeled off his latex gloves and dropped them on the heap? And then she saw him look down and notice the photo before turning and grinding his heel, tearing it down the middle before walking out.

Ranita and Naomi were left staring at the mound of photos and papers and letters, packages of ramen noodles, candy, and crackers. Deodorant and Q-tips, sanitary pads and underwear. Books that seemed to cry for help. Tenderly, Ranita picked up the two halves of her photo and brushed off the dirt, telling herself a tear could be mended, reminding herself of all that remained intact.

Kneeling, they collected their valuables and carried on, trying not to hear the pillage in the next cell down.

FOUR

Sitting in the DCF office, four days out, I'm getting another chance to practice my waiting skills. I tell myself I'm getting another step closer to my kids, but my spirit hurts, stuck in limbo with all the other broken-hearted families, flipping through magazines with last year's celebrity news or home-decorating ideas way beyond our budgets, if we've got homes at all. We stare into space, scroll on our phones if we've got them, and look anywhere but at each other, afraid that no matter what efforts we've made, we're still the bottom-dwelling kind of fish.

Finally, Miss Caseworker calls my name and I stand up and follow her to her little cubicle office. She's got a cheery wall calendar, hearts for February, and a philodendron, the one plant you can't kill, winding along the top of her partition. And a framed eight-by-ten family portrait. Standing a little behind her husband against a blue sky, her hand on his shoulder, she's smiling big, two little towhead girls who look just like Husband on either side of them. In real life, she looks tired and irritated. Her gray roots are showing and she's wearing a matronly suit and flats, and a blouse with one of those floppy bows at the neck that's got a crucifix tangled up in the fabric. Straight-laced, religious, and by-the-book. Everyone who's hustled knows you read the room and the people in it, and then make a connection.

I start in with my gratitude for being able to meet with her, praising the Lord for bringing me through and lifting me up. Miss Caseworker nods, but she's not exactly encouraging, and asks me how my reentry's going so far. She's looking at my eyes like she's wondering: *How'd you get those?* And I can't seem to keep from looking at my hand-me-down and shabby Goodwill clothes, pants faded and puckering in places, shapeless sweater pilling up across the front. I hate myself for being ashamed.

"It's going great," I say, and tell about how good it feels to be clean and sober, with my aunt Jessica, looking for a square job and going to meetings, *released to the community*, like my papers say. Radiating positivity, I chatter on about how much I'm looking forward to being a productive member of society again, while all I see on her face is skepticism.

We go over the situation: where I've been and where I am. She recites the hoops I'm expected to keep jumping: meetings, pee tests, job search. And fucking psychotherapy, every other week. Then she lists the thing I need to see in the distance and move toward: a three-bedroom place of my own. Since apartments that size in Boston start at $2,500 a month, getting one is nothing more than a thought experiment. I can only hope that someday, I'll be allowed to move back into the house with Val and the kids.

Though it pains me to bring it up, I ask about the TPR, just to make sure I'm not standing on a fault line. With chilling detachment, she breaks down how it works, how DCF can go for termination if it's been 15 months since you've had contact, and tells me the law was created to "free" kids for adoption and protect them by giving them "stable" families, instead of letting them linger without permanent homes. Sounds like being back with their birth families is slavery. And I know "stable" partly means richer. What she doesn't talk about is what it means to lose the only family you've known, and what it means to tell someone, *The law says you're not a parent anymore. Your kids are orphans and you've got no rights. As a mother, you're finished.* She never mentions what that's like for parents or kids. She likes the rules and regulations, I can tell. They give her something to hold on to, to keep from feeling bad, or feeling at all, about the people she's policing.

We go over her list of questions, each one making me more uptight. *What parts of being a parent feel challenging? . . . How do your childhood experiences impact your parenting? . . . When you experienced stress in the past, how did you handle that and learn from it? . . . What helps you stay strong for you and your family? . . . How do your culture and family traditions influence your parenting? . . . Who are the people in your family or community that you can count on? . . . Who counts on you? . . .*

Fuck. Another social services pro trying to split me open and look inside. My head's throbbing and I can't think straight. I ask can I use the bathroom and lean against the stall door, giving my face a rest from smiling and trying to picture something free and good. *My childhood experiences?* They thunder up and I see myself on punishment in the back hallway. Down in the basement. At the dinner table, so wrong I'm unwatchable. Clinging to love, if not rescue.

I push away what's gone and done with. And ask myself can I try and see Miss Caseworker as someone who can come over to my side, instead of blocking our chance to be a family again.

When I get back, her last two questions are hanging in the air like a funky smell. I push down my doubt and mistrust into a little space inside where they don't show, I hope, and get back in performance mode. *Who counts on you?* I talk about how I can be responsible, supportive, appropriate, resilient, and how I can't wait to have the chance to put in practice all the ways I've changed. *Who are the people in your family or community that you can count on?* "Friends and family," I say. But the answer in my head is: *I've got other program people groping for the light. I've got Jessie and Val. And Daddy's spirit, it stays with me. I've got a power greater than me. In theory, anyway.*

"What about the children's father?" she asks while typing, looking at her computer instead of me. *Didn't you bother to read the case file?* I want to ask, and say, "Deceased."

It still feels strange, nearly six years later, saying Jasper's gone. There he was, defining so much, even in his absence and his coming and going, that I almost expect him to resurface sometimes. Trifling though he was, he was persistent. And I can't stop asking the question I'll never get the answer to: *Was his overdose an accident or not?*

Miss Caseworker looks at her papers and asks about my co-defendant, "a Mr. David Quarles."

My whole body tightens up. DQ, pipeline to oblivion, he's out there somewhere. I shake my head, say, "Not a factor," and change the subject. She's studying me, and I'm halfway expecting her to ask did I get into any dyke mischief at Oak Hills, but thankfully, she moves on.

I see her measuring her words, using her skills and training to keep her balance and make sure she doesn't stray into caring too much for me and my kids. And she looks at me like she's trying to picture who I might have been, once upon a time, before I fucked up so bad. Searching for the girl I was, which I'm sad to say would work against me, truth be told. And though she can't help feeling bad for me, feeling pity, even, for the hard road behind and ahead, it's all hypothetical. A word problem. An algorithm. She'd like to believe in me, maybe. Or she does, in theory. But real life tells her that's foolish. Real life tells her I'll fail.

"When can I call them? And see them?"

Her eyes narrow in warning. And can I blame her?

"You can speak to them when your aunt Jessica calls them. Let's take it one step at a time, first things first. A supervised visit in a month, if everything's in order," she says, and I wish I could say I see hope or conflict on her face. Truth is, I don't see anything at all.

I nod like I'm thankful for any inch forward I can get. And swallow the resentment I feel, looking at her happy little unbroken family in the photo on her shelf.

Then I take the stack of papers I built behind the walls, feeling proud of every positive thing I could add, and hand Miss Caseworker copies of the letters I sent to DCF (most of them unanswered), stating that I want reunification, and she glances at them and flips through the contact log. But when I start showing my cards and letters and drawings and photos from the kids, she says she doesn't really need to see them; she's behind schedule, anyhow. And when she gathers up all I've given her and holds it out to me, what I really want to do is throw it in her face, but I ask, polite as I can muster, isn't she going to copy the letters and the log for my file?

She sighs and pulls open the office door and takes my accomplishments down the hall. And I'm just this side of pushing some of the papers on her desk into the trash or misfiling them. Fucking up her afternoon just a little bit. Or shoving her family photo to the floor. I control myself, but then, like my hand's got a mind of its own, I pocket a mechanical pencil from her desktop.

When I leave out of DCF, unsure whether to be nauseated at my begging or proud that I could take care of business, I need a cigarette in the worst way. I bum one off a sista standing outside the office, another mother trying to prove she can love her kids right. She gives me a light and I inhale with pure relief, savoring the burn, and walk over to a patch of brown grass and leafless trees across the street. And I can't help thinking about everything that's working against me.

I brought up all my evidence of self-improvement. My clean time, my GED, my list of work details. Participation in NA, meditation, Life Skills, Anger Management, Poetry Discussion, Spirit Circle, Restorative Justice Circle, A Book from Mom. Even woodworking. I babbled on about the birdhouse I made for the kids, describing how satisfying the painstaking work and love I invested in it was. I don't mention how I'd slipped up, eight months into my bid, and was in a stupor from the Vicodin I got, trading . . . let's not go there . . . and how I couldn't get the pieces even or lined up straight or sanded smooth, and it ended up looking like a bird trap house, and I've always wondered if the kids threw it out before they even got back home, like those chrysanthemums in that Steinbeck story.

And now I'm making a list in my head of my recorded wrongs. The truancy and boosting and incarceration. I've paid for my official crimes. But what about the ones I keep inside?

Some of the places I've been, they give me a sick feeling right here, in my middle, and I try not to think, let alone talk, about them. But they earthquake into the present, no matter how I try and refuse them.

I drop the butt, crush it out, and put it in my pocket to throw away later. Then it seems like a pair of trees call out to me, and I stand among these bare witnesses, doing a silent accounting of my crimes and the open sores I can't remember *not* having.

I try and banish the low-down feeling that crept through me in the DCF office, but I can't help it; I'm picturing my kids at the dining room table with Val, eating homemade cookies, peaceful and carefree. Their homework's done and they've had a tasty, balanced meal that they helped cook and clean up after. And soon, at their designated bedtime, they'll go to their soft, warm beds in the rooms I know so well I can close my eyes and see every view from the windows, every patched crack, every glow-in-the-dark star I stuck up on the ceiling.

Choose the free things, I tell myself, looking up through a tangle of tree limbs, thinking there must be an order I can't make out, and picturing them returned to green.

Time for a meeting. I choose one from my list that's close to Jessie's, look around to get my bearings, and head toward fellowship, wishing I had at least one true friend out here, someone who might have even visited me at Oak Hills, someone who'd be here now to pick the thread back up.

I'm hoofing it, and that feels good, until I see a bus coming. There's a crowd waiting at the curb, and in the crush of folks getting on and off I slip in the back door. Soon as I'm in, I look at the seniors, making their way to visit loved ones, see about their benefits, keep their appointment with the podiatrist. Young lions slouched across the back seats, and serious, determined kids with backpacks full of binders, looking around cautiously. Men covered with construction dust, hard hats and coolers in hand. Down-and-out sistas. Stooped old men. Just-getting-by folks of every age.

I see my people, seeing me. And feel the disappointment of everyone around. As we ride it builds, crowding out the momentary charge I got from getting over and snubbing the rules. Someone pushes the yellow strip and when the bus stops I slip off and resume walking, feeling shitty.

This morning I was too anxious and pressed to really look around at the rough, free-world waters I've been thrown back to, but now I try and take them in.

The main difference is more white folks taking over the best blocks and the nicest houses, buying shit up and forcing us out, "developing" the areas they wrote off long ago. Making something sleek and trendy from the mess of our lives. Building brand-new condo complexes nobody who's been living here will ever be able to afford. They buy. They "renovate." And stay inside until things change some more.

While change is coming, there's still no real parks. No real grocery stores. No banks. Plenty of empty 40s and plastic supermarket bags drifting by like landlocked jellyfish. Plenty of liquor stores and barbershops.

Seems like I can pick out every single smell that drifts over while I walk: frying onions and Sazón. Laundry soap. Exhaust. Coming rain?

I notice the shine of cobalt glass, and looking around to make sure no one sees me picking trash off the ground, I snag it. The edges are sharp and caked with dirt, but the blue is gorgeous.

There's still a brotha on the corner, selling oils and incense at his fold-out table. Egyptian Musk, Kush, Arabian Sandalwood. Maybe later, when I've got the cash. I look past the glowing neon of the check-cashing store to see they're still making a good living on the desperate, down-and-out, and undocumented. Passing a rec center I hear excited voices and trash talking and dribbling, as teens try to choose the safety of basketball and dancing and chess.

Passing by a storefront church I hear electric organ music and stop to listen, wishing I could find a way to sing inside the Lord's house. If they'd have me, that is. The real me.

Walking on, I see the flashing signs of Mario's Paradise Lounge, advertising liquor and relief. Now that's the church where I used to worship.

I slow down and stand here looking at the door, picturing the soft darkness with its colored glow, the jukebox music smooth and whiskey-hard. Making a good hurt. The party's started without me, but it never ends. It's right there for the having, on the other side of that threshold. All I have to do is go through.

And a straight-up jones comes over me, as I start down the maybe-I-can-have-one-drink path in my head. Close my eyes and I can almost taste it. Open them and say out loud: "Ranita, you know where one drink leads. Before you know it you're back on slow-death road and your kids are lost to you for good." I know I look like a nutball, standing just outside the door, talking to myself.

I think about Caprice and Aquila, one locked up again, the other dead, and try to forget how whiskey eases up the tightness, the sorrow, the fear and failure, and remember what comes next. I focus on the fact that I can look at myself these days, at least some of the time.

I do not go through the door.

And just as I'm thinking there's really nowhere, inside or out, that's safe from the present and past colliding, I see Vera Santos, coming toward me with a hug.

"Cherry," she says, draping herself on my shoulders. "Girl, where you been? I thought maybe you were taking a dirt nap."

I can't help laughing. She always was good for putting an entertaining spin on things, even though we were both checked out more often than not.

"Naw, I'm still aboveground." I hear myself say it proudly. For real, it's a low standard. Reminds me of the times I raised my hand for roll call in eleventh-grade study hall, while my heart and mind were elsewhere. *Ranita Atwater?* "Here."

She hugs me again and says how happy she is we're not done hanging out in this life and asks, "Where you staying at? Whatchu doing right now?"

I study her, trying to decide if she's lit. Hemming and hawing, I say I'm with my auntie, I'm pressed, I'm behind on my errands. I'm trying to catch a meeting.

"Meetings. You know they're just like buses, always another one coming, ready to be caught." She claps her cupped hands like they're trapping an insect. "Come on with me while I make a run to get some smokes, some grub. We can catch up, and then I'll drop you there."

I stand here silent, trying to make the right decision, and then follow her to her ride, though I don't really need anything she's offering, and nothing me and Vera have to catch up on is really good. We stop for cigarettes and Chinese food, and go back to her place, which I'm relieved to see is neat as a pin, everything in its rightful place.

She sets the food out on the coffee table and we dig in, half watching an NBA game while we shoot the shit, trading family news. I tell her about Daddy, and about just getting out of Oak Hills. She says her brother's locked up and she's got a new man.

"Saw Judy recently," she says. "She was with . . . what's that dude's name? Ike, that's it; we hung out, played some dominoes. All he talked about was tropical fish."

It's a comfort, being with someone who knows the deal, and before I know it I've had three cigarettes and I'm stuffed with pork fried rice and shrimp with lobster sauce and wishing my waistband was elastic. When she goes to the bathroom, I call out that I'm going for more water and take a look in her fridge and cabinets (okay, I'm not proud of myself, but I need some clues to Vera's state of mind) and I'm astonished and relieved at how everything's organized and lined up perfectly. She doesn't even have an everything drawer.

Then I look out the window and realize it'll be dark soon. I start feeling anxious about getting to my meeting, and when she gets back I say I've got to go. She offers me a ride, but I tell her I need to walk off the food I just scarfed, poor people's fitness plan and all, and she takes out her phone to get my number. I ask her to write hers down, dodging the embarrassment of being phoneless.

And in the beat between her handing me a slip of paper and me grabbing my backpack to go, she says, "You holding?"

My heart sinks, and a jumble of sadness and anger and fear shoots through me.

"Naw, Vera, I'm done with that," I say, shoving the paper in my backpack and standing up. I thank her for the food and smokes and get up out of there, heading for the place I need to be. At least there'll be a big pot of scalded coffee, along with some bargain cookies for us indigent, addicted souls.

When I come through the door, the meeting's started and someone's talking about Letting go, Letting God. I can smell the fear and loneliness, and I sit, shoulder to shoulder with my fellow strugglers, and listen to the announcements and the reading of Step 3: turning ourselves over to the care of God. And now it's time for the sharing.

A part of me still hates the sorrow broadcast. And it ties my tongue. Here I am, new space, new faces. And the same old wrestle to stake something. Keeping quiet's not a long-term choice if I'm gonna make it out here. But it's so hard to open, even a hairline crack.

I look around the room. The brotha who's talking, he's in the sub-basement, one clean day, he says, and trying to get a foot on the stairway going up. Another circles like a vulture, eyeing a handful of needy sistas who've got their guard down, just trying to survive. "Who else wants to share?" the leader asks, and I look at the floor. And a woman two seats over, I feel her watching me, like she knows I'm a chump. I try and read her with a hostile look, but I'm prickly hot along my neck and shoulders, hesitant to put my fears and failures and my just-out-of-prison story out there for everyone to feast on.

Feels like I've got a bunch of stones weighing down my pocket. They're too heavy and too stuck, and I just can't seem to turn the pocket inside out to get them loose. But I raise my hand before I can stop myself. "My name's Ranita and I'm an addict and an alcoholic," I announce, wishing that instead of starting with what I am, I could say what I'm doing about it.

"Hey, Ranita," "Hey, Ranita," "Hey, Ranita." Their voices feel like lapping waves.

"I've got three years, two months, and change clean. And . . ."

The quiet stretches out while I fumble in my pocket. I can hear the human noise . . . people gobbling up the cookies and slurping the coffee and clearing their throats, metal folding chairs creaking as people lean back and shift their weight.

I reach in, turn my pocket inside out, and pull one small pebble free. ". . . and the past's been heavy on my mind. . . ."

Most of them nod and some toss me an "Amen." They look at me to say they see me, hear me, feel me, and then they look down to give me some respect, some room. "Take your time," one says, real gentle.

I pull out a bigger stone and I'm off and running, relieved and scared shitless at the same time.

After the meeting wraps up, I throw Vera's number in the trash, then snag a few extra cookies and take a look at the bulletin board. There's a notice for a Queer Dance Party at a bar not so far from where I grew up. *First Fridays of the month, 10:00. Free. Dance jams, throwbacks, 80's, 90's, house.* Making sure no one's looking, I pull it off the board and stuff it into my backpack.

I come through the doorway into full five o'clock darkness, jangled. Stupid and clumsy and at a loss. Seems like I've forgotten how to do anything without being told.

I pick a path and start walking, and a few blocks away I hear singing and stop outside a big stone church. Choir practice. And it's sounding pretty good. Staring up at the heavy wooden door, hesitating as I think of Mama and her solos, I wonder am I welcome. Then I decide if this is God's house, then it's my house.

Pulling open the front door, I step in, and then linger in the vestibule, just listening, until I get up the nerve to open the inner door. No one seems to notice me as I slip inside and sit in the back pew.

Candles are burning and I smell incense and stone. Jesus is up above the altar, paining. I close my eyes and take in the organ and the interlocking voices, imagining what I'll say if they ask me who I am and why I'm in here. *My name's Ranita and I'm looking for my higher power, trying to figure out what it is I understand God to be, after all? My name's Ranita and I'm a sinner? My name's Ranita and I don't even know where I fit?*

I stay and listen to them sing one I haven't heard before. I may have been forsaken, but not by the music. I give myself up to its call . . . *Not by might, Not by power* . . . for God's spirit to be sent, and receive its medicine.

After a few more songs, when I start to get up and leave, the lead point of Miss Caseworker's pencil pokes me in the side. I sit back down and whisper.

"Please help me defy her in a different way.

"Please give me the strength to wind my story back. Accept what's done and can't be changed, from DQ . . . to Jasper . . . to what all came first. And own this present I've been fighting for.

"Please let me feel God's love."

FIVE

1996

Looking over her shoulder, she saw her mother watching from the kitchen window, wondering, no doubt, why her child didn't have the sense to put her shoes on and come in out of the rain. But Ranita kept walking toward her garden plot, enjoying the feel of drizzle on her skin, the wet grass between her toes.

On her way out the door, she had tried to unsee the injured look on her mother's face and avoid thinking of how payment might be exacted for their desertions, hers and her father's. If he wasn't at work, he was out in the yard with Ranita or listening to old soul and jazz records in his basement "lair," as Geneva called it, surrounded by all the second-hand junk she refused to have upstairs. Ranita couldn't help wondering if he'd chosen the lava lamp and painting of sailboats on black velvet to ensure that her mother would never come down there, though Geneva periodically opened the door to the basement and stood at the top of the stairs. And now that the warm weather had called them outdoors, she had taken to watching from the window.

For Ranita, rain was usually a bother that kept her cooped up inside or frizzed her hair, but as soon as she'd come home from school she changed into shorts and ditched her shoes and came right out, thinking about thirsty roots getting a drink as she inhaled the wet, earthy scent. Petrichor. It had its very own name, she'd learned, the smell of rain.

All winter she'd been stuck on dormant, and even the arrival of spring, her favorite season, hadn't stirred her alive enough to shove off the weight she felt, day in, day out. The only choice she seemed to have was turning further inward, despite how inhospitable that territory was. She rarely slept the night through, and she'd been going through the motions with her schoolwork, marking time as she tried to finish the seventh grade without pissing off her teachers and getting into trouble for just being herself. She hadn't been able to keep the thread of any novel she tried, and her father hadn't once caught her reading by flashlight under the covers after she'd been told it was bedtime. He had that uneasy look that made her feel even more alone. His forced, upbeat questions landed with thuds, and she alternated between evading him and wishing he would press her to tell him what was wrong.

She shuddered when she thought of Thanksgiving weekend last fall, when she'd come to the den while he and Mama were watching the news. Ranita had found herself at that doorway as if by sleepwalking, tears streaming down her face, and Geneva had stared at her and then looked at her father, just as she did when a leaking faucet or a drafty window needed fixing. He had sat on the couch, looking terrified, and then stood and stepped forward to hold her as her tears turned to sobbing.

"Let's go for ice cream," he had said, patting her back, "or to the movies. Skip church today and come help me at the shop."

Instead, she had returned to her room and her silence.

Six months later, when it was time for him to get started on his garden, he'd asked if she wanted to grow one alongside his. They could plant and tend together, he'd said, looking strained and uncertain despite his lighthearted tone. It would be like the times when they'd worked on her bike, or put in the little brick patio, or played with her snap circuit set. She agreed, with more resignation than excitement, but her mood had lifted once she started reading up on what to plant.

Each June Lennox put in vegetables. Tomatoes, beans, peppers, pumpkins, squash, anything that sprawled. Bold and untamed, his plants could barely be contained by the fence that surrounded the yard. He had never stopped sharing his awe at each wispy blossom's transformation into a curvy yellow pepper or dark zucchini, heavy on the vine, and he carried on about the virtues of growing what could be eaten. But it was flowers she loved best. On summer afternoons she had watched in awe as their neighbor Miz Martin emerged from the red and purple ocean of poppies and delphiniums that filled her yard. And when she'd asked her father, "Aren't flowers food for our eyes?" he had chuckled and added that they nourished the spirit, too.

She'd decided on some loyal perennials, and some annuals, too, with their short-lived bursts of color: cosmos, zinnias, and sunflowers, the kind with faces big as breakfast plates, and learned the Classical names so she could recite them for her mother's approval: rudbeckia instead of black-eyed Susans, echinacea for coneflowers. Ranita researched what each plant needed. The optimal season and month. Beds with drainage, alkaline or sandy soil. Sun or shade or both. Sprinkled on the dirt, or pushed a fingernail or a knuckle down, and this far apart. Some were so tiny she'd had to pour them from their packet onto white paper, and she worried most about those, hoping she'd done right by them.

After they'd all been planted, she had stood looking at the empty patch of ground and said, "You can't see them, once they're in there, Daddy. How will they find their way up? Why do you believe they'll grow?"

He had put his arm around her shoulder and reassured her. Trying to give them what they needed, she and her father had done their part.

They couldn't control the weather, but they would give the plants water and compost, though Geneva said it disgusted her, gathering peelings and eggshells and leftover food and then letting them rot.

"They'll grow toward the light," he told Ranita. "And most of them will thrive. Just you wait and see, Ranita Bonita."

She had gone to sleep dreaming of the pictures of flowers on the seed packets. And every day she'd gone out to see if anything had sprouted.

After coming in from the shop, Lennox went right upstairs to wash up. The little first-floor powder room, as Geneva called it, was for guests, and as she often reminded him, the oil from the shop left dark traces in the sink.

From an upstairs window he saw Ranita kneeling at the edge of the garden, barefoot, and went down to join her in the light, warm rain.

"Checking your crops?" he asked.

"They came up, Daddy," she said with quiet reverence. "The Susans sprouted. I gave them what they needed and they grew."

He knelt beside her and they looked together at the tiny double half circles dotting her garden plot.

"You're a real flower farmer now," he said. "We'll have to tell Jessie." And they marveled at the little bits of green that had pushed up and through.

Ranita heard the back door open and looked back at her mother, standing half in, half out of the doorway, under an umbrella.

"Dinner's ready," she called out. And they went in to dry off and change their clothes. When they came down, Geneva was putting the food on the table.

"Nita's a black-eyed Susan farmer," Lennox said, pulling out his chair at one end of the table.

"Is that so?" Geneva answered, sitting at the other end. "Well, we'll have to tend to your hair this weekend, won't we, now that the rain's had its way with you," and then she announced what she'd made for dinner.

There was enough food for two families. Spicy shrimp creole, Ranita's favorite, along with rice. Biscuits, butter beans, greens. And celery. Geneva served Ranita's plate, skipping the biscuits and beans and giving her small helpings of rice and greens. She and Ranita were allowed six shrimp each, but Lennox had a man's needs, and he could have more.

Ranita stared at the celery. It was her death vegetable. A waste of chewing. She hated the stringy parts and the watery, bitter taste. She even hated the color, as though it had tried for green and couldn't get there.

Geneva said it was a good choice for Ranita, because you lost more calories chewing it than were in it, and she gave her a huge helping. And as her mother held the plate out to her, Ranita pictured herself vomiting a wishy-washy-green celery rocket at her.

After devouring everything else, Ranita picked up a piece of celery, pulled off all the strings, and tried to get it swallowed, while Lennox asked what they'd be having for Sunday dinner and whether he should grill, and Geneva said she was thinking ham and sweet potatoes if Pastor Johnson was coming.

Ranita put down the celery, thinking she might throw up after all.

And then the deadly silence descended. And thickened. Until she was having trouble breathing. It would kill her, she was sure of it, all the not-talking, all the keeping things in. The only thing she heard was chewing and it was getting louder and louder, and she could feel teeth biting into her skin, eating her bit by bit, and if she didn't find a way to stop it, there'd be nothing left.

Staring at the dainty pink flowers choking the edge of her plate, Ranita opened her mouth to break the pall and tell about the math quiz she'd had that day. Word problems, which were way more interesting than the equations she had to practice over and over. She liked figuring out how to divide up pies and cupcakes evenly, how many cubes it took to build a staircase, what the common factors were.

As soon as she started talking, her mother interrupted. "What was your score?" School was the place where Ranita excelled, and the question reminded her that she mustn't let up and squander the academic future her parents had been denied.

"Ninety-seven," she said proudly, and her father clapped. "That's my Nita!"

Looking at Ranita's plate, where the only thing left was a pile of celery, Geneva asked what had happened to the other three points.

Lennox sighed and turned to Ranita. "What've you been discovering in your encyclopedias?" He called them hers, even though he had wanted them so badly he'd paid for them three times over on an installment plan and he spent more time than she did poring over them, late at night.

"I figured out what kind of pine tree Avery is," she answered, trying to steady her voice. "She's a *Pinus strobus*, eastern white pine."

"She?" Geneva said. "Are trees male or female?"

"Excellent," Lennox said, bypassing Geneva, and the word felt like a warm hug. "And how could you tell?"

Ranita explained about the long, thin needles in brushy clusters of five, the cone shape, the ridges in the bark. And the way the branches looked like wagon wheels, with a new round added every year. She wanted to say how she stood under Avery and gazed up, wishing she could reach the lowest branch and climb to see how things looked from high above.

Geneva did not approve of tree climbing, especially for girls. And she did not love Avery. She didn't even like her. The sap got on the car, and the tree was too close to the house to be safe, and she said again and again that they should really think about having it cut down, in case it fell and crashed through the roof.

While her mother finished eating, Ranita told what she'd learned about *Pinus strobus*, the boats and masts and cough medicine people made from it, and how it had been a peace tree to Native people.

"May I have more shrimp?" she asked, looking at her father, and he reached out for the bowl and put a ladleful on her plate. And before the consequences set in, Ranita started gobbling up her windfall, aware as she did so that she looked more like a beast than a young lady.

Geneva believed in portion control. She allowed herself 11 almonds between lunch and dinner. She declared that in their house they drank water with a slice of lemon, as opposed to soda. And on the rare occasion when Ranita did an outstanding job with her piano lesson, Geneva let her have a single red-and-white peppermint wheel from the covered milky-white glass bowl that sat beside the metronome.

Geneva weighed herself every morning and stood in the bathroom while Ranita got on the scale. When her breasts had started growing that year, Geneva had bought her a "minimizer bra" to make sure she didn't look "fast." And although Geneva said they needed to take action on "the chubbiness," Ranita felt comfortable with a little more cushioning. "Your body's changing," Geneva had said to her that very morning, frowning as she reminded her of the vigilance required to smell nice and clean "at that time of the month."

Lennox asked Ranita if she knew what the other trees around their house were, and she started in to answer, "Out back there's a black oak and a rowan, and that's—" but her mother broke in mid-sentence, "Just push back from the table, Ranita Atwater. Use the discipline I've tried to teach you. Use your self-control."

Ranita's eyes brimmed and her voice came out high and strained. "I was just trying to answer Daddy, and I don't understand why you're always on me. Do you want me to be hungry? Do you want me to—"

Geneva's hand came down on the table so hard the silverware and glasses trembled. "I can't, I *won't*, talk to you when you're like this. When you can speak calmly, we can talk."

She offered more lemon water, but Ranita didn't answer, focused as she was on keeping her balance. Sometimes the gap between her outside and inside was so wide it threatened to swallow her, and she had to *focus focus focus* just to keep from falling in. She tried to blink away her tears as she put her fork down and finished chewing what was in her mouth and swallowed. There was one more shrimp on her plate, but she'd had enough.

Her father tried to rescue her by returning to the topic of trees. Looking directly at her, he asked her to share what she knew now about black oaks.

"Well," she said, focusing on his warm brown face, "did you ever notice that on top, the leaves are shiny, dark green, but the undersides are yellow-brown?" She paused, gripping the sides of her chair. "And I found out they can grow one acorn by itself, or in clusters of two to five." She was about to tell about the catkin tassels, but she looked up and saw her mother, and her mind went blank.

Geneva had closed her eyes.

Her shoulders and head were turned toward Ranita. Her mouth was cinched and her arms were folded. Her eyes stayed shut. She had spoken with her body.

Suspended in time, Ranita tried her best not to disappear. She saw the minutes pass on the kitchen wall clock, and heard her father, speaking with his quiet, even voice, saying, "Geneva, really, how could you?" from a long way off.

SIX

My feet are dragging and I feel like a traitor, just for going to my first therapy appointment. Yeah, my head's real crowded today.

I hear Mama, telling me to toughen up and never air my dirty laundry, never show my fraying seams.

I hear the Oak Hills sistas: *You be careful with that couch talk. . . . Be strong and leave that shit to white folks. . . . Depend on who you know and trust. . . .*

I hear Auntie Jessie saying she doesn't believe in psychotherapists. Maybe not. But like with ghosts, that's got no effect whatsoever on their existence.

Getting ready this morning as best I could, I upgraded to the hand-me-down top she'd offered and wished I at least had some mascara to work my eyes.

I decided to do my nails and stared at the little bottles Jessie said I could help myself to. When I chose pastel and girlish, I chuckled at how little that fits me, and remembered the time DQ sent me for a spa day: Brazilian wax, pedicure, and manicure. I got acrylic, gold and purple paisleys and a rhinestone on my index fingernail, and glow-in-the-dark pinwheels on my toes. And here I was choosing posh pink.

I talked to myself in the bathroom mirror, trying to summon up a warrior spirit to confront the stranger who's got a key to my future and a license to walk through my head.

Now here I am, waiting for the bus way ahead of schedule, in case I have to fight my second thoughts. I may not have a choice about whether to go, but I can decide how to get there, and it'll be a winding path. Or circuitous. That would earn me a vocab point from Mama.

I head for somewhere that's not part of my story, and come to a gourmet market, over in an area where the fade to white's already been accomplished, and walk in like it's no thing, like I belong there. Truth is, I'm all anxiety as the doors slide open and I walk in and see the plenty, right up close. All the organic and farm-grown and high-end things not meant for me and mine.

Nuts and olives and *artisanal* cheeses, fresh-baked bread in paper sleeves, bottled sauces and pickles and jams. People's carts are overflowing, and they're pulling things off the display islands without even looking at the prices or slowing down. And as I take in all the bright, shiny produce stacked in perfect mounds, I feel a blaze of anger at my four years of bruised and squishy bananas and oranges, and when nobody's looking I pull an out-of-season organic mango from the bottom of one, turning and stepping away as the golden fruit comes tumbling down.

Fuck, yes. There it is, the rush from my little sabotage. And not too far behind is the shame of defaulting to my same-old same-old, and at making more cleanup work for someone like me. I picture Daddy shaking his head at my empty victory.

Jasper looked at things in terms of game. When money was tight, he decided boosting was like that, too, a triumph of stealth and will. He liked flirting with getting caught, outsmarting the store workers by slipping merch down his pants when they were close by. He wasn't too troubled by a guilty conscience, long as he was winning, and said he had no qualms at all about stealing books. Knowledge should be free, and he was just redistributing the ill-gotten wealth. Jasper would have his way if at all possible, and come up with an outlook that made it not just a forgivable lapse, but a right.

Thinking back on those days when both of us went low, this fruit's feeling heavy in my hand. But I hold on to it. I want to make my mango misdeed count for something, and I intend to pay.

I search for a pomegranate, but there's not a single one to be had. Still, I wander past the red and orange peppers that look too good to be true, past coffees and pastas and cookies and snacks of every kind, feeling more and more out of place as sweat breaks out beneath my boobs. Seems like an obstacle course, making sure you're tempted by everything on offer, the prepared and frozen bounty, the granolas and bakery treats. I go past fresh-butchered, free-range Cornish hens, lamb chops and grass-fed beef, past swordfish, jumbo shrimp, and salmon that mock me with their price per pound.

My mouth waters at the choices, and I feel like someone who just got let out of a cage (oh, that's right, I am), and I feel everyone watching me, expecting me to pocket something or make a mistake, and I'm getting madder, too, at the sideways looks from my fellow shoppers and the cashier line that's barely moving, and suddenly I decide to put the mango down. I'm out. And I should return it to the fruit section like a good citizen, but I drop it into a last-chance treat and magazine rack where no one will likely find it before it's decayed and spotted like the produce at Oak Hills.

I stretch out my arms and splay my fingers as I leave. I've stolen nothing. I'm empty-handed, still.

A few blocks away I stop by Walgreens for a toothbrush and a jumbo box of tampons, after four years of soggy maxi pads. I can't even afford a DIY perm, but I pull a satin bonnet off the rack, happy I won't have to make do sleeping in a T-shirt head wrap anymore, and then stop in Makeup for mascara and eyeliner, necessities on the self-worth pyramid of needs.

On the way out, I stop at the Valentine's cards and stand in the fluorescent glare, imagining what it would be like to send a classy card through the mail to Maxine, instead of hiding a kite behind the dayroom microwave, and picture her hearing her name during mail call and smiling loose and free as she loves me still across space and time. But what do I want to say to her? That's what I'd like to figure out.

Back in the open air, I keep taking the long way round, checking out the curving stoops and wrought-iron railings and brass-knockered brownstone doors, looking in past the custom drapes and blinds at the gut renovations and designer décor. Jasper's folks grew up over here, back when white folks ceded it as worthless territory and no one had the money to fix the houses up.

For real, there's nowhere that's not part of your story.

I head for more familiar territory, and when it's almost time for my appointment I open the door to the waiting room three shrinks share. And I swear, there's nowhere, except for Oak Hills, I'd less like to be, but here I am, taking a seat in a cramped vanilla waiting room with a handful of scratchy tweed chairs and blown-up photos of flowers on the walls. I'm staring at a field of giant daisies, waiting to be called.

My turn comes and I follow Mr. Therapist into his office and take a seat. Most of the social workers I've met with, they've been women, and I'm a bit surprised. He's clean-shaven. Slim. Salt-and-pepper, close-cropped hair. I peg him as early forties. And yeah, he's Black, at least on the outside. His sweater-vest and striped button-down are white-boy nerdy, and his grave expression and formal way of talking, they make me anxious.

We do the meet and greet, go over why I've got to be here, how this whole thing works. Every other Friday he'll be trying to get a look inside me. Make sure I'm not a danger to my kids. He'll decide if I'm good enough, recovered enough, righteous enough to get them back. After his preamble, he says, in a more casual way that feels like it might be an ambush, "Call me Drew," and I nod, feeling queasy at the offer and hoping to avoid getting overly familiar.

People love to talk about themselves, especially addicts. I've witnessed it time and again at meetings and groups. *Pass the blunt*, you want to say. *Give someone else a chance.* And sometimes, once I've gotten started, I've held the floor longer than I should have, too, high on the attention and release. Right now, everything in me's saying control the impulse to spill, regardless of Drew Turner's eyes, which look just like soft brown caterpillar fur.

Sitting on the hard-ass couch that's covered with cushy pillows (a contradiction designed to keep me off-balance and give him the upper hand, no doubt), I try and radiate composed and detached. And finally, I think maybe he's wrapping up. "So, Ranita, DCF mandates psychotherapy, but another way to look at our time together is to see it as your own personal journey. A place to share the weight of what you've been through and what you're managing. I know you're here because you want reunification with your kids. But you can get something out of this for yourself. It can be a win-win. . . ."

Right. I nod. And tune him out. His mouth keeps on moving like a ventriloquist dummy and I picture myself walking out the office door. I'm not a stranger to making a journey, and it's not like I haven't been working on myself and owning my shit. But that's among my people, a circle of folks who've been where I have. This one-on-one shrink thing, it's different, and let's face it, Drew Turner's getting paid. He's a professional listener, along with jury and judge. Well, I'm a professional, too, at showing people what they want and need. And he's no match for me. I've been keeping secrets all my life.

"We can begin where you choose, Ranita," he reassures me, "and you can do some of the steering.

"Alright," he says, when I stay silent, "one place we can start is with what it felt like when you first tried alcohol and drugs."

I look at the window, wishing I could raise the blinds that slice the view, though there's only a parking lot and a little bit of sky to be had out there. And then I toss him something to chew on. The first drink I had (Bacardi white and Coke, in Antoine's Pathfinder, I never will forget the taste, like sugary fuel) was in the ninth grade. And the first time I smoked a joint was with Jasper, at that basement party where we met. All I give Drew Turner is the basics. Not that the rum eased things up. Not that the weed made things more and less real.

"Jasper Nunn, from the file I know he was your children's father. What was that relationship like, at the beginning?"

Despite my efforts, I see myself. Off-balance. Ever hopeful. Caught between adoration and critique.

Do I share that? No. "He's dead and gone."

"I see that from the file, too. But what would you say has been his role, alive and dead?"

I look away. And while he's waiting for more, I'm checking out the office for clues about Drew Turner, but there's not a lot to go on. No personal photos, which figures. It's not his story that's up for grabs. Diploma. Social work certificate. Paperweights with colored shapes trapped in glass. Tissue box, which I plan on not needing. Framed prints of museum paintings. And a slew of books on the world of things that can go wrong, between and inside of people.

"Well . . . ," he says, "I'm sure there's a lot for us to explore there."

Sorry, I'm not up for hanging out with 16-year-old me.

He fishes around, asking about my home life, my school life, my friends and hobbies and interests, and I try and keep to the general, telling him I liked my classes and teachers in elementary and middle school and my report cards were always good. "Not perfect," I add, seeing a flash of Mama's frowning face. "I got a B in fifth-grade math, and in PE once." When I say I've always been a reader, I decide he looks surprised.

I see myself at the little branch library, in the warm lamplight, lost in the pages of a story. Later, I found out there were escapes that felt more complete.

Drew Turner wants to rewind my story, figure out my turning point. But I just took one step and then the next. It's not like I knew where I'd end up. And it's not that big of a leap from outsider to outlaw.

He's quiet, watching and waiting for more. Why, I'm wondering, if we're here to talk about my parenting and my kids, who by the way, I'm getting more and more anxious and desperate to see or even talk to as the days tick by, are we digging in the way back? *Why go there?* That's what Daddy would say when I tried to talk through the feelings that scared me, and when Jasper got long time with the feds, three states away: *Why dwell on the past, Ranita? Let him stay gone.*

"You know what? I'm trying for a new start. . . . I'm trying to turn the page."

He answers, with a firm, parental kindness that pisses me off, "Well, my job here . . . from the DCF perspective and also therapeutically, is to connect your future ability to parent with your behavior, past and present. The idea being that they don't exist alone, that they're all interrelated, and that exploring them will give me the insight I need about reunification . . . and also help you."

"And what if I don't need this kind of help to move forward? What if I've got what I need?"

I decide to hit him with an encyclopedia fact. "You know, there was this eastern white pine, *Pinus strobus*, outside my bedroom window, and I ended up learning all about it." His head is cocked slightly to the side like with pets, when they're trying to figure out where you're headed. I keep going. "Its sap flows in the spring and summer, and my mother . . ."

Fuck. See, I started talking and lost my balance. I reset.

"People hate the way the sap flows and gets on things, on cars and stuff. . . . But the thing about the sap . . . the point I'm getting to, is that *Pinus strobus* uses its own sap to close its wounds. It heals itself."

"Okay," he says, slowly, "things work that way sometimes. With trees. But maybe you've got to give therapy a chance to see if it can help or not. Like I said, this is mandated, and since you've got to be here, maybe it's worth choosing to give it a try."

How's it a choice if it's mandated? I don't say that, or anything else. Once the levee's breached, there'll be no containing the flood.

I do like Jasper's dog, who used to go boneless in passive refusal, and sit here blankly. And when Drew Turner's finally finished and I actually do get to walk through his door, I'm all keyed up, even though he did the talking and all I really gave him was ice in the wintertime. Feels like I'm breathing through something sharp, but maybe I can walk it off. After a stretch of blocks, Drew Turner's still in my head . . . *your own personal journey . . . DCF mandates . . . reunification . . .* and next thing I know, I'm going through the door of a corner store and heading straight for the candy.

Again, there's way too many things to choose from, and my eyes dart from Milky Ways to Gummi Bears to Twizzlers, Laffy Taffy, Kit Kats, Sour Patch Kids. I can't decide on anything. I want them all. Then I see the Reese's, which I couldn't get enough of growing up and haven't had for four long years, and snag the Pieces jumbo bag. I can't say I'm thinking I'll have a few now and there'll be plenty for later. I'm not thinking at all, just trying to get me some of this sweetness I know is gonna hit the fucking spot.

Once I've paid for it, before I've even left the shop, I tear off a corner of the bag with my teeth, tilt my head back, and start pouring it into my mouth . . . until I see, from the corner of my eye, the cashier looking at me. *Get ahold of yourself, Ranita,* I scold, and try to chew and swallow without choking. When I've gotten it down, I turn and make sure to hold my head up, hoping my lips aren't smeared with chocolate, and force a smile at the cashier lady, wanting to say that what she saw was an aberration and, even though it might not look like it, I was raised right. I do know how to act.

I try and slow my breathing down while taking in the bags of rice and nuts and different-colored lentils, and the smells of spices and honey-soaked fresh-baked treats. And I see a basket of pomegranates.

When I pick one up, my fingers remember the texture of the weathered skin and my eyes are tearing up, but I keep it together, going back to the counter and pulling out my few dollars, trying not to think of how my money's dwindling.

"Last of the season," the shopkeeper says, smiling warmly and looking me in the eye like respect is not a finite resource.

I tell her I don't need a bag, I want to hold it, and she hands me the fruit and says, "Enjoy," wishing me peace in Arabic. And the barbed-wire tangle inside loosens and softens into something bearable.

On the way back to Auntie Jessie's, I feel tender from the probing, and exhausted from the dodging. What I need is peace and rest. What I want is to see my home and my kids.

I try and bend my mind to better things, but it refuses, and I'm heading toward my bus connection when I turn instead of walking straight. I tell myself it's my feet that are doing the deciding, but I know deep down that tactic's an old friend that hugs you, even as it does you wrong. I put the pomegranate in my backpack and ignore the alarm bells going off inside me, heading for familiar ground. This is the going back that I can do.

When I see the bus approaching I hurry to the stop, and this time I get on at the front and pay, as if that'll redeem me. Grabbing a strap, I hold on, and travel into territory where I've got no business going. Waiting and judgment, impulse control . . . I've got Good Time certificates for the last one, but here I go, and I can't say I keep on trying to talk some sense into myself. I just surrender to the path I'm on.

We pass the places that grew me . . . corner stores and hair burners, playgrounds where the dribbling never stops and boys dream of NBA glory, hardware store and carryouts. And Atwater Garage & Body Shop. It's got a new name and a different owner, but for me, it's still his, and I can picture the tool chests and shelves of parts, the hydraulic lifts and stacks of tires. All I've got to do is close my eyes and I hear the banging and revving, the teasing banter of men at work, the R&B that was always on in the background. Somehow, Daddy's simply gone.

A few minutes later I get off, praying I won't see anyone I know, and when I round the corner I see Avery, rising above the roofline.

I move down the block until I'm right out front, until I see the spindly hedges and the missing piece of curbstone just before the driveway, and here I am, at the house I've come back to so many times. The beige siding's the same, but the front steps are crumbling, and even at nightfall I can tell the paint on the trim is flaking. Val's Corolla's out front and the porch light's off.

Looking at the front door, I picture Daddy opening it, relief and worry on his face, and welcoming me home with open arms, ready to feed and fix me. And then I see Auntie Jessie, blocking my way.

My feet are moving again, taking me up the strip between our house and the Wilsons', to a light shining from the dining room. I know better. But I step into the flower bed and crouch behind the boxwood Mama was always asking Daddy to prune into a geometric shape, and look in through the window.

I am on the outside. Gorging on my boy.

Holding my breath, I watch him write, filling out a worksheet, looks like. Still left-handed. Frowning in concentration. And then he puts his pencil down, slides his chair back, and disappears into the kitchen with his empty plate. It is not enough. *Come back; come back to me*, I choke on my unspoken cry. And my girl? I'm hoping for a glimpse of Amara, but she's nowhere to be seen. All that's left is an empty dining room, with the traces . . . place mats, pens and papers, half-filled glasses . . . of lives carrying on without me.

Then I see myself. Invading their privacy. And it comes back to me like a flash of fever, the one time I saw Mama undressed, without even meaning to. Running up the stairs, I'd yanked the bathroom door open, and there she was, stepping from the tub. Naked.

Our eyes met. She froze. Gasped. Shouted that I was bent on embarrassing, disrespecting, exposing her. And slammed the door. We never spoke of it, and she was even more distant than usual for weeks on end.

Feet sinking into moist black dirt, I see myself. Spying. Hiding in the bushes like a criminal or a psychopath.

And I smell myself. Sweat and armpit stink. Desperation and shame. All of it hits my nostrils at once, the body that brought me here, telling on itself.

Real slow and careful, I back up, one foot at a time, from the mushy flower bed, to the firmer grass, until I'm next to Avery. I put my arms around her as far as they'll reach and press my hands into the ridged bark, and then glance at my palms like I expect to find them sore from climbing and see Mama, waiting to punish me.

I move from grass to driveway and scuttle back to the front sidewalk, praying Mr. and Mrs. Wilson don't take me for a prowler, don't shoot, don't call 911, and walk as fast as I can without running, always a bad idea for Black folks when it's dark. I'm a stalker, a trespasser, at the only real home I've ever known.

Soon as I get back to Jessie's, I clean the mud off my shoes, thinking about how forensics can detect even the smallest signs of wrongdoing. I strip off my clothes and take a long, hot shower, trying to wash off what I just allowed myself to do.

Then I remember the pomegranate and take it from my backpack. *Punica granatum*. Fruit of death, seeds of eternal life. Fertility. Sexual power. Lure to the underworld. I wonder what all Daddy realized when he gifted me that first one. I picture the treasure inside, recalling that some say every pomegranate has 613 seeds, matching the number of commandments in the Torah. I like to think of them as infinite.

I find my rescued piece of cobalt bottle in my backpack, too, and wash it off, smiling at the stunning color, and I'm transported back to Maxine telling me about collecting sea glass at whatever beach she went to, and adding it to a jar. She'd shake the jar, enjoying the percussion, and spill out the cloudy blues and greens of her private treasure into her hands, feeling the edges that had been tumbled smooth and soft by churning waves and sand.

This here is city glass. Discarded recklessly. Unexceptional. Still sharp enough to cut.

Maybe I'll add to it, make a collection. Mama would shake her head at my coarse tendencies, after she tried to teach me better with her porcelain figurines. I find a piece of Tupperware in the back of Jessie's cabinet and put the glass in it, at least for now.

I've got the place to myself while Jessie's at physical therapy, and that's good and bad. Seems like when she's here and there's silence between us I can't wait to get some space and solitude. What exactly I'd like to do with it is a mystery. Walk around naked, breasts swinging, ass jiggling? Shout at the top of my voice? Lick my plate? And when she's gone I can't wait for her to come back.

I get the kites from Maxine out of my backpack and just hold the paper scraps in my hands, feeling wealthy. If I look at them one by one, it'll be like reading our story, at least the half I've got.

Just after we started talking and playing Scrabble, she sent me on a scavenger hunt. "You up for a challenge?" she asked, and I said yes, excited and afraid.

"It's a series of challenges, really, should you choose to accept them. Maybe it'll help with the mystery deficit in here."

First she asked could I find something beautiful in my cell, other than the photos of my kids. The whole next day I looked around, trying to think of something that didn't involve looking out the window. I was just lying on my bunk, my new cellie snoring above me, when I noticed the light coming through the bars, striping me like a tiger.

Next Maxine asked me to detect a change, it didn't matter how little, in the woods we could both see from our cell windows. I watched and listened for days, until I saw a great horned owl. "How'd you know the species?" she asked, and I told about me and Daddy's encyclopedia thing.

Finally, a word puzzle led me to the microwave, where I found the first kite. I wanted to wait and read it alone, and it felt like my pocket was throbbing the whole way to the chapel. My fingers shook as I unfolded it.

Two words, in caps: *WHAT IF?*

I return the kites to my backpack now, thinking about my first year at Oak Hills, before I met Max. There I was, trying to keep to what I knew and keep apart. Trying to get to the other side of my sentence on my own, as I prayed for the visits that broke my heart.

I take the pomegranate in my hands, promising myself I'm gonna wait to open it.

Sometimes you can't even imagine what's hidden inside. I knew Maxine was unique, but still, what an unfolding treasure she turned out to be. A revelation, after what all came before: the self-doubt, the silence and uncertainty, the measurements. The territory sacked and ceded. The being looked at, but not seen.

SEVEN

Ranita sat at the counter of her father's shop, doing her homework while she worked her Saturday shift. The radio, tuned to WILD by her father or Jam'n 94.5 by the mechanics Tommy and Blue, was a comfort. And along with their trashtalk and deep-throated laughter, the familiar smells of oil and metal and sweat made her feel less lonely.

The boys she'd always known had started coming by to stand around and talk about the rides they dreamed of getting and how to perfect the ones they had. Taking Antoine's lead, they gathered around Ranita and took turns holding forth about all matters automotive, and though Ranita tried to join the conversation, she found it even harder than jumping in for double Dutch.

Socially, the ninth grade was worse than middle school, where she had at least found a home of sorts singing with the jazz band. Though she never had been part of a girl posse, her current exile felt complete. Growing up, despite Geneva's tireless efforts to put a skirt on her and reproaches that she came home dirty and unkempt, she had slipped outside whenever possible to run free with the neighborhood boys, climbing jungle gyms and trees, playing dodgeball and kickball, speeding downhill on her bike. Fighting, when necessary. While the girls had kept their distance, the boys had made a place for her. Until middle school, when the rules shifted and she had no quarter. This year the girls still didn't want her. And the boys wanted her in new and unsettling ways.

Today they were arguing about which recent Mustangs were better, and Antoine had the floor. Ranita knew the '94's V6 engine made it little more than a show car before it went back to a V8 in '96, and she closed her textbook, waiting for a moment when she'd be able to share her knowledge.

Antoine and company moved on from Mustangs to rims, putting the options . . . long spokes, Japanese, mesh, center caps . . . to vigorous debate.

They talked past her. And when they weren't opining on cars or sports or hip hop, they teased her about whether it was jealousy that had turned her eyes green, if she could still do a no-hands wheelie, which she liked better, books or people. She didn't get much of a chance to talk, but she'd seen them checking out her body, and she felt exposed without the pre-teen weight she'd shed, and conspicuous, even in her oversized hoodies, from the breasts that had defiantly grown to 34Ds.

She noticed their voices getting louder, looser, more insistent. And she saw Antoine's body taking up more and more space as he held the floor. She hoped her father didn't notice the escalation, or his backward cap and sagging pants.

"Let's let Ranita decide whose engine is the biggest. . . ."

Nervously, she scanned the floor and saw her father straighten up in slow motion from the fender he was inspecting, wiping the oil from his hands and crossing the shop in a few long-legged strides. Nearly jumping when he realized Lennox was standing beside him, Antoine held out his hand.

Lennox kept his in his pockets and spoke firmly. "Lennox Atwater," he said, looking from face to face and stressing the name that was on the sign out front and the invoices stacked on the counter where they stood. "I'm Ranita's father."

"Daddy, you know Antoine. He lives two blocks over, and he's practically a walking encyclopedia on cars."

Lennox nodded and then told them he'd be closing soon and Ranita had work to do. They filed out and she finished organizing orders while smoldering with resentment. She was a 15-year-old high school freshman, not a little girl, and she was sick and tired of being sequestered from the world, and hearing how she needed to be her own person before she started dating. Plus, it had felt good, the attention, the warmth, the promise of a constellation, when it was so hard persisting as a solitary star.

Still, as she updated the calendar and filed paperwork, she couldn't help thinking how her father's antenna was suddenly operating and how accurate it was. Antoine had kissed her when he dropped her home from school the week before, and he'd been pressing for more.

If you didn't put out, to some degree, who would choose you? She'd overheard girls talk about blow jobs and using the back door, ways to pay your dues without risking a baby. Pregnancy was an F for Failure that landed you in exile, labeled with a bunch of other *F* words: Fast. Fallen. Finished.

In middle school health class, they'd been told that getting your period was a "natural" passage to womanhood, part of the awesome gift of making life. But it felt like pain and shame and a new way to fall, more cause for alarm and disgust than reverence. The day Ranita's had started, Lori Watson had pulled her aside to tell her about the swath of shocking red on the seat of her jeans and she had squeezed her legs together until class ended and she could get a bathroom pass, and then tied her jacket around her waist until school let out. With unaccustomed gentleness, Geneva had given her pads and put her clothes to soak. And then

Geneva's tone had turned ominous as she warned about the care Ranita would now have to take to keep herself chaste, and clean *down there*.

As they closed up the shop, Lennox grumbled, "Where I come from, men keep their pants up at their waists, where they're meant to be, covering their drawers. And they take off their hats indoors."

"Cap. It's not a hat; it's a cap." *Country. Antiquated. Ridiculous.* She named his shortcomings to herself and informed him that there was nothing going on that had anything to do with pant wearing, or cap wearing; Antoine and his friends were just expressing themselves, and just being guys.

"Ranita, trust me," Lennox said. "I know guys . . . men . . . *boys* . . . and that one can't get enough of the sound of his own voice."

Over dinner they were quiet and awkward, and when he suggested they go down and listen to some Aretha she refused and got to work cleaning up the kitchen. But as the music drifted up, she let go of her grudge and joined him for a few songs before kissing him good night and going to her room to finish her homework and get ready for bed.

Lying in the dark, she looked up at her ceiling stars and listed her faults. Bacne. Sloping shoulders. Fleshy nose. Freckles. Pudgy arms. Breasts that were a long way from round and perky, however big they were. Hair that refused taming and lame-ass clothes. Eyes that were a conundrum all their own. A lightning rod, but incapable, alone, of making her beautiful. She ached when she thought of the first day of algebra the fall before, when a group of boys had stood at the classroom door watching her enter, look for an empty seat, and then carry her books to a desk and sit. Seeing them track her movements, she had felt potent, and when she was seated she'd lifted her eyes to meet theirs. They had looked her up and down. And then looked at each other, shook their heads, and said, *Nah.*

Antoine knew her, saw her as she was. And wanted her. But whatever she did give in to, he wouldn't be touching her if she had her say.

Was it even worse, though, the way she sometimes touched herself? What would happen if all her desire was released, or recognized? Was it possible, she wondered, to shrink your wanting, to empty yourself out?

She got up and opened the window, even though it was cold and blustery, and she heard her mother's voice in her head, reminding her not to let out the heat they paid good money for. She wished she could escape her questions, let them loose and watch a gust of wind take them, but they kept pressing.

Was it better to be invisible?

There always seemed to be someone watching, judging, laying in the cut.

Was she her own or wasn't she?

Was her body a source of life or a source of pain? Sacred or sinful? The means of sovereignty or ticket to the underworld?

EIGHT

Turns out the waiting thing's a delicate balance. I kept the pomegranate too long, saving it for just the right time, and missed my moment. That's today's first piece of bad news, but I'm trying not to read too much into it.

I could make a long-ass list of what I've not got. No pomegranate. No voice. No money. And no Maxine.

Throughout the night I toss and turn. I can't stop thinking of her, and when the sun comes up I take out my kites.

After her *WHAT IF?* it was my turn to leave one. In the couple of months I'd known her, I'd learned how she could talk things up.

She'd told me how, even as a kid, she'd wanted out, sneaking from her bedroom window after bedtime and stretching out on her father's chaise lounge in their little postage stamp yard to look at the evening sky, even though the plastic-weave seat would print her skin and tell on her.

I had told her about climbing Avery, describing how it felt to be up high and almost hidden, doing the little comedy routine I'd performed over the years about Mama, ranting down below. I imitated her voice and body language . . . *and there was Geneva, worrying about my panties showing and threatening to disable and disown me, which was not exactly an incentive to come back to earth.* Maxine had reached across the Scrabble board and touched my face with a tenderness that was hard to take, making me wish my schtick had been funny enough to make her laugh. Making me wish I could have told it true.

I decided to see what she could conjure. *Tell me a pine tree,* I wrote, longing for the place where I'd found openness and shelter, both.

At our next private moment at the chapel, she made me feel like I was up in the branches, surrounded by the clean, fresh smell and bark against my skin.

And a month or so later, she left me her second question: *Favorite time of day?*

Truth is, they all have their virtues. Morning *can* feel like a new start. Though not necessarily, not today. Nighttime has its gifts. Bridge between today and tomorrow. Star canvas. Cover. And minefield.

And here I am, reliving my nighttime trespass at the house, longing for the kids I've got and not got. Just the chance to be in the same room would mean everything. And what would be the danger, with Val or Jessie there?

My worries and regrets, my questions, they ricochet inside me, no outlet, no rest. And on top of that, I'm trying to reason away my impatience at Auntie Jessie avoiding a conversation about any of it. *We can't solve everything tonight,* she said when I got here, and still we haven't really talked.

I know Amara's last report card was pretty good, but Jessie says she gets Bs without trying, so she's not too invested. I know she's in the Spanish club and runs track and she's late to everything, classes *and* extracurriculars. And unapologetic about it, though lateness is punished as an absence that leads to detention and, sometimes, failing out, though it's beyond me what the fuck they've got in mind with that. A kid's on the edge about school, or troubled, or has a long bus ride and shit going on at home that makes them late, and instead of finding out why, and helping, they push them out?

When I got locked up, my girl stopped speaking for almost a month. I had to pry it out of Daddy that she was taunted. *Your mama's in jail and she's never coming back.* When she started to speak again, it was with a serious edge she's never lost. Always mad, staging some rebellion, refusing to do something. Too tired to finish her homework and didn't want Daddy to check it. No, she didn't want to read to Theo. No, she wouldn't finish her food and she hadn't, *wouldn't*, brush her teeth. And if she did as she was told, she did it real slow. I know that move. I may buff that floor, but I'll take my time doing it. She's still got an attitude, and who can blame her?

As for Theo, he gets good grades when he's paying attention, when he's not trying to be a clown instead of a target. He loves art, reading up on animals, the Red Sox, and Pokémon. It took a while, but he got past getting freaked out by the police, clinging to Daddy when they saw a black-and-white and saying, *They take mamas.* Worried he'd get locked up if he visited me. Worried he'd be arrested for getting his letters and numbers wrong, for not paying attention in kindergarten, for crying. *Like a girl*, the class bully said. Soon he'll be aiming for tough, and I just hope I haven't squandered the chance to raise him into a gentle man.

And what about the rest of life? Grades don't begin to tell the story, I well know.

I get out my photos and go through them, stopping at the one we took in visitation, when I was a year in. I've stared at it so often I know it by heart, but I get the magnifying glass I saw by Jessie's recliner and take a closer look. I'm grinning, proud of the beautiful kids who maybe haven't given up on me, relieved that they've come to visit and we're still a family and I'll have proof of that to share and stare at once they've gone. But I can see now that Theo's clinging to my shirt and his anxious smile could shift into tears, easy. And Amara's expression, it's only technically a smile. It looks brittle enough to cut. Her arms are folded and she's stiff . . . and is she pulling away from me? It looks like she's pulling away.

I put the photos away and get dressed. Might as well accomplish something and get outside, since it's one of those midsummer days in winter that we're having more and more.

Stepping out into the blue, early-morning light, I do feel better. The streets are empty and quiet, and porch lights are still burning. I imagine crocuses pushing through the dead, soggy leaves piled up from last fall, and song from the birds that'll soon be coming back north. The city-hardened squirrels riding out the winter, they're out and scrounging to survive, and there's plenty of trees carrying on with little bent, trash-muddled fences around their trunks, roots buckling the sidewalk as they fight confinement. As I walk by I touch their different barks, grooved, rough and grainy, smooth and scaled, and the scars people have carved into them.

Music drifts from open windows, competing with car engines coughing to a start and things unanchored, flapping in the wind. I can tell where people are making breakfast from the smell of bacon and baking bread, and where the morning housecleaning is going on from the Pine-Sol and ammonia in the air. And there's the stink of garbage, too, having its say.

I go and surrender my pee for testing, looking forward to the day when this body might feel like it's mine again. And then I check my watch, and without really planning on it, I'm headed downtown to Val's job at Liberty Mutual, thinking if I time it right I can be out front when she gets to work. First and foremost, I'm gonna say hi, that and show her I'm doing okay. And then I'ma do my best to ask her help.

I know I'll look suspect, hovering around the door of her stately limestone building, so I bum a cigarette on the way and then pretend

I'm a working stiff, having a smoke before I punch in. I haven't seen her for months, but looking back, it's amazing how little she changed from year to year. *Steady wins the race*, Mama liked to say, delighted with her pun.

Every fall, like the vernal equinox, Auntie Val came from D.C. for a weeklong stay, bringing books and candies and gifts from the Smithsonian. Stuffed animals, fluorescent stars for my ceiling, that tin kaleidoscope. And we had Girls' Day Out, going to a movie matinee or Alvin Ailey, and then for tea downtown, in the café at the Public Library, where we had our fill of scones and profiteroles. . . . I loved saying that word. Her visits made me feel special, if not known.

But at our last outing, just before I met Jasper, I was furious. She wouldn't let me drive, even though I had my permit, and how was I supposed to learn if no one ever let me get behind the wheel? As we stood in line for tickets to some PG flick we'd compromised on, I tried to feel grateful. But our little routine was tired, and Auntie Val's buttoned-up, goody-goody ways had become a serious drag.

I knew Daddy had summoned her out of season, after he'd caught me creeping at night from the window and climbing down Avery to hang out with Judy. I'd found a spot with the renegades, and started skipping class. I still hadn't let Antoine or anyone else touch me, but I was riding with him and his crew after school. And I'd been out tagging, playing lookout while he climbed a billboard to throw up his name in fluorescent colors. I was tearing free, and nobody could make me feel bad or rein me in if I opted out of caring.

I remember me and Val, sitting in the theater, shoveling in our Junior Mints and popcorn instead of talking as we waited for the movie to take us elsewhere. And as the lights went down I leaned close and whispered that I knew Daddy had asked her to come and help right me. Then I asked her, acidly, why she was so sure I was fixable.

Now here she comes.

"Ranita, what are you doing here?" she says when she sees me, giving me one of her constrained smiles. "Is Jessie okay? Is something wrong?"

I put out my cigarette in the ashtray barrel by the door. "It's all good. I just wanted to say hey, keep you in the loop, you know. . . . I figured you're wondering how I'm doing out here . . . trying to jump back onto the spinning world."

Though I'm well aware she's not a hugger, I open my arms, and she takes one step toward me, then stops. "Are you supposed to be here, what with—" she says, stalling mid-sentence. Nice welcome back.

I drop my arms. "Seeing you's not forbidden, is it? I don't recall anything about visiting your auntie in the DCF rules and regs."

Without answering, she glances at the office building door, and she doesn't need to say a thing. I knew coming to the workplace wasn't in the playbook, but I repeat that really, I just came by to say hey. And because it isn't and hasn't ever been like that with us, she waits for the rest of the story. Dropping my pretenses, I say, "Look, I know it's not ideal, me coming to your *j-o-b*, but I need to talk to you about something." What I *need* to do, though, is keep my shit in check. My vibe is moving from anxious to confrontational, and I can feel the passersby looking at us.

"Okay, what's on your mind?"

Now that I'm here, I can't seem to say it. Val looks like the actuary she is, prim and proper in her work drag: skirt and pumps and silky blouse, and a girlish navy velvet headband on her graying, straightened hair. And my fraying, dirty seams are definitely showing. I've already lost the war, but I dig in for this battle and blurt out how I can't see why it would be harmful to have just the briefest visit with Amara and Theo, just 10 minutes or even 5, with her there to supervise, wherever she wants, and that would ease my mind and their minds and help me carry on with some hope and pride. She's staring at me, and I swear she takes a tiny step back, like my desperation and rambling speech are catching.

I hadn't really thought this out. Once again, I'm freestyling, and I know my pitch is falling flat. And I go where she and everyone else might predict: I tell her Daddy would support me, if he was still here.

She looks pained. But unmoved. And tells me she's not prepared to go against what's allowed. I argue harder, working against my goal as I pull out all the stops, until she holds her hand up like a stop sign. "Don't try and hustle me, Ranita. There's another way to try and approach things: Keep to the rules. Prove yourself that way."

Insulted, rebuked, ashamed, take your pick, I claim them all. And angry, too. Raising my voice, I demand to know, "Whose side are you on?"

She flexes her jaw and looks straight at me. "I'm on Amara and Theo's side. That doesn't mean I'm against you. I'm praying . . . and working hard, for you, and the kids, and our family. But I'm their legal guardian."

The truth hurts. And it does not set me free. I answer the only way I can: "I'm still their parent, Val."

She takes a deep breath. "I haven't forgotten that. I've been trying to keep things going, not replace you."

Did I mention that I feel ashamed? I kick the ashtray, sending sand and crushed butts flying, and she steps back.

We stand here looking across a three-foot chasm at each other. I want to cry. Or howl. I say I meant no harm, I came in peace. I tell her this is about the kids.

"You sure about that?" she says. And then turns and goes inside.

I look up at the dignified stone façade and gleaming windows, picturing Val, respectable and level-headed, riding the elevator up to her office and then looking out and down on me, and see myself through her eyes. Desperate, sneaky, and hostile is not an approach that makes folks want to go out on a limb. And I'm sure she's got to dig way down to find the little girl she came to see on those annual visits from D.C.

When I get back to Jessie's, I think I see that look on her face, the one where she's afraid of what she'll see when I walk in. I try and atone by throwing myself into making omelets and corn bread, and when she shuffles into the kitchen, looking even more stiff and bent than usual, I offer to help her with bathing, cleaning, errands, laundry . . . anything that needs doing. "Maybe later" is all she says, and I can see she's tempted to accept my offers, if only to soothe and support me, but she'd rather do for herself.

Jessie always has been a mix of whatever-you-need and don't-try-me. Though loyal, especially to Daddy, she did not mess around. She was real direct in telling even him if he was being trifling. But she had another, lighter side, especially in the decade when she was married to Cedric. She liked a whiskey sour before dinner, and she had a kind of sly sassiness that emerged when they played bid whist with their work friends from Medical Records at The City Hospital. Most Sundays she went to church, but she also got her fun on, and after a week of paperwork she and Cedric got dressed up . . . I can picture him in a suit and her in the shoes that matched her outfits . . . and went out on Friday nights to Slade's, or to hear some music at Wally's. After he died, she dated a little, hoping, I think, to find some steady company, but that fizzled, and she had her hands full, helping us.

I haven't seen any lightness in her since I got here, which is probably my doing. While we eat breakfast and chat about recent news stories, I see how tired she is, and ask is she feeling alright. She puts a nice face on things, pretends she's doing fine.

"I know it's not easy," I say, "me being back, and in your space."

"No. That is not a thing. You're welcome here."

Sighing, she tells me Gil says he's okay, but those overseas letters are meant to comfort, and they never tell the true story. "I just keep asking the Lord to please just bring him back to me whole, in his right mind. They come back broken and then take their own lives. And then, like every Black mother knows, it could go another way. He could come back and get killed by the police or someone who doesn't even think he's a person."

"I feel you."

Gil was 10 when she married Cedric, but she might as well have birthed him, and I was always jealous of their easy friendship, the way they laughed and played board games and gin rummy. They both loved amusement parks and every summer they went to Six Flags and went on rides all day. She was so proud when he graduated from high school, and I know it crushed her when he enlisted, one of the "few good men" the Armed Services are looking for, those low-opportunity Black and brown ones who make the easiest prey.

"If only we could protect them," she murmurs, shaking her head.

"There's no end of worry, whether you're home or away, inside or outside," I say, and then add, taking advantage of the opening, "Auntie Jessie, while we're on the subject of parenting and struggling, I've been wanting to talk to you."

She glances at the walker parked next to her, and without thinking I put my hand on the front bar. I know I've overstepped, but I launch in, "Jessie, when I got here you said get rested, instead of talking that night. It's been two weeks, and I know it's a lot . . . I know *I'm* a lot . . . but we have to talk."

"Talk. Weren't we just talking? About Gil. And before that, about the government shutdown . . . and the Hong Kong protests . . . and that madman punishing that CNN reporter for asking a question? And I've been telling you how Judy changed jobs, and what the cast of characters in physical therapy have been up to. We've done plenty of talking just this morning."

"Yes, we've been talking about the news. Auntie Jessie, I know you don't owe it to me, but it's hard, being back and not being able to talk about what I'm carrying, and not see or contact the kids, or know how they really are." I feel myself revving up, and hear a long line of people telling me to take it down a notch.

"I spoke to them last Saturday. They're fine."

I cut to the chase. "Did you tell them I'm out?"

It's not good, I can tell by how she looks away, and I brace myself for more hard truth. She might evade, but outright lying's not her way.

"I told them." She pauses, looks away. "They didn't have a lot to say."

Ouch. I just try and carry on while she pulls over the corn bread, cuts a piece, and slides it over to me.

"When are you allowed to see them?"

I'm praying Val hasn't called yet to report on my behavior this morning, but I know it's just a matter of time. "According to the rules, it'll be weeks before a supervised visit." I get busy with the corn bread, and pause to say, "Tell me how that's good for the kids? Everything depends on keeping the tie alive with Amara and Theo, though I'm not sure how I'm supposed to do that without seeing them."

She's watching me slather butter on the corn bread and then she says, "We can call them later. I know it's not the same as seeing them, but it's something."

For the rest of the morning and afternoon, I'm rehearsing and preparing. Trying to decide on the right things to say, on how to fill the little silences and know what to do if they're angry, or roll with it if they don't want to talk. I try and come up with some questions to ask them and lighthearted little comments if we get stuck.

I say, "Let's call," trying to sound at ease, and we sit at the kitchen table. Here's the contact I've been so bent on, and what I feel is dread. I can hear Val answering and I whisper, "Jessie, let me talk to her for just a minute," and she hands me the phone.

"I just wanted to say, before the kids get on . . . I'm sorry for this morning. And I'm hoping you can maybe forget it, strike it from the record, chalk it up to my janky heart running the show, instead of my head."

After a long silence, her voice is steady. Not warm, but not cold. "Something that's happened can't just be erased, but I understand . . . I mean . . . I don't understand, not being their mother . . . but I get it, that it's tough, what all you're dealing with. . . ."

"Okay, well, just . . . thanks again."

And into the awkward gulf between us, she takes a step. "I meant to ask you earlier, how's it feel, being home?"

I flash on Keisha and her *Where the fuck is home?* I know where mine is, but I'm not allowed to go there. "It's feeling like a lot, but I'm glad to be out. I'll give you back to Jessie now. Appreciate you."

Then I can hear Theo get on and chatter for a while, until she tells him I'm with her and I'd like to talk to him. I don't want to come at him too intense, so I just say how good it is to hear his voice. Then there's an awful stillness, and I'm searching for what's next.

"Well . . . how was school this week?"

"Okay."

"What did you do that was fun?"

"Fun?"

"Fun. Interesting." Then, thinking of Daddy and those encyclopedias, I say, "Tell me something you learned."

I guess he's got to think hard and long on that one, which is worrisome, and just when I'm wondering should I give up and hand the phone back to Jessie, he starts in on how he's drawing birds for a project on science and art, and "searching them up on the computer" to find out about their behavior and habitats. He gets excited talking about ospreys, and all I have to do is say, "Un-hunh," and, "Wow," and, "Okay," and he rambles on.

"You like birds?" he asks.

"Yes. Yes, I do."

"What's your favorite?"

I don't know what to say. Truth be told, I feel a kinship with pigeons, but I'm sure that's not the right answer, so I tell him I saw a red-tailed hawk out at Oak Hills sometimes and it was awesome and beautiful. And I say I love that flash of red you get to see with cardinals.

He says, "Hawks are predators. I like cardinals, too."

Then he asks for Jessie. She repeats for me what he says, that Amara, she's in the middle of her homework and doesn't really have time to talk right now.

"Alright, baby," Jessie answers, before hanging up.

Amara, she didn't even . . . Anyway, with Theo it started out rough and got better. I've never been good on the phone . . . the pressure to go with the flow and get to what matters at the same time, all while keeping the conversation afloat, it's too much. Amara didn't even want to say hello.

While Jessie rejoins the news loop, I sit down at her puzzle and try one piece after another that doesn't fit. Maybe it's time to try some speculating.

At Oak Hills, in meditation group, I usually tried to picture gently lapping ocean waves. And then a few weeks before my out date, I started imagining an Afrofuturist scene play out. Unlike Maxine, I'm just a novice conjurer, and so far, my visualization goes like this: The apocalypse is underway . . . and that's not futurist at all. Climate change. People's rights being snatched. Our bodies policed and controlled. Walling the suffering brown and Black people out. The rich getting richer. Maniacs in charge all over the world. All that's already going down.

Okay, I sound like Maxine, but that's the backdrop. And I'm wandering across the dry, barren rocks and sand that've taken over what the oceans haven't swallowed up, and I see a woman standing with her back to me. When she turns around, I see she's holding an ancient-looking clay bowl, smoky dark and red, and I know there's something familiar about her, though I can't see her face, and something special about the bowl. So far . . . sometimes . . . I've been able to see myself in the desert, seeing her. Not a stretch, right? But where I'm trying to go is holding that bowl myself and seeing it fill with water.

Sitting with my back upright, feet planted on the floor, I focus on my breath and try to get still. Fuck me, I can't turn off my head. I can't even see myself, let alone the sand or the woman or the bowl.

What I can picture is Val, mothering my kids. On her worst day, she's probably a better caregiver than me, and I'm sure she takes them on outings like the ones we had when she visited, and to museums. She's involved with their homework, and I'm sure her cookies are never store-bought, or even from a mix. She probably grows organic herbs and puts up pickles and tomatoes and preserves in those Ball canning jars Daddy had stacked in the basement.

Starting with the glimpse I got at the house, I'm seeing a slide show of her virtues, and my kids as beneficiaries. And an insight sinks its teeth in me and won't let go. Maybe the thing that's already been terminated is their need for me.

I'm groping for something that'll help me turn the page, wondering why I can't seem to get out of my own way.

Daddy used to ask me did I have a death wish. *Maybe so*, I answered. *What's so good about this life?* I never was sure who would have me, who was friend or foe, how to choose life.

Other species, they know what to do. Buds open when they can tell spring's arriving, though they're a bit confused these days, what with global warming. Morning glories close at night and unpleat their ruffled indigo petals with the morning light. Seeds know which way to grow.

From those encyclopedias, I remember learning how emperor penguins know when it's time to walk across the ice and make their babies and some kind of way they get back to where they were born. Knowing they can't make it alone, they go in a group. They know what time it is. They make a way.

And something deep inside pulls those gorgeous black-and-orange monarch butterflies to the same place, every year at the same time. Well, it seems like my GPS is broken. I know the destination, but I haven't got the strength to get there or the sense to know the route. And I want to think I'm wiser, weller, better than before, but I still can't tell winter from spring or up from down.

In Jessie's fridge I find the ingredients for turkey chili, one of the few healthy things I know how to make, and get cooking. When the pot's on, filling the apartment with a warm, spicy aroma, I lean on the windowsill, watching the lights come on in people's windows as the sun goes down, neon signs flashing into being and the murky sky taking on a sickly yellow streetlight glow, and I'm winding tighter and tighter as the streets begin to call my name.

Turning my back to the window, I look at the magnets that cover Jessie's refrigerator, trying to picture myself traveling to the places they're from. Everyone knows about Jessie's collection, and whenever anyone from church, or the senior center, or her job at the hospital went on a trip they brought one back for her. She's got Maine and Vermont, New York City, Atlantic City, Chicago and St. Louis, Aruba and Puerto Rico, to name a few. Maybe one day I'll take the kids somewhere and be able to add one to the mix.

Jasper used to say nomads lived the right life. In motion. Living in the moment. The Masai were his people, he maintained; he even looked like them. I've tried to roam, but never far from home base. And I've always tried to stay either in the present or in Planet Bookworld, Judy's supposedly lighthearted tease that had a sting, and keep the past at bay. Survival, in the now, that always felt like a big enough challenge, and better than getting ahead of myself by thinking of the future and possibly, maybe, probably, fucking it up.

I'm setting the table when my mind goes to a fantasy I'd never share, one I can barely admit to myself. Sometimes I daydream that I've got a terminal illness, and it's sad and terrifying, knowing death's coming for me. But it's also a relief. Too late to fight, I'm allowed a respectable surrender, a release from all the trying and failing and trying.

I realize I'm holding a plate so tight it's about to snap. And then I drop it and it breaks in half.

"Auntie Jessie?" I call out as I pick up the pieces, hating the panic in my voice, and take a kitchen chair into the living room, plant it right next to hers, and sit, arms on my knees, head in my hands.

She grabs the remote and clicks the TV off. Then she puts down the footrest and lays her hand on the back of my neck, lightly, and the feeling of being touched with kindness sets the tears to flowing. I'm pretty sure she's not up for this. No drama, she said, and I guess this qualifies. But she does not desert me. She keeps her hand on me, and I wish I could wrap my arms around her and be swaddled in one of those weighted blankets I saw at Walgreens and rocked to sleep.

"I want to choose right," I say, ". . . but maybe how I've been is just the way I'm made." I'm looking for something to focus on and calm down, but everything I can see from here . . . my few, pitiful belongings, the hideous crocheted blanket, the family photos, the sofa bed that's miles from the wall, and the jigsaw puzzle that looks like a bunch of chaos . . . all of it makes the tears come harder, and even though I'm trying to push them, along with the panic and noise, back down my throat, I'm keening now, shocked at the animal sounds coming out of me.

"Nita, Nita," she says, soft and gentle, and she's leaning over now, resting her body against my back, "that first phone call was hard, but the next one'll go smoother . . . and Amara, she'll come around, long as you stick with her."

I try and settle down, taking deep breaths like I've been taught, and she's rubbing my back in circles like you do with little children, humming a lullaby. "I remember you singing that to Amara and Theo," she says, softly. "It's been so long since I've heard your voice."

She's not alone. I wish I could total up all the ways I've fallen short and sing out one big, loud apology. I've loved my children. But I'm mute. And too many times to count I haven't put them first.

I'm trying to sit with that truth, thankful that at least my crying's letting up. She leans toward me and, bless her, bless her, she says, "Let me help you carry it, Nita."

Clumsy, stammering, I tell how I've worked on taking inventory, and on making amends, on the Eighth and Ninth Steps. And how now that I'm out and trying to earn back the right to mother, I need to keep on owning the ways I've messed up. How in the past, when I woke up to how low I'd sunk, I had to use again to unsee it, and I'm afraid that given the chance, a part of me will always choose numbness.

She takes my hands in hers and I can feel how dry and lined her palms are. I can see in her face that my pain is hers. She squeezes my hands for emphasis. "You've got to keep to the rules, that's true, and yes, Val told me about this morning. But you've got to forgive yourself, too, like you're asking everyone else to do, and live with . . . with the all of it."

Looking directly at me, her eyes shining, she says, "Nobody just chooses once, and then the work is done. All day, every day, we've got to keep on choosing, over and over again, who we're going to be."

When my cryfest is over, we sit together in the quiet, Jessie looking spent and me feeling naked. I look out the window and see Judy, carrying a six-pack of wine coolers, with a brotha in a Kangol cap and long leather coat. Jessie says buzz her in, and when I open the apartment door and stare at Judy she just stands there, mouth open and face a complete blank, and then seems to realize what's wrong.

"Oh. Oh yeah," she says, looking at the six-pack. "Aw, sorry, Nita. Me and Ike came through to say welcome home." Auntie Jessie stares at Judy until she hands over the six-pack to Ike and asks him to put it in the car.

I can't believe I considered staying with her when I got out. I thought, anyway, since she'd been in NA (in and out of, for real) that we'd be bonded. Maybe she's evolved, or maybe she's back on the ride. She's got no kids to fail, she used to remind me, and how she rolls is up to her.

Growing up, we didn't hang out, except at holiday dinners, when Daddy's extended family was unavoidable. Mama's kin were never there. It was like she'd sprung into being with no people, no past, and I learned not to bring it up. Working on a family tree project in second grade, I asked her whose names belonged on the branches above her. Eyes on fire, she grabbed the marker from me and drew a big *X* across her half of the tree and said, "This is the family that matters, right here in this house."

Judy had a seat at the table, but in Mama's opinion, she was an un-suitable companion. Too loud and too out of control. *That girl is trouble waiting to happen*, she'd say. And even though Judy was only a year older than me, *That girl's twelve going on twenty*, our paths crossed when I started skipping school in the ninth grade, and then overlapped more and more.

As sentimental as they come, especially when lit, she says, *You know how much I love you*, to me and everybody else, texting heart emojis and rainbows before she leaves us high and dry. She never did come to Oak Hills to see me, but she's here now. There's nobody more fun, more live, than Judy, but she always has been like one of those dust devils, blowing into town to turn things upside down and then moving on.

"Let's play some cards," she says when Ike gets back, and I decline. The only game I play is solitaire (and Scrabble, but only with Maxine). Jessie says she's tired and goes to her room, and now it's the three of us, sitting in the living room, no drinks to ease things up, though I sure as hell keep thinking about the sweet-liquor-lemon taste of a wine cooler. Judy shakes her head wistfully and tells Ike, "It's probably hard to imag-ine, but Ranita used to be wild."

Even sober, Cuz puts some music on Jessie's little Bluetooth speaker and gets in what Jasper called Judy[2] form, cracking jokes I can't help but laugh at, getting up to shake her very shapely ass. She was the best dancer at whatever party or club we went to, and I swear she's got no bones at all, just cartilege. In motion, like a reef shark, which doesn't usually bite. Man, how I wish I could get that looseness without heading down the road to perdition. She's still wasp waisted, thick in all the right places. Ike, he just leans back and looks at her like she's a go plate he's gonna have all to himself later.

After they've put a hurting on the chili, watched some basketball, laughed their asses off, and talked on and on about a whole lot of nothing, they finally leave, and I start on the dishes. Judy. Still appearing unannounced. Still bringing the buzz and ease I envied and never could seem to stay away from. She's like a virus that runs its course but stays in the nerve endings. Just when you think it's over, it shows up to bring on another fever.

NINE

1999

Her eyes were the exact color of ocean jasper. He told Ranita he had pegged it as soon as he saw her. A mix of green and ochre so rare it could only be reached at the base of a single Madagascan cliff at low tide. She had walked into the kitchen to get a drink, and then she was gone, disappearing down the basement stairs to the party, before he'd had a chance to find out who she was.

Jasper never stopped telling the story. How her eyes called his name, how it was love at first sight that made him follow her down. And how he'd searched for her in the smoky darkness, getting anxious and then angry that he could lose track of his destiny in a room that small.

She stood apart, against the wall, half blinded by the weed and cigarette haze and holding a red Solo cup of rum and Coke. She didn't really like the syrupy, medicinal taste, but it made her feel a little bit more comfortable in her skin and a little bit freer with every sip. She was alone, as usual. A misfit with a ponytail and freckles, wearing a baggy sweatshirt and generic jeans.

She'd told her father she needed to help Judy with a paper, and he let her go. He had tried to institute restrictions after he caught her sneaking out, but it wasn't hard to slip his oversight, caught up as he was in work, and in the sadness that seemed to descend and lift without any pattern she could recognize. Now here she was at her first real house party, feeling like a tourist. Judy was upstairs getting Antoine a drink, while he was over in the corner, rapping to some other girl.

Black Star and Jay-Z were on the box, and though she might have been standing still, she was dancing and rapping along on the inside. She'd had a lot of catching up to do in the three years since her mother's death, and her father didn't pay too much attention to what she listened to, up in her room. Geneva hadn't thought hip hop was music, and she didn't like soul, R&B, or anything popular. Even Aretha was a bit too raw and real for her. *Live from the neck up*, she had seemed to advise, *and if you're determined to open up your heart, then make sure God's the one you let in*. Even so, she hadn't even liked the church choir to get too out of hand.

Now they were playing Ranita's girl, Lauryn Hill. Miseducated, re-educated, she was having her say, and Ranita had been singing along with her in the mirror. Wishing she had that kind of fluid fire and confidence, even though it seemed like there was always someone ready to quench it. Tonight she was soaking it all in, being out there and in there with those who were freed up, skin bare, moving like one body as they danced and sweated and celebrated and sang along. She knew the words . . . "my emancipation don't fit your equation. . . ."

As "Everything Is Everything," came on, loose-legged, lanky Jasper walked up and took both her hands. He had finally found her.

"Come on, girl," he said, pulling her from the shoreline into the deep. "I know you're tired of holding up that wall."

He was a wild dancer, waving around like one of those inflatable tube guys her father wanted to put in front of his shop, unconcerned with how he looked or what anyone thought about him, and Ranita began to give herself over to the music and let the people all around her who were dancing out their joy and trouble buoy her up.

After a few more songs, Jasper said, "Let's put it on pause and go out back," and they went to the yard and leaned against the fence, watching people coming and going and smoking and making out. She tried to get a good look at him without being obvious. Sharp nose and Special Dark Hershey's skin. Wispy mustache and goatee, and chipped front tooth. Long, skinny body. And dyed blond tips on a spiky fade. He looked like a paintbrush.

He mentioned in passing that he'd just turned 20 but didn't ask her age. And he didn't give his backstory. He didn't say that after a year at Northeastern he hadn't had the will or the money to continue, that he'd been needed at home to contribute to the rent and help out with his ailing grandpops, that he worked as many hours as he could get at RadioShack. Whenever he did speak up about his aborted education, he said: *An intellectual doesn't need school to study. Knowledge belongs to everyone.*

Ranita wouldn't have argued with that. Her father was the most curious person she knew, and he hadn't gone past high school. She studied Jasper as he talked, drawn by his animated gestures and worldly certitude. He didn't really look four years older than her, but he spoke with authority.

After a monologue on the origins and future of hip hop, he asked what she listened to, and when she gushed about Lauryn Hill he said yeah, she was okay, but he was really into deeper shit than that.

"Wait, what?" she asked, hoping she'd misheard.

Looking away, he said, "The underground shit I'm into, it's just . . . you know . . . realer."

At first, Ranita didn't know how to respond without sounding strident and off-putting, and she knew brothas hated that in a girl. But she was personally offended. Ms. Lauryn Hill had been speaking directly to her, and she'd been listening to her record nonstop. In spite of telling herself to be noncommittal, she told him maybe he should get his ears checked; it didn't get any deeper or realer than Ms. Hill.

After a long, uncomfortable silence, he said, "You know what's really real? It should be illegal to have eyes as pretty as yours."

Squirming, she told herself to take it down a notch and be polite, and he picked the Lauryn Hill thread back up. "Word is she's crazy anyhow; just ask Wyclef," and went on about the underground, cutting-edge music he preferred. Not just hip hop. Rock, reggae, Go-Go, New Wave. He name-dropped songs and bands she'd never heard of, and as he got excited talking about his recent discoveries and how you had to get off-road to find the real shit, she watched his face, marveling at his intensity, unsure of whether to back up or lean in.

Eager for a chance to show that kind of devotion to something, she asked if he liked to read. "Was the 808 the shit?" he answered, and she could tell the answer was yes, even if she hadn't followed his drum machine homage. She said she'd been reading Toni Morrison and was now on *Jazz*, and without confiding that she wasn't sure she understood it, she asked if he'd read it and why he thought Morrison had decided to tell the story in a splintered way. He didn't answer, but he did declare that it ruined a book to pick it apart, dealing a final blow to the conversation: "You have to have the confidence to just let art live in you."

After pulling a joint from his pocket, he lit it, took a puff, and offered it. She looked at it, knowing that her two choices were taking it or looking childish and foolish. She didn't even know how to smoke it, but he helped her out: "Pull hard and hold it in."

She wished her mother could see her, openly spoiling her proper girl status. But it was just an image. She never had been good.

When the weed hit her, everything turned hilarious and trippy and loose, and they busted out laughing and couldn't stop. They couldn't stop kissing either, even though she felt woozy, but when he put his hand on the inside of her thigh a bolt of panic ran through her and she jerked away. "My bad," he said, "I moved too fast," and she said no, no, it was not his fault; she'd just had too much to drink and needed some water. And as they pushed slowly through the packed dance floor, a hand with a gun raised up above the crowd, and chaos broke out as the whole room started shouting and screaming and running to escape.

Grabbing her arm, Jasper pulled her through the back door with him, and they ran. They didn't hear shots, but they ran block after block, until they were clutching each other, panting, stumbling to a stop. And just as Ranita was saying they needed to find out where Judy and Antoine were and make sure they'd made it out, a car slid up.

"We left to get some munchies," Antoine said, "and missed the drama. First house party was one to remember, hunh, Ranita? Come on, get in."

Judy was looking from Ranita to Jasper and back again.

"So that's your name," Jasper said, bending down to the back seat window.

Antoine didn't offer him a ride. He just pulled away from the curb, until Ranita said, "Damn, wait a minute," and leaned out. "What about yours?"

He said, "Jasper. Like the gemstone," and blew her a kiss.

Hugged up against Antoine, Judy said, "Well, he was dancing to his own beat, that's for sure. The two of you can be nerdy together. Read the dictionary for your first date." And then she asked Ranita to sing something, "long as it's not churchy," and she complied.

As soon as they dropped her off, Ranita went to the encyclopedia, and found that jasper was an opaque silica, usually red, yellow, brown, green, or sometimes blue. Thought to absorb negative energy and bring tranquility. Known as a "supreme nurturer." She went to sleep thinking of how he had pulled her to safety, how she had swooned when he kissed her, how maybe she'd found someone who was even weirder than she was and alright with it.

A week later, he was standing outside her school when she came out, holding a fistful of purple hydrangeas he had cut with his pocketknife from someone's garden on the way there.

Soon they were meeting up every weekend, and then on weekdays, too, even if she had to climb from the window to reach him. He couldn't seem to get enough of looking at her. She was his Ranita, and even her eyelashes were perfect. If he played connect-the-dots with her freckles, he told her, he just knew they'd make an outline of the place in Africa where his people were from.

They lay cocooned at the attic studio apartment in his parents' house, gazing into each other's eyes as they told and retold the story of how they'd gotten together. He listed all the things he loved about her, including that she had her own opinions, and she tried to forget about his interruptions when she tried to express them. He showed her the new "serious" camera he'd bought, which would give him the medium he needed to realize his vision, and began trying to convince her to let him shoot "artistic" nudes of her. She started out with firm refusal, but he kept on asking, waking her from sleep or catching her on the way out of the shower. If she loved him enough, if she trusted him enough, if she was grown and confident enough, she would not withhold.

A month later, she'd changed her no to yes.

And a year later, she was marking herself with his name.

When he showed up at the little redbrick branch library that reminded her of an old-fashioned train depot, announcing that he was taking her on a surprise mystery trip via the Orange Line, she looked up to see who was blocking the warm circle of lamplight where she'd found some peace in Planet Bookworld. Reluctantly, Ranita let go of the novel she was reading and gathered her things.

"You know I don't like surprises." She said it three times as the train rocked its way toward the destination he would not disclose. The first two times he smiled and told her she had to trust him; it was worth the buildup; it was gonna be so good. The third time, he said, "You know what? I'ma call you Cherry. You know why? Sometimes you're a sweet, juicy cherry. Sometimes you're a wild cherry. And sometimes you're a sour cherry. I see which one it's gonna be today."

As they rode the train in silence, she tried to be sweet and trust him. She just didn't believe in happy endings, even in novels.

And then there he was, opening the door of a tattoo shop to the clanging of a cowbell and waiting for her to walk through.

All the artists were occupied, and while they waited for someone to come out and talk to them, Ranita's heart raced. She looked at the pictures on the wood-grain-paneled wall, designs you could choose and photos of the ones they'd done. Dragons and skulls . . . THUG LIFE . . . Christian symbols . . . flowering vines and hummingbirds. It had already been decided what she was getting.

Jasper had gotten her name down his right arm six months before, and he'd been asking when she was getting his. She had told him it wasn't that she didn't want one. It was the pain that scared her. She'd asked, "What if I can't take it? What if I want to stop?"

He'd chuckled. "You gonna stop at JASP? It's a hurt you're choosing, and once you get on the ink path you're committed. Nobody gets half a tattoo."

A guy came out front and introduced himself. Brody was tattooed up to his face, even on his neck, and trying not to stare, Ranita wondered if he'd started with one image and found he couldn't stop. She pictured the designs creeping one by one across his body to cover even his private places and wondered what he'd do when there was nowhere left to ink.

It was her turn, but she didn't stand. She told Brody what she wanted, and he had her write it down, making sure he got it right, and then looked from the paper to Jasper.

"That you, man?"

Nodding at her, he said, "That's right. She's mine and I'm hers," and pulled up his sleeve to show the RANITA that covered his forearm in bold, black Gothic lettering.

"Okay, then. You want that font?"

"I want cursive," she answered, pointing to just below her shoulder, "up here," where she could hide it from her father and Auntie Jessie.

Looking at the door, she told herself she could still say no, she could change her mind. But the mix of hurt and bravado she saw in Jasper's face brought out her tenderness, just as it had when they'd first undressed and she saw that he padded his scrawny body with an extra pair of workout shorts beneath his jeans. She stood and followed Brody.

In his cubicle, she looked at the bottles of colored ink, the fittings, the snaking drill, while he made a drawing and asked if it was what she had in mind. "Smaller," she said. "Thinner." He made his preparations and cleaned her shoulder. And then he started.

At the shock of searing pain she bit into her fleshy, scar-tissued cheeks to keep from letting out a cry and running for the door. Then she forced herself to look at the needle that was breaking her skin and pushing in the ink. The J was underway. She was in.

Distracting herself from the fever-pain, she found a knothole in the fake paneling that she could focus on. At least Jasper could give her one of his grandpa's pain pills when they got back to his place. Where was he, anyway? He had promised to hold her hand.

Out in the waiting room, he was lost in his latest reading obsession, The Art of War. He'd been talking about it nonstop, the philosophy of battle, strength in weakness, subduing the enemy without fighting. She felt as though she had to wake him from dreaming when she came out bandaged and ready to go. And the whole walk to the station he talked about strategic warfare, telling her to surrender to the reverberating ache.

"Why don't you ever take my advice?" he asked. "And why you got to blame me for what we agreed on months ago?"

Focused on the window as the train rocked and rattled through the tunnel, she left his questions unanswered, but she could tell from the way he kept playing with her hair and fingers that he wanted her attention.

She didn't have it to give. She was trying to hold it in, but her submission to the tattoo had shaken her, and she was angry. He was asking, as he'd been doing lately, why she didn't dedicate a song to him and sing it just for his ears. He hadn't even asked how her fresh wound felt.

She hated when he made a point of kissing her in public, but he whispered her name and when she turned to him he kissed her on the mouth. The people around them looked away. And then he said, "Can't wait to see how it looks, my name in cursive. But you might want to tone up your deltoid, make it look its best."

Staring out at the murky tunnel's armature, visible only in flashes from the train car's light, she tried to place when the faultfinding had started. Her smile was beautiful, but she shared it too often. She tried to put him down when she disagreed with him and used big words she thought he didn't know. Her breasts were big and luscious, even though they sagged. She withdrew her affection without warning, and she wouldn't even tell him why. One of her amazing, ocean jasper eyes was noticeably bigger than the other.

She tried to ignore his chatter and the long, thin fingers intertwined with hers, and then she heard him say, "Hey, Sour Cherry," and tuned back in.

Squeezing her fingers hard, he leaned in close. "I shoulda gotten CHERRY instead of RANITA. On my arm."

Cherry, wild, sweet, and sour. She could tell it was going to stick.

She shoved him away with her elbow. She wasn't sure she liked it, but a nickname was a sign of devotion, wasn't it?

TEN

All night long my mind and heart roam. I spend some serious time in anxious and low-down, and then get up and visit grateful, stop through positive for a minute or two, hit lonely and scared, and try to get to hopeful. Relaxed is somewhere I see in the distance but never reach. I rev up, move from one worry to another. Pray for serenity. Sputter and stall. Nighttime makes me stir-crazy and daytime's too bright. Even in this thin winter light, it makes me see too much, too much. Soon as morning comes, I get all jangly about what the day ahead of me will or won't bring, and lie here tapping my foot, my leg, my fingers, while my heart bumps around inside, aloose from what it's known. I keep seeing the sign that says your head's got to face the cell door when you sleep, so they can tell you're breathing flesh. And that's about all I am right now.

At 3:00 a.m. last night I woke in a panic, thinking DQ's out there, lying in wait, and maybe I'm drawn to what hurts me. Maybe that's the addiction I'm powerless over.

I try and be here now.

Starfishing my arms and legs on the sofa bed, I occupy the whole wide mattress, even if it is disorienting. In the unaccustomed quiet I stretch, try to let myself sink into the softness, just rest for a minute from all the holding it together and pushing forward. But my mind's humming, working through my failures, and there's plenty to choose from.

And what do you know, the corpse of my junkie past floats to the surface, making me remember the most perfect rest of all. Instant serenity. Complete relief. If you can keep on breathing.

My body remembers. The foretaste. The deliverance.

Oh, my Lord, will I ever get past this wanting? Own it or not, it's in me, a hook in the mouth. A craving embedded in blood and tissue and bone.

I've managed to keep the memories of dope and DQ contained, and now that they're rising, I force myself to remember the agonies. The arrest and public shame of court. Pulling up to Oak Hills in that van, *live on arrival*, like Wu-Tang said. The horrors of being caged. And a flash of watching myself get smaller and smaller as I fight to breathe, that comes back, too, but I zero in on my heartbeat, on my breath going in and out. I get out my affirmation index cards and read them over. *I am in control. I respect my body and my loved ones. I am stronger than temptation.*

It's been a whole lot, this sunup. I tell you what, though: I'm gonna follow through with my plan to celebrate with a fried shrimp dinner tonight, whatever else goes down.

I get up and turn the bed back into a sofa, and when Jessie comes out of her room to get ready for The Ride to take her to physical therapy I make tea and breakfast. And after she's gone I take that bath I dreamed of and add some dish soap from the kitchen to make it special. I'm alone and safe here, but I lock the bathroom door. Because I can. After the cellblock showers, I stay in the tub so long, just enjoying the soak, that I have to add hot water twice.

Once I'm clean I take stock of the body I'm trying to reclaim. This time I'm doing the looking, now that I've got a real mirror instead of the plastic square that passed for one inside. The 20 pounds I put on at Oak Hills are unavoidable, but that can be worked. My ass always was one of my better features, and it's still an onion; there's just too much of it. My titties are moving even further south. And my eyes, whatever they signify, have got serious baggage underneath them.

I put on the heavy sweat pants and fleece pullover Jessie gave me, and as I walk through the living room there's Daddy, staring at me from the bookshelf, reminding me that sooner or later I need to visit his grave. I go to the kitchen window and open it for a few inches of air. The street's calling my name: *Raaaaniiiita . . . come on out and play.*

And I do go out, because I have to. For the opposite of play.

I'm back at Drew Turner's office, looking at orange daylilies while I wait my turn, and planning on a different strategy than last time.

Soon as I sit down, I try and use up as much of the 47 minutes left (after the hello-how-are-yous) as I can, going on and on about the boring details of my week. Where I went, what I ate, what me and Jessie watched on TV, what time I went to bed, what I saw on the way there. I see him stifle a yawn. Fuck, I'm even boring myself.

Turns out he's not having it. He just waits, totally calm, until I run out of steam.

"Well, that's a lot," he gets in before I resume jabbering, "and I know it's overwhelming, everything you're managing . . . getting released, getting back on your feet, staying on track. But how are you doing under the surface? What's been happening on the inside, in terms of your feelings and thoughts?"

No comment, I want to say, like in the interrogations on those British crime shows Judy loves. *No comment, no comment, no comment.*

I feel like one of those beetles we pinned and dissected in seventh-grade science to study the soft and hard parts of their exoskeletons . . . their compound eyes . . . which parts of their wings were used for flying and which for protection.

I focus on his framed museum prints, which, really, I can make no sense of. Abstract art. The kind of thing that'd be right up Jasper's alley. Big splashes of color or dreamy tangles of lines. And though I have no idea what it's supposed to be, I focus on the one that's got patches of blue and mustard on top, brown and green at the bottom, and a giant stretch of red bleeding across the middle with a blank, ragged hole torn from the color.

I look everywhere but Drew Turner's face. It's a standoff, and it feels partway good that I'm making him wait. Then again, I hate other people's silence. I can't help the impulse to fill it, and because sometimes the best defense is a good offense, I say, "Let's talk about you."

Soon as it comes out, I realize I sound like I'm working a customer. On the inside he's probably cringing, but he gives a sympathetic face. My embarrassment and his kindness make me want to disappear into the escape hatch in the red paint across from me. Seems like he decides to let my misguided invitation slide, though, and I'm hoping it's not gonna count against me on the parental judgment score sheet. After taking a minute to look at his notes, he recaps our last session and then says let's look at my middle school years. He asks. I dodge. He presses on. And when I don't answer, he reminds me that more than mere physical presence is required to make therapy worthwhile.

Most of ages 12 and 13 I try to keep buried. But school, I think I can go there. "Sixth grade was . . . new building, new place at the bottom of the heap, below the seventh and eighth graders. New kinds of meanness and bullying. New focus on who was 'going out with' who, but not for me. New rules by the zillion. Teachers who didn't know me and presumed I was dumb and lazy."

The feeling I had of being too much comes back. "Too amped. Too attitudinal. Too willful. I raised my hand to share my opinion too often and asked too many questions. 'Because I said so, Ranita Atwater,' my homeroom teacher, Miss Price, said, over and over, when I asked why we couldn't choose any of our projects, why the MCAS test was the only thing that mattered, and could she explain the logic behind the rules they had for everything. In elementary school I'd never been sent to the principal's office. Now I was noncompliant, and I seemed to live there."

"So . . . 'be less' was the message," Drew Turner says.

Yes. Yes. Yes.

"And was there anything familiar about that, from your past?"

On the outside I'm blank and clueless. Inside I'm breaking down.

"Your growing up," he says. "Your parents, your family life."

"I guess my job was pretty basic. Get A's. Go to church. Respect my elders. My father had an auto shop. He was a workaholic. But we did things together. . . ."

"And your mother?

I try and swallow, but my throat's too dry and my voice comes out croaky. "Well . . . she worked two jobs, substitute teaching and giving piano lessons. Cooking and cleaning. Taking care of the house. Singing in the church choir."

When he probes gently past the facts, I look down and say, "I'm here to do better. To feel better. Talking about my mother isn't going to lead there. Now or ever."

He nods and backs off. And I've clued him in to the mess inside me.

When he asks about the shift to high school, I tell how it was new everything, again. I got used to the system and started in to proving myself with academics, even if I couldn't fall in line the way they expected. But I was starting over, alone, with even less goodwill. And the teachers' expectations seemed to get lower and lower.

I'd already read all the books assigned for freshman English, and passed on applying for the honors class. Why invite the scrutiny? Or the straitjacket of being the model of Black achievement? I decided to fly under the radar, and classes started feeling more . . . irrelevant. I still liked reading and knowing, but school seemed to murder that feeling.

My high school felt like a factory, and some days I couldn't seem to get out of bed for the assembly line.

Now that I've started talking, all the shit nobody cares about is pouring out. How they gave the ones with problems punishment, instead of help. How the college bound were mostly on their own with applications and essays and tests, and discouraged from trying for the better schools. They told the salutatorian who ended up at Yale she wasn't "Ivy League material." And how they let the ones like me, who were losing interest or confidence or direction, just drift and fall off.

He looks shocked when I say I never met with a guidance counselor the whole ninth grade and no one . . . teacher, coach, librarian, nurse, front office worker . . . ever reached out to catch me. I start telling how I stumbled through the tenth and eleventh grades, just going through the motions, and never went back for my senior year, and though I didn't plan to go there, the story can't be told without the thread that runs through it: Jasper.

I end up telling about how I met him . . . feeling he was kindred . . . and how quirky his devotions and his outlook seemed to be. And I tell about the force of his will, slipping his hold and getting pulled back in.

After dropping out, I was too mortified to go back and finish up. That seemed more repentant than renegade, and I'd have been older than everybody else. Until I had Amara, I was back and forth between the house and Jasper's, working at Popeyes, bagging at the grocery store, helping out at Daddy's shop. Shut down, numb and empty. Or roving with the pack me and Jasper became a part of, which always seemed to have Antoine as alpha. Looking back, the wild, impulsive way we rolled seems unsure and pointless, and I think I even knew that then. Mostly, though, it felt like freedom. The hook in my mouth got harder and harder to shake, but when I was using, everything glittered, and I was king and queen. And subject, too.

Some of the story I keep to myself. I'm not proud of it, but honestly, when Jasper got sent up for distribution and missed Theo's birth by a month, it was a relief, not having him coming and going, doting and chiding, getting up my hopes. I took the expensive calls and put the kids on the phone. Sent their artwork and photos and cards. Told them to ask God to bless him when they said their prayers. In his absence, I picked the name for our baby that meant "blessed gift," and he told me he'd added a tattoo of THEO to his left forearm, even though he was disappointed I hadn't picked a stronger name for him to live up to.

I'm surprised by how cathartic it is to talk about the Jasper years. But it shames me, the failure I chose, little by little.

Then Drew Turner jumps ahead to the recent past, asking about the role of David Quarles, and I try and act like I don't know why he's focusing on my charge partner and do some more shrugging. I want to plead with him: *Let's not connect up all the dots.*

I say I don't remember a lot of it. Which is not a lie. And I'm not planning on sharing the parts I can't forget.

I'll never tell about how amazing the sleep-floating felt.

I'll keep it to myself, how I turned to the street on occasion, trading my body for what we needed to get by. And how DQ, enterprising to the core, helped me see myself as a small-business owner, a pop-up enterprise in pretending and forgetting. *You're in charge, baby, even though you make them think they are.* My deeds were just transactions with strangers, nothing intimate about them, one-act plays about who wanted what, and who was the top. I switched off my feelings. Mostly. And my body went to work, no confusing questions of love or loyalty or God to cloud things up. I'll never tell about the last time, about the thing that stole my voice.

Seems like reckonings, at least in this life, are few and far between.

I throw Drew Turner a tidbit, something I really did dream, just before I got out of Oak Hills, to get him off my case: There I am on a peaceful little island, just off the coast of somewhere I've never been . . . with the turquoise water I've seen 2-D, in movies and postcards (and Oak Hills visitation), gentle on the soft, white sand . . . and I'm relaxing in my own little cabana-type hut that's open to the warm breeze . . . a roof for when it rains, but no walls, no doors. And I hear something moving next to me and sit right up as I feel the fear shoot through me. There's a crocodile in my little hut. Turns out he's living on the island, too.

"Okay," Drew Turner says, "that's telling. Do you feel David Quarles is a threat?"

That pisses me off, the conclusion buried in his question. And when he tries to get me to talk about what safety and vulnerability feel like, I turn the interrogation back on him, asking really, where did he ever know of that was safe?

Still, he pokes and prods, looking for how I'm made and how my parts work, looking for scars and bruises he can press on, while I return to the painting on his wall. It looks peaceful in that little blank space, relief from all the red.

I hear him talking in the distance. And finally, I say DQ was a manipulator, a seducer, a bottom-feeder. A wolf in wolf's clothing. But did I see that up front? It makes me sick to my stomach, revisiting it all, me finally free of Jasper and doing good, back on my feet . . . mothering alongside Daddy and Jessie . . . and then there he was, leaning against the bar at that club, ready to fill every empty space I had.

I see us. Drifting, floating, slow and lazy and easy, everything slipping away and me singing, slow and languorous, like I'm channeling Billie Holiday, until I'm fading, too.

"No," I hear myself say out loud.

"No?" It's Drew Turner, yanking me back to now.

Finally, I say, "Right away I was magnetized. I shoulda known better, after where I'd been. Then again, I've got a talent for trouble, like my . . . Anyway, David Quarles was over-the-top. All-in, from the very first moment, and still, not quite with me."

This feels like vivisection. I've started spilling, but I haven't told how I felt the night he claimed me. I'm about to say more when Drew Turner looks at his Movado watch and says, "We have to stop for today."

I want to clock him. I don't even want to be here, but I've got to recover from the ouch of rejection. Like *I'm* needy and want to overstay my welcome. I feel shitty enough already about what's coming clearer, about the things he's sucked me into sharing. And most of all about the sorry excuses for love I've known. I stand and grab my backpack, working at keeping ahold of the mad and everything it drags along with it. And I guess I want to let him know that I have not been a complete idiot, lowlife, bad chooser, that there has been a ray of light for me.

Before I go, I say with angry and embarrassing pride, "I have been loved right. Once."

After getting through the inner and outer doors fast as I can, I hit the same store as last time, and with all the free-world treats to choose from, I go straight for the Honey Buns, and soon as I've got them I duck into the back-alley driveway, tear open the plastic wrap, and wolf three of them down, one after another, just like I'm bottomless.

Disgusted, I lick the sweetness from my fingers and wipe my mouth on my sleeve. My body should have crime scene tape strung around it.

How the hell did I let that happen? Hard as I tried for mental toughness, I turned the ball over in the final seconds of the game. I let my guard down with Drew Turner. I opened up and let him in.

Emerging from the back alley like something from a horror flick, I try and brush the sugar from my clothes and stand up straight. And what the fuck. I see Leon Grambling glide a sparkly blue Escalade into a curbside space, parallel parking like he was born doing it, and zipping down the window to call out to me like not a moment has passed since I saw him over four years back. "Cherry, is it really you?" I open my mouth to inform him of my true name, but his cell phone rings.

"Just a sec, baby," he says, unlocking the door and leaning over to push it open for me. And I stand here, taken by a memory. DQ. I can almost taste him. He's on the tip of my tongue.

That was then. This is now. I am in control. But here's Leon, kicked back in his toasty, caramel-colored leather interior, surrounded by a musky-citrus cloud of weed. The smell picks my lock before I can get my thoughts together, and I tell myself to turn around, back up, keep walking, but I'm stuck at the curb, breathing in the sweet-sticky smoke and looking at the open door, thinking, not for the first time, about how Leon always did remind me of a sneaky reptile. Eyes so far apart they're damn near on the sides of his head. Elastic-looking lips and pointy nose. He finishes up his call and flashes me a toothy grin.

"Sure is good to see you, Cherry. Let me give you a lift."

Leon used to pop up out of nowhere on the regular, or he'd be hovering along the edges of whatever shit was going down, entertaining everyone with his little comical stories while he drove us around or made a run. He always seemed to be in the background, helping grease the wheels and making folks laugh.

Before I know it, I'm getting in.

The window zips closed, and here we are. Just like old times.

He's still ragging, still in monochrome, and draped with gold. "You wanna hit this sativa?" he asks, and I shake my head as he takes a long toke. I'm probably getting a contact high I should raise my hand and admit to at my next meeting.

The music on the box is slow and slinky, the leather's soft and buttery, and I feel my body melting into the heated seat. I tell myself I should be waking up, not relaxing, and putting my hand on the door handle instead of the armrest. But I ask myself how much danger I'm really in, shooting the shit for a minute with Leon, over three clean years underneath my belt.

"Nice ride," I hear myself say.

He beams. "You know I only fuck with Caddies, and this one's got a custom paint job. I know you like words. It's called azure."

Leaning my way, he says, "David Q's been out three months now, and just the other day he was saying you'll be joining us soon. And here you are, like we talked you up. Cherry, fine as ever, with those pretty-ass eyes."

Now I'm creeped out. I manage to answer, "No need for you all taking credit. I was out here doing my thing, walking my own path."

He chuckles. Tells me he's staying over in Quincy now. Fills me in on their latest stunts. And every time he mentions DQ a charge goes through me.

Then my mind starts tumbling toward another memory and my throat tightens. Fuck me. I am not going to lose it in Leon Grambling's Escalade, before I've even seen my kids. I take a deep breath, feel my belly expand, and try to call up a feeling of abundance.

And then, hit by the reverb of what Leon said: *he was saying you'll be joining us soon,* I see me and DQ, at the end of the line. Caught. Drugs and everything to do with drugs spread out all around us, and me slammed to the floor and cuffed and read my rights, using my phone call to reach Daddy, shaking and crying that I'm in trouble again, pleading and apologizing, thanking God the kids are with him, hearing them in the background, *What happened, Granddaddy? When are we gonna see her? Mama? Mama? Where are you?* I'm reliving the arraignment . . . possession and intent to distribute . . . when all I was doing there was trying to stay numb. Daddy's face through glass at Nashua Street, and that cut-rate lawyer who's telling me about the plea I've got to take.

I try to get back in the present. And though my tongue feels thick and lawless, I interrupt the funny story Leon's started in on and say, "I did just get out." I do not ask can a bitch get her footing before you try and pull her back into your mess? I say, "Look, Leon, I don't go by 'Cherry' anymore. And I've got over three clean years. That's what I want you to understand. My name, my real name, is Ranita."

"Cool. Cool." He smiles. "I'll pass that on to David Q." And putting his hand on the gear shift, he says, "Matter of fact, he's over at the crib right now."

"Hold up," I say, nearly shouting, trying to keep the fear out of my voice as I fumble to open the door. "I'm out, Leon. Out of Oak Hills and out of the game. You tell DQ that, you hear me?"

He gives me his reptile grin, looking all relaxed and patient, like he knows that wherever I've been and whatever I've chosen and whatever I say, I can still be eaten whole. I belong with them. I belong to them. And eventually, I'll come back home.

I get up out of that car like the devil's chasing me and hear Leon idling at the curb. I do not look back.

Nearly running toward Jessie's, I'm fighting with the cold and the wind, even in my new-old coat, and I stop for that shrimp plate, getting one for Jessie, too. I can't afford it, but I promised myself I'd celebrate like this.

Now here I am, coming through the door. Hands still shaking at my recklessness, my foolishness, I'm cursing at myself while I get the napkins, place mats, and plain, everyday dishes, anything but Mama's china. Jessie's making her way, moving real slow, from her bedroom.

I offer the shrimp, but she says her fried-food days are over. I should have realized, should have brought her something healthier, should have asked what she wanted. She says it's okay, she'll have the chicken from yesterday, and we say grace and dig in, and I inhale the shrimp, every piece of it, so hungry and relieved to be back home safe, at least for now.

I'm beat. Seems like I lived a lifetime between this morning and getting back here to have this meal. Stretching out on the couch beside her, I hope for a bit of peace. But I feel Leon and DQ tugging on me, and wish I could sing myself a lullaby. I should have read Leon, told him what a useless sycophant (a point for me) he is and always was. And it's pathetic, but along with telling him I'm Ranita, I'm different, I'm done with that life, I wish I'd told him that now I know what it is to be loved right.

ELEVEN

2014

Walking alongside Judy through the hazy dark, Ranita felt the heartbeat bass and club energy pulse through her body. She was still on the fence about getting in a party mood, especially sober. But there she was, freezing her ass off in Judy's red minidress, so snug and skimpy she could feel it riding up over her hips. "That's what you want," Judy said, pulling her by the arm. "Let it be known what you're working with."

That afternoon, she had found her father in his basement retreat, once all was quiet upstairs. She'd fed the kids lunch and they had made holiday cookies from a refrigerated grocery store roll and decorated them with the can of frosting they'd turned red and green with food coloring. Theo was napping and Amara was working on a Lego set Val had sent as an early Christmas present.

Ranita had come down to ask if he'd watch them while she went out with Judy, and he'd patted the spot next to him on the pleather couch and asked her to sit and listen with him. It felt good, the invitation to resume their song-trading practice, and that was the least she could do, since she'd come to ask something more of him than he was already giving.

He'd pulled Roberta Flack and Donny Hathaway from his vinyl collection and they'd leaned back and put their feet up on the old, scratched steamer trunk that was his coffee table. Ranita found herself singing along. And then it was her turn, and she'd gone up to her room for some CDs, searching through OutKast and Beyoncé and Kendrick, the kiddie singalong music and seventies disco that Theo loved to dance to, and all the stuff Ranita knew was too harsh or vapid or explicit to play for her father, until she found Ledisi and Lizz Wright. "I'm glad people still sing," he'd said when she put them on, "and I can put a foot in 2014 with a little help."

While he was deciding on the next cut, she sat there wishing she could tell him how low she'd been feeling since she heard about Jasper dying, how she was just getting up after being broke down for months. But her father's face looked so drawn. She didn't want to step on their playful, feel-good moment and make him take on something else for her, and she knew he'd rather not hear about her mourning or know what it had felt like down on the ground. He was just relieved that she was up again. And she was. She was putting Jasper to rest, and she wasn't even sure she needed more than an occasional meeting anymore.

After trading a few more songs, she'd asked her favor, and he said he was glad to do it, he was happy to see her getting out to have some fun. She wasn't sure fun was possible, but she was trying for an upbeat outlook, and Judy had stopped by to talk her into it. "It'll be good to leave Planet Bookworld, or wherever dreary place you've been living these days, and get out, be with people, remember life goes on." She'd insisted it would lift Ranita's mood to get dressed up, ignoring the protests that it was too cold out for party clothes and she had none to wear anyway, and offering the bright red dress and matching shoes she'd just bought. "They're perfect for you, Nita, and I'm driving, so you won't be chilly for long, and you know what? I'm feeling lucky. Who knows, we both might meet someone tonight."

Maybe so, Ranita had thought. You never knew when something would change the way everything unfolded. *Maybe so.*

As soon as they got inside the club, Judy was off to see what "the talent" looked like, and Ranita was standing at a high-top table, feeling only partway there. She *had* been feeling better, but now she couldn't get her mind off Jasper. Even though she'd longed to be free of him, and felt guilty relief along with sadness when he was locked up so far away, she'd pictured him bouncing back.

She had been at the house ever since, over three years now, and she had a handle on her recent lapse. She wasn't exactly completely sober every single day, but she'd been able to stick to one drink . . . or maybe sometimes one and a half. Still, she hoped being out at a club wasn't too big a stretch. And she wondered why she couldn't ever seem to say no to Judy.

Ranita clung to the table, wishing she knew where her cousin had gone and conflicted on whether to hope for a man to approach her or pray that she'd be left alone. And suddenly, standing next to her was a brotha with odd, wide-spaced eyes, dressed in royal blue and looking very proud of something. He put a champagne flute on the table and said, "From my compadre."

She nodded. "And what's your compadre's name?" And he turned and smiled. "That's David Q."

Determined not to be ordered up like bar food by his minion, she didn't look. He hadn't even asked what she was drinking, though she couldn't lie; she did love bubbles. Before he walked away, the messenger bowed from the waist and said, "Leon Grambling." He reminded her of a gecko, creepy but graceful, and she remembered an encyclopedia fact: they had sticky feet that helped them keep their grip.

Looking everywhere but at this David Q, Ranita stayed at the table and sipped. But she could feel him from across the room, waiting for her to come to him. Instead, she finished her drink and headed for the restroom, taking a quick, undercover glance as she went. Leaning against the bar, fine as hell, he gave off a mix of unavoidable and out of reach.

When she came out he was standing just outside the door, a glass in each hand.

"More champagne. What are we celebrating?" she asked.

"You. We're celebrating you."

The sumptuous give in his voice struck a warning bell almost too deep inside for her to notice, but she followed him back to the table she'd just left and felt her sadness step aside. After putting the glasses down, he released a smile, just for her, it felt like, that took shape slowly. When it was complete, it left her holding to the table's edge for balance.

After a long-drawn-out gaze, he said, "That's a nice dress you've almost got on."

She couldn't help laughing, and said it wasn't even hers, she'd borrowed it from her cousin, who was in the club somewhere.

"Naw, it's yours," he said, and nodded at the glasses. "Let's toast. To us. I been looking for you everywhere."

As a warm, liquid body flush crept from head to toes and fingertips, she stumbled, and he reached out to steady her. "I've got you; you're good," he whispered, but she thought she'd heard something rip and ran her fingers over her side seams, hoping she hadn't ruined Judy's dress before her cousin had even had a chance to wear it herself.

When David Q nodded at her glass, she told herself the one drink she'd had was pardonable and she would stop with that, but then he brought another, and she muted the internal commentator who never seemed to shut up and let her enjoy herself. As she sipped she looked him over. Sculpted mouth, even features, and flawless copper skin. Eyes so dark you could get lost in them. *He's prettier than I am*, she thought, pulling closer as he smiled again, little by little, as though it hurt.

When she asked what the Q stood for, he said he'd tell her, but she should know that words were his thing. And just as she was about to say,

For real? Me too, thinking how Geneva's one indulgence, florid vocabulary, had given them something in common already, he started talking again and she lost her chance.

"You might call me a wordologist," he said, "and I love me some *q* words. 'Quarry.' 'Quim,' I bet you don't know that one, but you should. 'Quest.' But my daddy's name was Quarles." Chuckling, he spelled it out. " 'Quarrels' woulda been more fitting. And his name's damn near the only thing he gave me." Ranita laughed along, wishing she had it in her to relieve the sadness of what he'd shared.

"And what's your moniker, sublime lady who just walked in and changed my life?"

Moniker, nice. He got a point for that one. "My name's Ranita . . . ," she said, and then added what seemed to go along with the borrowed outfit and the glass in her hand, ". . . but sometimes people call me Cherry."

"Black Cherry. My favorite flavor. I knew you were just right for me soon as I saw you, with those summertime eyes in December."

Fighting the urge to say they sometimes looked browner or greener, but it had nothing to do with the seasons, and pushing away the undeniable truth . . . the right one was distinctly smaller than the left . . . she finished her champagne.

She ached to sink into him now, while his desire was swelling, and as he leaned closer, she felt herself pulling free of Ranita, with her grief and her murky past, her failure to fit in or measure up, her stalled, mundane present.

As David Q brought another glass and another, she lost track of Judy and everything else, and when he pulled up to her house at 3:00 a.m., her father opening the door before she'd made it up the walk, she had renamed him DQ. For those little childhood trips to the Quincy waterfront, where she had pleaded for the indulgence of a soft serve cone, with its creamy, sugary, melting smoothness that was gone before she could take it all in. She didn't know how apt the nickname was: nearly half air, and full of chemicals. But the mouthfeel was so good it had to be sinful, so cold it hurt. By the time she made it past her father through the door, she had surrendered to free fall.

For their one-week anniversary, DQ gave her three dozen long-stemmed roses. And marked their first month with 24k rose gold earrings, bracelet, and chain. It felt so good, having more than she even really deserved lavished on her. She didn't ask what kind of hustle brought such plenty. She just lay back and enjoyed her prosperity.

He had cash; he had game; he had a platinum tongue. He'd be Leon's nigga in the afterlife and Ranita was his soulmate, the finest woman who'd ever walked the earth. Happy to speak of himself in the third person when the truth needed telling, he said, "David Q is the Black trinity: athlete, lover, fighter." Whatever needed doing, he was more than man enough to handle it, and even though he was pushing 30, he was still deadly on the basketball court. A winner in any arena where he decided to compete.

Jasper had never aimed for more than getting by, and his gas tank and bank account had usually been close to empty. His part-time gigs at RadioShack and CVS, the car wash, liquor store, corner shop, they had carried him from month to month, and whatever Ranita convinced him to put in savings would be suddenly blown on something like the Leica he needed to answer his artistic calling, something for himself. When he was short, he peddled the pills he used more and more to manage that getting by. Ranita started out objecting. Then looked the other way. Then resigned herself to the reality. Then got on board. When she thought about it, which she tried her damnedest not to do, it amazed her what a person could get used to.

The threesome with DQ and heroin started out with snorting. Which was not all that different, she told herself, from the E and Vicodin she'd spent nearly a decade renouncing and seeking. Then she walked into the bedroom and found him, belt around his bicep and firing up a spoon. He'd been talking about how she should try it, the high was cheaper, better, quicker, and she'd said no, she didn't like needles, that was not the tier where she belonged. But here he was, about to push off without her.

He let loose his pained smile and beckoned with his plushest voice. "You want some of this, don't you, Cherry Ranita? Come with me."

Loving, that's what it was, the way he invited her along, switching the belt from his arm to hers and hitting her first. And tender, how he held her as she sank back into warmth and peace and him, emptied, freed from caring how they'd gotten there or what would happen next.

Tied to each other, and to forgetting, they spent all day in a stupor if they felt like it. Had pancakes and ice cream for dinner. Didn't bother getting dressed. He never stopped talking large, even as everything about their lives contracted, but sleep-floating in his arms on the warm, lazy-river H ride was just too soothing to forsake.

The tether to the hard-won world of family, home, and work at her father's shop began to fray. At first, she slipped out while the kids were sleeping and tipped back into the house a day or two later, contrite and offering some story of how she'd been caught up helping out a friend and lost track of everything. It was temporary, she reassured them, but the absences grew longer, and she relinquished the parenting to Lennox, returning with tears and apologies and complaints of being under the weather, needing help, being overwhelmed with how much she loved them all. They were better off with her father steering; she knew that much.

Caught in the cycle of her departures and returns, Theo cried and Amara begged her not to go. And the shame and guilt she knew were waiting for her when she reappeared were unbearable. *You are a piece of shit, Cherry*, she told herself, looking at their faces as she came through the front door and seeing heartache, disappointment, and fear at the hope and relief they felt.

How was any of it explicable to them, to children? In her absence, Lennox tried to field their questions. *Where's Mama?* Mama's sick. *I could kiss it, make it better*, three-year-old Theo promised, *if she would come home*. When she was present, there was no way to hide the truth of the rung she'd come to occupy. She beamed a beatific smile, slurred, nodded off. She trembled, ravenous. She left again. *She'll get well*, Amara said. *I know she will.*

After she crash-landed at Oak Hills and began to crawl from the wreckage, her year with DQ would come back in appalling flashes. She lost every inch she'd reclaimed after Jasper and found a bottom lower than any she'd fathomed.

Throughout, her father held her, soothed her, pep-talked her, told her he'd be by her side. She'd been a handful in the Jasper years, but this was different; this was something else. He tried distracting her; he tried inspiring her. He fed her and put her to bed, as though she was an infant who could be loved into wholeness, and when he saw the story her bare arms and pinpoint pupils and jutting hip bones told he tried to protect her from herself, installing a lock on her bedroom door. Like him, she hoped she might be savable, but she had her doubts, and when he opened the door to bring her breakfast and saw her doubled over in misery, he removed the lock and she was loose.

Then came the graveyard spiral. And the night when she was taken to the threshold of freedom more than once, and found it in her to refuse death without choosing life, when she saw DQ with brief, horrifying clarity, and then dove deeper into blindness and forgetting.

A month later, just before they were nailed, Jessie reached her limit.

At the end of a week-long jag, awake but barely, at four on a Sunday afternoon, DQ dropped her at the house. She stumbled up the front walk like a vampire recoiling from the light, only half recalling how she'd stormed out three, four, five? days earlier, yelling, *Stop fucking trying to control me!* at Jessie and her father, and watched him back away, hands in the air.

She was home now and ready to beg, promise, borrow, whatever it took to get in and see the kids and make things good again.

After digging her keys from her coat pocket and finding the right one, silver, plain round top, she tried three times to get it lined up with the lock, focused only on seeing the love on her father's face no matter what she'd done, and getting to the kids and the care on the other side of the door. Finally, thank God, she got the key in the right place and fuck yes, she was home.

She pushed it, jiggled it, tried it upside down, but it would not go in. Even when she tried to force it, it refused. "What the fucking fuck," she whispered. Had she grabbed the wrong one? Had DQ switched her key with his? She started pounding on the door and was about to start yelling. Mama was long gone and who gave a fuck what the neighbors thought?

The door opened. And there was Auntie Jessie, on the threshold. Blocking her way.

Too stunned to argue or say a thing, she focused every bit of her energy on figuring the whole thing out. And the fog cleared enough for her to understand that this time was different; this was Jessie's line in the sand.

She looked from the doorstep upward. Jessie's suede boots were planted shoulders' width apart. Her arms were folded across her breasts. And her eyes were flashing. Ranita wouldn't have been surprised if she'd reached up and pulled a lightning bolt from the sky.

"Don't you come around here," she said, her voice steely and quiet, "until you're on the road to changing."

Ranita could barely process it, but she knew she'd heard right. She stood there, legs weak and rubbery, trying to get her mouth closed and hoping she hadn't drooled.

"You can run yourself into the ground . . . put that poison in your body. Kill yourself. It breaks my heart to say it . . . but that choice is yours. But you need to give these kids a chance."

"Jessie, wait . . . ," she wailed, feeling like she was being slapped awake. "Where's Daddy? And my babies, you know I love them. . . ."

"I'm tired of hearing what you feel for them, Ranita. 'Love' is an action word."

And then she took a step back, into the entryway. And shut the door.

Ranita stood on the porch, fumbling to collect herself and think it through. She tried the handle once more and stared at the closed door. She could not believe it. Auntie Jessie had put her out of her own house. And changed the fucking lock.

TWELVE

Woke up with the sour aftertaste of chumping out on therapy yesterday. Told myself I was going and walked in that direction. And then bailed.

My parting words from last time kept circling through my head. Almost out the door and I blurted out how I've known true love. Daddy said I always did have to have the last word, and I've paid for that little triumph with two weeks of chewing worry.

I was on my way to Drew Turner's office. I was. And then a memory of me and Max, entwined, flashed through me, and I had to stop and lean against a tree: the taste of mouth, our first deep kiss, the shock of my wanting. The blood beat in her neck. Me, touching my lips to her throat hollow, saying it had to be the softest skin, and her saying no, there were softer spots still to be discovered. Places protected and hidden, the way good news sometimes is.

I stood there leaning against that sturdy black maple, glad neither Drew Turner nor anybody else could see my thoughts. I was trying to be tough with myself and get moving, but I was making a list of the reasons not to go. My thing with Maxine is my business. It'll just sound like jail talk. It's one more minus, one more way I'm an unfit mother, one more reason Auntie Val will do a better job with my kids. And it's not just that I did my time laid up with a woman, though that wouldn't earn me any favor. What I don't know how to say is that choosing Maxine felt like coming home.

I pulled out my cheap-ass TracFone and left a message with the robot voice that picked up, saying I didn't feel well enough to come.

Tired, feet and heart aching, I went and sat on the cold metal bench in a little bus shelter and looked around at the places where folks have left their marks in pen and spray paint. Those writings and drawings, they save the lives of birds, Max told me, helping them know the difference between free air and the lying plexiglass that'll turn an ordinary flight into their last. Along with the bursts of bubble writing and bold neon tags, other messages were scrawled in black marker. *FAGGOT DESHAUN AINT SHIT. KAYLA GIVES HEAD. YOUR PUSSY IS TOXIC. WHRE R U?*

Now it's morning and I lie here staring at Jessie's smooth white ceiling, no cracks or water spots or cobwebs to distract me. Drew Turner's already churning up my messes, and now I've rejected the journey to self-discovery he's advertising. Another thing to add to the bad-choosing pile. And of all mornings to be feeling ashamed and meek, why today? This is the day I've been yearning for, when I have my first visit with my kids.

I force myself to get up and make some tea. Take a dish-soap bubble bath. Get dressed. And then I try on every piece of clothing I've got. Nothing looks right. The slacks, Mama would call them, from Jessie look office-y and wrong, and my jeans look wrinkled, worn, and tight. The secondhand pantsuit I found at Boomerangs is too fake-serious, and every top I try looks too clingy or too low-cut. I look like a secretary moonlighting at a strip club. *Would you give this woman kids to raise?* I ask myself, looking in the mirror. I try the dress Jessie picked up at a church thrift store, pastel flowers and belt and respectable neck bow, but in the end I look like either a liar or some grandma's easy chair. I figure one of the only things I got going for me is honesty, so I iron my least shabby jeans and put on a loose sweater.

For days I debated whether to show up with presents and, if so, what to get. Candy's bad for your teeth and cookies cause obesity, as I well know. Helium balloons look desperate. What are 8-year-old boys into? Superheroes? Transformers? And which would Theo choose? What do 13-year-old girls like that I could manage to pay for? In the end, I got them mugs, wrapped them in colored tissue paper, and put them in my backpack. And now I need to get outside and walk.

At Oak Hills, some folks did their time in laps around the yard, but their eyes were turned inward, there being so little to look at. The whole rest of the world had disappeared, and nature was way over in the back of beyond, like Daddy used to say, past the fences and wire.

Someone at a meeting once talked about this Japanese tradition called forest bathing. Slowing down and immersing in nature and wandering, without a destination. Tuning into the smells and textures and sights. Clearing out the clutter in your head and breathing it all in. At Oak Hills, I did what was available, a long-distance bath. Which is a contradiction in terms. But you work with what you're dealt. I got to know every bit of that little landscape I could see from my cell window, even before Max's challenge. I'd watch the trees lose and get, lose and get their leaves. Wait for glimpses of the animals that lived out there. Geese, once the weather turned, leaving their green shit trail. Raccoons and squirrels. A deer now and again. Owls and that hawk.

When I came through the gates five weeks ago, the lifeless February landscape seemed to sum up my life and my chances, but now that winter's started easing up, I'm out here reclaiming these sidewalks. Sometimes I pretend Daddy's walking alongside me, quietly noticing without the need to point things out.

It's still overwhelming, everyone out here doing their thing, walking where they want, and I'm still expecting to be called out for stepping out of line. Sometimes I feel out of synch, strung together all uneven, like a bargain basement marionette. But I walk, even at night, though the dark has its dangers. Feeling my muscles flexing and my feet against the pavement, I will myself forward. And now I notice different things than I used to. I like watching the moonlight shrink to nothing day by day and then return.

While I'm walking I'm rehearsing how to act, and I just hope to keep from being the wrong Ranita, and saying the wrong thing. The phone calls with the kids, even with the stumbles and the lack of flow, the little collisions when we start talking at the same time and the awkward silences that scare me, they're getting easier. But what if the kids ice or sass me in front of Miss Caseworker? How will that count against me?

It still surprises me to see men walking by. The only ones I saw at Oak Hills, besides Daddy, were either COs or the rare stranger-visitor. I saw a brotha yesterday who was fine enough to turn my head, which sent me into a where-do-I-fit tailspin for a minute. And when the space invaders approach, catcalling and undressing with their eyes, I feel a twisted mix of things. Repelled by the license they feel to bid and make a play, and grateful, too, for the recognition. I do like I've been taught, smile as politely as I can to keep the peace, and continue on my way.

When white folks approach I keep walking straight ahead. If the sidewalk's not wide enough for everyone, it's them who'll be stepping aside. If they wanted to know why and had the nerve to ask, I'd tell them, *It's the very least you can do. Learn some history.* It's useless. Morally small. And when white women smile at me, I walk by like I don't even see them. *That's for your Trump vote,* I'd like to tell them, *and for every other time you sold us out*. Morally smaller. A self-indulgent scrap of individual, internal politics with no impact whatsoever. Still.

From the corner of my eye I see a *Kitchen Help Wanted* sign in a café window. An hour and a half before I've got to be at DCF, I decide to go in and check it out. And as I come through the front door and open my mouth to speak, the man behind the counter dismisses me without even looking me in the face. "Not through here. Come through the back door in the alley," he snaps, even though there's not a single customer inside. I try to ignore his tone and ask does he know who I should talk to about the sign, and he points to the door I just came in and says, with Oak Hills coldness, "Like I said, out there to the back."

I swallow hard, pushing my hands into my pockets so they don't go off on their own. Nodding as polite as I can manage, I don't say a word. I know the way he's looking down on me, and I can see he thinks I should beg for the chance to work this dead-end job. As I walk out of there, on fire with all the disrespect I've ever known, my anger's moving through my body, and along with it I feel the rush of getting ready to tear loose.

I know I need to get off the street, get myself together, soften up my heart. A coffee shop with steamed-up windows looks warm and cozy, and I go inside and order the cheapest thing I can think of, tea and toast, and once I'm sitting there sipping, I feel my fury at the restaurant guy, who's probably just a poor asshole mad that he's stuck at the bottom like me, start to dim. *Common ground*, I try to tell myself, *focus on the common ground*.

Soon as I'm calmer, I feel something stirring around underneath all the mad, and I start scanning the street through the steamy window, even though I'm a long way from DQ's habitat. He's out there somewhere, and it wouldn't surprise me one bit if I saw him driving backward down a whole block like he sometimes did, and screeching to a stop right here. I know I'm on his radar screen, and he's resourceful. His ass has come back from the next life with Narcan more than once.

The weight of freedom and choosing, the aching for lightness, numbness, sleep, it's all coming down on me, and it doesn't take a whole lot to trigger me. A look that says I'm unworthy, and I'm 6 . . . 12 . . . 13 again. I recite one of my affirmations: "If I know my story, I can change it." And that puts me in touch with my truancy in therapy, where I seem to be running in the opposite direction of knowing.

Time to catch a meeting. I need all the help I can get today. And even though I've been speaking more, this time I sit and don't say a word. I don't know what might pour out if I do open up my mouth, but I say it in my head: *My name's Ranita. . . .*

Afterward, once I get to DCF, I'm so keyed up while I sit here waiting that my whole body aches. Looking down at myself, I realize I should have spent more time on my ironing. My shoes are scuffed at the toes. My sweater's pilly. My hands are rough and ashy. *Cheap lotion's to blame,* I want to say in my defense.

I try and fast-forward to the picnic I'm gonna have with the kids one day, watching butterflies and sipping lemonade while we relax, carefree in the open air, beneath a stand of leafy trees.

But here I am, back on punishment, Mama's and the state's, confined and remorseful and yearning. Trying to imagine an open door.

I try and see them at the waterside with me, okay with whether or not we catch a fish.

Instead, I see myself leaving them with Daddy so I can get my high on. Slipping out and tipping back in, no explanation, no excuses. Just the useless apologies they've heard before.

I try and picture tucking them in at night, with the love they need and the answers to their questions.

But here's Jasper, stopping through with a stuffed penguin for Amara, feeling like a hero for just coming over, proud he's made a baby, even if she's not a boy, and going on about how she's his heart, his pretty girl, his angel. Then he's gone before she starts needing something from him and it's just me, only a fraction more together than he is, and our girl's asking where is he, why'd he leave, is he coming back.

Jesus. Struggling to get my balance in this present-past jumble, I'm just praying not everything my kids remember is bad. Reaching for the safety of low expectations, I own that nothing good will come of this. They'll look right through me. I'll say something stupid, something wrong. I'll find nothing at all to say.

Miss Caseworker comes to get me, giving her most uninvested look yet, and explains that for now we'll visit here at the office and if that goes smooth (smooth*ly*, I want to tell her, channeling Mama) we'll do it again.

And here are my kids, coming through the door. The last seven months I've seen them in my photos and fantasies (and Theo, in the glance I stole), and I'm shocked at how big and stunning they are.

My name's Ranita, and I'm a mother. No matter how far down and far away I've been.

I hug Val whether she likes it or not, thank her for bringing them, and watch her leave, after reassuring us that she'll be back in exactly one hour.

"Mama," Theo says, and I answer, "Yes, baby," grateful to him beyond measure, "you're a sight for sore eyes."

He's got his hat on backward like he's trying for tough, but his face is soft and shy, and he's missing his front teeth. I wonder where he's found to put all his tears.

Amara cuts her eyes and looks past me. She seems older than 13 . . . boobs already, just like me . . . when did that happen? And she's standing with her womanish hip stuck out. She's tried to slick her hair down, and it's crying out for braids or freedom. Stepping closer to Theo, she puts her arm around his shoulders, and we stand here as Miss Caseworker recedes to the sidelines with her pen and notepad, unsure what's next.

I feel Daddy with me, in me, and picture his heartbeat lighting up the both of us.

My name's Ranita, and I'm a daughter. No matter if he's spirit now.

I'm the only one smiling, but I can't help it, and like a hostess, I say, "Well, have a seat." I give them their presents, feeling anxious as I hand them over, and my kids have had enough manners sown into them to thank me politely, but it's hard to tell if they like the presents or if they've already got mugs with their names but better, or if these are as shitty as the price would suggest and they'll go unused.

Just like at Oak Hills, I feel the visit slipping away as soon as it begins. I can't help glancing at the big wall clock as the conversation sputters and some of my questions flop and end in painful silence. Amara's on the muscle, and Theo's doing such a bad job of being stoic. And Miss Caseworker's over there like a storm cloud at a picnic, witnessing every fumble.

Last week, she went over the rules of engagement for today: She'd be observing; Val would bring them; it was critical to be prompt. She suggested I bring some activities, to *fill up the time.* "Like what?" I asked, angry that she thought we'd just be going through the motions, and that she thought she knew them better than I did. Maybe a game like Uno. Or a video, as long as it was appropriate. Did she really need to say that? Does she think I'd show them porn? I took her advice with the Uno, and picked up some playing cards at the dollar store.

I pull the Uno and playing cards out to fill the quiet, and both are hits. When Theo wins at Uno, he does a victory dance, while me and Amara watch and smile. We play gin rummy, which I let them both win, and I try to get a conversation going about school. Theo says lunch and recess are his favorite subjects, and I nearly jump in and scold him, then remember the bite of Mama's disapproval and hold my tongue. Amara talks about being more than ready to leave middle school, like it's an old sweater she's outgrown, and when it really hits me that she'll be starting high school next year it takes me a minute to recover. Well-versed in playacting, I keep on pulling from the draw pile and discarding like

I'm all good. I didn't see either one of them for their birthdays this year, though I sent cards, and somehow it didn't sink in that she's a teenager, and moving out of reach.

I think back to my 13. Mama. She was the story of that year.

When it's time to say good-bye, Amara lets me hug her. And Theo's blinking away tears as he wraps his arms around me.

I plan to get out of here before I have to watch them walk away with Val, but before I leave I ask, "Wait . . . what are your favorite colors?"

It sounds random, like some creepy stranger, trying to get close. They look surprised, but Theo smiles big. "Mine's blue!" Amara, she plays it cool and says, "Red," shrugging, with a halfhearted roll of her eyes, like she can't be bothered with such a lame question. "I guess it's red."

The whole way down the stairs my legs feel shaky, and after hurrying through the door and down four blocks I make myself stop and get calm enough to see where I am. For a minute I recognize nothing, though my eyes are open. And then there's a tree and a bench I haven't noticed before, and I go and sit there, even though the seat's dirty and one side's lower than the other and there's a pile of dog shit close by.

An encyclopedia fact comes back to me, about the give-and-take relationship we've got with trees. They make oxygen for our use, and we make carbon dioxide for theirs. As I exhale I picture this stately elm drawing in what it needs from me. Inhaling, I see myself receiving what it's releasing, and giving thanks.

Then a piece of glass catches my eye, and this time it's the emerald green I know from Tanqueray, and I free it from the dirt, rub it on my coat, and put it in my backpack, hoping it'll read like something other than a weapon if somehow (there can always be a reason) the cops stop me.

Over and over, I relive the visit. Looking at it from every angle, zooming in on the details, going wide, playing it forward and back. It was hard, but so much better than at Oak Hills, when the vibe was funereal and there was no escaping the price to be paid once they'd left.

THIRTEEN

Oak Hills
2016

They listened for their names. Visualized their people coming through the trap. Bargained with their higher powers. Today, God willing, they would get a visit.

If they heard their names, they answered with relief and often, tears. If they didn't, there was another absence to add to all the others, as they receded further and further from the free world.

Ranita felt blessed. Her family was coming. She focused on her little bit of forward motion, and even with what would follow, she couldn't wait to be with them, a year in and clean.

Back at the jail, post-arrest, her father had been two feet away and unreachable, on the other side of the glass that was magnifier and mirror. She'd watched him mouthing words she couldn't hear, until she pointed to the phone she was holding and the one beside him. Before he left, like everyone else, she had pressed her hand to the glass and he'd done the same. How well she knew that palm that was nearly twice the size of hers and oil stained. When she moved hers away, obeying the order to return to her cell, and his lingered on the glass, she had choked back sobs.

At Oak Hills, the glass partition was gone, but she knew the passage through the trap was still a trial. If he made it there after the hour-and-a-half drive, he'd be sitting with Amara and Theo, along with all the other expectant families, waiting to be called.

Marooned on the waiting room pews, worn-out elders tried to keep control of the kids they had in tow. Dressed in matching outfits, boys in navy and girls in pink, hair freshly done and skin lotioned, they chased each other round and round, until a frown from a guard or a warning from a grandma brought them in line. *Want me to tell your mama how you're acting?*

Why couldn't they just sit quietly? The elders shook their heads and tried to get ready for the metal detector and the stamp, the heartbreak and the inexplicable situation in which they found themselves, the making do and acting happy, and all the questions they were so unequipped to answer.

Too much to manage, and not enough help or time or money or energy or thanks. Kids who would not obey, pressing with their *Whys*. And them . . . aunties . . . grandmas . . . left to deal with it, no good explanation for why Mama had been taken way up here, why she was gone again, no good explanation for any of it. When would they get there and why did the bus ride take so long? Why did the bathroom smell that way and have no toilet paper? Why were there no toys to play with? Why did they search the youngest one's diaper? Why didn't the man in blue ever speak to them, even to answer their *Whys*? Why was Mama living so far away? Why did they have to wait so long?

How could they explain any of it? And how could they unravel why sometimes, even though you came all the way up there on the bus (because the car needed fixing or was taking someone else to work) and you'd done each and every thing correctly, abiding by the rules for dressing and touching and talking and being, they called a Code 99 and locked the place down. And you turned around and went home, without any good explanation of why they couldn't see Mama that month. *Because*, they answered, *just because*.

Matter of fact, they had questions of their own. They'd like to ask why anyone thought it was a good idea to degrade and shame parents in front of their children, to separate them and punish them, and why their children's glistening and newly braided hair was seen only as a way to smuggle contraband. They'd like to ask who, after all, would want to keep people locked up for a living? *I'd rather be on unemployment*, they thought. *I'd rather be on welfare for the rest of my gotdamn life. Look at that one over behind the plexiglass and the counter now, thinking he's something other than a slave.* They might have had no choice about doing as they'd been ordered, but they could decide to never, ever give the guards the satisfaction of looking them in the eye.

After Lennox had surrendered his driver's license and produced the kids' birth certificates and proof of guardianship, he put their outer layers of clothing, along with his watch, wallet, eyeglasses, and phone, in a locker, and deposited a quarter in exchange for a little orange key. "Wait," he said, gently pulling Amara back to remove her barrettes, and then opening the locker to add them and get another coin. Jessie was still talking about the blow of having to surrender her gold chain with the praying-hands pendant to a CO's custody after she'd made it into the trap.

They found seats beside another family while a drug detection dog walked past, sniffing at their legs. Most of those who sat waiting knew the dog would not stop at them; there was nothing to detect. Still, they couldn't help tumbling back to the lurking ambush of the countryside and the stop-and-frisk terror of the city, and it never ceased to unnerve, the knowledge that they could suddenly, disastrously run afoul of the law, which had never meant to serve or protect them. At last month's visit, when five-year-old Theo had reached out to pet the dog, the guard had cut him off with a cold, knife-edged, *No touching. He's working*, and Theo had cried. He hadn't stopped mentioning the rebuke, and today he clung to Lennox's arm as man and dog walked by.

All around them, restless and nervous kids goofed, argued, wove in and out of the benches, but instead of pinging around with that restless energy, Amara and Theo sat motionless and deflated. When Lennox smiled at the three stairstep kids beside him, the toddler hid her face in her grandma's sleeve, the middle one smiled and pointed to her missing front teeth, and the eldest said, "Hi, mister. Their mama locked up, too?" Grandma apologized, pulling him closer, and launched into what she'd told them on the bus about how to act. And then they were called, and she was getting to her feet, pulling her string of little ones along.

"Why can't they call *us*?" Amara asked with sullen sadness.

Again and again, Lennox looked at his wrist, though the only thing to see was a pale band of freckled brown skin. He pulled the locker key from his pocket and put it back three times. The slacks and button-down he wore whenever he was not at work were well within the rules, but he looked at the dress code posted on the wall in English and Spanish. For men, *No blue denim pants. No cargo pants. No double-layered clothing. No sweatsuits. No hooded sweatshirts or jackets. No T-shirts. No pockets with holes.* It was more challenging for women, as Jessie had found; she'd been turned away once for excessive pockets. *No skirts with slits. No skirts more than three inches above the knee. No shorts. No skorts.* What in God's name was a skort? he'd asked her. *No tank tops. No halter tops. No scarves. No low-cut tops. No formfitting stretch pants. No bathing suits.* Another question for his sister: Who would wear a bathing suit to the penitentiary? *No sheer clothing, with or without a bra.*

At her first visit, Jessie's underwire bra had set off the metal detector and she'd been taken to a little room for a pat-down search at the hands of a stone-faced stranger. After standing with her arms outstretched, pulling the wire away from her rib cage and her waistband from her belly, lifting the bottoms of her feet while trying to balance on one leg like a ridiculous flamingo stuck in the least exotic of places, she had come braless, in a pullover that was roomy enough to hide the evidence of her drooping middle-aged breasts, but not too baggy to prevent entry.

When their turn finally came, the heavy metal door rattled open and shut behind Lennox and the kids, and they were taking off their shoes and putting them in a bin, turning out their pockets, getting the black-light stamps on their wrists, and walking through the metal-detector archway. Through it all, Lennox stood tall and looked past the cold, dismissive glances of the guards who puffed out their chests with self-importance and shook their heads at the failure of his family, his people.

He answered the question on the clipboard he was handed, *Have You Ever Been Convicted of a Crime?*, writing a big, bold, uppercase *NO*.

Coming through the buzzing gates with a child by each hand, he moved toward visitation, looking down at their feet and their three gleaming shadows on the buffed linoleum floor. Fourteen, 15, 16 steps and 23 to go until the next door, a right turn and then 12 more. Now sitting for the final wait, he watched the door.

As soon as she entered the room, Ranita heard the voices of children and saw the mothers, grandmas, aunties, and sisters who sat with them, and the few men who stood out like trees on the prairie. There was Daddy, sitting with her babies, who were almost too beautiful to bear.

Kids chattered and jumped around, trying hard to entertain them-selves with out-of-date *Highlights* magazines and a few worn or disabled toys. A truck with three wheels. A doll with matted blond hair and sight-less blue eyes. They argued and complained. "This one hit me." "That one teased me." "That one took my seat."

A boy stood apart, arms folded and tucked to his body, silent and wary of his disappearing, reappearing mom. A toddler, dressed in the denim and Timberlands of a miniature man, stiffened in his mother's insistent hug. A family played gin rummy with a deck of limp cards.

The Oak Hills women ached for these visits, proof that life and love go on. And once they came, they weren't sure they could endure the stilted positivity. The walls, with their fake wood paneling, seemed to close in, and the cheerful posters of panda bears and smarmy memes mocked. The lit-up soda and junk food machines enticed, only to over-charge and disappoint, and the overseers looked on with pity and indif-ference.

Still, there were miracles. The hugs for bodies craving touch. The loving faces, returned to them briefly, smiling in spite of the mournful mood. A mother played peekaboo over and over, glowing at how she could make her baby smile. A couple stared with hope and longing into each other's eyes as they claimed this now.

Trying to refuse the blank, surveillant eyes of holstered guards that ravaged every intimacy, Ranita made her way to the children who sat eerily quiet and the father who was still showing up for her, nodding and saying, "Afternoon," to those she passed as she heard Lennox's voice inside her head: *We speak to each other, wherever we are. . . . It binds us . . . it says we're people, whatever they think or say or do.*

She gave her father a quick squeeze and a kiss, and then squatted down to Theo's height and tried to put her arms around both kids. Ama-ra's arms hung limp and Theo reached for her, then pulled away.

As soon as they sat down, the visit started slipping through her fin-gers. They'd just arrived, and her first thought was how long until they had to go.

"How you doin', Nita?" Lennox asked, and she answered, "Fine, I'm doing fine." They'd always been good at talking without going anywhere painful.

"How've you been keeping busy?" Lennox asked.

"Hmmm . . . I've been reading again. It seems to help. And cro-cheting."

She asked about school and after-school and the neighborhood kids, but every try at conversation, lighthearted or probing, fizzled. She sent them to the vending machines she wasn't allowed to use, hoping her father would say something real about how they were doing, but he just sat between the chairs they had vacated, looking morose. She knew his credo: keep on providing; keep on loving. How did you talk about a thing like prison without making things worse?

"You feeling good, Mama?" Amara asked, seeming older than her ten years, when the kids were back at the table and digging into the snacks. Resisting the urge to promise that this time she'd conquer it, this time her recovery would take, she said she was working hard at being well.

Looking over at the photographer who was setting up, Ranita asked, cheerfully, "Want to take a photo, the four of us?"

No one spoke or moved. She saw her father look over at the back-drop of turquoise water and palm trees, and then at the door.

Ranita had seen other mothers showing their photos around and she wanted one, too. Nodding at the family getting a picture taken, she said, "Look at them. Seems like it's a good thing, doesn't it? We can both have a copy, and that way we'll be able to see us, all together, any time we want. We'll be seeing the same thing, maybe even at the same time."

Amara and Theo looked at each other. Lennox said, "You all go on then. Let it be the three of you," and when Ranita stood the kids did, too, walking with her to wait their turn. Ranita paid for two copies, or her father did, since it was his money on her books, and when their turn came they arranged themselves in front of the 2-D beach, her on one knee with her right arm around Theo and Amara on her left, almost touching her.

When she held one of the copies out to her father, he shook his head and said, "I'd prefer a different reference point." She put it on the table in front of him, hoping he'd change his mind, and sat back down to look at herself with her children, frozen now in time.

The air felt thick and heavy, and they tried for goodwill, but it was a carcass picked clean. They'd gotten Doritos and candy and soda from the vending machine. Taken a photo. Exhausted their news and their pretenses. And Ranita wished she had things to share, but she was on pause from life. What could she tell them? She'd stood for count at 6:00, 11:15, 4:30, and 9:30. She'd gone to chow. Watched a spades game and listened to stories about plants with taproots and watched women sneak affection in the dayroom. Buffed the floor. Gone to chow twice more. Cried herself to sleep with regret and loneliness. She was story-poor.

They sat silently across from each other, running out the clock.

And then, leaning across the table to take their hands, Ranita went somewhere she knew was a misstep as she opened her mouth. "I hate to see you leave. When you're gone I miss you so bad. . . ." She saw Amara's face hardening, but she couldn't seem to stop talking. ". . . I picture you at the house, or at school, or playing out back. . . ." She saw Amara balling up her fists, but kept going, ". . . and it's so tough, being away from you, sometimes I feel like my heart's breaking. . . ."

And that was it. Amara blew, "What about *us*, Mama?" Ranita felt the faint spray of her daughter's spit on her face as she shouted, "It's like we're locked up, too!"

Her cries shook her skinny ten-year-old body and Ranita looked over at the CO standing on the wall and was flooded with shame. He watched but registered no compassion, no mercy, no regard at all, as Ranita got up and went to her daughter and took her in her arms and Theo buried his face in his grandpa's side, asking, "Granddaddy, why can't Mama come home with us?"

When the tears subsided and Ranita went back to her chair, Amara slid the photo closer and stared at it, before saying, "You'll get better, Mama. I know you will."

Ranita felt the last minutes of what she'd prayed for expire with mourning and relief. And just before the time was up, she couldn't help asking, "When you think you'll come again?"

She watched them disappear from view. And now it was time to pay for her good fortune. And prove the body's innocence.

Herded into a private room, those lucky enough to have had a visit faced three COs, one a "female" who'd been detailed there for the protection of the women inside. "You know the routine," she said with icy detachment, making clear, in case they missed it, that the whole thing meant less than nothing to her.

They did know the routine. They'd learned it after every visit. In the search for serious contraband. Returning from a funeral, the hospital, a trip to court. And whenever some CO felt like it.

With no choice but survival, they stripped like they had so many times, looking straight ahead and looking back to all the other takings embedded in their cells. Human-cargo passages and auction-block appraisals. Escapes and captures. Rapes and other unrecorded conquests. Lynchings to entertain others and warn their kind. Chain gangs and coffin cells. Firehoses and dog whistles and flaming crosses. Police on the other side of the gun and on their necks.

They handed their clothes over for inspection, baring the bodies that had kept track of their mishaps and hurtings, of the accidents and want and illness and aggression that had left their marks, along with the things they chose to say in dark blue ballpoint ink.

Their flesh said: *Here's where I fell off my bike, where I scraped myself climbing that fence, where my adolescent bacne bloomed. This is from my C-section with my first-born, and here's the mark from fighting off that Klansman CO. Here's the cigarette burn my ex gave me to remember him when I tried to get free. Here are the traces of the tracks I used to hide and this is my first boyfriend's name, inked half*

my life ago. The fat around my middle is the story of canteen chips and empty calo-
ries, of salt and starch and sugar that have passed for nourishment inside the walls.
And this is where I muscled up, lifting and planking to defend myself and fill the
time. Here's what my body's got to say about the days and months and years spent
where doctors and dentists and fresh air and sunlight have been in short supply.

They spread their feet apart. Lifted each one to show the sole. Wig-
gled their toes. Leaned forward and shook out their hair. Folded each
ear forward, tilted their heads back to expose the nostrils. Opened their
mouths wide, lifted their tongues, rolled their top and bottom lips.
Raised both arms.

Lifted their breasts and their fat rolls. Pulled their innie belly buttons
open. Ran their fingers through their pubes and spread their pussies.
Squatted. Coughed three times. Turned around, bent over, spread their
ass cheeks, coughed again three times.

They tried to go elsewhere. Concentrated on the doorway, bit their
cheeks. But they could feel the inside wounds, the tally kept from the
punishments, the things they had been named and deemed, the ways
they had tried and fallen short. From the poisons in their blood and
lungs that had seemed like liberation. From the ones who broke and
entered, using kinship and prayer as passwords. From the daily wound
of being reckoned less than human, the toll of being thrown away like
trash.

Silently, they chanted: *This is my body. It is still here and it is still mine,*
and it has known worse than this, along with its portion of pleasure and kindness
and love. It was mine. It is mine. It will be mine. But it is also just a body, and I
can leave it and go past hurt, past feeling, past anything you can do to me in here
today.

FOURTEEN

Just as I was starting to wonder if wellness and recovery were mirages, two milestones are giving me hope. One: I got a part-time gig. Turned out Jessie had a connect with a former co-worker, and she called and asked if his friend's restaurant was hiring any kitchen workers. I heard her telling him, "She's a good person [*debatable*] and a hard worker [*she hasn't seen much evidence of that*], and she really needs this job [*truth*]."

Honestly, I was amazed when it came through. The pay's crap and it's dirty, smelly work, scraping plates and manning the dishwasher, mopping and scrubbing and restocking tableware, but I could get down on my knees I'm so thankful, after putting in an application for every job I could think of and getting nowhere. I got one callback, until a CORI check put the kibosh on it.

I tell you what, you may get freed, technically, but you're stuck with your old leaf and nothing else to turn over. *No* to anything involving money: cashier, teller, Western Union. *No* to anything that involves a key or the chance to steal: office worker, hotel maid, night maintenance, inventory worker, warehouse stocker. To anything where there's a security risk: airport checker, van driver. *No* to anything with kids: daycare worker, counselor, teacher. Go back to school to get a different kind of work? *No* to financial aid. Get help while you're looking for the job no one will give you? *No.* A driver's license to help you get that job? *Suspended.* Help with getting a roof over your head in public housing? *Hell no.*

Sometimes I swear I hear the whole universe: people, institutions, clouds, stars, all saying *no* in perfect harmony. To survive I've been doing housecleaning, odd jobs, and errands for some of Jessie's rehab buddies and friends from church. But this kitchen thing's a step up. And there's no toilets involved.

There is one special thing about the restaurant. Sometimes they play opera and I picture everyone in the kitchen singing what all they've got to say instead of talking, and imagine myself stepping up to belt one out. Seems like I've been able to take opera music back from Mama's choke-hold on it, and I do love the drama of the arias. After all, I've played the diva more than once, mostly a down-on-her-luck one, truth be told, but I like to think I had a little bit of diva style.

Until something steady breaks, I'll go to the kitchen gig whenever they need me, which is not often enough. Being under the table, it won't help a whole lot with DCF, but it's something, and I get to eat dinner for free when I'm there, even though the work steals your appetite. By the time I get home, what with the worrying on top of the work, I smell like a wet mop and a garbage disposal, and I can barely stand. After Oak Hills, where the longest most of us really work is 5 hours, and mostly you can finish your job in 45 minutes, the 10-hour shifts are a bitch.

Milestone Number Two is moving into my own place this week. It's a "garden studio apartment," which means a no-frills room belowground with a month-to-month lease that someone at my regular meeting's giving up. Val helped me out with a little loan, and the landlord's letting me take over the lease. I've got a feeling it's not really up to code . . . the lights flicker and power goes out now and then, like in other parts of the world, I guess . . . but it's mine, and when I got the key I nearly cried. Before I brought over my little bit of stuff, I got a House Blessing candle from a botanica and sat in the empty room while it burned.

The room's not what I've pictured in my head, especially with the bars over the windows, but at least they're not for keeping me in, and through them I can see two skinny red oak trees. I've been watching . . . one day all trees have is buds and then you wake and they're covered in green lace . . . so I don't miss their turning point.

Anyway, I know this place won't do in the long run. When I told Miss Caseworker about it, she reminded me, even before I finished my sentence, that the kids can't come there; they'll need their own bedrooms for reunification to even be considered. I took some deep breaths and nodded. And then, like I was channeling Mama, I said, "I was merely apprising you of my progress toward self-sufficiency."

She looked at me with new curiosity, like I'd shape-shifted. And I jumped on that to request that she "consider the possibility that we revisit the appointment times that have been set forth, in order to accommodate my new employment hours" . . . and to "request that I be permitted to participate in the relapse prevention group despite the fact that the registration date lapsed on the previous day." I could practically hear Mama singing out her approval, telling me, *That's how it's done, Ranita.* Eyes wide and blinking, Miss Caseworker tried to take it in. And answered no. And no. She's sticking to the rules, and no matter what fancy words flow out of me, she's sticking with her doubt.

When it was time to leave Auntie Jessie's, I sat by her recliner. She'd watched me dart around all morning, losing the thread of what I was doing, checking and rechecking that I had everything.

"You come back and see me regular, now," she said. "And don't forget, I'm expecting that invitation over to your place real soon, you hear?" I nodded, but I knew she wouldn't be able to do the stairs.

"I'ma try not to be a disappointment," I whispered, leaning my head on her shoulder. "I'ma do my best."

She kissed my forehead, like I was a little kid. "That's right, Nita. Keep on choosing. And remember I'm a phone call and a bus ride away." I called her three times that first day, just to hear her voice.

Well, the actual moving part's easy if you don't own shit. Judy drove me over with my things. I had the clothes she and Jessie gave me and the stuff I combed through the charity shops to get. And Jessie gave me kitchen supplies to get started with. I was really touched, knowing how tight her money is on her fixed income, even if she's too proud to talk about it. I've seen her reusing tea bags and tinfoil and washing out freezer bags, adding water to the liquid hand soap to stretch it, and fixing rice and beans again and again and pretending it's by choice.

Everything I've got is second- or third-hand. Three chairs that are barely on speaking terms. A small pressed-wood table from the Salvation Army that I painted, the top bright blue and the legs green, still starved for color from Oak Hills. I'll have to wait for a couch. Judy helped me get a mattress and a boom box on craigslist, and she gave me an old box-shaped TV and VCR/DVD player that mostly works, though all of a sudden it'll spit the movie you're watching out like it tastes nasty. And I know it'll be months and months before the kids can maybe stay overnight, but I can't help thinking about how this place will feel to them. I got them fleecy pillows, and found some turquoise cloth place mats at the dollar store, where I've been stocking up on supplies. I can't get enough soap and lotion, tampons and toilet paper, hair product. I know I'm hoarding, but I can't help it. Those things we couldn't get on the inside, they're precious.

Of course, Judy wanted to hang out after we finished moving. "Come over to our place," she said, though it's really hers. Ike moved in three months ago and has yet to pay any rent. We sat there on his sprawling black leather sectional sofa that barely fit in the room, next to a huge fish tank he brought with him that had one fish in it. Jasper was way into tropical fish for a minute, and I knew their names and habits. Ike saw me looking at the orange-and-black tiger oscar and said, smiling, "I had others . . . zebras, mollies, tetras . . . but Oscar here, he owns the block. Soon as I put him in, he took over. Killed the others off."

Trapped, too beholden for the help Judy'd given to get up and leave, I watched Oscar patrol his big, empty house, while they drank pink Moscato and played video games, imagining themselves with assault rifles and answering to no one.

While Judy was in the bathroom, Ike pulled out a vape pen and took a drag. I hadn't seen one, but I knew everyone was using them, out in the open, too. The mist he exhaled didn't even smell. Easy and covert, no problem. He held it out to me and I didn't even bother saying, again, that I'm in recovery. I wanted to take it, slip it in my pocket, and split, but I just shook my head and pretended to be interested in what Oscar was up to.

Ike jabbered on about how he's looking for a way into the weed economy. "Why the hell not, that's what I'm asking. We got politicians and law-and-order types getting in on it . . . white folks get richer and niggas stay locked up . . . there's a goddamn fortune to be made, and I want me a piece of it, you feel me?"

Judy came back and chimed in, "I know that's right. We could be entrepreneurs, but we can't even get in the game."

I felt a wave of sadness for Jasper and so many others, locked up and vilified before they changed up the rules, and tried to shift the topic from drugs to what I've been reading, but they didn't seem eager to discuss speculative fiction by Black women.

Somewhere in the middle of my hour-long sentence on that couch they started asking had I met anybody. "You still look good," Judy offered, which didn't exactly feel like a compliment, and then she said Ike had friends they could introduce me to. "Tall, dark, slim goodie . . . I know your type, Nita."

I shrugged, not really wanting to think about what my type is. "My mind's on other things."

"Well, you must be wanting some *company*, after all that time at Oak Hills."

I shrugged, looking as casual as I could, and then Ike, who's got no standing whatsoever to say anything the least bit personal to me, said, "You wasn't down there at Oak Hills bumpin' pussy, was you?"

A raunchy grin showing all his fillings announced how he felt about that possibility. If only he knew what a cliché he was. The only answer I wanted to give him was to slam his mouth closed so hard it might dislodge a filling or a tooth. But I'm sad to say, and thankful Maxine never has to know it, I performed a shallow chuckle and changed the subject.

Damn. With skipping out on therapy, I've had a dismal shadow visiting me pretty much nonstop, and now another shame ghost would be stopping by. I was so grateful to get back to my little crib that I kissed the inside of the door once I had it closed and thought about how to make the place homey.

The next day Val brought a few of Daddy's things over to Jessie's for me. His fishing poles and tackle box, and his best set of tools. Cuff links and tie clips and some of his cologne. Taken by a wave of grief and guilt for not honoring him proper, I shoved everything except his model ship-in-a-bottle into the closet, and then put my photos of him and the kids in the frames I found at Goodwill. And even though they're just plastic, they give the pictures more dignity than when they were stuck to my cell wall and curling at the edges. I looked at my stilted visitation picture and decided to put it away for now. And what to do with my ugly crocheted throw, one of the first positive things I did at Oak Hills? I thought about tossing it or putting it in the closet. But always a softie for unloved things, I folded it across the foot of my mattress.

I wish Daddy could see me here. I've survived in an Oak Hills tomb, stayed for stretches with Jasper and DQ, crashed with people I didn't even know, and bounced back to Daddy's house again and again. But I've never had a place of my own.

At first, I put my blue and green city glass in a little ceramic bowl I found at Goodwill and set it on the windowsill. Then I decided it looked meager and weird. And I imagined what Miss Caseworker would say. The edges haven't been worked soft and the kids might cut themselves if they picked up the pieces. I moved it to the top shelf of a kitchen cabinet.

The first few nights I pulled a blanket across the windows, making sure nobody could look down in here and see me. Then I thought about what the sistas at Oak Hills would do about the situation, and took myself to a discount fabric store over on Morrissey. Found some bright teal-colored remnants, and went back to the dollar store for tension rods, then folded over one end of the fabric to make a casing. I was wishing I hadn't refused to learn to sew in Home Ec, but it's amazing what you can do with safety pins.

Standing in the middle of the room now, I look around. I need things for the walls. And some decorative touches. Mama didn't do house-plants, but some green would make a difference. Anyway, this room is mine. And even though the mattress feels like a raft, down on the floor, it's good here. I like sitting at my own little table. Taking a bath again, and having some privacy. I close my eyes to the places where the tile grout's breaking apart and the caulking's coming loose, and lean back on the scallop shell bath pillow Jessie let me have, now that she can't get in and out of the tub. And let me tell you this: the best new possession of all is the shower massager Judy gave me.

Time for a bath, matter of fact, and for a session with the handheld lover that's all about my needs. I end up calling out Maxine's name and then lie here, feeling even lonelier, and before the water goes completely cold I get out of the tub and take the kites from their new home, up in the cabinet beside the city glass.

The third one she left for me is one of my favorites: *Do you want to dance? It's free. I'll be at the chapel.*

When I got there, she opened her arms. "We'll have to imagine the music, unless you can sing. Me? I couldn't carry a tune if my life depended on it."

"I used to sing," I said. It would be months before I'd tell her why I stopped.

I walked into her arms and we danced, barely moving. Every part of us touching that could, our breathing synched and making a kind of music. Both of us were fully dressed, but I could have sworn we were naked.

Later, lying on my bunk, I kept reliving it. We'd danced for five minutes, tops. And we hadn't even kissed yet, but it was like we were making love. I was present, clean and sober, awake. And I'd never felt more alive or more myself.

I get out my cards to play some solitaire and tame the wildfire that burns beneath my skin, and it does feel calming, watching the four lines of cards build and unbuild. Ace King Queen Jack Ten, you don't have to wonder how to put them down. And every time you play, you think you've got a chance.

Maybe I should check out that Queer Dance Party, see what it feels like. No harm in just looking. The flyer I got from the meeting bulletin board's up in the top cabinet with the city glass, and I pull it down and check the details. Then I perch on the edge of the tub and paint my toenails Metallic Sapphire, wondering does it make me look femme or not. It's making me feel cuter, however it reads, even though my feet will be covered.

I do my eyeliner and mascara, adding some smoky eye shadow and choosing wine-red lipstick, and put on the black jeans I found on consignment, wondering how them being tight on my ass will play with this crowd. My black bra and a gray top that's clingy enough to show my boobs, but loose enough to hide my middle. I hope. Maxine said queer folks, freed up from the patriarchy to some extent, anyhow, tend to be body positive. I'm going with that *It's all good* feeling.

I put on the black suede boots Jessie gave me, now that her heel-wearing days are over. And staring at myself in the bathroom mirror, I decide to free my hair (hoping my mind and ass will follow) from its elastic, and let my kinks be wild. A backpack doesn't seem right for a dance party, so I shove my lipstick, brand-new house key, wallet, and phone into my jacket pockets, and soon as I walk out of my new front door I'm feeling charged up by the open air and the winter's-almost-over feeling that's got people in the street.

Feels good to be out and moving, even if I do feel myself getting wound up the closer I get to the bar. As the Orange Line train jerks and clacks along, I look out at the tunnel walls, wishing I could dodge the fluorescent lights for the cover of darkness.

When we get to my stop, I sit here, avoiding the eyes of the folks across from me, unsure all of a sudden about this little adventure, and then I jump up and put my arm out to keep the doors from closing, and soon I'm stepping on the escalator behind a group of rowdy teenagers who remind me of my young self, shouting and running and carrying on like they'll live forever. I picture Amara with them, hoping she has friends, the law-abiding kind who believe in the future. And on the way up I spot the shine of red glass down on the platform. It feels ridiculous how much I want it, but I ride to the top and down again to pick it up. It's an unbroken circle, the bottom of a votive candle, maybe, and I add it to my coat pocket, thinking it should clean up nice.

When I get to the address, I realize, from the faded letters on the brick smokestack out front, that the building used to be a brewery. Great. The whole way here I've been trying to prepare myself for the fact that for most of the people at this here party, drinking will go with dancing. Now I know alcohol's in the foundation of this place, even before it became a bar. Yeah, I managed not to pick up at Mario's, but that's the little neighborhood "lounge" that time forgot, and I'm feeling mighty anxious about this outing, this place . . . this queer thing, and something to sip or inhale or smoke always did make me feel a little more right in my skin.

It's not quite party time, so there's a line taking shape out front, and a patio where folks are gathered. And I'm standing at the curb, trying to look casual, checking out the crowd. It's upbeat and mostly young. Plenty white folks, but Black and brown and Asian, too. And some of everybody's here. Those giving girl are in tutus, spiffy vests and wing tips, baggy Carhartt. Some are mommy-jeans frumpy, wearing tunics and those hiking sandal-shoe things, and others are looking fresh in heels and skirts and jeans even tighter than mine. Those looking boy, they're a mixed bag, too. They've got on everything from plaid shirts and sneakers to tailored pants with neon argyle socks, muscle shirts and skinny jeans, cargo pants. Some are refusing category. And the young and beautiful and underdressed strut by slowly, catching everybody's eye.

The hair's all over the map: Afros, gelled spikes and expensive, messy-on-purpose salon cuts, massive corkscrews and high ponytails, blond tips, turquoise and purple and magenta streaks, buzz cuts, Mohawks, locs. My hair's fitting in, but then it seems like anything goes. Still, no one would look at me and think I belong here.

While I'm standing on the edge of the patio, trying to look like I'm waiting for the rest of my group to arrive, a gorgeous brotha with a shaved head and gold hot pants comes strolling over, his big gold hoop earrings bouncing, and asks me do I have a light.

I give him a friendly smile. "Sorry, I don't smoke anymore."

He bows dramatically, like he's addressing royalty. "Thanks anyway. And I know you've heard it before, but you've got a bad-assed walk and a big, beauteous smile to go with it."

I bow back, feeling myself go into performance mode, while on the inside I'm choked with doubt. I wish I could summon Wild Cherry for the night, keep her sober, and then box her back up.

Standing apart, I'm looking at the folks on line. Hoping they're not watching me. Some I would have recognized for queer . . . they're yelling that they're different, or at least not hiding it. Others, like me, they just look like everyone else you see around the way. But they all seem so comfortable with themselves, so confident in who they are. So free.

The line starts moving. I tell myself, *Go on, get in it.*

But I stand watching as the partyers, amped up and already dancing bouncing chatting laughing together, go inside, one by one, until only the tail of the line is still outside.

It's not too late, Ranita; go on.

From out here I can hear the music pumping, and I want to be able to see what it's like in there, to step into the crowd and move with them, let myself go and feel their sureness and freeness lift me. It's only dancing, I tell myself. An opportunity. Not a bid.

Standing on the outside, wishing I had Maxine with me, I watch the last few people disappear inside. And it crushes me, but I can't do it. I can't go through the door.

FIFTEEN

Oak Hills
2016

The first time Ranita got up the nerve to speak to Maxine, she had been trying to get to Planet Bookworld.

She'd watched her at chow and in the dayroom, unable to look away from her proud, unfettered bearing and the salt-and-pepper locs cascading down her back. Next to "warrior" in the encyclopedia, Ranita thought, should be a picture of her.

She'd heard the talk. *That sista always got her nose in a lawbook*, people said, with a lot of respect and a little jealousy. *Talking legal strategies, feminism, racial justice, liberation, 24/7.* And she'd been to the hole for fucking up a predatory CO, that was the word.

Hoping to find a novel she hadn't read, Ranita had gone to the Oak Hills "library." She thought of it with quotes, far cry as it was from the refuge of the local branch with its warm lamplight, worn wingback chairs, and what felt like an infinite supply of books that might transport her. "Hey," she said as she entered, and Maxine looked up from the habeas petition she was working on with a long-termer still bent on freedom. Their eyes had engaged, and when they finally broke contact Ranita turned to a new batch of donated books and found *Parable of the Sower*.

The next time all she managed was a nod. Reluctantly, she'd gone to a meeting with Naomi, who never let up on urging her to attend, for which Ranita felt alternately grateful and irritated. It was hard to do your time, let alone avoid temptation, on your own, but she didn't like being someone's project.

Except for that Vicodin relapse that set her back with a D Report and a new reservoir of remorse, she had been clean for a year and a half. But she still had only one foot in NA. She caught a meeting now and then and spoke as little as possible, as she'd seen plenty of people do: put nothing on the line and get the buzz of affirmation. *Keep coming back.* And she tried to, but she still hadn't figured out how to regulate the opening up.

Everyone was so broke down, so exposed. So ashamed. And proud that they'd gotten themselves there and were speaking, even if the destination was a windowless room in prison and what they were sharing was a low they'd never imagined.

She tried to get a sense of Maxine under the guise of checking out the congregants. And maybe she was imagining it, but she thought she felt some kind of invisible fiber humming between them. Bravery might be too high an aim, but she didn't want to be cowardly in front of her. When Ranita's turn came around, she said, "I'm not that big on talking," and a few who'd heard her run her mouth during chow and rec raised their eyebrows. She heard someone suck her teeth, and glanced up to see Maxine, looking right into her. Pulling her eyes away, she said, "Anyway, I'm here; I'm surviving. That's all for now."

When Maxine started speaking, Ranita held her breath, and then tried to look nonchalant while listening to her gentle, raspy voice and the story she was giving up. She talked about struggling to find strength in the seemingly small aspects of life that are there to be noticed and recalled. And the only shame she spoke of was past tense.

When Ranita saw her in the yard the next afternoon, sitting by herself and working a crossword as she tried to catch a breeze, she made a point to walk by, say hey, give her a smile. And when Maxine smiled back her face changed from majestic to radiant, arousing and unsettling with its plain delight.

When Maxine sat down with her the next morning at chow, she nodded and asked about the book that lay open next to her tray, "That the one that made your day at the library?" Ranita said yes and chattered on, feeling foolish as she gushed about how much she loved Octavia Butler and how lucky she felt to have found a novel by her that she hadn't read. Then, feeling exposed, she turned to the dispiriting globs of congealed oatmeal and eggs on offer that morning and thought about the bread and sweets she still had left from the last time she'd made canteen and the veggies Eldora offered from her little garden plot.

"You a reader?" Ranita asked, fighting the shyness that had made her look away.

"Always have been. History, biographies, politics."

Ranita nodded. She felt like a lightweight in those areas. "I'll read anything, but I prefer fiction. It saved me, growing up. Even so, I got away from it . . . in the dark times, you know."

"I do."

"Found my way back, though, here in captivity."

Yes, Maxine said, you had to find some kind of light to steer by. But in terms of novels and stories, she admitted to being unschooled. She'd always been drawn to what was factual, and the arguments and theories around those things. As she listened, Ranita felt defensive, and tempted by her accustomed all-or-nothing settings. She wanted to know this woman, and there was some kind of kinship between them, she could feel it, and she decided to resist her impulses to either retreat or go into crazed battle mode. *Just talk with her,* she told herself, *find out who she is, let her know you.*

Sounding more tentative than she intended, she asked, "In those history books . . . don't the facts depend a lot on who's doing the telling? Seems like they're no more objective than fiction. Seems like what gets left out . . . kept out . . . says as much as what isn't. And aren't *we* usually excluded?"

Maxine's eyes sparkled. "You're right; there's always a slant to the telling. That's part of the draw, isn't it? Looking for, looking at the bias, the angle . . . figuring out the counter-story. But at least nonfiction's working with things that can be verified . . . records, documents, transcripts, photos, data . . . and fiction feels . . . unmoored."

"Nonfiction feels safer?"

"Well, I've never thought of myself as someone who plays it safe, but I guess that's what I said. Truth, when you can come by it, does feel . . . surer, I guess."

Eager for the exchange and the chance to express herself, Ranita stepped from the shoreline. "So novels and stories aren't true? Here's where I'm unschooled, but can't all that data be made to say what you want it to, and even lie? And aren't there different kinds of true?"

"Hmmm. What I ought to say here is that you can challenge that with more and other facts, and data. But I'ma shut up and listen while you tell me about the powers of fiction."

Ranita paused to collect her thoughts. There *was* one kind of nonfiction she'd always liked. She pictured sitting with her father as they took turns opening an encyclopedia volume at random and sharing their discoveries. Both players won, though they called it a game, and those details had seemed magical.

Coming back to the present, she said, "Novelists might be making up and rearranging what happens and who it happens to. And where it happens . . . yeah, that too . . . but it's still got to be true to how people are, to how things work in that story world. And to what's already happened . . . to history . . . what all went down before the story starts and while it's unfolding. Seems to me fiction's based on all those truths . . . like . . . like *Beloved*'s based on what it was like to escape slavery and get caught, and what one actual woman did about it. Or . . . you'd like this example . . . in *Sula*, Morrison says the Black folks live 'up in the bottom,' after they've been tricked into getting the hard-to-farm land in the hills, when it's the bottomland they were promised. She's showing a truth about people, with that one phrase."

Maxine's utter focus was thrilling, and unnerving. She seemed to be listening with her whole body, and Ranita wondered if anyone, besides maybe her father, when he hadn't been managing her mother, had ever listened to her like that. What would she pick up on that Ranita didn't even mean to reveal?

She kept going. "Novels tell the truth. The inside kind, about what's going on here," she said, touching her belly, "and here," pointing to her head. "People like to think fiction's less serious than other kinds of writing, and I'm here to tell you it can make the real more bearable. But that doesn't make it escapist. Or flimsy. And I don't think novels and stories just give you a picture, like a photo with words. They comment. They speculate. And the making up and rearranging of the facts are about showing what is and has been true. And what could be."

Maxine picked up a strand, "A photo can comment, too, though, can't it?"

"Yes!" Ranita said, her voice rising. "You're right." She thought of what she'd learned from Jasper about the role of light and mood, composition and context. His photos had tried to suggest what might be happening beyond the frame. "There's lots of ways to tell a story, I guess. Novels, they've always been what speaks to me clearest. And they prove you're not alone." Fighting embarrassment at the tears in her eyes, at how things were spilling out, she said, "I think . . . ," and then found herself tongue-tied.

"Tell me, Ranita. I'm dying to hear what you think."

Ranita laughed, and eased up. "It might not be about the people rising up and demanding change, like what you read about, but I think
the way novels and stories ask you to imagine things being different is
revolutionary."

"Indeed, my sista. I just don't know that much about them. Which
means I'm lucky to be in your company."

When they moved on to current politics, fascism, to be specific,
Maxine got even more fired up. *Damn*, Ranita thought, *she does go hard*, as
she listened to her break down how the whole MAGA restoring national
greatness thing . . . and claiming to speak for the people . . . ruling by
terror, white supremacist groups acting as the new Klan with more pal-
atable names . . . none of it was new; it was a program, a design, and you
had to look at who and what was financing it, you had to see its prece-
dents, its reach. "We know it's a recurring Reconstruction nightmare . . .
we know the Jim Crow laws inspired Hitler," Maxine said, and Ranita
nodded, wishing she had put that together on her own.

She couldn't argue with anything Maxine had said, but the facts she
seemed to see by weighed Ranita down. She followed the news as much
as she could stand to. She voted, or at least she had, and hoped to again
when she got out, if that right wasn't taken from her. But a wave of self-
doubt washed over her, and she sat back and said, "Maybe, next to you,
I'm not that political."

Maxine leaned toward her. "No? Hasn't everything got a politics to
it? Opting out, that's a stance, too, isn't it?"

Fighting irritation at both herself and Maxine, Ranita answered, "I
didn't say I've opted out. I'm just saying . . . ," and watched Maxine wait
to see how she would finish that sentence.

"I'm just saying I'm not on it every waking moment. I know your
rep, though. Legal expert, activist, soldier. Superhero."

And there was that sunglow smile. "I'm not looking to rescue nobody, so we're good. I'm just looking for some conversation, some substance, some argument. Seeing as we're both in this here cage, we might as well spend our time as best we can."

They worked on getting down the tasteless food they'd both forgotten while talking, but the August heat stifled their appetites. Ranita thought about the ripe, sweet juice of the tomatoes Eldora had been growing and imagined sharing a full, succulent harvest with Maxine.

They circled back to reading and family, and Ranita showed Maxine the visitation photo of her and the kids that she'd been using as a bookmark, and Maxine asked if she'd joined A Book from Mom, so she could read to them during visits. She explained that after Amara had decided she was too old to be read to, Theo wasn't sure he should keep liking it and they'd let it go.

Maxine said she'd come by books the hard way. Her folks had told her, *Get up off that couch and go outside*, as though all of her reading made them nervous. "Lately, people say Black kids suffer from a word deficit, and there I was, doing my part on that front, and they shut me down." She told Ranita about the time she was reading about Henry Box Brown, transfixed with the ingenuity of mailing himself out of servitude, and her father came in and said it was bedtime and made her turn off the light, just as the story reached its climax.

"I think they were worried about how their strange Black child would make her way in the world. As you can probably imagine, I was not girly. And neither the reading nor the 'tomboy' thing made me too popular on the block, either. My ways couldn't be drummed out of me, though. And as for reading, I just did it under the bleachers after school, and under the covers with a flashlight at night."

Ranita had nodded in recognition, thinking of how she'd been teased for being nerdy and speaking proper and had tried to submerge both, and as she listened to Maxine she could feel the tented covers and see the little circle of private light. She could feel Maxine's determination to know a liberation story, even if she was told to close her book and her eyes.

"I wonder," Maxine had asked, "is being read to something we've got to outgrow?" And then the announcement that chow was over blared. As they stood, Ranita had pulled two Atomic FireBalls from her pocket and offered one on her open palm.

"Dessert?"

Maxine's fingers had brushed hers as she reached for it, and it took all of Ranita's self-control not to hold on to them.

And now here she was, the next day, coming toward Ranita with a rubber-banded Scrabble box tucked under her arm.

"Looking for some substantive conversation?" Ranita asked, realizing as the words came out that she sounded flirtatious.

Eyes full of mischief, Maxine sat down. "Today I'm looking for some exercise."

"Exercise?

"That's right. Come on, let's play some Scrabble. Exercise our minds."

Ranita shied away, wondering why she couldn't be proposing something like Parcheesi, where you just roll and move your token. She loved words, and growing up she had competed to see how many points she could score for arcane diction, but her family had seldom played board games. Lennox had once brought a Deluxe Scrabble set home and unpacked it, charmed by the lazy Susan board. But after playing twice, Geneva had rejected the game as slow and interminable, declaring it unfair that you could win with small, commonplace words, and saying grown folks had things that needed doing. It had been shelved in the hall closet and forgotten.

Ranita wanted to want to play. She wanted to keep the exchange with Maxine going, and she wanted to see if she might be good at Scrabble, or enjoy it, even if she wasn't. But maybe sometimes it was better to opt out of trying than to give it your best and fall short.

She felt sweaty and nervous, but she reached for a lighthearted tone. "I don't know. I've got a feeling you're too intense for me and you play to win."

"You'll make up for that with fire. Maybe you try and keep it hidden, Ranita Atwater, but it's there for all to see," she answered. "I'm looking at you . . . taking in what all I see . . ."

Please, Ranita thought in the space before she completed her sentence, *don't mention my eyes.*

". . . and I can tell you're an atomic fireball."

Damn. The flirtation was on. "I thought maybe I was a Gummi Bear or a caramel. Something sweet and soft and chewy." Ranita was shocked at her own brazenness and Maxine's eyebrows went up as she smiled.

"No." She shook her head, her gorgeous locs dancing past her shoulders. "Not a chance. Sweet and hot. And I know the taste of you burns long after the candy's gone."

Ranita didn't even try to look away. She just basked.

Maxine said Ranita should go first and get the double word score. "But," she added, resting her hand on the box, "we'll play if and when you want."

Ranita took a minute to see if her yes would be a decision or an assent. "Let's play," she said, and then watched Maxine pull the rubber band off the box and start unfolding a faded board. Hoping their hands might touch, Ranita helped her turn over the letter tiles, all wooden except for one made from cardboard, with a *Y* drawn on in pen.

"What happened to that one?"

Maxine paused in turning the tiles facedown, even the cardboard one, though its letter and value were not secrets, and looked into Ranita's eyes. A trace of sadness came across her face. "You know, there are losses, big and small, along the way. And still we play."

Ranita's chest hinged open.

They picked from the tiles, undisclosed mysteries except for the cardboard square that could be asset or liability, and began.

SIXTEEN

Judy comes through. Again. *Let's hang, go by this or that person's crib, go get some food, watch something that'll make us laugh* . . . She wants an upbeat running buddy. What do I want? I want a distraction from myself. She asks me to go with her and Ike to a house party. Watch some basketball, eat, look on while other people drink and play cards. Before I can stop myself, I say yes.

She says they'll be back for me in an hour, so I get busy pulling myself together, and when they pick me up she's in a very good mood. Too good to be unenhanced. She talks through the whole ride with the music up loud, like we're in a club where you've got to shout. And when we're getting out of the car, I catch Ike looking at my ass and throw him a don't-try-me-muthafucka look, and he smirks and looks away.

"My name's Ranita," I say as we walk into the house, and I'm half expecting the room to answer, *Hey, Ranita*, and for me to name what I am and always will be. Everyone's drinking: beer, hard lemonade, prosecco, white and brown liquor, but I say I'm all set, looking at the cool, sweating longnecks and shimmery glasses in other people's hands and wondering how come they can stop at one, or two, or even three drinks, but I've got to climb inside the bottle and try to drown myself before moving on to stronger poisons. I'm standing along the edge of the party, watching people come in and find a spot in front of the giant plasma TV, noticing how when they get here they're polite and stiff and then the drinks unwind them. And I'm left behind.

I try, but I can't relax or get with the festive mood. I can tell everyone's looking at me funny. Knowing I'm in recovery, maybe, knowing I just got out. I shudder to think of the ways I might have encountered some of them before. And one woman keeps looking past me while I'm talking, and when she speaks down to me, like I knew she would, my neck starts getting loose and I can feel a *bitch* taking shape in my mouth, and I know it's gonna feel good when it comes out. Seems like Judy can feel what's about to happen, too, because she comes over and takes my arm and walks me to another room, letting me know to keep my shit in check. Back in the day she told me she could always tell when I was about to go off by the way I tilted my head back.

I feel like cussing Judy out, too, but instead, I escape to the bathroom. Will I ever be able to enjoy myself like other folks? Should I go back home? I look at the shag rug underneath my feet and remember being on my knees, combing fibers to make sure some tiny bit of goodness hadn't hit the floor and gotten lost in the little twists. I'ma try to carry on.

Soon as I open the door, I see a man scoping me out from down the hall. Handsome brotha. Big shoulders, stocky. Bald head, bushy mustache. The wiry, pointed goatee looks a bit vaginal, but I bet that would be news to him. He works his way over little by little, sipping on his drink along the way, while I stay put and watch him come. His cologne reaches me before he does, and I try and screen it out.

"Hey there," he says. "Can I get you a drink?"

"No thanks, I'm good." I should have gotten a glass of club soda to hold on to, so no one would ask.

"No? You sure?"

Smelling the Jack and ginger in his glass, I say, "Promise. I don't drink."

He looks a question at me, and even though it's not his business and I don't know why he can't just take no for an answer, I say, "Used to. Don't. Can't."

His eyebrows lift and I want to say, *Really? Come the fuck on. Everyone above the age of twelve knows someone in recovery.* What planet is this guy from?

We have one of those dumb conversations about how we know the hosts and where we live and what we do. He sells software or something like that; I'm only half listening. He tells me he's from New Jersey and asks, "You a Bostonian?" I nod, thinking how I've barely ever left the city limits, and then, for some reason, I say, "But I'm just getting back into town."

We chat about this and that, and he drops all kinds of knowledge on me. What teams and players are the best, who'll be the first NBA picks. What kind of bourbon is aged longer. Blended versus single malt scotch. What laptops and headphones are top of the line, why Bose is really not that good. I do a lot of nodding and pushing the button that'll keep his monologue going, thinking about what it would be like to kiss him, what his mustache and goatee would feel like, whether I've still got enough straight in me to break him off a piece.

Fuck me. I see a pair of familiar faces across the room. DeQuon and Vaughn. I always did think of them as a rhyming unit, and they're edging toward me, holding their drinks above the other partyers. A quick glance at the crush of bodies tells me I've got zero chance of getting away, so I just lean back against the wall while the connoisseur keeps talking, and grit my teeth.

"Cherry, is that you?" Seems like they speak in unison. I don't bother saying it's Ranita now.

They take turns hugging me and Vaughn spills his drink on the carpet and laughs it off. I gag at the whiskey on DeQuon's breath and pick up the inviting aroma of weed in their clothes and hair.

Vaughn says, "Hey, man," and introduces himself.

"Peyton," my new acquaintance says, and they ask him how he knows me.

"He doesn't." I get it in before he can open his mouth. "We just met."

"DeQuon. We been knowing Cherry since . . . forever, seems like."

"That's right. We even knew her back when she was Ranita."

"I'm still Ranita."

They're both smiling. "Alright. You still got those pretty green eyes, I know that much."

I deep-breathe for patience, and don't bother asking if people's eyes usually change color over the course of their lives. Then Vaughn says, "Aw, man. Wild Cherry did some crazy shit, back in the day."

And here we go.

"Remember the time you stood up in Antoine's sunroof . . . what car was that? I think it was the RX-8."

He's right, but I look away, hoping he'll drop it. Instead, they carry on with the story, alternating the narration.

"So anyway, Peyton, Antoine was driving, and Jasper, Ranita's . . . anyway, he was in the front passenger seat." He looks at me, "Am I right?" and keeps going before I can answer. "In the back it was me, Cherry in the middle, and then Vaughn."

"And it was December."

"That's right, but the cold didn't stop her."

"Naw, she got on the console and stood up, waist-high in the sunroof."

"And then she took off her top and her bra . . . it was emerald green . . .

can you believe I remember that? . . . and people say weed fucks with your memory. She was waving her top in one hand and her bra in the other, like Celtics pennants. . . ."

I'm looking through the crowd for Judy, wincing at the image that's been forced upon me, wondering why I can't just stay in the present for a fucking minute, and they're laughing too hard to finish the story, until Vaughn recovers enough to say, "There she was in the middle of winter, flashing everyone we passed. . . ."

They're cracking up, and Peyton's looking back and forth from them to me, and I'm just standing here, absolutely sober and fully aware of how unfunny and embarrassing this little snippet of the past is and probably always was, unless you were as high as we were.

Another story of our escapades gets told, and I can't make myself listen or laugh or even smile, but I can see the dynamic duo glancing at each other, sharing the silent insight that not only am I no longer crazy; I've become a killjoy. And then someone who's still fun catches their eye, and they move on.

Soon as they're gone, I tell Peyton, "Cherry's a former nickname. I'm Ranita."

And then Judy signals me that they're ready to go and I tell Peyton my ride's leaving, nice to meet you, I'm out. He's asking for my number and I'm giving it. A touchstone? I haven't given my new digits to a possible friend or a possible date. A misstep? Maybe so, but God how I want to be held. And instead of just saying good-bye, he kisses me on the mouth, and I don't know whether to be offended or impressed that he knows what he wants, which is apparently me, and goes for it.

He calls before I'm even home and asks me out to dinner tomorrow.

Warmed by his wanting, I respond to the bell I recognize. And now I'm shaving my legs and pits, doing some downtown grooming, taking a bubble bath. My black bra's in service again and I put on the new black panties I found on clearance at Marshalls, suck in my belly, and pull on my consignment jeans, feeling thankful Black men don't usually like skinny.

Peyton picks me up in his Lexus, and when I ask where we're headed he says it's a surprise. Which maybe should have been my cue to walk. I hate surprises. At the pricey steak joint that turns out to be our destination, he insists on ordering for me, and I want to assert my newfound, little chance at choosing, but it doesn't seem worth the trouble. And after all, he's paying, at least I hope so, or I'll be working off my meal in the kitchen. He also orders a glass of wine before remembering my *Can't* from last night, and I play it off and try not to watch him drain the full-bodied red from his glass, wondering how I'll manage the sex-with-a-stranger thing sober as I dig into my steak and have my fill.

He's got all kinds of info for me about what series to stream. And questions about where I've been and why I'm back. I sidestep his curiosity, realizing while I'm doing it that this is no way to get to know him, but for real, I just don't have the energy or the motivation or the positive outlook to share my story with him. I was scraping plates and mopping floors all day, and I've been dragging myself up from my bottom for a good long while now. Matter of fact, I'm afraid that addiction-incarceration stink is in my skin and blood and bone.

Doesn't seem like he can detect it, though, or that it matters how little I've said, because before I know it he's paying the bill and we're headed to his place. And before I can say, *Touch me there*, we're getting it on. Turns out we're skipping right over the foreplay (except for a brief ADW Bushy Mustache and Goatee) to the getting laid. Part of me's grinding, but instead of getting lost in arms and skin like I'd hoped, I'm watching from across the room. Lord knows, I've seen or done most everything two bodies can do to each other, but I'm still over there looking, from a critical distance. For what feels like way too short and way too long, he's pounding away, and before I know it he's finished.

Now we're lying here next to each other, awkward with unearned closeness, and he raises up on his elbow and says, "You good?"

"Oh, yeah, baby," I say, "you were great," feeling more than a little sick at how the line tumbles from my mouth.

" 'Cause I got some more where that came from," he whispers, pressing himself against my thigh. Seems like his imagination isn't big enough to include what he might accomplish with his mouth besides talking.

I don't want to have to tell him what to do. I don't want to explain that, for the both of us, this was about loneliness, scratching an itch, curiosity, or taking a worn path, and that instead of pretending, we should let it be. I don't want to explain where all I've been. And I don't have it in me to make my story feel alright to him. He's one person I don't owe an explanation or apology.

I sit up and start looking for my bra and panties. "Gotta get going," I say, and then I feel the air in the room change. He's not ready for me to go. He's feeling neglected and abandoned. And I'm gonna deal with it.

"That's it, then? You're just gon' up and leave?"

"I've got a real early start tomorrow, and I need to be getting home."

"You'll need a ride. . . ."

"I'll manage," I say, longing to feel the open air.

He reaches over and grabs my wrist. "Just tell me why you're leaving, all of a sudden."

My panties are midway up my thighs, but I freeze and try to keep my breathing even. *Is he more intense than angry? Will I have to get ugly? Can I distract or charm him into letting go? What can I reach for? How will I have to pay?* I start counting and praying . . . *One, two, three* . . . and notice, of all things at this moment, that the trim I gave my pubes is uneven . . . *four, five* . . . and my toenail polish is chipped . . . *six . . . seven . . . eight—*

"Ranita. Ranita. Just tell me when I'ma see you again."

"Peyton," I say gently, easing my hand loose. I stand and move within reach of the metal dresser lamp, then get my panties the rest of the way up and grab my bra and jeans. His anger's filling up the room now and I should keep my mouth closed and get up out of here, but I just can't.

"You think you want to know me? You think you want my story? I'm an addict who just got out of prison. And I've got kids, which along with those two things I just told you means I'm working through some serious shit. I did what all you can imagine to get my high on, and to survive. And now I'm about putting my life back together and being a mother again." I forget about the bra and pull my top over my head. "This here was benign enough, tending to our needs and all, until you took it somewhere else. No, I did not come. And no, we will not be doing it again. . . ." In his eyes I'm seeing fury and contempt, too. I can hardly breathe.

"What happened to Wild Cherry? Where the fuck's she at?"

Snatching up my shoes and backpack off the floor, I head for the door, and he shouts a parting shot as I walk through, "You need to get your shit waxed, now that you're out!"

Asshole. I'm on the verge of shouting that what he's really mad about is being a lame-ass fuck, but I shut the door and head for the elevator, praising God when it shows up. I push the emergency stop button and reassemble myself, stuffing my bra into my bag and struggling into my jeans and shoes, getting out the jagged rind of city glass I found this morning before I resume my ride to the lobby, where I try and exit past the doorman with my head held high.

Once I'm outside I slip on my jacket and gulp in the air that's still Boston-chilly, even mid-April. I hear Nina in my head, wishing I could throw back my head and sing out, *Tryin' to find the ocean, lookin' everywhere* . . . Wishing I could walk and walk, and find myself somewhere I've never been.

Clearly, fucking is not one of the free things. Never has been, and I know this better than I know most truths. I'm cursing my loneliness, my blindness, my story. Cursing whatever made me go along with where he took things, like I didn't have any say-so. I start toward home, scanning the street for his car as I go, glad to be walking free, even though I left my socks behind and my shoes are rubbing my feet raw.

I walk and walk. And come to Mario's. I swear it calls my name.

This time I grab the handle and walk in. My people, the bottom scrapers, here they are. The silent, brooding, after-hours users, looking to tune up or blur the edges or all-the-way lose themselves. I walk up to the bar and order a ginger ale, and the bartender smirks like I'm a chump or a cheapskate.

It's all playing back in my head while I wait, and I've got a little, throbbing crevice under my sternum, the kind I used to get when I'd lied or done somebody wrong. I'm the tiniest bit relieved that I liked the feel of Peyton at all. And that relief shames me.

Me and Maxine, we made no sentimental promises. She's lost to me behind the walls. And I still feel like I cheated on her.

She turned me out. When she asked was I good with her kiss, with her touch . . . there . . . and then there . . . and then there . . . it was a revelation. Nobody'd ever bothered to find out what I wanted, and at first I didn't even know how to answer.

It was unforgettable, both of us right inside the groove, riding it like the needle in an album track, and whatever little Oak Hills space we were stealing for ourselves was all we needed. No drink. No drug. Just us, right there, open and awake. Looking, eye-to-eye. I let myself feel it all. The slow, tender sinking in. The pleasure, the trust, the going to the center, the trembling that went on and on. Our bodies and our rhythm were all that existed and we lost all sense of whose limbs were whose.

And now I'm sitting here wondering, what does it all add up to: loving Maxine . . . hooking up with Peyton.

When the bartender brings the ginger ale I put my face to the glass to hear the little bubbles before I drink it down, and go over to the jukebox and flip the heavy plastic lists of songs. The crowd in here is old and so are the music choices. Every title brings back a flood of memories, and I choose "Natural Woman," push my hard-earned quarters in the slot, and decide to take a break from sorting out what Ranita is and isn't, and focus on my tired body and my aching feet.

One of the kites from Max comes back to me. I don't need to see the paper; it's unforgettable.

A force in your life, not seen by the eye?

When I got it, I thought I could have spoken volumes on that question. All the things that drove Mama, and my inheritance from her, they qualified. All the things that organized church and state and school. All the codes imposed and unchosen. All the hidden things I'd tried to evade. I decided to answer with a positive, and when I sat down with Maxine at chow I named Daddy's greatest gift to me, which had a huge part in keeping me aboveground.

"Curiosity," I said, and she smiled.

"Yeah, I see that. It's part of your life force."

"And what's your answer?" I said. "Or you just asking the questions?"

"My answer," she said, "is constructive defiance."

I kick off my shoes and dance with abandon, feeling my breasts jiggling and swaying in a way that would have mortified Mama for the family, for the race. And I guess because no delight exists without its opposite, I feel the banished girl I used to be, rising to the surface, before I wrestle her back into her tomb. I'm in the church of Aretha, and I put aside who's looking or what they think, and give myself to the music.

SEVENTEEN

I've been carrying on, leaning on my weekday routine. I pick up a kitchen shift and go to work. Catch a meeting, come home and fix a little dinner. Eat it by myself. The late nights and weekends, they're harder. No structure, no release, I feel myself wind tighter and tighter.

One night I was down here trying to ease my restlessness with an Afrofuturist novel when Judy rang the buzzer. I crept over to the window and peeked from the little gap between the curtains, then looked around at my little home. Here I am, making a start, and I don't need any help fucking up. It felt shabby, but I pretended I was out.

Add Judy to the list of who and what I'm dodging, right below Drew Turner.

Last night, as I listened to a wild, lashing rainstorm I pictured destruction, starting with the water finding a small way in, through a missing shingle, then the ceiling swelling like a malnourished belly, then a slow, stubborn dripping with buckets on the floor, then an all-out flood.

I've been telling myself I'm protecting the story of me and Max. And I'm not sure what difference it makes that I've been loved right. I made it sound game changing. But the jury's out on what kind of counter-weight even the right kind of love is.

Anyway, it's time to settle up my therapy debt, anxious as that makes me feel. Drew Turner called and offered me a midweek slot, and I knew I'd worked the sick excuse as far as I could take it. And the shame chorus raised its voice: *You fighting for your kids or not?*

Now I'm in the waiting room, staring at giant daisies, wishing I could masquerade as someone stronger and prouder.

"It's been a while . . . ," he starts off, once I'm in his office and the door's closed, "five weeks since our last appointment. I hope you're feeling better."

I make myself look him in the eye. And I think I see kindness there, but then again, I've got zero judgment, especially where the male species is concerned. I play it out, trying to save a little face.

"I'm well again, thank goodness."

Then, after glancing at his notes, he gets right to it. "You said last time, when we were wrapping up, that you've had a healthy relationship. You've been 'loved right' was how you put it."

Avoiding his eyes, I nod.

He keeps at it, trying for a way in. "What made it healthy?" "How was it different?" "How did you know it was right?" When none of those questions works, he shifts. "Can you say how my asking about it feels?"

"Intrusive," I shoot back.

"Okay," he answers, "but you did bring it up. And I wonder what you think about that."

I sit back and grab a pillow. "Why is it you've got these soft pillows but a couch where it's impossible to get comfortable?" I sound whiny, which pisses me off. Then I sigh and admit to myself that I did open the damn door.

"Why don't you take the lead, Ranita, and decide how you want to get back on track."

I picture myself, afraid when things got deep with Max, trying to play that go-away-closer game she wasn't having any part of, and take a step.

"Even though it's just been two sessions, and even though I didn't do a whole lot of answering, your questions got me remembering. And it hasn't been easy."

He leans forward and I take a deep breath. "I guess there's been a whole cast of characters and truths, trying to have their say. David Quarles . . . Jasper. My teenage slide toward trouble. My grown-up failure to . . . to practice what I felt."

He's looking, listening.

There's all that from before, stirring around, and there's the more recent past, too, speaking out. "My father passed. Fifteen months and twelve days ago. You're probably thinking it's time I stopped measuring it so close, but I've gotten used to tracking time this way."

"Okay, I hear you. Do you want to tell me about your father? What he was like? What he means to you?"

I guess I'm looking less composed than I think. He hands me the tissue box and I don't want to, but I take it and put it on my lap. And I can't hold back the tears any longer.

"Daddy wasn't a big talker. Seemed to run in his family. But he was always there. Providing. Inspiring. Recognizing me. We had our little things we did together. . . . His love was a great big *yes*. And him ending up a single parent . . ."

I think he looks surprised. "My mother died when I'd just turned fourteen. Not that I want to go there."

He nods, respectfully. And I wish I could admit to him, to anyone, that she never left. That she's still haunting around the edges of my life when she's least welcome. And that I sometimes wish I could go back to the future and skip whole chapters of my story. Or inhabit someone else's.

"And then there's the captivity," I say. "There's been nowhere to talk about that last, four-year chapter, and what it's like trying to walk out of that skin into the future, when you can't help looking back."

"That's a lot for anyone to carry. We can start with Oak Hills, if that might feel more doable, and work backward."

Keeping it in, now that I've found someone who can stand to hear where I've been, it's just not possible. I start retching up the undigested truth.

"In prison," I tell him, "you're reduced to a body. But denied what any living thing needs. You're just breathing flesh that can house contraband, and cause violence, and run. You're strip-searched. Counted and penned. Summoned for joyless feedings and herded from place to place. Denied privacy, and tenderness, and almost anything colorful or beautiful to look at or listen to or play with or touch. Education . . . voting . . . any tool, any basic human thing's considered coddling. Maybe we should even have to pay for the costs of our confinement, that's the thinking now, while our very incarceration . . . and the work we do for almost free turns a profit." I'm building up steam, and he's holding to the armrests of his chair.

"You're banished to the most barren landscape anyone could imagine. You're a thing, a crime, a number, beyond care and beyond hope. Punished and degraded into submission, or at least compliance. Day in and day out. And I swear genetic memory's for real, because it feels like you're reliving lifetimes of shit. Being a commodity. Being bred. Being three-fifths of a person. All of that's echoing, day in and day out. And when they let you out you're supposed to keep it together and build something from the ruins." My eyes are tearing up and my voice is raw.

"People are all up in arms about free-range chickens and taking milk from cows that never leave their pens, but where's the sympathy for the human captive who'll be returning home, if they've got one to go to? I'm telling you, it's a failure-to-thrive blueprint."

Drew Turner looks stricken. "I hear you, Ranita. You've got a gift for going to the heart of things." Yes, Daddy liked to say I was *incisive*. That was a great big compliment. And a high-score word in Mama's book, even if she disagreed on the value of that.

"Long story short, that's where I've been," I say, "and yet, there was something . . . someone . . ."

He waits, giving me room. *Come on, Ranita*, I tell myself, *go there*.

"What I said about being loved right . . ."

"Yes. . . ."

"Maxine. Oak Hills. Two years plus left on her bid."

And now that I've broken my silence, I'm wondering how to make him understand. A parade of images of us together shuffles through my head. "I could never total it," I say. "It was like a house with endless rooms. And I guess I'm still figuring out what all it means. Maxine invited me to see and be seen. To be all-in." I look away, adding that I haven't exactly been doing that in here.

Gently, he says, "I know it's not easy to come here and open up, and building trust is a process. Believe me, I'm aware that this context, it's difficult for our people, and I respect that. My mother was no end of upset and disappointed when I became a psychotherapist."

I can't believe he's getting so familiar. Neither can he. He pulls right back. "In any case, the path to revealing ourselves, and to understanding and acceptance, it's a winding one with stops and starts . . . setbacks . . . and forward motion, too."

I try and tell about Max's fierceness, Max's softness. The things we shared, and imagined. What all got exercised. And then I sum it up, after all: "She was the water in the rock."

After a pause I stumble forward. "It wasn't a gay-for-the-stay kind of thing. It was . . . substantive," I say, smiling inwardly. "But . . . I guess . . . I think . . ." Fuck, why can't I get it said? "Maxine's so clear about who she is . . . 'gold star,' like they say, and not afraid to live that out loud. I guess . . . my story feels harder to sort out. And I'm not brave like her."

Drew Turner says, "Maybe everyone feels afraid. And maybe you've got more courage than you think. You were brave enough to get clean. To come back for your kids. To come back here."

"That's bighearted. We both know why I'm here. 'Mandated' was the word you used."

"Yes, but that's not the only reason to be here. And it doesn't mean bravery's not required."

I rest for a minute, relieved at doing what seemed impossible, and then make myself push out the rest. "I think of people asking, 'So, is Ranita a lesbian, or what?' And I don't even know the answer. I keep imagining the names people use, applied to me. Sus. Bulldagger. Deviant. Dyke. Maxine's got no problem with any of those words. She knows who she is, and people can reclaim slurs, anyway, turn them into strengths. Queer is a wide-open umbrella, she says. But for me, every question seems to lead to another. Am I queer? If so, am I queer enough?"

He offers me this: "There's no single path to being who you are, or one way to be authentic. For some people, being able to choose a word, or having a category that describes where they fit, that's a comfort. But that's just not true for everyone. You don't have to pick a label for yourself. And maybe being Ranita doesn't mean one fixed thing."

"Maybe." And then I picture Jessie and Val in church . . . with my kids . . . nodding along with the congregation while the sinners get named.

"My family, my aunts . . ." That's as far as I get in explaining, but I'm thinking of how Val told me on an Oak Hills visit that our neighbors, who seemed like decent people, put their son out when he got sick with HIV, and how someone from the church choir tried to beat the gay out of her daughter when I was in high school. And Mama, she's speaking from the grave on how she always knew I'd shame her, the family, the race.

"And then there's DCF . . . ," I say.

"I respect what you're facing on the family level," he says, "and we can work on that. And I hear your concerns. But you should know that what we talk about is confidential, and I can't reveal it to DCF or anyone else . . . unless what you tell me poses a danger. Sexual identity does not constitute a danger." This does ease my mind, though I wish keeping it secret, what with the way that eats away like a sore that never heals, was not what I need.

And then I blurt out something I didn't even intend to say. "It's kinda hard, getting with the word 'lesbian.' It's not like it's a slur, but it sounds like a diagnosis. Or like a person with webbed feet or someone who speaks backward, and I can picture them being in one of those dioramas at the Unnatural History Museum. 'A millennial lesbian engrossed in daily tasks.' And also, there's this. Nobody says, 'She's a straight.' 'He's a gay.' "

He laughs. "I hadn't thought of that, but I hear you . . . it's a noun, instead of an adjective."

And then he says, "Ranita, I want to reassure you that I feel comfortable in supporting people in their coming-out process." He waits for me to meet his eyes, and says, "And I'm familiar with that process myself."

What? My mouth is hanging open. "Are you saying what I think you're saying? Are you telling me you're *a gay*?"

He smiles.

I shout loud enough for the people and the flowers in the waiting room to hear me, "Well, that's a fucking relief!"

He laughs. I laugh. We laugh together for quite a while. It blows my mind. Me and Drew Turner, under the same umbrella.

Then he says he wonders how it feels for me when he says our time is up.

Damn. Why'd he have to cloud the feel-good moment? I own up to being "a bit thrown when you say the meter's run out" but keep the angry to myself. He asks what might make it feel better, and I say I'll think on it. Then I realize one answer.

In one of my Oak Hills groups, before we ended all the vulnerable unveiling, we went around the room and everyone said a feeling and a hope. *I'm glad I held space with you all, and I hope the remembering gets easier. . . . I feel grateful, and I hope it's bearable to be awake. . . . I feel connected to you all, and I hope I'll be able to carry that with me this week. . . .*

Drew Turner asks do I want to try that here. Yes. I do. I think for a minute and then say, "I feel a little bit prouder than when I walked in and I hope I can keep that going." He nods and I say, "Now you. It's your turn."

"Okay, let me see. I feel more enlightened. And I hope I'll see you in two weeks."

This time, after leaving his office, I don't stuff myself with sweets. I can't lie, though, I do get some Atomic FireBalls but have only one right now. I take my time walking, looking around at little things, noticing the trees, stopping to window-shop. At a botanica, I pick up a 7 African Powers candle, for some extra help. And at a corner store I get myself some pears.

As I sink my teeth into one that's sweet as candy, savoring the juice that's on my hands and chin, I get a familiar, prickly feeling on the back of my neck. A reprisal's coming. And there are quite a few transgressions to choose from today, along with my appetite and pleasure. Telling secrets. Owning my truth. And not being shamed.

I hear Mama's voice: *I can hardly bear to look at you. What punishment do you think is fitting?*

No. Just fucking no, Mama. You're dead and gone, and I refuse you. Now get the fuck out of my head.

Reaching in my backpack, I pull out my list of meetings, the paper wearing thin at the fold lines. Maybe I could use a change of perspective. Drew Turner mentioned communities and support groups, and

LGBTQ+ NA meetings, and I need to check those out. But for now, I see there's a meeting in Cambridge, zenith of open-mindedness if there ever was one; at least that's how it sees itself. If the traffic's not too bad, I should be able to catch it.

I hustle over to where I can pick up the bus, get on and squeeze in with the rush hour folks, and curse the fact that there's nowhere to sit, though plenty of able-bodied young men are taking a load off while others stand. Daddy, always gentlemanly, would hate to see it. When we cross the river, I'm still standing, but I'm focused on the positives: venturing out, getting a fresh outlook. I get off in Central Square and walk through the have-nots drifting and begging and stalled among all the Cambridge haves.

Everywhere I look there's construction, biotech companies making this city less and less affordable, and I stop and stand on tiptoes at a spectator hole in the wooden fence to see what's getting built, with all the commotion and noise. A huge metal skeleton's taking shape as machine-giants heave the dirt and rocks. I know what each one's called, from when Theo was mad for construction vehicles: there's a backhoe, a digger, a front loader. I wonder what they've found underneath there, what things from the past are in this ground. Way down, I know, are the relics of the people whose land this was, the Massachusett and Wampanoag. And then closer to the surface is the recent past. What parts should be left to rest in peace?

After walking past the smokers in front of the Y, I circle back and bum one off a millennial in a custom-tailored suit and fine, soft leather shoes. We stand there smoking side by side until it's meeting time, and go inside.

Really, it doesn't feel all that different from my regular meeting, though there's more white people. I hardly ever come to Cambridge, though I remember hanging out there sometimes back in high school, standing around the T stop, acting like we were doing something bigger than standing around the T stop. Folks over here are always congratulating themselves on how woke they are, The Republic of Cambridge and all that shit. Yeah, right. Except for Area Four and the projects up on Rindge, there's only a handful of Black and brown people who can begin to afford renting, let alone owning, here.

I grab coffee and help myself to the cheapo blue tin butter cookies Auntie Jessie loves and take a place in the circle, near the door. Someone opens the meeting and just like everywhere, we chant the Serenity Prayer and they ask is it anyone's first meeting. A skinny girl who looks all of 15 raises her nail-bitten hand. She's chewing her lips and bouncing her legs and looking down, but she smiles when she gets her newcomer chip. White, the Color of Surrender. I've got a collection of white chips over at the house.

Today there's a speaker, and it's the guy who gave me the smoke. He talks. And talks. The floor is his, and he takes his time and a few other folks', too, gracing us with every thought he's ever had on the roots of his addiction, looking at it from every angle (even a mechanical engineering one, which is what he says he studied at MIT), sharing his brilliant insights. Yeah, what's new. Just another case of the white boy's disease: the delusion that you're the center of the world and we're all dying to hear about every breath you take.

A young sista with a stunning face and bangin' body turns herself inside out, telling about her self-esteem issues, her lying boyfriend, her no-show friends. Her uncle's visits to her bedroom when she was only six. Fuck. I mean, sometimes the meeting shares make me want to run for the door, the corner, whatever kind of stupor I can get to first.

The 15-year-old gets three words out and starts crying. We don't even get her name. And even though we let her know we're with her . . . this is the first day of the rest of her life; she's not alone; she's stronger than temptation; she can and she will . . . she gives up trying to speak her truth, and everyone moves on.

A Latin brotha talks about his drunk papi, his drunk tía, his drunk siblings. After taking his place in a long line of users, he's trying to steer another way. Next week he'll have 18 months clean and sober, God willing, and he's looking forward to getting his gray chip.

I look around, see no one I know, and raise my hand.

"My name's Francesca and I'm an addict." It rolls right out, the romantic-sounding name I wished I'd had growing up, and it feels good, too. I say I'm visiting from another part of the city (I almost say another planet). I want to say I'm mourning the woman who's lost to me and wondering how to claim what all I am and feel, but my heart's pounding and what I do get out is this: "Feeling a little shaky, nothing new about that. But . . . today, I . . . I came out to my therapist. That went okay, though I was so anxious I'd gone AWOL for a couple weeks. Anyway, the hard part . . . what's got me off-balance . . . is thinking what the fam would say."

I get no judgment and plenty of affirmation. They congratulate me for stepping up. Tell me my life is mine. Console me. Say keep trying, keep the faith, keep coming back.

Instead of lingering when the festivities are over, I get myself back to the bus. Feels like it takes a lifetime to get back across the river, but it gives me time to think about the meeting. As tongue-tied as everyone else in my family is, I felt triumphant, managing to say what I did. Even if I pretended I was someone else.

Did I feel freed up, doing that? It was a release, for a minute, saying I was Francesca. But it felt shitty, too, like a betrayal. And after I said that name, I told the story I'm stuck with. Same old Ranita, carrying the same old baggage, no matter who I unpack it with.

EIGHTEEN

Oak Hills
2018

As the canteen line inched forward, Ranita began to waver. Maxine was on a tear about being forced to patronize the company store, and even though Ranita had marked her sheet to get one of the three greeting card choices that she cycled through every few months, maybe she should make something with her own hands for Amara and Theo, instead of buying another card that looked as canned and flimsy as the *Timeless Love* it promised.

Every two weeks the women of Oak Hills who had money on their books lined up for their necessities. Socks and hair grease, Tylenol and toilet paper. For the things that could be traded or used to settle up their debts. For the noodles and peanut butter, sardines and Velveeta that might keep hunger at bay. And for some small pleasures that Ranita maintained were also needs. While Maxine talked politics, Ranita was dreaming of sugar.

Getting closer and closer to the front of the line that wound along the cinder-block corridor, she could see herself unwrapping the little cellophane to get at the caramel squares and tasting their milky-chewy melt. She would try and stretch them out until next time, pacing herself and alternating with the M&M's and Atomic FireBalls she was also planning on getting.

Maxine didn't believe in making canteen for discretionary items. You might not have a choice about buying the deodorant and tampons and toothpaste, she'd said way more than once, but the rest you could decide to leave alone. If she did buy from the only store there was, like her people before her, who'd been bound by sharecropped fields and factory towns, she wanted to do it with her eyes open. "Look at all the products we make," she said. "For free, once again. And we line up like willing slaves to pad some corporate pocket."

Ranita nodded. Everyone had to find a way to do their time, and the lens of politics was part of Maxine's. She had no choice but seeing, and speaking what she saw. And she was right. But Ranita could not begin to say how big it felt to have a little something sweet, a little something tasty, when you were in cold storage. How sometimes it felt like your survival depended on getting a canteen Honey Bun.

"Seriously, Ranita," Maxine said, building momentum, "think about all the products we make inside . . . electronic cables and T-shirts, mattresses and flags. American flags, if you can believe the grotesque irony of that. Lock up all the Black folks and then make us produce the flags for the country that's been demeaning and exploiting us since they captured and enslaved us . . . after they've kept us from voting and owning anything, trapped us in city food deserts next to toxic waste, with shitty schools and shitty jobs and shitty food and a shitty place to live . . . no access, no exit . . . policing every breath we take . . . feeding us menthol cigarettes and drugs and blocking us from health care . . . and pitted us against each other and against the folks who should be allies, hoping we'll kill each other off. . . ."

"Max. Okay. I feel you. I overstand. But you're gonna break me.

This here situation's what we've got to work with, and sometimes, some chocolate and some peppermints, they help when the sun goes down and you're pacing your cage. They keep you getting up in the morning."

Maxine paused to steal a kiss on Ranita's neck, knowing the shout would be coming, *INTIMATE! NO TOUCHING!*, then said the line needed speeding up; she had to get back to the novel she was midway through.

"Okay. You've been talking trash about the principle of being here, and now it's the pace of the line that's the problem, and you've got something else to do, though I'm glad it's reading fiction. But you're not just keeping me company. You're in line, right behind me. Lemme see what's on your sheet."

"What I've got on this sheet is my business, Ranita Atwater."

"Un-hunh. You gon' be able to live with yourself if you get some Jolly Ranchers?"

Maxine smiled. "I *should* keep my Black ass away from here. Truth is, though, I was dreaming of green apple all night long."

They laughed out loud. "It's okay. The ancestors, they'll forgive you."

"I hope so. Exigent circumstances."

Ranita kept the playful banter going. "You're my conscience, Max. You're the Oak Hills conscience, matter of fact. And I'ma share my Atomic FireBalls with you, like always. Even if I just have two, one'll always be yours."

In the pause that followed, Ranita joined the women all down the line in dreaming of the brief sweetness to come. Caramels and Jolly Ranchers and M&M's, peppermint wheels and root beer barrels and butterscotch discs, Mary Janes and Kit Kats and Atomic FireBalls. So good, so fleeting, it made them young and free again, running in the soft summer air until the streetlights came on and their elders called them home.

Reverie interrupted, Ranita heard Maxine behind her, picking the thread back up. "Sharing. That's exactly what white America is not prepared to do. And in terms of what *this country's* got to work with . . . in terms of the resources at hand, it costs more to lock people up than to provide some decent education, jobs, opportunities, but that would mean giving us a chance, giving us a share. . . ."

A true conscience never sleeps, Ranita thought. *Thank God, for real.* And maybe she would rethink the greeting card. She knew she was artistically challenged, but maybe she could create something halfway decent like the other mothers she'd seen, making cards and pictures that showed their love.

Back in her cell, popping a caramel in her mouth and making it last as long as possible, she gathered her resources. She had the white, unlined paper she'd gotten in a trade for dental floss. A floppy prison-issue ballpoint pen. Q-tips. Four little pleated med cups that she'd found, discarded. The M&M's. And a paper clip she'd discovered and pocketed on floor-buffing detail, contraband, because it could become a weapon. Really, though, what couldn't?

Sitting down at the "desk" that was no wider than her shoulders, she tried to unsmell the mix of dank cement, the salty trace of ramen noodles, and the sour breath of her fellow captive who lay just two feet away. Lizette had watched her getting things ready from the upper mattress she never seemed to leave, and then turned to face the wall to resume settling up her debt to society by sleeping away her time.

Deciding to begin with sky, Ranita folded the paper and went over and over the top half of the front with her blue ballpoint, taking care not to tear through the weave, until there was almost no white showing through. Then she unbent the paper clip and punched tiny holes in the dark blue background.

Under the pinpricked night she decided to make butterflies. Did butterflies fly at night? Could you just not see them in the dark? She wondered, wishing she had a way to look it up, and put the question aside in the name of artistic license. After making the outlines of their open wings with the pen, she put a few drops of water in one of the med cups and added an orange M&M, the way she'd seen it done, letting it stay in just long enough to soak off the color and not the chocolate. And then she dabbed the orange liquid onto the paper with a Q-tip, making the faint, watery-orange wings of what she'd decided was a monarch.

Next she made a yellow one, thinking it actually looked like the cloudless sulphur she remembered from a butterfly info deep dive back in middle school, and then a blue morpho, her favorite, which she hoped to see in person one day. As she dabbed on the color, she pictured herself getting the chance to see just one real butterfly, any species at all, with her kids. Watching it land on their shoulders. Looking at the wings up close before it flew away.

At the bottom of the paper, where the grass would be if she had any green to work with, she made sunflowers, and then colored in with the ballpoint up to the edges of the wings and petals, though she knew it didn't really make sense that you could see the butterflies and flowers like that at night.

She thought of the glorious sunflowers she had grown that one summer. Geneva had grumbled that they were loud and pushy, towering over the other flowers and growing every which way to turn their faces to the sun, and that she felt like they were looking at her. *She wouldn't mind these*, Ranita thought. *They look tame and quiet enough.* Sadly, the M&M's had given up only a hint of color.

Ranita sat back and looked at her work. She saw parodies, nothing like real life or even the encyclopedia pictures she'd grown up on. The things she'd chosen to draw didn't even go together, and it wasn't a card. It was a folded piece of cheap paper that wasn't even substantial enough to stand. She felt poor and bitter, at her resources and her skills, and put her hands in her lap to keep from ripping it up. This was what she had to give. This was her real.

Later, when Maxine asked how the card making went, Ranita didn't want to show her the subpar product of so much effort. After dodging, she admitted that she'd had something more special and less amateurish in mind. "My butterflies look anemic, and my sky's splotchy, and the flowers . . ." Her eyes filled with angry tears as she said she'd wanted to make something beautiful, she'd wanted to give Amara and Theo butterflies, and she wished they could open an envelope from her and a million gorgeous bright paper butterflies would spill out.

"You can send them butterflies. Not a million, but enough to stuff an envelope. I'll help you cut them out. Right now, though, why don't you show me what you made. The point's not really whether it looks professional, is it? It's that you went to the trouble."

When Ranita finally showed her, Maxine looked around, checking for overseers, and hugged her. "It's lovely, baby, and it came from your heart. I'd moonwalk if I got a handmade picture from you." And then she added, "What about doing the edges with nail clippers? Maybe that'll make you feel better about it. Come on, let's play some Scrabble, change the vibe," she said, reaching for the board, "and you can revisit your card later."

Their games sometimes stretched on for days, and before pausing when rec was over Maxine would draw a sketch of the board so they'd be able to resume later. She might take a break from law and politics, but she was still determined, still all-in. She worked her tiles, intent on maximizing her score, holding out for the triple-word square and the 50-point bonus for using all her tiles. Ranita had won a few games in the first few months, but the focus that required was more than she could sustain each time. She called Maxine the Scrabble Dominatrix, and admitted to herself that winning was fun, but mostly, she was grateful to be playing.

As usual, Maxine was going hard and taking her time. Ranita saw her moving around the makeshift cardboard letter on her rack and knew not to hope for a Y.

As usual, she was pressing her to hurry up. "Come on, Max. I'm growing old over here waiting on you to play your word. We need to institute a time limit."

"Yeah, yeah, you keep threatening that, even though you take as long as I do. Patience, my sista, I'm getting there."

Looking at her rack of letters, Ranita didn't know why she was pushing. What word could she make without a single vowel? She watched Maxine, wondering how she managed to shift things from can't to can.

When Ranita had been studying for her GED, Maxine had helped her get ready for the test, coming up with ways to help her learn the material for geometry, physics, and chemistry that she'd either missed by dropping out or forgotten. Maxine had done the Cabbage Patch or the Stanky Leg, or moonwalked when Ranita got the answers right. She had come up with mnemonics and added little pictures to the flash cards they made, chuckling at how rudimentary her drawings were, and when Ranita teased her that they looked like prehistoric cave paintings she had just laughed. "That would have been when the goddess was worshiped, so I'm good with that. And what does 'prehistory' mean, anyhow? Is there really such a thing?"

Ranita marveled at how she never stopped delving, questioning, conjuring.

When they realized they'd both been to the same little patch of Franklin Park in the same August of the same summer (probably in the same jammed state), she had made Ranita feel every part of it. There they were, sitting on a bench in part sun, part shade, bright blue above them, leafy trees and curbside wildflowers all around. Kids running and unburdened, for that little bit of afternoon, anyway, as an ice-cream truck jingled its way closer. She and Max, side by side and free. Popsicles purpling their mouths. Sun on bare skin.

How did she invoke her magic, Ranita wondered, with all that she was seeing and carrying? She hardly ever talked about her own pain, except at meetings, and even then, she didn't dwell there. And until a week ago, she'd never mentioned the thing she was known for, taking down that predatory CO.

For days, aware that something was weighing on Maxine, Ranita had tried to be extra tender. Spooning her, once Maxine's cellie had left for floor-buffing detail and they'd stolen some privacy with a blanket, Ranita could feel how knotted her shoulders and back were.

Ranita had an inkling of what was wrong. News had traveled, fucking up everyone on the unit, that a CO had escalated from watching while they showered to assault, and Ranita figured that it had struck an even deeper chord for Maxine. "You know I've got you," she had whispered, and Maxine had opened up. Shaking her head as though haunted, she told Ranita how she'd been dealing with a wakened memory, and how vivid it was, years after the fact.

She'd been on laundry detail, the last one in there, pulling sheets from the dryer when she felt someone in the room, and realized she'd turned her back to the door. "Before I understood what was happening," she said, trembling, "he got me by the neck and shoulders and pinned me against a table.

"I knew he'd raped. And gotten away with it through size and strength . . . authority and fear. But I'm sturdy and strong, too . . . *big boned-ed* they said when I was growing up . . . and these days, if at all possible, I don't back down."

Swept up in her own backward tumble, Ranita rested her head against Maxine's shoulder blade, picturing the triple-spiral tat that was right there, underneath her shirt.

It wasn't really a conscious, thought-out choice, Maxine had said. Her face so close to his, she was sure she saw him search her eyes for fear, and her body seemed to take over. Groping behind her, she got ahold of an unplugged cord and yanked, swinging the iron at the end of it, and though he blocked it with his shoulder, he was off-balance enough for her to pull away and knee him in the groin. When he went down, she kicked him there again, as hard as she could. "And once he was on the floor," she said, "holding his crotch with one hand and his shoulder with the other, and I was standing over him, the cord with the iron in one hand and metal rod in the other, his face crumpled like a wet paper bag and he started bawling."

She turned around to face Ranita. "I might have looked fierce to him, like Shango or something from his worst Black nightmare, but inside I was all confusion and panic. What should I do? How would he retaliate if I let him go? What would be the price for defending myself? Would I ever be believed? Adrenaline and fear were shooting through me at the corner I'd backed myself into. And then he started talking.

"He blamed his own body like it was the true perpetrator. And while I was listening to him disown all responsibility, I was reliving how he'd treated us like we were subhuman, calling us *piece of shit lowlifes, bitches, hoes*. He put the blame on everyone . . . father, coach, neighbor, teacher . . . who'd wronged him. And on his own body. They were co-conspirators.

"He lay on the floor, moaning, as though he was the only one who had ever been hurt into being who he was."

Maxine said she couldn't stop looking at his whining face. Or his hands. Delicate, soft from paperwork, they'd filled her with rage. "Those hands had locked our cells," she said. "Written us up for D Reports. Roughed us up and shoved us down the stairs. And they had held us down and tried to take our souls."

Ranita breathed into Maxine's neck as she felt her own ghosts stirring, and the hands she hadn't been able to fight off. She felt nauseous. But she didn't turn away.

"I pivoted," Maxine said. "I made a choice. I told him I wanted him to remember me next time he started in to hurting somebody with less power than him. I saw he was right-handed, and I stomped on that one, breaking as many fingers as I could, and left him there, howling in pain."

She laid her head on Ranita's breast. "I did pay. With a trip to the hole. A D Report. Losing my Good Conduct Credits. Getting more time. He said he'd caught me stealing from the laundry, and found contraband on me. But the story he told was that he'd hurt his hand when a machine fell on it. Saving face for being bested by a lowlife bitch.

"When I got out of the hole he'd left Oak Hills, by choice. I wrote up a complaint anyway, to make a record. And I try not to think about it, but it's in me, like it or not. It comes to life sometimes, like it did this week. I *hate* how afraid I felt. But my body remembers.

"I don't fight unless I have to, and I'll tell you what . . . it took something out of me to hurt him like that and hear him cry in pain, miscreant (that word's for you, Ranita) though he was. It was . . . it is . . . an ugly feeling. But except for turning my back to the door, I don't regret what I did. Everyone's got the right to defend themselves, and to stand up, too, for those who can't."

After she got the story out, they'd held each other, until Maxine's cellie came back. They took the blanket down and tried to carry on, but Ranita hadn't been able to stop thinking about it. Even when she was making the butterflies and night sky that morning, it seemed like the memory had become hers.

She heard the call for afternoon meds, and looked across the Scrabble board at Maxine, who was adding up her score and replenishing her tiles. It was Ranita's turn, and she looked at hers. Still all consonants.

When rec was over and she'd been returned to her cell, she got the nail clippers from her footlocker. She'd seen Naomi use them to scallop the sides of a poem. Slowly, carefully, Ranita worked her way around the edges of her card. When she was finished, she decided it was good, even with the fact that the little half-moons didn't come out even on two of the sides. And when she held it up toward the ceiling, she saw little points of starlight, coming through.

NINETEEN

Two weeks ago, Miss Caseworker called and asked me to come in and meet with her. The whole way over there, I was wondering what I'd done wrong.

When I walked into her office, I was surprised to see her photos and personal knickknacks gone, and boxes full of files stacked against the walls. She told me she was leaving, going to another service center, and someone else would be taking over her cases. The idea of starting over again with someone else made me kinda nervous, but I couldn't say I felt sad to see the back of her.

I recognized her replacement from the week before, when she was watching from the sidelines, making me nervous. I was happy she was a sista, though in truth, some of us are harder on our own than others are. People like Mama, who want us to be done with overcoming and only show the world our successful, upright faces. Or those riding solo, striving to rise no matter who they've got to step on. Black or not, I was thinking she could still be the overseer type.

But I felt different about her. I thought: Maybe she knows something about where I've been. Maybe she loves someone in recovery. Maybe she's fucked up, herself. Most Black families include somebody who's seen the underside, even if we look away from them. Well, I don't know all her personals, but as soon as I met her I liked her friendly, heart-shaped face and her no-bullshit way.

Instead of sitting behind her desk with me on the other side, she sat next to me at the little round table Miss Caseworker used for folders and forms. Before we went over my file, she asked about me. I started with how I'm doing great and feeling like the bad times are behind me, and then I found myself being real. Talking about what all I felt about getting out, keeping my balance, moving forward.

We talked about how the first supervised visits felt, and what my hopes and fears look like. Then she asked about Amara and Theo, their personalities, likes and dislikes, attitudes toward school. Jessie and Val, the roles they've played. And Daddy, I even went there. She mentioned her 10-year-old twins, who go to a special-needs school. I started relaxing, and we discovered we grew up not far from each other. Turns out she is different. And she's got a name, too: Ms. Barnhart.

After another supervised visit when they insisted on playing Monopoly (I kept my mouth shut about it being an ovation to capitalism, for now), Ms. Barnhart called me into her office to meet. When she told me they'd had a private social worker do an evaluation, I felt the burn of betrayal. You could have knocked me over when she revealed her investigative work. "I've visited your kids at home with your aunt Val," she said. "I've visited your aunt Jessie, and I've talked to your psychotherapist. And I'm encouraged by what I've learned."

I was pissed at the invasion and the secrecy, even though the news was good. What if it hadn't been, and she'd stumbled onto things I've tried to leave behind? I was ready to vent my resentment when she floored me.

"Ranita," she said. "There are valid reasons for the rules, but they don't always work for the good of families. I'm not going to disregard them, but I'm going to relax them just a little bit . . . off the record." She looked me in the eye. "Unofficially. I'm going to give you some room to do your repair work."

No fucking way! I was hollering inside, but I nodded calmly. And in my heart, anyway, I was singing out, *Hallelujah.*

"We'll still have our check-ins. And some supervised visits. You'll stay with the therapy. Go to meetings. Keep up the clean urine scans. If any of these things falter, we go right back to the supervised visits, and the leeway is over."

I said okay and did my best to look like I was taking it in stride, but I had to wipe my eyes a couple times.

"I'm giving you a chance here, because I've got a good feeling about you and your family. But don't play me. Don't let it blow up in my face, Ranita. Don't make me regret this."

Instead of jumping in her lap and hugging her like I wanted, I told her I'd do my best to live up to her trust, thanked her quietly, and left. And the first good thing that's flowing from the new situation is this: Auntie Val agreed to bring the kids to Jessie's for a visit, and let me be there, too.

Now I'm headed over on the bus, wishing I'd left time to walk in the June weather instead of being in this tin can that chugs along, moving down-and-out folks from one frustration to another. After checking the news on my new smartphone, I put it away and try to get some uplift from the way my people soldier on, struggling on and off with canes and bags and strollers, taking care of shit despite the fact that the police killed another Black man today. Despite our deficits in words and health and shelter and freedom. And the widening wealth gap, the open rise of white supremacy, the . . . Fuck. Let me look around for something free and good.

I get off and wait for them out front. I feel nervous and unsure, but

I'm hoping for my TCB mama persona to kick in, wishing I could get some mothering my damn self. When Val pulls up, Amara and Theo spring from the car, and without even speaking to me, Amara marches off while I'm saying bye to Val and opens the front door, like she's in charge. At first I'm trying to overtake her, but then I think, *Why argue?* Instead of being the rule enforcer, instead of saying, *Walking ahead of your elders is disrespectful*, I'll let her speak her mind the way she can. She knows the way. And Auntie Jessie was there when I was not.

Amara's ringing the buzzer as me and Theo come through the door, and on the elevator I try and search her face, but she's looking away, and knocking before we can catch up. When Jessie opens the door, they're both all over her and I want to say, *Careful*, but I don't want to interfere. I stand here feeling grateful. Jealous, too.

Amara shows me around like I've never been to Jessie's, like I wasn't just staying here. The kids stop by the puzzle table for a minute and Theo puts a piece in right away, and Auntie Jessie kisses him. "Theo, you're a drive-by puzzler," she says. "Me, I've got to sit and focus before it comes together." Well, I'm no good at all at puzzling, and she's right: she's got the patience for it that Daddy had for fishing.

When I say I'm gonna make some peppermint tea, Amara tells me, "Auntie Jessie keeps her tea bags up in that cabinet. And the kettle's over there." I just thank her and ask does she want some.

She shakes her head. "Was tea *your* drink of choice when you were a teenager?"

I've been remembering 13, all right, along with other years, and it was desolate. I'm not sure I liked anything at that point, and I can't think what did feel like a choice. At 16, I favored rum and Coke, and Jasper. And later, following in his footsteps, I added Vicodin to the list.

I'm putting the kettle on while I try and keep in 2019. And I'd like to point out that she just recently became a teenager, but I reach for the tea bags and keep my mouth shut.

She's standing in the doorway, half in the tiny kitchen with me and half out, and I make small talk to try and keep her here. ". . . I guess I got into tea while I was staying here . . . started trying the herbal ones . . . chamomile, Lemon Zinger, peppermint, seemed like they made me feel better, calmer. . . ."

Feeling her intense focus, I'm wondering what she's homing in on as I chatter, and getting more and more uncomfortable. ". . . and then when I moved, I forgot to take the peppermint . . . coming and going, you do lose track of things. . . ."

And she strikes.

"Coming and going, that's your thing, isn't it? You and Jasper both. Lucky me. Lucky Theo."

She's knocked the wind out of me. But she's not wrong. Still, I want to say people are more complicated than they seem and not everything about her dad was bad. He was shit on follow-through. Controlling. Confused and hurt and a long way from grown. But there were pluses. And my choices got even worse later. Jasper had his own special outlook, when it was good between us that was intoxicating.

Amara calls me back to now with another punch to the gut. "How long you plan to stick around this time?"

I open my mouth and then close it, like a landed fish.

My first two years at Oak Hills I did a lot of apologizing. In cards and letters, at every visit, on the phone. And I guess I moved on after that, to saying how I know being a family again is a process, I know I've got to show my love by doing right.

When I think I can talk without breaking down, I stop fiddling with the tea and lean back against the counter so we're face-to-face.

"You want to understand? So do I. I'm sorry, Amara. Sorry for being an unreliable, mixed-up mother . . . and person. For giving you a father who was as . . . as unable as Jasper . . . though he did have his good qualities, especially early on. I'm sorry for not putting you and Theo first. For not sorting out my troubles and trying to run from them with alcohol and drugs. For dragging you through the prison system. I'll be apologizing for the rest of my life and it'll never be enough."

I'm tempted to say what I've heard in The Rooms and behind the walls, that I'm not the same person I used to be, but I know that won't land. And what I did and didn't do, those are still parts of who I am. Instead, I say, "I'm making different choices now."

She's looking away, toward the window.

"I'm not trying to act like I've got it all together, like the pain in me . . . or what all happened . . . has disappeared, and I won't make more mistakes. I know I've got to keep proving I'm not going to bail."

From the doorway, she just looks at me, says, "Your water's boiling," and walks away.

After Auntie Jessie (over)feeds us all their favorites, mac and cheese (not from a box, the real, baked casserole kind), clementines for Theo and pears for Amara, I clean up while they relocate to the living room. I can hear them talking and laughing together, and when I finish I see Amara's stretched out on the couch and Theo's squeezed himself into the recliner next to Jessie. I listen in, I admit it, and hear him telling how he still misses Daddy so much he cries at night sometimes.

Jessie puts on the first Star Wars movie, one of their traditions, they say, and they're giggling at the bar scene, where all the freaky creatures are hanging out together. From the doorway, I watch them. Amara's laughing freely, not fronting, not shut down. For the first time in recent memory, she looks like a kid.

Resisting the urge to try and be a part of their Star Wars thing, I let them be, and go to the kitchen to make microwave popcorn. While it's popping, I lean against the windowsill. It's beautiful out, with a warm breeze that's carrying hints of fried onions. People are out, doing their Saturday afternoon things, taking it slower than on weekdays and stopping to chat. One man's washing his car, and a group of women are sitting on the porch together, sipping from tall icy-looking glasses. Someone's hanging laundry on her back porch line, and kids are bouncing to some hip hop chant. And the trees are getting thick with leaves.

Sometimes seeing things as they are is still tough. But I stand here looking, taking it in, and let myself feel all of it. *I get it, Daddy: this is the point.*

When the popcorn's done I divide it into two big bowls. Trying to be as low-profile as possible, I give Jessie and Theo one and sit down on the couch next to Amara, not too close and not too far away, and put a bowl down between us, savoring each time her fingers collide with mine. When the movie's finished they plead to watch another, and this time it's one of the Indiana Jones flicks, also their tradition. I make more popcorn and fall asleep while they're at the Temple of Doom.

When it's time to leave, they look glum, and then Theo says, "I'ma draw you a picture, Auntie Jessie."

"You do that, little man. I'll put it right on the fridge like I used to."

When Val comes for them, Amara says, "Bye, Mama," without even realizing what she's called me.

I stay the night at Jessie's, like I do some Saturdays. Help with her groceries and the cleaning and the laundry, even though she protests, saying I shouldn't have to wash her clothes. "Come on now," I say. "I want to help." And today, since she's only been to church a few times since her stroke and Val goes to a different one, I offer to take The Ride there with her.

I'm glad I can help with her walker and getting her in and out of the van, but then I feel uneasy. I intend to get her settled and then leave and come back after the service. My reputation precedes me, like they say. But I hardly know anyone, not even the pastor, and Jessie's introducing me proudly, looking happy to have me there with her. When she asks me to stay, I hem and haw, and then go in, making sure not to look at the stairway to the basement.

It's a good feeling, sitting alongside Jessie, surrounded by the warm, swaying bodies of my people. It brings back the past, for better and worse, but I know the singing will soothe my soul. It's hot up in here, and I guess the bodies and the need for salvation help dial up the temperature, but I'm going with it, liking the human heat, the being shoulder-to-shoulder.

And now it's time for the sermon. And today it's sin and fornication. On the sacred bond of marriage between a man and a woman, righteousness, godliness being the only path, what with how busy Satan is. The warm glow of togetherness evaporates and I notice the sweat spreading beneath my breasts. I'm feeling judged. Rejected. And trapped.

I put my arm through Jessie's and try to focus on the love in the room, but I'm afraid the magic's gone. I picture Mama up there, singing a perfect solo. How will I get through this, stuck as I am in the middle of the pew? And then the choir gets going and I forget myself in their interlocking, passionate voices. The congregation's joining in, waving their hands, and pieces of the hymns that were sown in me return. Along with a feeling of panic. I swallow hard and lean against Jessie, and she takes my hand. And I wish I could sing along. I want that fullness, that quickening I used to get from singing, but I can't help feeling a menace close by, in the next pew, downstairs, on the other side of the stained-glass windows.

Closing my eyes, I try to let the music back in. I want to stay and I want to go. And I decide to ride it out, keep alongside Jessie and keep my mouth shut. Take what's being given and try to let go of the rest.

When we come through the heavy wooden church door, back into the daylight, Jessie's searching my face. "You alright, Nita?" she asks, while we're waiting for The Ride to pick us up, one hand on my arm and one on her walker.

I force a smile. "I'm fine."

"Well, you've got a funny look about you."

"It's nothing. Things . . . they can just get a little stirred up some-times."

And then the van arrives and I throw myself into helping her in, re-lieved that her question gets lost in the shuffle. Once we're back at her place I've almost managed to forget the last two hours, and I help with the chores and cook her some dinner, before making my way home.

I'm playing back pieces of the morning in my head: *You alright, Nita? . . . sin and formication . . . a man and a woman . . . give me Jesus . . . I cry at night sometimes . . . coming and going . . . you and Jasper . . . lucky me . . .*

I get in lotus, focus on my breathing, try to see my desert bowl. It's empty.

But I get up off the floor and I throw myself a solo dance party, which I've been doing on the regular. I pull the curtains closed, drape scarves over the lampshades, and pick an upbeat house music channel on Pandora. Then I put in my earbuds and dance like my life depends on it.

TWENTY

2005

The Late Jasper Period, as Ranita thought of the five-year stretch that ended with his federal prison bid, was all about internal flux. During Middle Jasper, she'd swung between showing out . . . jumping in public fountains, stealing restaurant glassware, blowing her temper at the merest slight . . . and crashing out. As her behavior settled, the oscillation moved inward.

Leave or stay, the question arose more often as the debits piled up. Aborted education, marginal employment, addiction, inertia. Ideas and imagination that translated into nothing. Plenty of book smarts and zero follow-through. She had to admit that the negatives applied to her as well as to Jasper. Together, they seemed to go nowhere, but then again, he was the known world, and she'd come to adulthood by his side. And what about the pluses?

There were his talents. For photography. For philosophy. For off-the-beaten-path insights. He had his own angle of vision. He understood her. And who else would even know about ocean jasper? Who would view her eyes that way and say so? He saw her; at least she thought he did. Put that in the plus column. Obsession? That was debit and credit, both.

She hadn't been able to put the leave-stay dilemma to rest. What was she doing with her life? What was salvageable? If she left, maybe she could begin again. She had pictured herself keeping the exit door wedged open with her persistent questions. And then, just after she'd told her father she was working her way free, she sat on the edge of the tub, staring at the pregnancy test +, and felt it swing shut.

Whenever Jasper had told her to loosen up and let herself receive the pleasure he had in store for her, she had tried. But mostly she'd pretended to like what he wanted and imagined for her. *Let's spice things up, Cherry, check out some new shit, innovate*, he'd said. He liked to try different positions; he liked to fantasy role-play; he liked to do it in places where they might get caught. She'd drawn the line when he wanted to explore asphyxiation, but yielded when he turned her over and took his pleasure from behind, pushing her face into the covers until she could barely breathe. What did she like? He didn't ask. She didn't know.

One afternoon, on a trip to the library for books and videos, he told Ranita that he'd gotten the inspiration that sex in a utility closet was something they should experience. It would be transgressive, his new favorite word. And he assured her it would be safe. *Why don't we just go to your crib, where we have protection?* she'd asked, and he'd convinced her it would be okay as he coaxed her through the door into the cramped space filled with brooms and cleaning supplies and started unzipping her. They didn't have to wait. She could trust him. He'd pull out and they'd be all good.

Now she was pregnant. And along with the practical questions, her panic at what would happen to her body flared. She would have to be examined, and the one time she'd been to a gynecologist she had nearly fainted when she felt the speculum. What if she couldn't handle the growing and swelling, the looking and feeling misshapen, the habitation, by a being who depended for their very breath and nourishment on her? And what if she couldn't endure the pain of giving birth?

She had decided, even before her period started, that she would never have kids, but now she tried to sort through her feelings. Maybe parenting would give her discipline and direction, hold her accountable, inspire better choices. At the same time, she tried to face the reality of how hard it would be, even if she somehow turned out to be good at it. The first hurdle, in any case, was telling her father.

"Let's wait for him out here," she said, stepping into the backyard. "It's warming up, and being outside helps ease my nerves."

"Don't worry, baby. He's not the wale-on-you-for-messing-up kind of pops."

Poor Jasper, she thought, kissing his temple. He knew from that kind of dad. But love could rewrite things, couldn't it?

"He's not. But I don't think he's looking to be a grandpa yet. Not till I go back and finish school. Get settled into a good, steady job. Get married." What went unsaid was how her father felt about Jasper. And about her, for picking him. She knew he'd never stopped hoping it would run its course, and now, maybe, that had been settled.

"You can still do school and work. We're doing good, and you've got even more clean time than me." It was tempting to collude in his fantasy that they'd be in it together, parenthood and everything else, and be alright. The truth was that he'd never launched and neither had she. She was still bouncing back home and depending on her father, off and on. Still working shit jobs, off and on. Still getting clean and sober, off and on.

"You know my position on the marriage thing," Jasper said, walking over to the rowan tree she'd named Devon way back when. She didn't want to hear it again, how Jasper was *philosophically opposed*, how the government shouldn't force people into relationships, how a marriage certificate was a paper trap that ruined the ability to love freely.

She followed him to the joint of the first thick branch, the armpit, he called it, saying the tree looked like it had put up its arms in surrender. They had to search for it, but it was there and always would be: *Jasper + Ranita.* He'd carved it with his Swiss Army Knife into Devon's shiny-smooth, copper-blue bark, right after they met, and though it had felt good to be wanted, she had hated seeing him do the tree like that. It wasn't right, staking a human claim at the tree's expense.

She'd told him how rowans had meant courage and protection to the ancients, how their red autumn berries, drops of blood shed by the eagle that was a goddess's protector, signified life and creation. How bees loved their creamy white spring flowers and their wood was used for divining rods. He'd pushed forward anyway, and she remembered standing there, watching him digging his blade into the beautiful tree, and doing her best to swallow it and let it go.

"Found it. And I'm with you because I want to be."

Yeah, she thought, but marrying, that wasn't what was pressing on her. She didn't say, to someone who knew his father's backhand, strap, and fist, that for her, disappointment was an acute and lasting punishment. She was dreading what she'd see on her father's face. It would be worse than what had gone down when they were fishing at the reservoir a year ago. Plus, telling him would make the whole thing real.

She looked at her watch again. "I wish he'd get here so we can get this over with. Telling him, it'll suck . . . but he'll help me figure out what to do."

"Us. He'll help us. And you know what to do."

She just looked at him. They'd been around that bend, and she was not having another argument about her right to choose whether to give birth.

He plowed ahead. "Let's talk names. You give everything a girl's name. What about boys' names?"

"Avery's for girls and boys. So's Devon. And maybe it's a girl."

"I think it's a boy, Cherry. Let's name him Duncan. It means 'dark warrior.' It's perfect."

She let him go on about what to call the embryo he'd decided was a boy, and gave in to her own anxieties. There seemed to be layers to her worrying, and she pictured the diagram of the earth's innards that she'd discovered in her more inquisitive days. Crust, lithosphere, asthenosphere, upper mantle . . . each one a different color. She was down in the lower mantle, where she tried to keep things buried, and her fears were wreaking havoc.

What would surface when the baby was born? Was it escapable, being the kind of mother she'd had? She could remember no time when Geneva had been affectionate and playful, and as she grew, her mother's antipathy seemed to thrive, as well, and venture into the open. Geneva's final year had been one of either blatant conflict or passive aggression, and although Ranita told herself it had been in self-defense, she had proved her own capacity to match her mother's smallness at the end.

What if she couldn't feel, let alone act out, the love she was supposed to have for her child? Or what if she tried so hard to be the opposite of Mama that she ended up smothering or swallowing her baby whole? What if she ended up carrying on the tradition that rang so true: *Black women raise their daughters and love their sons*?

What was keeping Daddy? she wondered, and then she saw that Jasper was leaning on Devon's trunk and gouging the bark with his knife. She whispered amends to the tree, and Jasper said, "It's okay, baby. I don't blame you, for wanting a girl. Maybe we'll get one next time." When he was finished, he stood back so she could see. *Jasper + Ranita + Duncan*.

Before she could clarify her apology, she saw her father through the kitchen window. "Put that away," she told Jasper, pointing to the blade. Her father didn't need to learn her news from his knife work.

"Ranita Bonita," he said, coming out of the back door. "I didn't know if you'd be here for dinner, but I got fish to throw on the grill, just in case. You're welcome to join us, Jasper." Ranita didn't have to wonder how to read Jasper's silence. He never wanted to eat with them or hang around their house. It was her father's place, he said, not his.

She didn't know how to begin. Jasper had reminded her that she was grown, and she didn't have to confess to her father or involve him in their plan, but Ranita knew the only chance she had of doing a good job raising a baby was with her father's help. Jasper had insisted on being there when she told him, and the only sense Ranita could make of that, when Jasper could see how little respect Lennox had for him, was his pride in fathering a child. He couldn't be displaced now. He would be part of Ranita's life, forever and always.

When Lennox said he'd go in and get dinner started, Ranita made herself speak up. "Wait, Daddy. There's something I need to tell you. She could feel Jasper's anger flare and added, "Something *we* need to tell you." And then she blurted it out. "I'm pregnant."

Her father couldn't seem to get his mouth closed, even though nothing was coming out of it.

"I think I need to sit down. Come on inside and we'll talk."

Ranita glanced at Jasper, unsure of whether to hope for him to stay or go. "Well, I'm not hearing any congratulations," he said. "I'ma leave this to you, Cherry. Call me later."

She and Lennox went in and prepped the dinner, working together without talking. He didn't need to say he was disappointed; she saw it in his stooped shoulders and worry lines. When he looked at her to ask how spicy to make the marinade, she saw grief. But when they were outside at the grill, he told her he'd be right there with her, whatever she decided to do, and added, "I'm not a big believer in Jasper; that's not news. But if you have the baby, you don't have to worry about whether I'll be decent to him, or whether I'll help."

She was grateful. And thankful that her mother wasn't there to see her fulfill her expectations in yet another way, though she was pretty sure Geneva would say an abortion was even worse than a child born of sin and stupidity.

After a week of anxiously weighing the pros and cons, Ranita made her choice. She could do it; she had Daddy and Auntie Jessie. And surely Jasper would be able to kick in some support. Besides, the past was not always prologue; she would be the mother she hadn't had. When she told Jasper, he raised his fist in victory. And although she suspected he was privately relieved, he stormed off when she told him she'd be staying with her father once the baby was born.

She went back to regular meetings and managed not to use. She missed the euphoria, the relaxation and contentment, the feeling of being free. But the true problem with sobriety was seeing things as they were. Jasper was more debit than credit. And she was more bound to him than ever.

All the love she felt when the baby started kicking overwhelmed her. The fear of using despite the love she felt never went away, and the entire pregnancy she was anxious over what kind of home her misused body was for new life. She anguished over what she would feel giving birth, and what she would and wouldn't feel afterward. What, she couldn't stop wondering, could make a mother turn away?

Her labor was a 16-hour purgatory. She went elsewhere. She begged and cried and cursed and pushed. She prayed for the baby to come out, and prayed to be left intact. And she tried to unsee Jasper's horror at the pain and the ugly struggle of giving birth. He tried to stay the course, hold her hand and coach her breathing, but he had to step away. "I'll be right back, baby; I just need a tiny break." She tried to roll with that, but the third time he said it, she exploded, "I don't get a fucking break and I'm doing the work. The least you can do, since you're not the one being torn open, is stand by me."

"You're right; okay, you're right," he said, looking embarrassed in front of the nurses. "I'm here for you; I'm here."

After the final push, she tried to read his face for disappointment when the doctor said they had a girl, but all she saw was someone shaken and numb. She was spared having to argue against the name Duncan, or Jasper Junior. Less invested in what they called a girl, he didn't fight Ranita's choice.

Loved, that's what she wanted her daughter to know about herself. And when she held Amara to her naked breast, she was amazed that something so beautiful had come out of her. But Jasper looked frightened, as though he was trying to find his image in her wrinkled, patchy, vernixed skin, her swollen eyelids and conehead, misshapen from the passage through. He said he'd take that bathroom break he'd been needing and be right back.

When he came to the hospital the next morning, he removed a bandage from his wrist to show Ranita the tattoo, *AMARA* in italics, that he'd gotten that morning. "Wow," she said, "that must have hurt, going over bone and all," and she couldn't help wondering if he was leaving his other arm free for the son he hoped he'd still get.

"I wanted it to hurt," he answered, eyes brimming. "Once I saw the pain you went through, getting her born. This way we're tied to her and tied to each other." She watched him as the silent tears turned into the ragged sobbing that sometimes overtook him, which he'd never been able or willing to explain. And she would never be able to forget what happened next: when he started crying, her milk let down.

Once she was back at the house, he came by to see them most days but never stayed long. He wanted to hold the baby, but as soon as he had her in his arms he was giving her back to Ranita. And as Lennox pointed out, he never helped out with anything practical, washing clothes or changing diapers, cleaning up or fixing food.

When he stopped by with balloons for Amara's two-week birthday, Ranita immediately noticed how jangled and restless he was.

"Come on, you've been watching her since I got here," he said, after ten minutes of pacing the room.

"And you've been watching me watch her."

"Yeah, but what's there to look at? All babies do is sleep and eat and shit."

She *had* been staring at Amara ever since she'd been born, and there was plenty to look at. Skin flower-petal soft. Fingers and toes, all there. Ranita put her face against the fluff of hair and inhaled. She watched her yawn. She watched her breathe. She was perfect, and Ranita didn't want to miss a thing.

When Amara woke crying, Ranita moved past the cracked nipples that were sore to the touch and the haunting feeling of her body not being her own and put her on her breast. And as she got used to the feeling of being milked, she was able to focus on the fact that what she had to give was everything her child needed. Ranita was just right, not too much and not too little.

Still watching, Jasper said, "I think she's got your ocean jasper eyes. And she's lighter than me, but she'll brown up. You know how they say the edges of the ears tell what color she'll be, and look at hers."

He wanted Ranita to put the onesie that said *Daddy's Girl* on her. "Later," Ranita said. "I'll put it on when I finish feeding and change her."

He came close and whispered, as though the baby could understand him, "Can't wait to get some of my sweet Wild Cherry again. . . ." She ignored him. Torn and stitched, like she'd told him, still aching and burning, she felt like someone had driven a minivan through her. Sex was the last thing on her mind.

As he watched her nursing, Ranita noticed his dilated pupils and recognized the look in his eyes. Love and hurt and separateness, all knotted up together.

Her father knocked softly and then popped his head in to ask if she needed anything, nodding hello to Jasper before he left.

Ranita began singing a lullaby. Eyes closed, she could feel Jasper's will, as though he were tugging on her other breast. *Me, pay attention to me.* Then she heard him say he had to go, there was somewhere he had to be.

She looked up from her miracle, swaddled and sleeping against her. And he was gone.

As Amara grew he came and went, missing her first smile, her first grasp of a rattle, her first solid food. He came through with stuffed animals and miniature big-people outfits, and made brief mischief with her, more playmate than father.

Money never stopped being short and Ranita wished she could shower her girl with riches, but she gave her imagination free rein, and became whatever age Amara was. Ranita got on the floor with her to build cities out of the colored wooden blocks Lennox bought. They sorted shapes, and finger-painted, and had nighttime picnics by candlelight on the living room floor. Made a playhouse from a neighbor's washing machine box and a tent from a blanket over a clothesline. Made up their own alphabet song, with "*J* is for Jessie's shoe collection, *E* is for 'Eating Eggs Every Easter.' "

Jasper would vanish, and as soon as she could just about imagine herself free of him he'd reappear and pull her close with artistic cards and books, mixtapes and quirky little trinkets. He mailed them, then left them at the house, tucked in the back screen door. And then he showed up in the flesh. But by the time Amara started preschool, she was calling him Jasper instead of Daddy.

TWENTY-ONE

Here I am, handling my business. Dealing with the past and present. And believing in the future, at least some of the time.

Coming home one night I ran into Antoine, and after he tried to convince me to hang out and I managed to refuse his will he told me about a gig doing data entry and phone orders at an auto parts warehouse. Hard to believe he led me to a square job, 30 hours a week, but it's true. The manager knew Daddy, which means he probably knows all about my fuckups, but he decided to give me a chance. The work's so boring it could make you weep, but I know from auto parts.

Yesterday, when I got off work there, I dragged myself to a shift at the restaurant. Soon as I can afford to, I'll be quitting, but there is a kind of bond between us phantom, back-room workers. Most are recent immigrants. The supposedly unwanted. Who nobody can do without. Anyway, I'm beat. But today's another milestone. I'm going to Sunday dinner at the house.

Val's picking us up, and I know she's all about being punctual, so I get to Jessie's an hour early and make sure we're out front when she drives up. And now that we're on the way there, I'm nervous, and the closer we get to our destination, the more I run my mouth. And as we pull into the driveway, I picture myself lurking in the flower bed and feel like I need another bath.

In the light of day, the house looks exhausted. The paint's worn and the siding's warping in places. When Theo opens the front door, I help Jessie through, kiss my boy, and grip the newel post. Daddy should be right here, at the bottom of the staircase, pulling me close.

I go directly to the hallway bathroom, turning my back to the mirror, and ride out the grief storm.

"You all right in there?" Auntie Jessie calls out as I'm retouching my eyeliner.

"All good," I say, opening the door and following the smell of biscuits to the kitchen, where Amara's sliding plump golden rounds off a cookie sheet.

"Hey," I say from the threshold, noticing the walls are a crisp, clean white, instead of the lemon yellow I grew up with. Amara's wearing one of Mama's flowered aprons.

"Hi," she answers, looking at the biscuits instead of me.

"Those smell mighty good. You made them?"

She glances at me briefly with a mix of pride and resentment. It *is* like looking at a younger version of me, and it's a lot, especially since me and Drew Turner have been revisiting my younger selves. And just as I'm trying to keep my balance, she says, concentrating on the biscuits, "I know how to do a lot of grown-up things. I've had to learn."

Okay, then. Punch to the gut, straightaway. And effective in its low-key ease. One step forward, one step back, that's the way this thing goes. I want to argue, deny, apologize, flee, but I stay and take the charge.

"I feel you. Can't wait to taste them, and maybe you can teach me what you've learned. My biscuits always came out dry."

Then Theo comes running in and reaches for one. "Not yet," she says sharply, holding up the spatula like she might swat him, and he pulls back his hand, looking hurt, and asks what he can do. She tells him, "Go set the table," and then Val comes in to lift the pot lids and get serving dishes.

As they buzz around me, I stand by the counter, looking at the kitchen stool where I sat to get my hair done. I see myself trying to sit quietly while Mama greased and combed and pulled it so tight, getting it to mind, that I had to bite my cheek to keep from crying, which was strictly forbidden.

It's hard to get my eyes to focus, and I stand over at the fridge, pretending to look at what's anchored there with magnets until the signs of their daily life come clear: Theo's drawings of baseball uniforms, school and sports schedules, emergency numbers, a dinner and chore chart, and this year's school photos. I nearly gasp when I see Daddy's copy of that visitation photo, wondering did he put it up, after all.

I turn around and watch my people working together with their own rhythm, attuned, without even needing to talk.

"Tell me how I can help?" I ask, and when no one answers I try not to feel slighted and decide to go to the basement and see if I can find a few things I've been remembering. I'm seeking good news, but when I start down the stairs I feel like I'm descending into murky water, submerging step by step into my befores. I stop, consider bailing on my plan, and then hold the railing and keep going. And at the bottom I'm swamped with hide-and-seek . . . covert sex with Jasper . . . trading views, at six, of what we had *down there* with the neighborhood kids . . . sneaking out with my bike. Standing up to Mama. And being with Daddy in his hangout cave. It looks like he stepped out for something and he'll be right back. There's even a record on the turntable. I'll have to work up to seeing what it is.

Thumbing through his albums, I remember his listening parties.

e his room. Going up the stairs, I hear Mama calling out to me,
 clomping; you sound like a hippopotamus! In the upstairs hallway I
 fingers over the encyclopedia spines. Even after everyone was
g what they needed to know, Daddy said he was sticking with

low Theo past the closed door of the room that used to be mine
nto his, which is way different from the one me and Daddy put
 for the baby, then toddler, then four-year-old he was when I
 here. I try and memorize each detail: the Red Sox champion-
ter and the drawings of team uniforms and animals on the walls,
mforter with the planets and beanbag chair that looks like a giant
, Lego creations and penny jar and little trinkets on the dresser.
ads his Pokémon cards on the bed for me to see, and shows me
 baseball mitt.

'll have to play catch," I say, hugging him, "but you gotta take it
 me. It's been a while."

re we head back down, I pause in the doorway of Amara's room
e a peek. The walls are a collage of posters and magazine pho-
op stars and rappers, and selfies she's printed out and glued on.
to linger and read the room for clues, but I've got no parental
to snoop. The dresser top's full of nail polish, earrings and neck-
air supplies, and there's a shelf full of school binders and books.
lored Christmas lights are strung from one corner of the ceiling
her. And the constellations I put up are still on the ceiling.

en it's time to eat, the aunties stand awkwardly, waiting for me to
 a seat. I'm touched by their sensitivity, but I sit next to Theo on
 that faces the window and leave the seats at the heads to them.
le's practically groaning with food, just like Sunday dinners used
vhether or not money was tight. We always did our best to make
bundant and special. Today it's pot roast, greens, corn on the cob,
ce, and biscuits. And lemon meringue pie.

Here's Marvin Gaye and all the Motown gro

War. Donny Hathaway and Sly. The Dells an

field and Roberta Flack. Earth, Wind & Fire a

When I pull out *Songs in the Key of Life*, I s

weed on the open double-album cover, pulli

one side with my library card and letting the

back and go to the secondhand couch Mam

tacky and Daddy loved, and settle into the wo

holding the shape of his body. I always felt

what I think of now is all the things, his and n

I get up and walk through his space to the s

mostly labeled, the boxes are filled with outg

Mama's handbags and shoes. Things that long

Daddy planned to tinker back to life. My stuff,

Val, I guess. I find three boxes of my CDs, an

the board books and toys that were mine and

looking for that tin kaleidoscope. I can picture i

blue diamonds on the base, green where you tur

plode, a red starburst around the hole you look t

After choosing a few CDs to go along with

doing, I go upstairs and drift to the living roc

needles and yarn to make a place beside Jessie.

with two comfy-looking sofas and a bold, thi

room like a museum, and the only time I wen

the piano, which was torture, except for the br

of a peppermint wheel. It's still here, the uprigh

wanted. After she was gone we did a lot of livin

doing it over we just stuck with the hard, scrat

had always been there and wore them out.

When Auntie Val announces ten minutes til

As we pass the serving bowls, I try to take modest portions, and notice that everyone else's plates are heaping. Now it's time to say grace and Theo volunteers. "Dear God, please bless this food we thank you for . . . and bless everyone who's here, especially Mama, who's back home . . . and please bless Granddaddy, too; he's up in heaven, but he'd really rather be here with us, because Amara's biscuits were his favorite food ever." We all smile, especially the biscuit-maker, and then Theo glances at me and says, "And bless my dad; he's up in heaven, too, but Amara says him and Granddaddy aren't hanging out." Sad, and so very true. A shadow drifts across Amara's face.

And speaking of shadows, the last time I sat here, I was back from DQ's, trying to shake him and my habit, but they were both stronger than me. Strung out, not able to keep food down, I was just moving things around on my plate, and all of them . . . Daddy, Jessie, the kids . . . looked so mournful and disappointed. An avatar for failure, I could barely stay put, and as soon as we stood up to clear the table I said I needed to use the bathroom and bounced. Left without saying good-bye, just walked out the door and called DQ. It's a lot to live down. It's a lot to live with.

I hear Jessie's voice and realize everyone's waiting for me to answer. I don't even know what she asked. They're watching me, and Amara's eyes are boring in with that laser focus of hers.

"You okay?" she asks, and then she gets up and goes to the kitchen for a glass of ice water and puts it next to my plate before sitting back down.

I say, "Thank you, baby," and I'm still having trouble eating, but I take a sip, and little by little, as the laughter and stories continue, I move forward in time. Val starts talking about the meals we had on her visits to Boston, and I remember she always did talk with her hands, even though the rest of her was reserved.

Come on, Ranita, I tell myself. *It's your first Sunday dinner with your family. Come back. Be here.*

I taste a biscuit and praise Amara for how moist and flaky it is. And since I seem to have one foot in the past no matter what I tell myself, I share a feel-good story that I'm hoping might help repair the bond with Auntie Val. "Remember those trips to the movies, when you'd get Junior Mints and let me put M&M's in my popcorn? And that time I convinced you to see *The Matrix* and folks were all loud and rowdy, talking to the characters, telling them what to do? And Auntie Val, you shocked me so bad by shouting, 'Get him, Morpheus!' that I jumped, and popcorn and M&M's went everywhere."

We all laugh, and talk about other movies we've seen together, the games we played on summer nights, the art projects we did. And I think of a little thing I loved as a child and passed on to Amara. "Remember when we made those kirigami paper flowers and watched them bloom when we put them in water?"

I do," Amara said. "I remember *everything*."

She stresses that last word and the silence stretches out.

Then Theo tells about the time they were putting on a puppet show and he couldn't remember the lines Amara had given him, so he made up his own, taking the story line in a whole crazy direction and making her nuts. Absent for this episode, I listen from the sidelines, and then chime in with one I thought of just this week. "Remember how Theo used to play with Auntie Jessie's elephant collection? And he called el-ephants ambicants?"

Giggling, Theo shares the story, probably more from being told than remembering it himself. "Then Granddaddy said, 'Not ambicant, Theo. Elephant.' And I smiled and said, 'Yeah, ambicant.'"

It's a relief to focus on the good times, but I can see Amara's face getting ornery. Though I know I shouldn't, I plow ahead anyway, "And remember how we'd make a tent by putting a blanket over a clothesline and pretending we were explorers, or camping in the woods?"

When she says, "You're all about back in the day, like it was paradise," everyone puts their forks down and an awful, thick curtain comes down on the reminiscing. She looks more pained than triumphant, and I want to reach out to her, but I know better. Once again, I sit here, trying to think of what to say. Then, looking out the window, I see the birdhouse I made, hanging crooked in the rowan tree out back, looking even more ramshackle than I remember, and I could cry that they kept it.

Saving the day again, Auntie Jessie speaks up. "Well, I'm so full it's sinful. How 'bout we tune into MSNBC and see what shenanigans they've been up to in D.C.?"

I help her get settled on the couch with her feet up on the coffee table, thinking Mama would be appalled at that, and when I'm about to walk away she says, "Nita. Remember, choosing. And patience."

I go back over and kiss her on the forehead, happily taking in her cocoa butter smell, and go to the kitchen, grab a dish towel, and start drying. It's weighing on me that I'll be leaving soon, now that dinner's over, and I can't help picturing the kids coming to my place to stay over. As I put away the last dish, I remind myself to slow my roll.

When everything's clean and put away, I go and stand at the back door, scene of so many punishments, and squint out at the yard, overtaken now by grass and weeds. It's June and Daddy's garden beds are empty. I open the door and walk out.

Under Devon's feathery leaves I find Jasper's carvings. Though I asked him to scratch out *Duncan* and put in *Amara*, he never did, and I'm tempted to obliterate the whole thing, but I won't assault the tree again. Like Eldora said, each part's precious to the whole.

I adjust the birdhouse so it hangs straight and walk around front. And then I see Val helping Jessie through the front door, the kids behind them, and my heart sinks that it's time to go. I say good-bye, pass on the ride Val offers, and start walking.

I'm minding my business, doing some reckless speculating in my head about the three of us reviving the garden, thinking it's a good thing the seeds we plant won't be depending on me to know up from down, when I hear the voice that always did remind me of brown sugar kicking in.

"So you just gon' walk on by?"

My heart lurches.

I stop and look around and here they are, kicked back against the azure Escalade, feet on the edge of the curb. David Q, in the flesh, his sidekick beside him.

Didn't see them. Didn't even sense them coming. My guard's down, what with all the spilling my feelings and believing in the future, but here he is, and I can't help noticing how good he still looks.

A greedy smile splits Leon's face, and looking from DQ to me, he says, "I knew we'd all meet up again, sooner or later, Ranita-Not-Cherry. What's good? You keeping busy?"

Like a fool, I stand here talking trash with him, while I feel DQ changing the atmosphere, making it crackle and buzz. Maybe meeting with Drew Turner gives me the feeling that I've got this, even though DCF can block you from your kids for just keeping the wrong company. Maybe I can't help that reckless urge to ride the edge.

I say I'm good, taking care of business, working my program. And for some reason, I add, "Believe it or not, I even went to church two weeks ago."

"No shit. Well, feature that. You say your prayers for peace and brotherhood?"

"You know I did. Said one for you, too."

He chuckles. "Well, you know I need someone besides the devil on my side." And then he spins one of his funny stories about going to church with his granny, doing everybody's voices and making me laugh about the outlandish hats everyone had on.

DQ speaks up, "They call them fascinators in England. Now there's a word for you, baby." And now that the attention's on him, he says, "Damn, girl, it's been a minute. You're still fine as hell." But I see him checking out my frumpy clothes and ponytail puff. I hope my eyeliner's not smudged. And it fucks me up that I still want him to want me.

I don't say a thing. Mama taught me the power of silence, that's for sure, and I just look at him, wondering what and who he's selling these days, while his smile tightens.

"Can't we have a conversation? Don't you owe me that?"

Owe you? I feel the volcano rumbling.

"Look, Cherry, if you're all set with your new life, then it won't hurt to talk to me. Leon's got shit to take care of, but you and me, we can go inside for a cup of coffee and catch up proper."

Leon lingers, making sure he's been dismissed, and then tells DQ to text him when he's done and crosses the street. And I'm wrestling with three options. Run in the other direction. Avoid a confrontation and play it off. Be strong enough to withstand the past and present converging. I refuse the coffee, tell him he can say what he's got to say right here. And I've resisted going in and sitting down with him, but now out here in the open I feel like prey.

Leaned back, stretched out along the car hood like he's in charge of something, he reminds me of that hungry crocodile that slinked into my dream. Somehow, he manages to look relaxed and on edge at the same time. The eyes are dark and empty, but in his face I see outsized wanting. Brokenness. And a touch of mean.

"How's the little man? How's Amina?" he asks.

"Amara."

"Aw, damn. Amara, that's what I meant. How's she doin'? She must be, what, fourteen, fifteen now?"

I act like he hasn't spoken and soon as he can he changes the subject back to his favorite one, DQ, and goes on and on. I might as well be a mannequin. Or a mirror. I'm not really listening, but he's talking, using words like "phantasm" and "habituation." And I'm thinking of a couple *q* words . . . "queasy" . . . "quicksand," as I watch his mouth.

Then he says, "You still sing?"

The word pings around inside me. *Sing Sing Sing.*

Instead of answering, I look him over, moving from the eyes downward. He is a beautiful specimen. Same jacked arms and shoulders and flawless skin. Same loose-jointed ease in his body. But then the layers peel back like the pages in those science textbooks that show what's below the surface, bone and muscle and organs and arteries, and it feels like I'm seeing past the skin.

"Damn, I've missed you, baby." His voice is slow and sticky. "A part of you's stayed with me, and I know a part of me will always be in you." Really? What shitty movie has he been watching?

"Remember, Cherry Ranita?"

"I remember."

I take my time going backward, and then come forward, to the present. And in the man across from me I see a boy who was never anyone's priority, whose only meal some days was the free school lunch, who waited for a visit from his father that never came. A boy in a man's body whose center never would be filled. I see neither honesty nor remorse.

"We always were soulmates," he drawls, "right from the very start."

I keep my voice even and direct. "Dopemates. We were dopemates."

Straightening up, he frowns and glares. He's towering over me, arms folded.

"You know what?" I say. "A whole lot of shit went down at the end. And you never wrote or sent word. You never reached out with a lawyer, with cash, with any help at all for me or my kids."

He looks puzzled and off-balance, and I feel my feet on the pavement, look at the oak tree right beside me, focus on my breath going in and out.

"You deserted me. And the biggest disappearing act of all was just before we got busted. That night. You know which one."

He's flexing his jaw now and stepping forward. "Come on, baby. We were both half-blind and sleepwalking."

I stand my ground. "No. I remember. Fortunately. Unfortunately. I remember it all. How you reeled me in, how you turned me to the needle, and the street, too, if need be. I remember that night, and I know you do, too. How you sold me. And left me."

One of his hands is a fist, and the other's holding it. Body coiled like a cottonmouth, he tries another smile on me, and this one contains as much malice as charm.

Feeling my backpack dangling from my shoulder, I picture the brass key to his place in the inside pocket. Seems like it's giving off a thermal glow. And I wish I could say I feel empowered from standing up for myself, but my legs are wobbly.

"I thought there *was* something real between us, at the start. Turns out you're a scarecrow with empty words for stuffing, and a hollow where your heart should be." Before I walk away, I say I've got business with the living.

And when I'm two steps away I hear his silky voice. "Saw that girl of yours the other day, getting off the bus."

I freeze. And I swear I feel my own racing heart drop down and hit my feet.

"Amara. She's just like you."

My neck gets loose, and my head tilts back, and my face goes hot and tingly, and I start some deep breathing, trying to decide before I turn around which Ranita is called for. The volcano's restive, but I come at him with ice.

"What did you say?" I ask, evenly, quietly, as I turn around.

"She's the spitting image of you, Cherry, and just as fine."

I get as close as I can to his face. The taste of copper fills my mouth.

And I speak slow and deliberate, just above a whisper. "You know me, David Quarles. I can do the time if I need to. You come near my daughter and I'll fuck you up before you can say, 'Quell,' and enjoy doing it. Try me if you've got a doubt."

Taking one slow-motion step backward, I hold his stare, flashing on Jasper talking about his German shepherd: *You gotta meet his eyes, make sure he looks away before you do, or you belong to him.*

I take another step and another, backing away, and DQ must see the crazy in these summertime eyes, because he doesn't move or say a thing. But I hear Maxine's voice echo through me, telling her story of taking down that CO, and I'm reliving all the times I couldn't speak up or act up, all the times there was nobody to defend me. I want to choose love and peace. I do. But I will protect myself and mine.

I hold down my nausea until I can get a few blocks away and duck into an alley, where I bend over and throw up. I'm dry heaving even after I'm empty, and someone walks by and glances at me without even slowing down. Just another down-and-out sista, heaving her guts.

Digging in my backpack, I find some tissue and wipe my mouth, my face, my eyes. And then I find a convenience store and buy a bottle of water and a pack of cigarettes and a lighter. Soon as I'm outside, I light up. It takes three tries, my hands are so unsteady, but now I'm sucking in the smoke with pure relief.

I down the water and smoke half the pack, lighting one with another, while I walk. *If I can get home,* I'm thinking, *if I can walk it off and get home I'll be alright.* I barely notice what I'm passing as I picture myself stepping into the rivers Maxine conjured up, Chesapeake, Potomac, Housatonic, Neponset, Charles, and calling on every good thing I can think of.

Soon as I'm inside my place, I lock the door and lean back against it. *Now would be a good time for you to show up, Power-Greater-Than-Me, as all the things you are, all the things you look like, all the names you're called.*

Looking at myself in the little mirror next to the door, I touch my throat. Fresh as that night feels, I expect to see bruises. Still, I look like I've aged a decade, like I've been to hell and back.

I hum it now, the last thing I sang . . . *Lead me, guide me . . .*

It still belongs to me. And for better and worse, so does Cherry.

I have been loved right. I say it to myself like I said it to Drew Turner as I get the kites from the top cabinet shelf. And instead of going in order like I have been, I dive in and pick one at random.

I pull the one she left for me after the first time we made love: *What's your body saying this morning?*

At breakfast she dropped the hint that I should check "the mail," and all day long I thought about the question, about her, about the places we went and how scared I was, and then soon as I saw her at dinner it was all good. She didn't bring up the kite, or what it referred to, or press me at all. She just smiled, easy and gentle. She was telling me about "misogynoir," a new term that excited her with the way it got at our truths.

"Yeah, it's perfect," I say. "And by the way, my body? It's singing."

I've got a lapful of notes here from Maxine. And in my head are all the things and places I asked for: flora and fauna, weather and the elements, pleasures, lost treasure, adventures I might still have.

Though I've memorized them, I read through every one. And I wish I could say the love undoes the hurt, but here it all is. And here I am, sorting through the wreck.

TWENTY-TWO

2014

Night of the living dead, that's how Ranita thought of it. After she got clean at Oak Hills, it came back to her with excruciating clarity, the bottom where she'd settled, instead of crawling up and out.

She stood on the street, brown skin blue in the moonlight. Jittery. Needy. Yielding. December, and Ranita was at the curb, dragging her heavy feet forward and shivering from her bare legs and scanty jacket, and the red minidress from Judy that hung loose on her now, while DQ stood back in Canada Goose. It was past time to get their high on, and they were selling their asset: Black Cherry.

Smelling the blood of the wounded, a shark pulled to the curb and slid his window down.

She tried to look seductive, though on the inside she was a mess of gnawing hunger, as DQ stepped forward to make the pitch, telling him, like they were homies, how she had talents, carnal and otherwise. She could even sing.

Ranita's inner alarm went off, but she could barely hear it underneath her fiending, and she got in the car, without even a nail file to defend herself, without even looking at the license plate. *DQ's on it*, she thought. *He's got me.*

The shark wove through the dark streets until he found a dead end. And when they got in the back she put herself on autopilot and went to work, tuning out his bad breath and cheap cologne and dirty fingernails, pretending, just as much as she had to.

She'd have what they needed soon if she could just hold on.

Watching from the front seat, she saw herself exposed in the moonlight, one knee digging into the safety belt buckle and the other jammed against a cupholder, and heard him say, "Sing for me how much you like this dick."

She tried to shrug it off, nasty-talk him, work faster and harder. Sing, for him?

He said it again, and this time it was an order, with "bitch" added for emphasis.

No. Still no. She saw that she'd lost one sandal, and there was her skirt, up around her waist, once more. But she was clear on one thing. He had paid for pussy, but not for one of the few good, clean, fine things she had in her.

She was carrying on, trying to get the job done, when he grabbed her shoulders and pushed her off. "Sing me a lullaby, bitch. Sing me something," he commanded as her head banged against the window and came to rest between the seat and door. And then he was doing the straddling, and his hands were on her throat, squeezing, pressing, as she gasped and clawed and kicked, and then easing up.

Again he pressed, and through the dizziness, the burn spreading through her lungs and neck, the spots throbbing in her eyes, he came in and out of focus. She saw him in shifting pieces: eyebrow, hairline, teeth. And then he eased the pressure, asking had she found her voice yet, before starting in again. She fought. Gasped. Clawed at hands and face and heard the panting, the grunting, the rampage from his gaping maw, catching two words, "cum dumpster," that she would never manage to forget.

Maybe it was better to let him end her, the thought bloomed in her head and then broke apart and formed again. She was prey, just as low-down as he thought, and always had been. She was a body he'd paid for, and she never had been free.

The serenity she'd never been able to keep ahold of was on the other side of the pain and denigration, she knew it, and maybe she could just give in. Not to the demand to sing, but to a relief that was more than temporary, to a rest from all the fucking up and trying and fucking up.

Ranita could barely see herself, but she could still feel him on her, in her. His stale sweat was in her pores. His breath and spittle were on her face. The hairy flesh of his stomach expanded against her with each breath. Each time he eased his grip and pressed down again she receded a little further.

And then she saw Amara and Theo, their faces grief-stricken. Motherless instead of mother-absent, back at the house with Daddy, waiting on her to call, waiting on her to get her shit together and come back and live the love she felt.

Inches from hers, his face came clear. And it proclaimed pleasure, along with hatred and rage. He had her pain and fear to fix on, and his power to decide if she would breathe, and soon her dying would be his never-ending thrill, and she'd live on as a piece of womantrash he'd snuffed. He'd get off, replaying his fun, while her people mourned.

She saw herself. She remembered her name. And she heard a faint thread of music from deep within. Focusing there, she tried her best to nod. *Yes*, even if he didn't let her live, *yes*, she would sing.

Reeling, coughing, and sputtering, her voice barely above a whisper, she got it out as best she could. "Lead me, guide me . . . through the darkness. . . ."

She sang. Neither music nor plea was for him. But satisfied, he had his way and finished, then put her out of his car like something he'd scraped from his shoe, throwing a dollar bill and her sandal at her before shutting the door and speeding off.

Ranita sat on the curb, dry-retching in spasms. Her panties were gone, but she tried to untwist her skirt and get it back where it belonged. She was alive.

Stumbling to her feet, she limped the three, four, five blocks to where she'd gotten in the car. And DQ was gone. Too numb to reason, too sickened and wobbly to figure it out . . . had something happened to him . . . had he been picked up . . . was he okay . . . she made her way back to his place. And as she searched her jacket for her key, he opened the door.

Heaving, sobbing, she staggered across the threshold and into the bathroom, and it was a mistake, she knew it, but she looked in the mirror and saw a face she barely knew. The neck was finger bruised, and broken blood vessels marked the puffy, dark-ringed eyes. They were those of a feral animal, injured and cornered, unable to bite its way free. Her throat was throbbing, her pussy was raw, and every muscle in her body hurt. And it all spilled out: his pleasure in her pain, her living and dying and living, his command, her song. Each word racked her, but at least, she told DQ, "We've got the plate; we can find him; we can fuck him up."

He stood in the doorway. Scratching. Silent.

Ranita knew that for junkies like the two of them, only the next hit was sacred. There were no rules that could not be broken. Still, she was dumbfounded. He hadn't been where she'd left him, and no explanation seemed to be forthcoming, but she waited.

After hemming and hawing, he finally said he didn't see the plate, or he saw it but didn't write it down, or he wrote it down but lost it. In the pause that followed, she saw her body, once again abject, helpless, prone. And when DQ spoke it was to ask one question: "You got the cash, though, Cherry, didn't you? We got paid?"

The only answer was oblivion, more oblivion. Ranita sat on the floor, teeth chattering, skin crawling, and looked up at his deadfall eyes. Maybe this was the afterlife, minus the peace.

TWENTY-THREE

I've been to two more Sunday dinners, and after conferring with Jessie, Val's letting me take the kids on an outing. It's not the sleepover I've been dreaming of, but it's progress, and all week I've been debating where to go in this July heat.

Soon as I ring the bell and Amara opens the door, I've got to get my mouth in check about her outfit. First off, her shorts are rolled up so far they show the black of her behind. The top is tight across her ample chest, and cropped to show her belly button. She's wearing flip-flops. And she's got makeup covering her freckles, which feels like a personal affront.

I know Val didn't see her before she left for work and it's on me to act parental. I step inside. "Soon as you roll down those shorts or change them, and put on a whole top, we can go."

She stomps up the stairs, slams some doors, and comes down in a stretchy top and jeans that show every inch of her beautiful, blossoming body. At least most of her skin's covered. Theo comes running down, his bony frame lost in baggy clothes, and I get a flash of Jasper on the night I met him. Trying to shake it off, I announce, overly upbeat and cheerful, that we're going to the Franklin Park Zoo (where today kids get in free).

After fighting our way onto a packed bus, we're separated from each other by what feels like a million hassled people, and I'm feeling like shit for not being able to drive us, and then we fight our way off and walk toward the zoo. I can't help scanning the street for azure, but it seems like the coast is clear.

In we go through the Zebra entrance, and there's a whole mess of whining kids and jumping-up-and-down kids and kids begging for something from the souvenir shop. Mine show no excitement at all, which doesn't worry me until I've already got the tickets and we're going through the gate. I pull them aside and ask do they want to tell me what's up. Theo says he went to the Stone Zoo last month with his class. "And what about you?" I ask, turning to Amara and feeling mad at the whole situation. "What's your issue?"

She glances at me briefly like I'm the most backward swamp creature she's ever seen, sucks her teeth, and looks away.

Struggling to get my breath and my balance, I force myself to speak. "You all want to go see the animals or not? I've already bought my ticket, but if you've got a better idea, share it and we'll change the plan."

They shrug, and we move toward the Serengeti, stopping to look at what the exhibit tells us is a wildebeest. And I'm reading the background displays out loud, saying, "Look, this says it migrates five hundred to one thousand miles when water gets scarce," going on like some kind of automaton tour guide and then pointing out how mismatched its body looks. Reminds me of brothas coming out of prison, upper bodies swole out of proportion from all the weight lifting. I'm talking about how interesting the wildebeests are, how they live in big family herds and how the babies can walk as soon as they're born, when I give up in mid-sentence. I'm working hard, but not only are we not on the same page; we're not even in the same book.

We keep walking and I keep trying.

Then Theo says he wants to see the lowland gorillas, and when we get there we stand and watch them pace around the rocks and the sorry excuses for trees, and I think my heart will break for them, locked down in this fake, empty place that I'm sure doesn't smell or sound or look like home, under constant scrutiny and aware enough to realize the whole rotten deal. One's curled up with a piece of plaid cloth, looking like Lizette as she slept away her time. Another's grooming a youngin with its back turned, like the hair braiding in the dayroom. What the fuck? I guess you can take the sista out of prison, but . . . My kids are silent, and even though I'm trying hard to turn the vibe around, everything feels heavy and loaded and stale.

"Incarcerated," Amara says, staring straight ahead, "and they didn't even do anything wrong."

Okay, then. This is how she's gonna roll. It is not good, not at all, and why I thought looking at caged, deprived, bored-to-death animals was a good idea I'll never know. Feels like a turning point's coming.

Maybe it's just another test. She's defying me, any way she can. Provoking me into mothering so she can push me away. Whatever the reason, she takes it further, stepping out of her flip-flops and onto the foot-high wall, and with her body spread out against the glass she slams it with her fist. The sleeping gorilla sits up and zeroes in on her. And I'm just thankful for the plate glass.

Everyone else in the tropical forest, most of them white, they're looking at her, at us, and moving away.

I take a quick glance around to see where the guard is, and notice the eyes of a man, toddler in tow, checking out my 13-year-old daughter, and sparks fly inside my head, but there's nothing I can do about him; he's just the landscape where we live and always have. I hiss in her ear, "You're working me. Deliberately. Now act like you were raised right and get down from there!"

"It's always about you. And if I *was* raised right, what did you, or Jasper, have to do with it?"

The witnesses are hovering, and my spitting image has taken complete leave of her senses and committed the Black child's worst offense: showing out in front of white people.

After what's seemed like progress. The first time I'm in charge. Why? Is it that I chose the zoo? Made her change her shorts, and have no car? My false cheer and pointing out facts about the animals that she and Theo can read themselves? I don't know from 8- and 13-year-olds. I don't know my own children. And with so many fuckups in my long roller-coaster ride to the underside, there's no pinpointing the moment when they were lost to me.

Just as the zoo police starts coming toward us, I say, real slow, and this time with a don't-make-me-hurt-you edge, "I *said* get down!" and Amara, she smirks and steps back, casual and sassy and slow, onto the ground and into her flip-flops, and says, "You are so extra."

Well, she's nailed me; I've got to give her that. When I'm not inadequate, I'm excessive.

The guard's here now, saying there's no climbing on the wall allowed and please don't disturb and disrespect the animals, and I'm apologizing and saying, "We know, Officer. I'm sorry and she won't do it again." And as he walks away she turns, and shoots me a hurt and hateful look. I'm so struck by what all I can see in her expression that I can't say a thing.

I'm stumped. Shaken. In public. My daughter sassed me like a straight-up white girl, and the only saving grace is that she didn't call me by my first name.

If I stay silent, I've got zero say-so that's real and earned and I've got no call to tell my kids what to do, today or ever. It's over for me being a parent, even without the TPR. And if I step up and discipline her, harsh and strict like Mama did, I'll drive Amara from me, and lose her in a different way. Theo's beside me, watching it all unfold with big, worried eyes, and I'm trying to draw on my support group wisdom on *limit setting* and *parenting your teen*.

I take a beat to collect myself, then step in closer and try to sound firm. "I hear you, Amara, and I know just where you're coming from. But it's my say-so or nobody's. You feel me?" She glares at me, and I can hear her digging in the concrete with her flip-flop toe, and I'm thinking, *Please just do as I say*, when she walks over to Theo and puts her arm around his shoulder and says, "Come on, let's go."

I exhale, more relieved than I could ever say.

We move on to the giraffes, which are, thank God, roaming around outside, and Theo's asking me about why they're made like that and why they don't tip over. I have no answers. Amara's not saying a whole lot, but at least she's taking a break from throwing me shade.

Everything else, the dusty Outback with its baffled-looking koalas and kangaroos, the caged birds, is a haze. The Kalahari lions, always my favorite, seem too worn-out to make a sound of threat or protest. We sit on a bench and eat the turkey sandwiches I brought to save money, and they go down dry and tasteless. It's a good thing, I tell myself, that the kids don't seem interested in the souvenirs I can't afford.

There are no more outbursts, but our first solo outing's been a bust, and the whole ride back to the house I replay it.

It's always about you. I hear myself saying that very thing to Mama, if only in my head, as she lit into me. *Ranita, why must you try my patience? Ranita, I can count on you to do the opposite of what I want.*

We're riding along glumly when Amara says, "Just tell me, what were you thinking?"

"What? Come again?"

"What were you thinking when you picked Jasper? Why him? And then why us? Isn't being a mother partly about choosing the father? Or were we accidents?"

Even more confused and stuck, I feel for a toehold. "You were wanted; you were loved. And he had his good qualities."

"Like what?"

Confused, stuck, silent, I hear her questions ricochet around my head. Why? *Did* I pick him? After a loooong wordless stretch, when all the negatives are tumbling through my head, she gets up, says, "Never mind," and grabs a ceiling strap two seats away.

I'm remembering how Jasper waged battle. Strategic. Cunning. Roundabout. No Sun Tzu for me and Amara, though. Our reasons might be subterranean, but our ends, our weapons, our attitudes, are plain to see.

Watching her stagger as the bus stops and starts, Theo beside me looking close to tears, I face the fact that I'm as language poor as my father. I know so many words, plain and fancy, so how is it that I can't use any of them? And though I try and get a footing in the positive, I'm slipping into a downside inventory.

When we get to the house, Theo runs in as soon as Amara unlocks the door, saying he's got to pee, and I stand on the crumbling porch steps, feeling like I need to do something to rescue the day, get something said, connect and make her see.

"Look," I say, reaching out to touch her arm before thinking better of it. She steps away and turns to face me, and I feel the force field of her resentment.

"Amara, look, I know it's not much, but all I've got is the truth. The two of us, me and Jasper, as parents . . . and each in our own ways . . . we were young, and we are all *kind* of messed up." I get a flash of Maxine and her lawyerly ways and think, *jointly and severally liable.*

"He wasn't a parent at all, was he? And you . . ." She doesn't bother finishing her sentence.

The truth is hard, even when you think you've faced it. "No. He wasn't. And I was shit. But it's not like we set out to fail you. And it's not like we didn't love you. He had a habit, and then I did. We were lost, unwell, each in our own darkness. . . ." I try to collect my thoughts. "You asked me to tell you something good about him.

"I fell for him right away," I tell her, "but I was only sixteen when we met. He was smart . . . and intense . . . and quirky. Different . . . like me, I guess. He knew about all kinds of stuff, and he liked reading and researching things, like I did. He dabbled in philosophy, and photography, and lots of things, but I guess that's what he did. Dabble. Anyway, my favorite thing about him was . . . he had a huge imagination."

She nods, looking heartbroken. And says, just above a whisper, "I guess I was hoping for something more . . . specific."

And I swear she looks away when I say good-bye.

And now I'm at the door of Mario's Paradise Lounge. Again. It pulls me close, whispers, *Come on in here, bitch; you know you miss me want me need me; you know I'm written in your cells.* And this time I walk through the door and into the dark and up to the bar, pull out my hard-earned cash, and order a Hennessy on the rocks.

I can almost taste it while the bartender's pouring, and when it comes I tilt the glass back and forth, listening to the ice cubes clinking, watching them slide and bump against each other. I lift it, taking in the amber color and inhaling the charred-wood smell with a hint of sweetness, my nostrils coming to attention and my mouth watering. My hand's shaking, but I get the glass to my lips and close my eyes.

And I take a sip.

It burns, just like I remember, and scorches through me like a thunderbolt as I knock it back.

TWENTY-FOUR

1996

The summer before Geneva died, the mother-daughter conflict that had existed for as long as Ranita could remember escalated into gray-zone warfare. Along with being a time of flower farming and erasure and losing Lori Watson, the summer of 1996 contained relief and revenge. Would she have tried for appeasement if she'd known how brief Geneva's life would be? Would she have made that last year play out differently? Only later would Ranita see what she'd only had a vague sense of at the time, that adopting her mother's weapons was about more than survival, and it had cost her the high ground.

With Geneva gone, and not gone, Ranita would remember her own acts of defiance, which had seemed minor and necessary at the time, with reverberating guilt. Turning off the light when she exited the room to leave her mother sitting in the dark. Asking had she put on weight, her dress looked tight. Watching her stumble on the front steps and walking away. Closing the piano fallboard just as Geneva sat down for a duet. Ranita refused all peace accords, even offers and concessions, even the absence of strife. Did the lack of a negative make a positive? She didn't think so. Still, withholding peace and indulging the temptation to match her mother's spite left her feeling empty and small, and once she'd lost the chance for either a reckoning or a truce she tried to forget as much of that year as possible.

But the memories nested, wounding afresh with the twisted logic of Geneva's punishments and the truths of her judgments when they surfaced.

The day after school let out, Ranita and Lori were stretched out on the floor, an open box of Entenmann's chocolate chip cookies between them as they chatted about which boys in their class were cute and which girls' exclusions could be as devastating as they were casual.

Ranita and Lori had stumbled upon their growing friendship during the awkward milling around after church let out. Lori had asked if she'd done the social studies assignment that was due the next day, and they had gone to sit outside while their mothers circulated. That had led to bike-riding and homework sessions after school. It seemed to Ranita from the tentative opening that anything might happen, and as they enjoyed the cookies they talked about what the rest of the summer held in store. They could ride their bikes and go for ice cream. They could go to the movies. They could go to the neighborhood pool.

"Maybe you can come to the Vineyard with us in August," Lori said.

Ranita was torn between excitement and reality. Unable to picture her mother granting permission for such a thing, she didn't know what to say, and in the space where a response belonged she replayed an argument from the summer before, when her father had announced that they'd been invited to a customer's Squam Lake house.

"They don't think we can afford our own family vacation," Geneva had said, "but I'll not be anyone's charity case."

Gently, Lennox said, "Why do you think that's what the invitation means?"

Our own family vacation. Ranita had driven with Lennox down to coastal Maryland several times, most recently when his father had been sick. But her mother hadn't come, and Ranita didn't think a trip to see an ailing grandfather she hardly knew qualified. She spoke up, "We've never had a family vacation. Maybe they're just trying to introduce us to the concept."

Geneva flashed her a warning look. "Do you know what vacation meant when I was coming up? It was a chance to make some extra money picking oranges, or raise the money for my school clothes washing windows and floors."

"Okay," Lennox said, holding up both hands, "I never got anything we'd now call a vacation either. Every summer was a stay-at-home vacation, full of being outside, fishing, and helping out in the garden and the house, too . . . anyway, this isn't about the past. This is about now." Ranita had smirked, and then felt bad about it, but really, was there anything that wasn't about the past?

Geneva was wearing her perpetual frown. "It'll be just fine for the two of you. You can fish. And Ranita can show herself off in a swimsuit that barely covers her . . . flourishing body. I don't fish and I don't swim."

Ranita pictured her mother sinking like a stone to the bottom of a murky lake.

"Well, you can sit on the shore, or deck . . . whatever it is they've got," Lennox said.

"And do what? Get skin cancer? Make conversation with people I don't know or even want to, who think they're better than me?"

Here we go, Ranita thought. Her mother always went there. But it looked to Ranita as though the people at church liked Geneva. They admired her singing voice and organ playing. And her piano students seemed to respect her. Even though she was demanding, she kept her temper and her ire in check, saving them for the daughter who sucked at sight-reading and pedaling. Ranita was the one without friends, and she was willing to risk a trip to the lake with people she barely knew to go *somewhere*. But Geneva's resistance had settled the matter, and they hadn't gone to the lake house or anywhere else.

"I don't know," Ranita said to Lori. "Maybe." Her face grew hot as she imagined telling how things really were in her family, and revealing that her mother would never, ever let her go.

"My mother's signed me up for some kind of lessons she thinks I need in August," she lied. "And who would water my garden?" It was all she could come up with.

"Couldn't you have your lawn person do it? Or your parents? What are you growing there, anyway?"

They went to the window, where Ranita pointed out her little plot. It looked so small and vacant from the second floor. She listed what she'd planted, adding, "They've sprouted, but they're still just seedlings, so they're hard to see."

"Okay," Lori said, like she was striving to believe her. "My mom's obsessed with her roses and she's got a vase of them, cut from her bushes, in almost every room. It's nice, having flowers inside, long as you don't have to pick them. You'll have more bouquets than you need in no time. And no thorns to deal with."

As they stood looking out, Ranita noticed Avery's branches stirring in the breeze. She wanted to step closer to Lori. She smelled good, and Ranita wondered if her skin was as soft as it looked. "Want another cookie?" she asked, turning from the window.

Back on the floor, they chattered on about what the eighth grade would be like. "We'll do inequalities, and linear equations," Lori said. "In science we'll be making homemade batteries, and we can be partners." Ranita let herself smile freely. She would love to be science partners with Lori, and she hoped having a best friend would help to temper the trouble she always seemed to be getting into.

She glanced up to see her mother filling the doorway, a furious thundercloud about to let loose. There was no way out, except through the open window.

Geneva's voice started out quiet and clipped, but as soon as she got going Ranita knew it would be bad. She began with what a shameful mess Ranita's room was and moved on from there to her taking cookies from the kitchen without asking, the pitch of her voice rising as she pointed out how Ranita was lying on the floor like she had no home training, and not giving Lori a napkin to keep the chocolate from getting on her good clothes. By the time Geneva arrived at Ranita having no business whatsoever stuffing her mouth with sweets, she was in a full-on rant and lightning seemed to be flashing from the doorway.

Ranita hung her head until it almost touched the carpet, praying she'd be the only target of Geneva's building rage, hoping that having an accountant father and a mother in the church choir would protect Lori. While her mother carried on about her faults, Ranita kept low to the ground and focused on the carpet, noticing the different blues in its mix. Counting the little shag fibers, she tried not to gag on the fake-floral carpet freshener smell, and tried not to cry or vomit while her one friend witnessed her pretty, talented mother's madness and revulsion for her.

It was the end of her and Lori, she knew it, the introduction and conclusion of having someone over. She tried to look down and close her ears to the speaking voice that was as foul and turgid as her singing voice was lovely and clear. She concentrated on keeping down the chocolate chip cookies that she *had* inhaled in a way that was totally piggish . . . they had looked so good through the little cellophane window on the box and tasted even better than they promised . . . and tried to focus focus focus on the carpet that was a mere inch from her mouth as the tirade peaked, and she felt girl secrets and having a science partner and ice cream and riding free slip away.

When Lori had left, Geneva reappeared in the doorway and snatched the cookies off the floor. Ranita followed her to the bathroom and watched her tip the remaining half box into the toilet and flush.

Ranita hit her with a standout vocab choice, "Deplorable," and went outside to her flowers.

At dinner that night she didn't touch a bite of the meal her mother had cooked. She sat silent, staring at her plate, and said she didn't feel well when her father asked what was wrong. "All those cookies," Geneva said, shaking her head in disgust.

"May I be *excused*?" Ranita asked as she stood, picked up her plate, and went to the kitchen, where she shoved everything her mother had put on it down the garbage disposal and turned it on, feeling a rush she hadn't expected as it churned the food and kept up its metallic grinding, empty but still chewing.

The Lori Watson kibosh, one of Geneva's greatest hits. When Ranita couldn't refuse its playback, she relived the carpet smell and the mortifying shame and, as often as not, another flashback from the age of six came with it.

Down in the basement, she'd been playing "house" with Bobby and Ayana. They had all been in the same kindergarten class, and on the weekends they romped through the neighborhood until their mothers called them home.

Bobby had designated himself the father, and assigned the role of mother to both Ranita and Ayana. "Lemme see what you got down there," he said, pointing to their crotches. All curious, the three of them took down their shorts and underpants. And looked. Until the door to the bulkhead banged open and a wedge of sunlight sliced through the shadowy dark.

They heard her before they saw her, footsteps coming down, down, down until they reached the bottom step and Geneva stood there, blocking out the light.

Ranita felt her favorite shorts with the whales on them around her ankles, but it was like freeze tag, and she couldn't make her arms reach down to pull them up. Six feet away, her mother loomed, a displeased and vengeful god.

Ranita's panic crowded out her breath and sent her senses into overdrive. She smelled the gravid basement that her father would panel and inhabit in later years. Damp and earthy, with traces of leafy decay. She saw Geneva's slanted shadow stretch across the room, and tasted fear in the back of her throat. She heard the footfalls of hard-soled shoes coming toward her, and saw Geneva looking down at her, down into her, eyes ablaze.

With a restraint more frightening than one of her rants, Geneva told Bobby and Ayana to pull their pants up and warned Ranita not to touch hers. "You like showing what's private, you can live with that." Once Bobby and Ayanna had been set free and scampered up and out of the bulkhead into the light, Geneva slammed the metal doors closed and slid the rod across to lock them. And then she pulled Ranita up the stairs by one arm.

Feet caught up in her shorts and underpants, Ranita had stumbled and tried to right herself, bumping her shins on the way up and suppressing her tears. She knew better than to cry, even though her punishments were not the hitting kind.

"Step out of them," Geneva said, pointing to Ranita's shorts, snatching them up as soon as she'd done as she was told and announcing her sentence. She would stand in the little back hallway where her mother wouldn't have to look at her, until her father came home. "Consider yourself lucky I don't use a belt on you like my parents did," she said.

"But my clothes . . ." Ranita tried to raise her voice in protest, though she knew it was futile to say how terrible her half nakedness felt. What if someone looked through the back door window? What if Daddy came home and saw her like that? Before Geneva shut the door, she said, "Maybe this will teach you to keep your pants up and your legs closed."

Ranita stood shivering, exposed and shaken by the anger and aversion she'd seen in her mother's eyes, and surrounded by three closed doors. One went to the kitchen and one led outside, where a rectangle of yard appeared in tiny pieces through the metal wire her father had put across the window to keep intruders out. The third one, to the basement, they had just come through. And tucked right inside that door was the kaleidoscope Auntie Val had brought for her, she'd seen it on the way up the stairs, and she longed to tiptoe over and open the door to get it, but Mama would catch her; she knew she would.

She felt the air on her skin, down there, where she was not supposed to touch, or linger when she washed up, or look.

She wasn't too good at telling time yet, even if she had been near a clock, but she heard the ice-cream truck on its afternoon round, and she'd been out there forever when her mother cracked the door open, gave her back her clothes, and left again.

Lunchtime came and went. Then snack time. She was hot and her stomach roared like a tiger. She needed to pee. And she stood on the black-and-white swirly linoleum so long she couldn't feel her legs or feet, but she was not allowed to sit, her mother had said so, and she didn't want to get caught out for something else.

On the other side of the kitchen door she heard the fridge open and close, and cutlery clinking against plates and bowls. She heard her mother getting herself a cool glass of water from the faucet.

Ranita wouldn't tell her father. Or Auntie Jessie. She knew Geneva was the boss of her, and she didn't want anyone to know what her mother had seen. She burned with remorse and confusion and shame. And she was so tired from the standing and standing and standing, and from being bad.

She recalled little else from being six. And what she did remember still felt present tense.

Geneva would default to that back hallway confinement over the years, especially for running with the neighborhood boys and coming home dirty. *But what's so wrong with getting dirty when you can just wash off?* Ranita asked, earning an extension on her punishment.

She developed ways to pass the hours of exile. Singing silently. Saying her prayers. Making up stories about the seafaring adventures of two sisters, Fazoo and Fazizzle, aboard the boat they'd built together. Pretending she was Cam Jansen, solving mysteries; then Annie, time-traveling with her brother in their magic tree house; Esperanza, writing herself into the world; and Janie, finding love with Tea Cake before rabies turned him vicious.

And along with 6, 13 was largely a conscious blank.

Years later, she would try to remember the good things about that time. The straight-A report cards and not her time in the principal's office. Her homemade battery producing light and the class projects she'd done with whoever else wasn't paired up. Helping out at her father's shop and basking in the playful ease as she learned how an engine worked to the backdrop of soul oldies. Going with Val to the movies and then for tea and scones. She tried to hold on to those, but it seemed as though the whole of 1996, shadow and light, got swallowed.

The final time her mother ordered her to the back hallway, Ranita was still aching from the loss of Lori Watson a month before. She stood in exile for a moment, looking at the three closed doors. Through the burglarproof wire across the window on one she could see her garden, teeming with color. And on the other side of the kitchen door she could hear singing. She looked at the third, which led to her father's basement retreat. After rushing home at Geneva's urging, he had talked Ranita down from her high-wire defiance and returned to work, leaving her contrite for alarming him and entrusting Geneva to deal with the consequences of her latest trespass. Looking at the doorknob, Ranita remembered the time when her kaleidoscope had been just on the other side of that door and she'd been too afraid to turn the knob and get it.

Fuck this, she thought, enjoying the taste of the curse word she had taken to using, in her head. She opened the door to the basement and walked through, and when she got downstairs she put on a Cassandra Wilson record, *Blue Skies*, one of her father's favorites, and sat on the couch singing along. The music helped to soothe her anxiety at the showdown she was provoking with Geneva, as she'd started calling her, also in her head, but whatever happened, it had been worth it, the view she'd claimed from way up high. When she heard her mother come down the stairs, Ranita didn't even meet her eyes. She carried on reading the liner notes while Geneva stood facing her, hands on her hips, fuming.

"I'm done with the back hallway thing," Ranita said, her eyes still focused on the album sleeve. "I'm done with church. I'm done with getting on the scale for you. And I'm done with dresses and skirts. You can think up new ways to punish me. Ground me. Take away my privileges . . . but wait, I don't have any."

When she stood up, she was nearly eye-to-eye with her mother. "Beat me, if you like," she said, hoping she sounded fierce and unafraid while on the inside she was quaking, and trying to steel herself for the coming explosion. And then her mother startled her by reaching over and pushing Lennox's glass lamp off the table, turning her back on the broken glass, and stomping back upstairs.

Ranita resisted the impulse to clean up the pieces of what she and her father called the genie lamp, though the only wish it ever granted was time with him. She hoped, to no avail, that he would find it and ask her what had happened. She sat back down, listening to the rest of his record, and relived that afternoon's ascent.

They had just come back from a long-winded sermon, and she was itching to get out of the uncomfortable skirt her mother insisted on and back into her real clothes. As they left the church, her mother had told her to straighten her hem and stop slouching and try not to look a mess.

"Can't you get off my case, just for a minute?" Ranita had asked, blinking back tears, and Geneva had given her typical response: "Life is a trial, Ranita; you need to get a thicker skin."

On the drive home Ranita imagined Geneva singing off-key as she lost her voice. She tried to tune her out, especially what she'd said about Pastor's concern for everybody's soul. When he was in the pulpit, Ranita did her best to picture a big black rectangle, like she'd seen in tabloid photos of disgraced celebrities, spread from his eyes to cover his whole body, but when she'd had to walk past him after the service she couldn't help looking at the gray and black hairs poking out of his nose and feeling sick.

When they got home, Geneva went inside while she checked "her crops," delighted with the audacious sunflowers, turned toward the light. She could hear her mother through the screen door, "Come in and change out of your good clothes," but she was looking up through Avery's wheel-spoke branches. The sun came through them, dappling her skin with dancing light. It was a long way up to the first branch, and even with a ladder she didn't think she could reach it. But up was where she wanted to be.

She ran inside, taking the stairs two at a time, and lifted her bedroom window as far as possible to remove the screen as she'd seen her father do in November, when winter became undeniable. And after pulling off her pinching church shoes, she climbed through.

Once she was out there, she was surprised to find that she was not afraid. Avery's needles were soft, and she caressed the worry lines on the dark trunk and gripped with her bare toes as she turned and edged her way into a place to sit. With the bark pressing into her bare skin, she wished she had taken the time to change into jeans, but still, it was magnificent up in the green. Swinging her legs, she looked down from her perch and inhaled the rich pine smell.

It was childish, she knew it, but she pictured herself on horseback, riding free. She saw herself up in a crow's nest, ocean as far as she could see.

Hearing the screen door bang shut and watching Geneva come out and walk around the yard looking for her, she tried to keep still and become part of Avery, but her mother must have detected movement in the branches. She started yelling.

"Ranita Atwater, what in God's name are you doing in that tree?!? And in a dress. I can see your underclothes!"

Careful to keep her balance, Ranita got to her feet, curling her toes around the branch for traction. And then she was climbing, pushing up into the leaves and branches to see what Avery and the animals that lived there saw and knew, pulling herself up to the next branch and the next, as though climbing a spiral staircase.

"You come down here this instant!" Geneva shouted. "Lord in heaven, you'll fall and break your neck!" She started crying, and ran inside to call Lennox home.

Holding on, her feet sore, Ranita went higher. She passed a bird's nest and a squirrel walking a tightwire, and saw past her yard, past the black and gray and brown shingle rooftops of her neighborhood.

She looked down through the branches and clusters of needles and saw her mother, staring up. She could hear and feel her panic. Her father would be there soon and she knew she'd be in serious trouble when she came down, but it was worth it.

Her mother saw her up there, out of reach. *Her eyes are open*, Ranita thought. *She's looking at me now.*

TWENTY-FIVE

When the morning light comes in over my slipshod curtains, I wish I could stay here under the covers and keep on with my private repenting for fucking up at Mario's. All night long I pled guilty to being a loser, alternating between punching and hugging my pillow, crying, cursing, praying for strength. But now I've got to get my ass up off the floor and go to work.

Waiting for the bus, I'm focusing on a gorgeous purple crape myrtle when a dude comes up and tries to catch my eye. Soon he's pitching me, asking do I live around here and where am I going and what are my plans tonight because he's free, and I try and give the shortest answers I can without being rude, but he's not getting the picture. I think about saying, *I've got a man*, to get rid of him, but I'm too pissed at his assumptions, and just say, "Look, I'm not interested." He mutters, "Bitch, you got mileage," walks a few paces away, and gives me his back. We're alone on the corner, no one else in view.

I'm noticing the sun on my arms, the music from passing cars, the thick summer light. But now I feel him looking daggers at me, and I'm just this side of losing it, telling him where I've been and what I've seen and what I'll do if he does not step off.

He's inching closer, and I'm working on keeping my fists to myself as I feel all the voices and bodies that have had their way with me, wondering why women are never safe, even when we're doing something as mundane as waiting for a ride, as basic as going to a meeting, trying to carry on or change our lives in some microscopic way. And praise God, here comes the bus, pulling to the curb and saving me from eruption.

But on the corner by my workplace there's a holy roller handing out leaflets on sinning and repenting or facing judgment, and wiping out the curse of abortion. By now I'm spitting mad, and I hold up the leaflet he hands me and tear it in half, and just as I'm about to shove it in his face and ask who appointed him decider when he doesn't even have a pussy or a womb my boss steps out to have a cigarette. I suck my outrage back into my mouth and down my throat.

I have made it here, to my job. I have not opted out of the trying that might end in failure. I have hurt no one but myself. This is its own miracle.

After I'm settled in my cubicle, I take a deep breath and look at the latest school photos of Theo and Amara that Val gave me. And here I am, my body in this morning, my mind and soul in last night.

Soon as I tasted the sweet burn of Hennessy, nothing but me and that drink existed. The first sip I savored, and the rest I downed without a pause. Head ringing, I put the empty glass on the bar and caught a glimpse of myself in the gold-veined mirror. *Ranita, is that you?* My life kaleidoscoped before my eyes.

I saw myself on the front porch, at the piano, in the garden, at church. In school and at the library and on my bike. Stumbling from the basement, and at the movies with Auntie Val, laughing and making paper flowers bloom and standing on the wall at a basement house party. Caught out by Mama and lost in encyclopedia facts. Getting schooled at Daddy's shop.

I saw Mama in folds of white satin and Daddy at the waterside.

Sleep-floating and beneath some stranger and curled up with a book. Standing bare breasted in the sunroof and sinking into temporary nothingness. Hand raised. Drifting further and further from the classroom shore. Saying my name to a circle of fellow addicts and standing up for count. Waking below ceiling stars, above Naomi, next to Jasper, and alone on Jessie's sofa bed. Nearly fainting as my skin got marked. Birthing, nursing, building wood-block cities, singing lullabies.

I looked down from Avery's branches. I saw a fish too small to keep.

I watched my people disappear from visitation and saw myself, drawing butterflies. Stripping and going elsewhere, open, entered, bruised. Seeking refuge, seeking rest. Hungry, apologizing, blissed out, ashamed. I saw Amara jumping rope and Theo's missing-front-teeth jack-o'-lantern smile. I saw myself holding a pomegranate. And between closed doors. Clean and dirty and clean. Loving. Leaving. Surrendering and fighting. On my knees.

I saw Maxine. Across the table. Beside me. In the chapel. Skin to skin.

I felt a world being conjured from her throat.

Staggered at the sum of me, I gripped the edge of Mario's bar with one hand and pushed the glass away with the other. As tempting as the promise of numbness felt, as tiring as it was just keeping aboveground, I made myself take another look. What about the garden seeds? Reunification? A bowlful of water? Song, pouring from my mouth?

Carefully, I stepped down from the barstool, got my balance, and walked out.

I pointed myself toward home and kept my eyes on the sidewalk in front of me as I listened to the steady sound of my shoes on the pavement, and when I got inside I closed the door and slid down to the floor and sat back against it, unable to stop thinking how my fingerprints were on that glass. Proof of my fuckup. At least, thank God, Goddess, Jesus, Allah, Buddha, the Orisha, Earthseed, it was a drink and not a hit, a smoke, a pill, a snort. It would not show up in my pee test. And if I confessed, it would stay inside The Rooms.

Grateful for the mindless tasks I get at work, inputting invoices and parts like in my teenage years, I focus on getting to 5:00. I think I'm keeping it all on the inside, repelling human contact of every kind, but another clerk, Theresa, she stops by my desk and asks am I okay. "Yes, yes," I reassure her, fronting like I've always done. It's just a headache that won't seem to go away.

Later, at the diversity training for recent hires, I sit here, part of me going over my lapse and part of me trying not to lose my job for cussing out the white man who's explaining to me how discrimination works.

Just before quitting time, Theresa reappears to say a group of them are going out for drinks and I should come. I'm not used to white folks reaching out with friendliness, and it takes me a beat to respond, along with deciding how to navigate the drinking part. While I'm sorting that out, she says, ". . . or not, whatever. . . ."

"No," I say, before she walks away. "I'd like to go. It's just that I'm . . . I'm in recovery. A drink's not something I can do." Feels like a lie, given what went on last night, but it's the truest truth. She smiles and steps closer, whispering, "Me too. The others get a beer. I stick with soda or iced tea." And when she gets back from her break she brings me a coffee, and won't let me reimburse her. When I thank her, the simple kindness of her gesture makes my voice crack, and after she leaves I sit here on the verge of tears.

I can't believe I've ruined my sobriety. I can't believe I have to start my counting over with one clean day, hour, minute. And I can't decide if I'm a loser for picking up, or a winner for stopping at one drink.

When the clock hits five, I drag myself to a meeting, and sit near the door through the anniversaries and the sharing. I'm tempted to stay here on my hard little chair and keep silent while the meeting wraps up. *Who really needs to know about my slipup?* I ask myself. *What difference does it make?* It's tempting to just let the "Keep Coming Back" slide on by, but something in me says, *Speak up, speak up while you can, and own what happened. Get yourself somewhere to lean.* And here I am, raising my hand.

I introduce myself, though most everyone here knows me. "My name's Ranita. . . ." I fix my eyes on a spot on the floor, and after everyone says their "Hey, Ranitas" seems like I feel all the sorrow I've ever known rise up through my body and threaten to come out in a tsunami of shaking and tears. I hold it back, think of how to start.

"Take your time, sis," someone near me says, and I hear a wave of "Amens."

I try to get my story arranged inside my head to make the best possible impression, and then give up on that. "Here's the bad news. Last night I picked up. After three and a half clean years. It feels like shit." I cast around for the right words. "And . . . and I'm not trying to dodge it, write it off as nothing . . . but there is . . . some . . . good news." I'm taking my time, like they said, but I can feel people start to fidget, and I know patience can be in short supply, no matter how much goodwill they're putting out there. I need to get on with it.

"I know where one of anything leads, but if it'd been a stronger poison I would not be here confessing today, or walking away. I'd be hustling for more. And I'm not saying . . . or thinking . . . I can start that up and manage it. So the bad news is, I found myself . . . no, strike that; I *took* myself . . . to a bar I been managing to walk past, or go into and not pick up . . . I took myself there. Ordered a drink. And downed it. The good news is . . . I stopped at one."

I know they're wondering what kind of recovering alcoholic-addict goes into a bar and expects to do anything but drink. The fucked-up kind? Guilty as charged.

They're telling me to *speak on it*, and I summarize how the special outing I tried for went awry, how Amara reproached me publicly, reminding me what messed-up, absent, shitty, low-down parents me and her father were. Are.

"There it is," I say. "I've been trying to move forward, like a new story's possible. But I was stuck back in the old one, and for a minute . . . a minute that passed, praise God . . . I couldn't figure out why I should bother working so hard to turn the page." I sigh and wipe my eyes with my hands. "It feels like shit. I feel like shit. I'ma keep trying. That's all."

The meeting wrap-up's fuzzy, and while I'm getting some bitter coffee and the brothas are thumping each other's backs in solidarity, a fiftyish-looking sista in cat-eye glasses comes up to me and comments on the coffee and how tasty the cookies I've been shoving into my mouth are.

"I've seen you here the last couple weeks," I say, brushing crumbs from my mouth and boobs. "Ranita, but I guess you already know that."

"Flora."

"How long you been coming?"

"Oh, twenty years, off and on. Every now and again I need a tune-up." She chuckles. "Listen, though I don't mean to intrude, I wanted to say something about what you're going through with your kids. Don't give up. Don't. Mantente fuerte. I been there, and the fact that your daughter's fighting you means she hasn't given up on you. You hanging in there, staying the course, that's what's important."

I want to pour out my heart to this sista-stranger. "I put so much hope into our little outing, and it seemed like it was going good. We were getting closer; at least I thought so."

"You probably were," Flora says. "That might've been what spooked her. You know what, though? It'll be up and down. And it's funny, you might be able to get custody again by trying your best to keep everything all simpatico. But your only real hope of getting another chance with your kids is by dealing with the ugly."

I'm nodding, trying to take in what she's telling me while I reach for another cookie, and then she smiles. "And didn't you say she's a teenager? One of her part-time jobs is to challenge you. Fasten your seat belt, m'hija, it's a rocky ride, even in the best of times, and you might need to work on some radical acceptance, dig into the Four Noble Truths. You meditate?"

"I . . . Not really, though I try. It's hard to get still enough sometimes." I don't admit that the feeling of relaxation itself undoes me, and that's the goal.

"Keep trying." She touches my shoulder and rubs it, adding, "My two cents, is all."

I want to, but I don't tell her that it's only recently, with my desert bowl visualizing, that I've gotten past the worry that I'm not doing it right. Enough confessions for one day. I never have been big on hugs with strangers, and I surprise myself by asking Flora can I have one, feeling like a sappy fool, and the warm feel of her hands on my shoulder blades is so good.

"Claro," she says, putting her motherly arms around me and squeezing. "I've got abrazos infinitos. They're free."

We talk some more, and she offers me a little bookcase she's getting rid of. "Maybe you can refurbish it, use it for your kids," she says. "I'll have mi sobrino bring it over to you." And before she leaves, she brings her hands together at her heart and says, "Namaste, Ranita. Namaste."

When I get home, I return to my bed, remorse my only companion, and remind myself that a mistake can be a pivotal moment. I try and imagine a body of water big enough to lose myself and salty enough to lift me up, and I swear my bed becomes a raft, tossed and turned all night by a restless sea.

I wake up feeling shitty. Not less than yesterday, but not more either, just on a shittiness plateau. And think about skipping out on therapy. We've been meeting every week. I guess he can tell we're heading for the deep, but I'm not feeling it today, dark and seedy as it is where Drew Turner's excavating. And I can't even tell him what's right at the surface: picking up at Mario's and seeing my life flash before me, just like I was drowning. It would probably be a relief to get it off my chest, but I can't afford to give him any ammunition that'll count against reunification. Speaking of which, being absent for my session will have the same result.

I arrive five minutes late, but I do get here and take my place on the couch, wishing there was a seat belt I could fasten before going backward.

Today he's asking about the feeling that using gave me and I'm trying to tell about the pull of nothingness, of being hollowed out and somehow full, but words don't seem to capture it. I wish I could somehow make him understand how the hurts, and unfortunately, everything else, too, melted away with dope, and what it feels like to trade in the mercy of forgetting for clarity. While I'm thinking about how to answer his question on how that awakeness feels, Drew Turner says, slowly, carefully, "Many people dealing with addiction have experienced trauma. . . ."

I focus on the painting across from me and rant inside my head, channeling Maxine, feels like. *Trauma. Which one? Captivity, racism, state violence, state control, centuries of exploitation, misogyny . . . ?*

"It can be buried," he says. "Something we don't talk about . . . that hasn't stopped hurting. It can be something from childhood that's still running the show."

His words settle in the quiet.

I can hear people on the other side of the door.

I can hear my shallow breathing.

And the clock ticking.

And my heartbeat skirring.

I am tender to the touch. My eyes are open, but I cannot see. And I feel leather-covered buttons, pressing into my 12-year-old skin.

Down in the tiny space I've squeezed it into, I can feel my secret turning, stretching, wanting out.

I want to tell.

But I've been keeping it in for a quarter century, and I'm afraid it'll feel even realer if I speak it; I'm afraid it'll bloom into Technicolor life if I share it; I'm afraid I'll break apart from shame.

I breathe deep and look at Drew Turner. Maybe he's willing and able to meet a Ranita who won't make the others even smaller and dirtier. Maybe he can know and still respect me. Maybe, maybe I can rest.

I close my eyes and see myself, at the top of the stairs.

I am 36. I am 12.

I am one entire bruise.

It comes out in jumbled pieces, but I tell it how I lived it. And when I come up and out of the church basement, Drew Turner's here, and in his face I see endless compassion and not a trace of pity.

"You're the only one I've ever told," I say. "You must feel special. Like you won the Powerball."

I did come close to telling once, or close to letting out my hurt, if not the cause. Thanksgiving weekend. Mama and Daddy on the den couch, watching the news. And me in the doorway.

Earlier that night, as I ate my portion of turkey leftovers, along with about a tablespoon of stuffing, she'd tossed a pebble into the still waters and left me flailing in what felt like rapids.

"Pastor's thinking of leaving for Detroit," she said. A church there needed him, and she knew it was selfish, but she wished he wouldn't go. "Not that that means a thing to you, Ranita," I remember her saying, "since I have to make you go to church these days."

I kept it together until she excused me from the table. But when I got up to my room one tear got free and before I knew it I was sobbing like I'd been gutted. When I showed up in the doorway of the den, they looked like they'd been caught in oncoming headlights, bystanders to a crash or a horror movie stalking, fear all over their faces while their nightmare caught up to them. Frozen in place until Mama looked at him to deal with it, and he got up to hold me. Neither one of them had the faintest idea what to say to me or how to ask what had happened, what was wrong.

I wiped my nose on my sleeve, even though I knew what Mama thought of that, and my sobbing finally slowed and died out, until the only sound in the room was my hitching breath.

People always ask survivors, when they're trying to decide whether to believe them, why they didn't fight back and why they didn't tell. It's staggering how big the fellowship of the violated is in The Rooms and behind the walls, and I've heard the pain that echoes from those questions countless times. For real, though, I am haunted for my silence, by the ones who must have come later to those basement prayer sessions. More hungry ghosts.

Drew Turner doesn't ask me why I've never told. He helps me hold my grief and make an anchor to the present. And he brings the news I need.

My eyes and mouth and nose, my arms and hands and fingers, legs and feet, backside and insides, neck and chest and skin, every place that should have been private, every part that's vital to the whole, it's mine. It's alive. It deserves love.

"You are here," he says. "You are yours."

He gives me some resources to check out. Survivor networks. Groups I can tap into. Yoga. And after our put-yourself-back-together ritual, I leave his office, feeling shaky, but a little bit lighter, until I stop to lean against a building and flash on a jumble of memories, things inescapable and things unhaveable, wondering what else will be dragged into the light.

My people are out in the warm weather. Washing their cars and sitting out front with cool drinks, telling stories, laughing, playing cards, freeing up their tired bodies to music. Running through the shimmering spray of water from a sprinkler or a hose. Shooting baskets. Planting

flowers in whatever space they've got. Trading "Afternoon" with me as
I walk by.

I'm amazed at how we carry on with the daily, what with everything
it takes to hold your head up and declare that you're a human. On
the lookout for all the free things I can see and might reclaim, I come
across a piece of glass that looks like nothing special, amber brown and
scratched, part of a medicine bottle, I suspect, for tonic or pills, and a
piece of milk glass, like that bumpy white candy dish Mama kept on the
piano, and add them to my pocket.

"It'll never be gone, will it?" I asked Drew Turner before I left his
office.

"It can play a different role in your story than it has." His eyes were
soft, like usual. "It's a part of you, Ranita, but so is everything about you
and your precious life."

TWENTY-SIX

1995

From the top of the stairs, Ranita looked at the door to the basement office, where the Tuesday afternoon prayer meetings happened.

For the last few weeks she'd made excuses to her mother, but today Geneva had told her she was going, she'd be outside the school to pick her up at three sharp, and she was lucky Pastor Johnson had taken a special interest in her.

That he had. *Your mother tells me you're an excellent student, honor roll, top of your class*, he said. *We must tend the spirit and the body, as well as the mind. . . . I'm his servant. He works through me. And you can call me Pastor J.* Like a friend, she'd thought, or at least friendly. A friendly minister who saw some promise in her that her mother didn't, who would read scripture with her, develop her understanding, deepen her faith.

By the time Geneva picked her up at school, Ranita had taken off the leggings she brought each day in her backpack to put on before classes started. Her mother wanted her looking like a young lady, in skirts and dresses, so Ranita had come up with a strategy, and now that she was back in her skirt and headed to the church her legs were covered with goose bumps and it felt like she was breathing through cotton wool.

As they pulled up, she had sat looking out of the windshield as she tried to get her breath. "Go on, Ranita; he's waiting." Her mother said it twice.

And now here she was, at the bottom of the stairs, though she couldn't remember walking down.

The first time, Pastor J had explained that he had to help her, had to *check her for sin, arrest what was taking shape in her, make certain she was intact.* Afterward, once she was home, she had gone straight to the bathroom to clean herself, that last word echoing in her mind. From a vocab quiz she knew its meaning. Uninjured. Entire.

The door opened.

And the furniture polish and pipe smoke and limey aftershave smells collected in her throat. "Come in," he said, and then blocked the egress with his huge body once she was over the threshold. He motioned to the couch with a welcome? A command? She tried not to see his hands, and then perched at the edge of the brown leather, avoiding the diamond-shaped tufts with buttons at their points.

He shut the door and turned the lock.

"But why?" she asked, when she felt the couch sink with his weight. What had she done wrong that she had not been punished for?

Here she was again, cold and limp, her skirt all bunched and scratchy around her middle, and his hands and his voice and his heavy manatee body, and his big breathing, and the wool smell of his suit and aftershave and his nose hair and the hand that was hurting her and the hand with little sprouts of hair between the knuckles covering her mouth, and the couch buttons and the screech of her shoes against leather.

This time she didn't close her eyes. This time she bit her cheek and her tongue, too, focusing on the iron taste, and looked up at a spidery crack on the ceiling. The fading began with pinpricks in her toes and fingertips, and then spread through hands and feet, arms, legs, torso, until she came apart like perforated paper.

From a distance, Ranita heard Pastor J tell her to pull her skirt down. And then she felt the absence of his weight and scooched backward, bringing her knees to her chest to cover them.

He shook his head, as though it made him so sad and disgusted, what he'd had to do, and just like last time he reminded her, "Our special time here, it's our secret, ours and God's. He is always watching, but it's our secret. Your mother . . . your family . . . . the whole congregation, they'll all know about you if you tell. They'll all know what I had to do, and they'll be sorely disappointed. In you, Ranita Atwater. In you."

They *would* be disappointed, Mama and Daddy, Auntie Jessie, Auntie Val, the church, her people. She knew they would. But she wasn't sure God cared one way or another about her.

And now she was in the hallway and the office door was closing. In her mouth was the metal. In her skin, in her everywhere, was the tobacco, and the cologne, and the buttons, and him.

And she wanted to go, but she couldn't figure out the stairs; she couldn't get her body parts to work together; she couldn't find up and out. And her vision was blurry. Turning, turning round and round, her breathing fast and ragged, she heard the office door open behind her, and groping for the wall her hands found the railing, and she stumbled up, tripping and cutting her shin on a metal stair strip that had pulled loose from its rubber tread.

Her mother waited in the car with the engine running. "What took you so long?" she asked when Ranita pulled the door open and climbed in. Unable to meet Geneva's eyes or speak, she turned away and looked through the side window at the thinning October trees.

"How did you get that?" Geneva asked, pointing to Ranita's leg.

"It's nothing," she answered. "I can't even feel it."

TWENTY-SEVEN

When going backward is so overwhelming I'm stuck in neutral, my desert bowl visualizations help. I always begin the same way, me thirsty and sand as far as I can see, but what happens next varies. Sometimes the mysterious woman holds it out to me and I take it into my hands. Sometimes I notice the half-buried bowl and free it from the sand myself. Sometimes I offer it to someone else. I try and be at peace with however it unfolds, while staying hopeful. The bowl hasn't filled with water yet, but I'm hanging in here, waiting.

I've been seeing Drew Turner twice a week for help with what all's been surfacing, with the call to remember, so I might be able to forget. I've been to one survivors' group. And I've tried an online yoga class that I streamed on my phone. Like with meditation, it's hard relaxing, being still.

The grief comes and goes. Last week I was walking in the park at lunchtime when I saw a carefree girl flying a dragon kite while her folks watched. For real, you never know what someone's been through, but there I was, crying as I saw a lightness of spirit in that thin brown girl that I couldn't remember feeling. I left work early. Spent the rest of the day in bed.

Got back up the next morning and kept on keeping on.

I've been steady with work, meetings, therapy. Twenty-two sober days now, with the help of my new sponsor, Flora. I've even gone for overpriced coffee with Theresa. And I've been reading up a storm.

I've hung in with the kids, too, carrying on like the zoo trip shitshow didn't faze me, and I think it must have been cathartic for Amara, since there's been no open warfare since. I asked them to pick the next outing and they wanted to see *Avengers: Endgame*, so we went to a matinee at the theater on the Common, where we got our favorite snacks and enjoyed the free-for-all experience, the audience amped and talking, to each other and the screen. Took me back to those outings with Val.

Since we were so close to the Public Garden, I suggested we go on a swan boat ride. Daddy took me once and it's been on my list of things a family in Boston oughta do together. They couldn't believe how slow the boat went, how small the pond was, but I was happy. Slow and small was feeling alright to me. Then we walked around, people-watched, sat on a bench eating hot dogs. And then last week they let me come along to Jessie's for puzzling and cookie baking. All in all, there've been some rough spots, but I keep on showing up.

Another thing I've kept doing is hoping Val would give the rules another bend and let the kids have a sleepover at my place. I invited her to come over and when she said yes I had to swing into action to get everything ready.

I scrubbed like mad, remembering the weekend housecleaning ritual from growing up, Mama's eagle eye making me nervous not to do a "slipshod job." I sprayed and scoured. Steel-wooled the cooktop and faucets and sink. Polished the windows and mirrors. Took a toothbrush to the bathtub grout.

Cleaned myself up as much as possible, too. Almost felt like I was going on a date. Put a hot oil treatment in my hair. Used the belching iron I got at Goodwill to press my clothes. Moisturized my skin and soaked my feet. Brushed my teeth so hard my gums bled.

I got a bag of clementines and arranged them in a wooden bowl. It's the kind of homey touch you see in magazines, on a coffee table. But you need a couch for a coffee table to make sense, don't you? Well, I've got neither, but I do like the way the orange looks on the blue tabletop, and the way the bookcase from Flora looks after I painted it red.

When Val got here, I was so anxious I broke out in a sweat. Then I tried too hard. "Let me show you around," I said, which was idiotic. You can see the whole apartment soon as you cross the threshold. I pointed out the futon chairs that fold out into beds, the games and books from the library sale, the healthy food choices in the fridge and cabinets.

As she looked around, I couldn't help seeing my place through her eyes. And the unavoidable truth was, it looked *common*, one of Mama's favorite put-downs. You could stand against one wall, spit, and have it hit the opposite one. The little stove and fridge looked like they belonged in a playhouse. Nothing matched. The framed pictures were dime-store tacky; the fold-out futons were neither chairs nor beds; my mattress was on the floor. The bowl of fruit was a pathetic try at domesticity, and Daddy's ship-in-a-bottle looked trapped and senseless.

I was about to apologize when Val turned to me, and just as I was trying to decide if her smile was mocking, I could see it reached her eyes.

"The place looks real nice, Ranita," she said. "You're doing great."

Since then she got me started on a knitting project, patiently showing me how to cast on, do the different stitches, follow a pattern. I was all thumbs at first, dropping my needles and my stitches, but I've been practicing, and the weave's getting tighter and more even, and I'm making fewer mistakes. My first project was a mugly scarf, but Val said keep it, remember my progress. I'm working on mittens for the kids, even though it's July.

Now the sleepover's a reality. They're coming today and I'm trip-ping. It's what I've been hoping for, but it might feel a whole lot differ-ent than a short visit, or an outing that gives us something definite to do. Let's face it, though, it can't go any worse than the zoo trip. Like Daddy used to say, you can't fall off the ground.

When Val pulls up with Amara and Theo, I'm waiting out front, praying no drama kicks off and watching out for uninvited guests. When she drives away, I tell them how excited I am we've got this time to-gether, sounding corny and fake upbeat. They just follow me in with their rolling overnight bag and bump it down the stairs. And when we get to the bottom, before I put my key in the door, I surprise myself by saying, "Look, you being here means more to me than I can say, and I'm just grateful you're willing to give me a chance. . . ."

"Isn't that what we been doing since you got back?" Amara asks.

"Yes. Yes, it is." I cannot believe how stupid she can make me feel. It's the teenager's special talent; that's what Flora says. I'm on the verge of warning the kids not to expect too much, but I hold my tongue, and soon as we come through the door I point out the table and bookcase, hoping they'll notice their favorite colors, and the games we can play later, and show them the tiny bathroom I tried to spruce up with bright touches I found on clearance. Their toothbrushes are waiting in a cup along with mine.

They walk around the room, checking everything out, pulling back the homemade curtains to look up through the bars at the street, and I'm hoping they can't see the safety pins. Amara stands there a long time, looking out, which makes me anxious. From across the room, I say, "You know how I named the trees at the house when I was your age? I was thinking about what to call those oaks. Got any ideas?"

She says nothing, and even from behind her body language says *who gives a fuck?* It cuts to the quick, acting like I haven't spoken, like I'm not even here, and I offer lemonade and go to the kitchen to collect myself.

When I come out, they're bent over Daddy's bottled ship, saying they remember it from his basement cave. Then Theo runs over to the clementines, asking can he have one. Amara wants pears, and while I'm cutting them into wedges she comes and stands right next to me at the counter. She's two inches away, so close I can smell her candy lip gloss and Vaseline, and I want to pull her into my arms and squeeze her tight, tight, but instead I try and carry on slicing without missing a beat. Anything to keep her standing right here by my side, almost touching me. I imagine her putting her arm around me, leaning against me, or walking away, more likely, but she stays right here until I finish, and then reaches out to get the bowl and takes it over to sit with him.

"This is cool, Mama," he says, unfolding his futon and stretching out while he peels a clementine. "Try yours, Amara; see how nice it is." She sits down on hers but doesn't open it or say a thing. Then she points to the burnt-orange throw and asks, "Is that Auntie Jessie's?"

"No, I made one for myself, too." Then there's just the sound of Theo slurping. I fight the impulse to take out the half mitten I've been making as concrete proof of my devotion and mama skills, telling myself I don't have to do everything today and this is not show-and-tell. "Well," I say, trying to fill the blank space, "how about ordering some pizza? We can get it from a place a few blocks over, and even have it delivered." They love, love, love pizza, they say, and then go back and forth about what to get on it.

While we're waiting for the food, Theo asks do I have any games on my phone. I suggest he do some drawing and get him set up at the table with watercolor pencils while Amara puts in her earbuds, leans back, and checks out. It's gonna be a long night. I ask Amara twice what she's listening to before she takes one earbud out, answers, "Cardi B," and puts it back.

I just nod, thinking how much nerve it takes for me to be upset, but is that music for 13-year-olds? I'll have to take that on later, no doubt about that. For now, I hope the pizza gets here quick.

I hand her the iTunes card Theresa gave me, saying, "Maybe you can use this, get yourself some more music." She puts it on the floor next to where she's sitting, and when she goes to use the bathroom Theo motions me over and whispers that she found the iPod on the playground and Auntie Val doesn't know about it and she can't add music to it without using the internet connection and Val keeps a strict watch on that. *Good going, Ranita.* I've given her a present she can't use.

When the pizza comes, we clear Theo's pencils and paper from the table, "just for now," and while we put out place mats and plates he tells me he's drawing David Price, his World Series hero. He asks how many pieces of pizza he can have, and when I answer, "As many as you want," he puts three on his plate. *Wow,* I'm thinking, *this kid's got an appetite, what with the four clementines he's polished off.* We all sit down and dig in, and he tears through the first and second pieces, and then stalls on the third, looking defeated.

"You don't want that, baby?" I ask. "You full?"

"I'm sorry," he says, looking down. "I tried." I nod and he says, "Sorry," again.

"Hold up; it's okay. I was only asking; I'm not *mad.*"

"I bit it, and now nobody else can eat it. I been wasteful. I know."

I sense a stifled cry beneath his words, but Amara speaks before I can ask what's up. "You have to finish everything on your plate in afterschool."

"Miss Penny said if you know what's good for you, you'll eat it. And I was always messing up."

"Okaaaay. Tell me some more about Miss Penny."

He shrugs, and again Amara speaks, liking the chance to be the designated talker, it seems. "Miss Penny's all about rules. You gotta do everything just like she says. Once she tried to get Theo to eat raisins and he wouldn't do it. Raisins are his death fruit. When I got there to pick him up at six, he was still sitting at the table with his little red boxful. He'd been there since four thirty, and missed all the games and homework. He wasn't allowed, until he finished everything. His head was down on the table. That's against the rules, too."

I'm flashing on the back hallway, and detention, and here she is, Volcano Ranita, hot and ready to blow. I try and speak evenly. "And what happens if you break the rules?"

He finds his voice. "I try not to, but I keep on messing up. She's mean."

I go and get the ice cream from the freezer and start scooping it into bowls. Inside my head, I vow to put my foot up the bitch's ass. I'll go over there . . . and make her sorry . . . and . . . *Get a grip, Ranita,* I tell myself. *Get a damn grip. Just listen; just see what they've got to say.*

"What kind of mean?" I ask with phony lightness, coming back to the table.

The story pours out. "She didn't let me play. Basketball or soccer or anything. She said I was a troublemaker and made me clean up while everyone else was playing. And when I was doing my homework, she talked to me like I was dumb. 'Can't you *do* this? Don't you *know* this? Weren't you *paying attention* in class?' Like that. If I tried to talk up for myself, she said I was being insubordi . . . something. . . . She gets beyond mad when you don't act like you know she's the boss . . . But she's not the hitting or even hollering kind of mean. She's the I'm-a-treat-you-like-you're-nothing kind of mean. But you know what, Mama? That can hurt as much as fists."

"Yes." I do know.

I'll have to think on how to find out what he knows about fists and what to do about Miss Penny. For now, I do what I've been taught and push something sweet to soothe. "You-all used to love chocolate ice cream. It's just the store brand, but . . ."

"It is good, Mama," he says, beaming a smile at me, and I feel a surge of love. My chest's too small to house my heart.

I get up and kiss his temple, and that little inhale at the hairline, shea butter and shampoo and him, smells too good to describe. "Look at how beautiful you are, Theo Atwater. You always were smart, and kind, and curious. Don't you let this Miss Penny, or anyone else, step on that or make you doubt yourself. I promise you, I'll be dealing with her."

Amara rolls her eyes. "Uh-oh, someone's gonna be going off. Let me know when so I can make sure I'm absent that day."

"Not like that. I won't be making a scene. But I will be taking action, don't you worry." Then I change the subject. "What about you, Amara? How's track and field going?"

"It's okay. I'm good at running. I like winning."

She talks about the hundred-meter and hurdle, the relays, and what they do at practice. And then she mentions that her coach, "Mr. Wilson, but we call him Anthony," thinks she's special, and he's working with her one-on-one, sometimes after the other girls have left. She looks shy and proud. "He says I could maybe do the citywides in high school. He says he sees something special in me."

Special . . . one-on-one . . . after the other girls have left. My skin's buzzing and the hair on my neck wakes up, but I keep my voice calm. "That's great, baby. I know you can make the citywides if you work at it." I don't want to sully this thing she's feeling good and proud about. Sometimes people come correct. Good, nourishing intentions, they do exist in the world. But.

It's an acrobatic feat to prepare your kids for the real, while keeping them open and loving. They learned to be wary and careful with the police early . . . too early, these kids of mine. But I haven't had the first, formal White People Talk with him, or the Sex Talk with her. And I haven't tried warning them without scaring them about the predation that's out there, masquerading as help. I will look and listen, even if I think I can't bear to know the answer.

I've just started earning their trust, and I'm working hard at building a good-times bridge, but now they're looking at me, puzzled. Waiting. Sitting in my first-ever very-own apartment, opening up to me while I'm swamped by the past. Finally, I manage to say something.

"Well, that sounds real positive, and if not . . ." Fuck, where am I going with this? "Look, I meant to say I'm sure he does recognize your specialness and talent, because it's obvious. Anyone can see it." My statement's rosy, but the vibe's awkward. Loaded. Wrong.

"Listen, I'm sorry I sound negative. I'm working on . . . I've been looking back. . . ." Oh, fuck, I'm ruining our sleepover and I don't know how to do this. I'm fighting for composure, but my fingertips are numb and prickly and I get up so fast I knock my chair over, mumbling that I'll be back in just a minute as I set it right, I just need to use the bathroom. When I've closed the door and I'm alone, I sit on the toilet seat and take slow, deep breaths until the dizzy fading lets up.

My heart is breaking for Daddy, and I miss Maxine so hard I could roar. And I can't help thinking about what they're up to at Oak Hills. And I'm glad I don't have to report back to them on how it's shaping up out here.

Back at the table, I try again. "Okay. What I want to say is, growing up, some things were complicated. Difficult. And in my recovery . . . and in therapy . . ." Yes, therapy. ". . . in therapy, I'm working on ways to deal with it." My breathing is thready, but I pause and feel my feet on the floor and my hips and legs against the chair.

"Sometimes . . . things happen, and you push them down, below the surface. Because they hurt. And then those things, they can feel like they're stalking you . . . like they're waiting around the corner to jump you or trip you up, and . . ."

Amara's focusing in on me, leaning toward me, squinting. And I'm trying to stay right here, wishing the adult in charge would show up.

I notice the mostly untouched ice cream's getting a skin on it, and I tell them they can get fresh scoops if they want, but they sit quietly.

"And . . . ?" Amara says.

"And . . ." I press the balls of my feet down and focus on this body of mine . . . starting with fingers and toes and moving inward and up. . . . I can't seem to speak, and from their frowning faces I can see I've got them worried.

"What I'm *trying* to say is . . . it can wreck you, in the end, to keep what pains you to yourself. I know we're just figuring out how to be together again, how to be a family, and I want our time to be special and fun . . ."

I stop myself from biting my cheek. And say, "But even more than that, I want to be a parent you can come to, who can help you with whatever it is you're dealing with."

It's dusk, that softest time of day, and my kids are looking at me with tenderness. When I get up and turn on the light, my hands are shaking, and they stand, too, and help me clear the table.

I suggest we play some Scrabble. Think of it as a practice round, I tell them, glad to be moving us into lighter territory and thinking of the fun deficit of my growing up. I found a tired old set at a yard sale, the kind of thing they call vintage so they can jack up the price, and I don't really know if the kids will like a word game, but I wasn't so into it either and now I miss it something fierce.

When I got it home, I searched through the tiles for a Y and started carrying it around. Felt like an amulet, and I liked being able to reach in my pocket and touch the little rectangle. If I could figure out how to get it past the mail screeners, I'd make myself a replacement from cardboard and send it to Maxine. I like to imagine her opening the envelope and finding the letter that would make her set whole.

I return it to the box and watch Theo pick each tile deliberately, like his care will bring good luck. Once we're playing, Amara helps him, not making his words for him, but guiding. And as she moves her tiles around on her own rack, strategizing, maximizing her score, I feel glad for her willfulness, even if it's hard for me. She'll need it to make her way.

I look for special meaning in the words they make, storing every little thing I notice so I can go over it once they've left. I want to know all the things I've missed but remind myself that no one really wants to be their mama's meal.

When we decide to pause the game, Theo opens up his futon bed and stretches out to watch a video, and I offer to braid Amara's hair. "I've got skills," I say, telling how it helps to have something to trade at Oak Hills.

She shrugs. "Okay, if you want."

"If *you* want. Just offering."

She wants. And follows me into the bathroom so we can wash her hair. As I peel down to my tank top, I see her looking at my shoulder. I paid an Oak Hills sista who was good with a needle and a ballpoint pen to camouflage Jasper's name with foliage, though I can still make him out in the thicket.

"You erased him," Amara says.

I tell her I just gave him some context. And as I get her positioned over the tub and turn on the water, I ask what she remembers about him, bracing myself.

"Mostly I remember him being gone. I didn't see much of him, except on your skin."

I soap and rinse, then say, "I thought of something specific, something concrete . . . about his imagination." She's quiet, waiting till I go on. "Maybe you remember how he always had his camera. His photos were . . . penetrating. Beautiful. But he was never satisfied with them, in the end, and he only printed or mounted a few. They were never good enough. I used to have boxes of negatives and contact sheets . . . maybe they're somewhere at the house. In any case, looking through the camera lens seemed to tame his demons. But the more he got caught up, the less he looked.

"Anyway, back when you were just a toddler, he started taking photos of shoes he'd found abandoned on the street. A suede moccasin flattened by car wheels. Mismatched heels, one black leather, one peach satin, on their sides and just touching, between curb and car. A polished men's Oxford, perched on a pile of household things . . . toaster, pillow, rickety chair . . . eviction aftermath, looked like.

"He never arranged or even touched them. He snapped them just as he found them. And then he'd make up stories, and we'd riff about who'd left them and why, what they'd meant to their owners, whether they knew they were missing and were coming back. *Shoe Stories*, he called the project. He dreamed of it becoming an exhibition . . . an installation . . . a coffee table book, but, well . . .

"Anyway, that's what I loved about him. His eye. The way he paid attention. The way he noticed something discarded and saw a whole world in it."

"Tell me."

"Well, just the other day I saw a shoe story, though I almost walked right by it. A glint of gold caught my eye and I noticed a pair of party shoes, black patent leather with shiny ankle straps, side by side on the sidewalk and toes lined up against a stockade fence. I pictured the owner holding on to the fence with one hand for balance while unbuckling them with the other.

"Maybe their feet hurt. Maybe they no longer fit the evening's mood. Maybe they'd had enough enjoyment from them, and wanted to share the wealth. Or maybe it was habit, and they always lined their shoes up right next to their bed, like me at Oak Hills. Maybe they'd been wearing them to please someone, and decided they'd had enough and stepped free. Maybe they had to run."

She's quiet while I'm rinsing, and I'm wondering why I had to go dark with my speculating. And then she says, "I saw what you carved into the tree out back. The one you call Devon."

My heart careens. "Jasper carved it, not me."

"Was there a baby before me?" she asks. "Why aren't our names there?"

I'm struggling for how to explain.

"Soon after we met, he carved his name and mine. I didn't like it, marking the tree like he owned it, but he carried on, driven by what he wanted . . . one of his flaws. Then, when I was pregnant with you, he was sure you'd be a boy." I pause and watch her face for hurt, but she's giving nothing up. "And he was fixated on the name Duncan. He liked the meaning."

" 'Dark warrior.' I looked it up."

"Yes. He added it before I knew what he was doing. I thought about marking it out, or having him put 'Amara' once I'd named you. But again, I didn't want to do more damage. It seemed pretty hidden. I should have at least talked to you. Explained. But one of *my* flaws is pushing away the truth and burying it.

"He put all three of our names on his body. And I got his, though it wasn't . . . exactly . . . freely . . . I'll leave that for later. I thought adding the leaves and brambles would help me go forward.

"But also, marking yourself with someone's name . . . it's not the same as showing up for them. It seems like action, but it can just be a sentimental tribute. Cheap talk, that's what Auntie Jessie would say."

I'm massaging her scalp. Her shoulders have relaxed, and I'm praying a channel's opening between us. And I wish this closeness could go on and on, but I don't want to push my luck. I dry her hair and wrap it in a towel, and we go and sit with Theo.

Seems like having her back to me eases things up, and I'm thinking of the times I combed and plaited her hair before school, when I was on my mothering game. She would talk about her schoolmates and what she thought the characters in her storybooks would do after the last page. I'm happy for the chance to recapture it, her on the floor between my knees, my fingers in her hair, and as I oil her scalp I'm also thinking of Maxine. How we tended each other in this way.

I make sure to go easy, remembering how I stifled my cries as Mama yanked out the tangles and pulled my hair smooth. Amara asks can I cornrow the front and keep the back loose, and by the time I'm done she's yawning and my hands are hurting and it's late.

She runs to the bathroom to look, and I hope she's pleased. When she comes out smiling, I can't believe how beautiful she is.

"Thanks," she says, beaming. "It looks great."

"Anytime."

After more pizza and ice cream, Theo picks a chapter book and we read out loud. And when I say it's time for bed, we make up the futons together, wash up, and settle in. And once we're stretched out and the lights are off, I can hear their breathing. Maybe in time I can tell them about Maxine. It would be awful for something so good to fester in secret, down there with the things I'm ashamed of.

I risk disrupting the peace by talking about the grief I feel for Daddy, and ask how they're feeling about him.

"I miss fishing with him," Theo says. "I caught a *humongous* spotted bass the last time we went."

Amara laughs. "That fish gets bigger every time you tell the story."

They've got questions I can't answer about what kind of boy Daddy was and how he started fishing. "Auntie Jessie and Auntie Val would probably like to tell about him, about home. I only went fishing with him twice. The second time I was too . . . restless to appreciate it. The first time was just after Mama died; we were both in a sad and silent state."

"You never mention her," Amara says, "your mother, our grandmother. I guess you were too heartbroken. I know she'd been gone a long time, but it felt like she was all over the house. Her dishes and her piano, the curtains and things she sewed and embroidered, her figurines and furniture. But no one ever talked about her."

My belly clenches. "Well . . . she had a beautiful, operatic singing voice, clear as a bell, perfect pitch. And she gave piano lessons."

"To you?"

"I was criminally mediocre," I say, trying for funny and clever, and squirming under Amara's scrutiny. "I think everyone was relieved when I quit."

I'm stumped about what to tell them. "Let's see. . . . She wanted everything done just so. She was proper, but not shy and retiring . . . forceful, I guess I'd say, a polished iron fist without the velvet glove. Upright and uptight, I used to say in my head. And not . . . not so easy for me to please."

"Mean?" Theo asks.

I do not know how to do this. It's important to know who your people are, no question. But right now, this is beyond my limits. Can I say, like I did to Drew Turner, that I'd rather not go there?

"She was a lot of things, like all of us. Let's talk more another time."

Amara's eyes and attention are fully on me as I shift the subject.

"Listen," I say. "I don't know if you can hear me when I say this, but it's true. Maybe this will ring a bell, Amara. Theo, you were probably too little to remember, but I used to say, 'MLY. DF. Mama Loves You. Don't Forget. And Amara, you'd look at me all serious for your age and say, 'Amara Loves *You*.' "

It's quiet. Real quiet. And I'm hoping what comes through is not that I said I loved them while I answered the siren call of numbness, because what kind of love is that? they might well ask.

I step out, no cover, praying for the best. "No matter what trouble I was caught up in, underneath it there was love. An aquifer. At Oak Hills, I said it, too. Every night. I pretended you could hear me, like it traveled on a special sound wave, all the way to the house and through the doors and windows, to reach you in your beds."

They don't answer, but the silence doesn't feel hostile. It just is.

After a while, I hear Theo's breathing shift. And just when I feel myself drifting off, I hear Amara's whisper. "Mama?"

"Yes, baby."

"I just wanted to say . . . sorry."

I turn to face her and see her eyes shining in the dark. "Sorry about what?" I answer quietly, trying not to wake Theo.

"About what's hurting, what you've kept inside."

It takes me a minute to get my words out. "That means more than I can say. Now you free your mind from trouble. Think good thoughts and get some rest."

Me? I don't do much sleeping. Thrown back to this reservoir that has somehow decided to receive me, I just listen to the music of my kids breathing, and float.

The next morning I make pancakes in the secondhand skillet Jessie gave me. No, they're not from scratch, which suits us fine. Sitting with them, I try and see myself walking in the desert, finding that bowl. And here it is. Hands hold it out and I accept it. And it doesn't fill with water, not yet anyway, but I'm at peace with what's to come.

"Next time," I say, with a big smile, "let's go to the Children's Museum." Amara gives the littlest smirk, but I catch it. "Those things aren't just for little kids," I say, "and we've never been there." I almost said *the science museum* but caught myself. I used to try and make up for my misdeeds by promising something I couldn't deliver. With the price of tickets, they sure don't have in mind for folks like us to learn about science. It's out of reach, but there must be other choices. I picture Daddy at the reservoir.

"I've got Granddaddy's tackle box and poles," I say. "Maybe we could go fishing before the summer's over."

Hope, I see it on their faces. And I can't help seeing what comes along with that: fear.

Val rings the buzzer and I reach for them. Theo moves in for a hug and Amara, she takes her time but comes close in the end. What I'm about to say feels risky, and I know it'll embarrass her, and maybe make her want to remind me that she's not a baby, or even a child, but I do it anyway. I whisper, "MLY. DF," before I let go.

TWENTY-EIGHT

2004

It was a time of back-and-forth.

Ranita caromed between Jasper's attic quarters and the house that was still home. Between working the fryer at Popeyes and helping out at the shop. Between the pills that brought a blessed blur and the clarity that she wanted in theory but found harder and harder to manage in practice. Sometimes she lamented that she was a lost cause at 21, and sometimes she maintained that she didn't even have a problem.

Lately Jasper had been reciting "Invictus": "master of my fate," "captain of my soul," and it irked Ranita, since he had never plotted any real course or stuck with anything. He'd started a band, though he couldn't sing and the only instrument he played was air guitar. Decided he would get into training German shepherds, though he couldn't even make his own dog respond to "Stay." Filled his saltwater aquarium with designer fish that died when he forgot to clean the tank. "Everything he does is half-assed and halfway," said Lennox, who had taken to calling him Half Jasper.

Jasper had the problem. Jasper *was* the problem. But as Ranita told her father, she was working her way free of him and, in fact, reality was the problem.

She pictured her father looking at his watch. She was supposed to be at the shop hours ago, and she hadn't showed or called. Once again, she'd left him shorthanded.

He would be scrambling to answer calls, process payments, order parts, and jumping in to help Tommy and Blue with a converter or a busted headlight. She knew he was wondering where she was, regretting that he'd trusted her to show. And it made her heartsick to fail him again, but she could not get up. Way apart from the world in Jasper's musty, airless room where the shades stayed drawn, where the dishes and sheets were unwashed, that's where she belonged. Daddy should have known better than to count on her.

Three days later, she roused from a dim stupor and went out for food, thanking God that the third floor's external staircase allowed her to avoid Jasper's folks. What did they think was going on up there, she often wondered, no movement or sign of life for days at a time? When she got outside and saw things blooming, she remembered it was spring and shed her jacket on the banister, welcoming the sun on her skin. And instead of going to the corner store, she went home.

When Lennox got in from work and found her in her room, he woke her to ask if she had eaten, and she opened her eyes to see relief eclipse the disappointment on his face. He cooked her favorite meal, convinced her to shower, and called her to the table.

"I was out back yesterday," he said as they sat down to eat. "Remember that summer we had our side-by-side gardens?"

It seemed like a lifetime ago, but she listened as he went on about the abundance of that season. He often mythologized that summer glory, either despite or because of its happening just that once. The following year, subsumed with unexpressed grief, the two of them had hardly left the house, and she had never taken up flower farming again.

Looking back, she tried to see herself as someone who could make things grow.

"I remember," she said, picturing how the black-eyed Susans had untwisted their dark little stick-brush bundles and spread open.

She could see that he was waiting for her to continue, but she had no more to say about a moment that was long gone and nearly beyond reach. Through her gauzy fatigue, and the craving that stirred beneath it, she saw him looking at her shoulder. He'd never asked about the tattoo, and as usual, she was torn between feeling thankful she hadn't had to defend her choices and bereft.

"Come fishing with me tomorrow," he proselyted. He still thought love was a curative. He still thought his medicine might work for her.

She nodded in agreement, the easiest response. But when he woke her at five, she tried to get out of it. "I'm just too tired, Daddy. I'll go next time."

He wasn't having it. He turned the light on, put a mug of coffee on her bedside table, and stood in the doorway, waiting, as she forced herself to sit up and tried to unsee the clothes and books that covered her bedroom floor like the still, sad aftermath of a storm.

She slept against the car window the whole way there and surfaced from a dream of fighting her way through cloying foliage, feeling foggy and defenseless. And agitated. Throughout the trudge to his accustomed spot, she worked at hiding her gnawing jones and tried to figure out why this was the day she was following through, after years of promising to go. He helped her bait her hook and reminded her of how the reel worked, and there they were at the reservoir as the sun came up, their lines disappearing into the water.

It was so still and quiet that Ranita felt sure she could hear her father's heart beating steady, while hers skittered between sluggish and alarmed.

His hold on the fishing pole was loose, passive, even. And his contentment as he sat there, awake and shining like a wide-eyed boy who was new to fishing, was getting on her last nerve. Hands worn and knobby, with the dark oil traces her mother had hated . . . hair graying at the temples . . . weary shoulders bowed, he was 47 and 9, both. And he was all-in, while at peace with whatever unfolded.

She thought of the other time she'd gone with him, after Mama died, when everything had seemed muted. She'd read up on mourning traditions, and wished they'd been the kind of people to tear their clothes or keen or fall out on the floor with grief. Maybe, out in nature, they'd at least talk about Geneva and her sudden defeat. But the quiet, like the water's surface, had gone undisturbed.

She knew she'd be spared taxing conversation. But she never could figure out what to give in to and what to fight, and everything about being at the water's edge grated on her. The wide-open space. The cloudless sky and stagnant water. The silence. She was wounded, jangled, dying for either furor or rest.

Trying to sit still while the sky lightened up in slow motion, she wished she could hit fast-forward on the whole outing, though she told herself to breathe deeply and choose serenity, accept what all the moment was and wasn't. She used to know the names of the evergreens around her, and the fish species at Blue Hills, too, but she couldn't call them up. She told herself those words were still there, somewhere in her addled mind. She told herself to be happy that her father had brought her with him to the place he loved best.

But the quiet was a torment, and she couldn't wait to catch a fish and get back to what she knew. If she couldn't nest, folded warm and numb and safe, she wanted to tear through open sky. And her father's assent to whatever happened at the end of his fishing line, since he'd done his thing by showing up and putting it in the water, felt like a rebuke.

The water had no current, no flow, and she watched the glassy surface for a tug, a nibble on her line, a sign of something, anything, happening down below. The only movement was the tremble of the pole in her jittery hands. And then she let go of trying to be there and be still, and started talking trash.

"I'ma catch so many fish you won't believe it," she scatted out, jazzy and way too loud. "I'ma put you to shame."

Lennox glanced at her and then at the water, the sky, the trees. And she gave in to the momentum of her stunting, to the rush of cutting loose.

"It's not a competition, Ranita," he said quietly, when she was spent. "It's this." He held his pole with one hand and spread the other in a wide semicircle. "The point is this."

She couldn't really hear him over the static in her head. There they were, stuck at the water's edge with nothing happening. Nothing. And she was getting more worked, more fevered, more *angry* that she hadn't caught a single fish. The point? The *point*? There was no meaning, not to this exercise in aimless waiting nor to anything else, and he had the nerve to criticize her and hold forth about the fucking point.

Finally, finally, she felt a nibble and jumped to her feet to claim it, the ticking of the reel sounding louder and louder against the quiet, and there it was, above the water's surface, a fish much smaller than she expected from the way it had fought.

Her father was shaking his head. "Yellow perch," he said, and looked at her. "Too small. You've got to let it go."

Ranita held in the shriek she felt building, but she couldn't control her anger. "It's mine!" she yelled, embarrassed that she sounded more like a toddler than the woman she was supposed to be. "I caught it. It's mine!"

Despite the guilt burn beneath her breastbone, she had no intention of letting her fish go, and she told her father how she'd noticed he was pretty good at taking fish lives, at hooking them and watching while they stopped breathing, at putting wire through their gills and bringing them home to gut and scrape and fry up.

As she got to her feet her shoes slipped on the dewy grass, while she looked at the thrashing fish that was only half the size of her hand.

"You never rob the water."

He spoke quietly, kindly, reminding her of the code she knew. "You leave some for later. It's only right to take the ones that have had a chance to grow. You never fish what you can't eat."

One foot higher than the other on the sloping bank, Ranita tried to keep her footing and get ahold of her impulse to chuck his expensive pole, along with the fish dangling from its line, into the water. She was throbbing with shame now, and she wanted to change course, but the only thing she seemed to be able to do was keep to the path she was on. She threw the pole to the ground.

"Whatever you're telling yourself right now, Nita, that little fish does not belong to you."

Hardly able to bear the compassion and puzzlement she saw on her father's face, she tuned him out.

Hook in its mouth, the tiny fish flopped and gasped on the grass, and Ranita tried to keep a sob from crashing through her.

"Suit yourself, then," her father concluded, "and live with that. Have what you want, instead of what you need."

He spoke just loud enough for her to hear him. And she prayed that he would just turn away. But he kept on looking at her, his disappointment and all that helpless love of his all over his face.

TWENTY-NINE

All week I've been playing back the sleepover. And I can't help wondering about the questions I'm left with.

Just how deep are the wounds I've caused? After what felt like a bunch of big steps forward, what'll be the next step back? And what's Theo keeping inside? Has he been bullied, done the bullying, or both? Beyond Miss Penny's rule, does he sit on the sidelines, watching? Is he in the mix? And if he's in, what's the price of boy belonging? Have gangs and guns already got their magic pull? And is he already seen as dangerous, at eight?

Is there any way to keep either one of them safe?

I return to the church basement. To the marks made. Night of the living dead and the year that nearly finished me, it all comes calling, too. In fact, seems like the two obsolete keys in my backpack from that year have got wills of their own. I take them off the little ring, put them on the table, and stare at them. *What am I supposed to do, remember or forget?*

The buzzer startles me and I peer out, recognizing Judy's shoes and legs. And I wonder has she ever, in her lifetime, called before coming over.

I buzz her in and open the door, and I can tell by the way she clomps down the stairs that something's wrong.

"You sure you don't have anything more, not even a hard cider?" she asks when I offer lemonade.

"Judy. Really? You know me; you know my story. You *should* be trying to support me."

"I know, I know. I need to get to a meeting my damn self; I need to make a change. I'm getting ready to get ready to try and maybe quit."

Right. I'm not judging, but I'm not pretending with her either. No comment.

Half crying, she gets her story out in fits and starts. Turns out Ike's married and he's got a double life. He's been lying since they got together, coming up with excuses for why he's got to be away every two weeks. He's got to watch his grandbaby. He's got to take care of his sister in Hartford. He's got to take his mother to the doctor. He's got to work the graveyard shift.

And his wife, she thought he had to travel for work, until he forgot his phone one day and she looked at his texts, dialed Judy, and told him get the fuck out.

Done crying, she moves on to the practical. "Can I stay with you, Nita, just till I can get myself together?"

I go to the kitchen for more lemonade.

Judy's my people, in more ways than one. She's helped me get back on my feet. And I think of all the second, third, fourth . . . you get the idea . . . all the chances I've been given. I think of how Daddy and Jessie and Val have stood by me, and by my kids. What do I owe here? Do I need to pay it forward, stand by my cousin and take her in?

I look at her, sitting in the little room of my own I've just now managed to somehow get, bent on more than lemonade. She'll take me down, without even meaning to.

"Wait," I say, coming back to the table. "Why do *you* need a place to stay?"

"He's at my place. When his wife called I went straight off on him and walked out. Left him sitting with Oscar, on that huge fucking couch he jammed in there."

"But it's your apartment. What you need to do is put him out and get it back. You see how small this space is, and the kids . . . we just now finally had a sleepover . . . and they'll be coming again. I've got to keep it together here, no deviations from the path."

She smiles, weakly. "Deviations. You always did like fancy words."

"Look, Judy. Let's call Antoine and get Ike gone."

Staring at the table, she says, "I thought he loved me. Nothing's real."

"Loved you? Seems like the question's not whether, but how. And one thing that's *for real* for real is your name on the lease. You get what you settle for. And you don't have to give away what's yours."

Sighing, she reaches for her purse. "I'ma go by Antoine's." Before she gets up she nods at the keys on the table. "What do those open?"

I don't know what to say, and she's out the door and up the stairs without waiting for an answer.

Now it's Therapy Friday, and I don't even think about not going. Seems like maybe the worst is over. I've even stopped minding the giant flowers. My favorites are the wild violets, and I doubt Drew Turner knows it, but they're really weeds.

He starts by checking the weather, asking how I'm feeling about my sentence in the church basement, and what it's been bringing up.

I share one thing I've been thinking. That it's caused me no end of pain and anger to use the honorific "Pastor," what with the respect that title gave him as a man of God, and the power he misused. And Drew Turner says I can choose to call him something else. I'm gonna think on that.

I'm still talking about the beautiful, ordinary aspects of the sleepover. Sitting down to eat with my babies . . . doing Amara's hair and playing Scrabble and kissing my boy while he sat at my table drawing. And then the closeness and peace when we were down on the floor together.

"I was afraid I wouldn't, you know, step up."

"And what does stepping up mean?"

"Handle shit. Show up. Be strong. Take care of business, like Black women do."

He's nodding, saying without words that he feels me, and I guess the affirmation makes me reckless, because I hear myself declare, "I've always wanted to be a different kind of mother than the one I had."

He's watching me, real still, trying to decide if I can and will go there, and then he tests the waters.

"In our second session, I think it was, as we were getting started, you were direct about not wanting to talk about your mother . . . and we've steered clear, up to now. . . ." He's propping open the door I cracked, letting me decide do I want to go in, or at least take a look inside.

Here we are, finally. *Mama, it's always been about you.*

And like Drew Turner said, everything's connecting up.

What a gift to pass on, a fucked-up-mother inheritance. But even if fucked up was what you got, what kind of Black folks criticize the ones at the bottom of the totem pole, the mules of the world, like Zora broke down? Yes, Mama was the knot I'll always be untying. But she had it rough, and she sacrificed for me, in ways I don't even know.

I collect myself and go into the routine I've refined over the years, turning the ways she made me feel small and wrong into a funny story. Offering up what she found fault with, the ways I erred and fell short and failed to win her affection and was way too much, as comedy. I'm doing my Geneva show, imitating her posture and operatic voice, joking about her convoluted punishments.

Mostly, on the rare occasions when I've talked about Mama, that's how I've gone at it, like she was a character in a sketch comedy or sit-com, like her words and deeds caused slapstick trips and falls that hap-pened to someone else.

Geneva sang everywhere, even on the toilet. . . . Geneva folded her arms and trapped me in the back hallway, and I got smaller and smaller, until I could almost fit through the keyhole and slip outside. . . . Me quitting the piano was proof of divine intervention. . . . I was so fat she counted out the eight green beans I was allowed for dinner. . . . When she kicked the bucket, I shoulda slipped my report card into her casket and said, "See ya on the flip side, Moms, now that your eyes are permanently closed" . . . She ran from the kryptonite of my kisses.

Drew Turner's not laughing. Or even smiling.

His eyes are caterpillar soft, like usual, and reflecting back my sad-ness. And he's waiting, but I don't know how to tell it real.

"It's nothing," I hear myself whisper. "She didn't abuse me, or any-thing like that. I guess that's why I can joke about it."

I'm doing a new variation on the evading from our early sessions, trying to keep the tangled mother-daughter skein wound tight. But Drew Turner, he tugs the thread I've left hanging.

"How *did* she treat you?" he asks, and then waits patiently for me to answer.

Oh man. Have I got a right to complain? I've heard family stories on the street, in The Rooms, behind the walls, that could make my hair straighten and fall out. And I always thought if I *was* going to breach the code of loyalty, I should lead with her strengths, with what an unwav-ering force she was, and how good she was at so many things. And her musical talent, which never had a fit scope. One image plays at the edges of my memory, and then takes shape: her uplifting solo of "Precious Lord."

I came up in an "unbroken" family, in a house we were on our way to owning, with a backyard and books and enough food on the table. I had a mother who was talented and polished, who had two years of college and could sing and cook and sew, and a father who earned enough from his own business to support us, most of the time, and who stayed by me through thick and thin. Mama seldom hit me. She didn't starve me. She didn't leave. And her high expectations, they were a kind of privilege, weren't they? I was luckier than most. Luckier than my own kids, truth be told.

I don't even have to wonder did she have it hard, though the facts I've got are few. Coming up in Florida in the sixties and seventies. Going to eight different schools while they moved around for work. Secretarial instead of music school. Breaking with her family and never going back. She used to say, *Ranita, you must toughen up; you have no choice. Trust God. And expect as little as possible from people.* She held herself apart, composed and locked away. Who knew what was going on inside?

If she hadn't died, maybe she would've softened. Let me know her. Let *me* soothe her. If she hadn't died, maybe I wouldn't be stuck with grief for going low right along with her, at the end.

I grab a pillow and squeeze, glance at the painting across from me. "It's such old news. . . ."

Gently, Drew Turner says, "Like we've been finding, there's really no such thing. Especially in here."

I look down, trying to figure out how to begin, what to say without an unspooling that'll break me down.

"She . . ."

The pain and doubt are settling in my belly, and I'm clinging to the performance and silence I've been practicing since . . . since always.

Looking across the room, I try and see myself flying into the tiny space in the painting, torn from the red and big enough for one, but I can't get off the ground. I close my eyes and try to feel my ancient bowl, but my hands are empty.

"She . . ."

I can't finish it.

I see myself opening my mouth to sing, and bile flowing out.

Then I look over at Drew Turner sitting here investing in me, and maybe even caring about what all's happened and whether I can get my secrets told. Down in the lower mantle there's heaving and buckling. And I think, *What the fuck? What am I here for?* If I can't say it here, with someone who maybe gives a damn, there's nowhere I'll be able to do it. He's been giving me a glimpse of what speaking the truth feels like, of having somewhere I can be all my Ranitas, of doing more than just surviving.

"She might have loved me . . . in a perpetuate-your-genes kind of way. But she didn't like me. She renounced me, in ways plain and extravagant, again and again."

There, I said it, and feeling sadder than I think I ever have, which is its own accomplishment, I let go of the performance and give up my story. The pain of being unwanted, of never measuring up.

Drew Turner waits, giving my words a minute to settle. I can't believe I've snitched on her. And I can't believe I thought the worst was over.

And then he asks were there times when I did get Mama's approval.

"For getting A's in school. But that was the expectation. And it was mixed. Sometimes it felt . . . like I had to pay for excelling. Sometimes it seemed to make her mad."

"Be more," he says. "And I'll define what more is."

Yes. We talk about that and he asks, "And your father?"

"Mama, she was a gale force. And Daddy, he tried to stay standing, but like I said before . . . he wasn't exactly fluent, in trouble or feelings of the unpleasant kind. His sisters, they're cut from the same cloth, though I owe them everything. Actions speak louder than words; that's their credo. But I've always been stumped by one thing. Isn't 'talk' an action word?

"Anyway, Daddy was the through line in my kids' lives, and he never did give up on me. I can't really think of a time when I didn't feel his love. And he tried to give me the code, the habits, the interests that had worked for him. I feel them in me, even if I've gone astray. Wonder, curiosity . . . stillness and patience, though I haven't excelled at those."

Remembering him out loud like this, I can't help crying, and I'm embarrassed, but glad for Drew Turner to get a glimpse of what I've lost. He points out that the parental messages I got seem like a contrast, and asks how I see the overlap. I try and think that through, but figuring out how Mama and Daddy fit together, that's gonna take some work. With a flash of Amara's questions about me and Jasper, I think I can see why Daddy chose Mama. But I never understood how and why he stayed. Loyalty? Inertia? Weakness? Compassion? What was the glue?

Enough, I want to say, *enough*. I'm so drained and tired I'd like to stretch out on this couch, hard though it is, and rest. But my fatigue must not be visible, because Drew Turner keeps on pushing.

"It's a lot, figuring out what was going on between the adults in our lives. And it's hard to see the folks who raised us as people with their own stories, apart from ours. But even just focusing on what you've said about your mother, there seem to have been contradictions."

Yes. " 'Hold your head up,' " I say. " 'Be ashamed.' "

I see six-year-old Ranita, caught with her pants down and confined, half-naked, to the back stairway, standing for hours as my humiliation sank in, while life continued on the other side of the kitchen door. I bite my cheek and vow to keep this episode to myself.

"Uplift," I say, "by tearing down."

I think for a minute, and then tell how she cooked and baked and filled the table, but I was consigned to hunger and shame.

"And what does a child deserve and need?" he asks.

Surely I'm the last person with parenting wisdom to share. "I don't know; that's a hard one. Lots of things, I suspect, but I'm not a shrink. You're the one with the answers; you tell me."

"It's not a test. I'm interested in your thoughts here."

I name the things I longed for. "Affection. Attention. Affirmation. I'm starting with *A*, looks like."

"Okay, what else?"

I name what I failed to give my kids. "And *S* is for 'steadiness,' 'security,' 'showing up'. . . ."

He nods and I think some more.

"I guess I'ma leave the alphabet approach and say a child needs freedom, but rules and limits, too . . . sensible ones, meaningful ones. It's not like I think yes is always the right answer."

"That's astute. Let's circle back to that. Sounds like there's a story there."

Indeed. "So keeping with your question," I say, "maybe most of all, you need to be loved for who you are."

And now, trying to keep my tears in check, I add, "People say I'm old-school . . . what with some of my music tastes and being bookish. Anyway, some of those old-school ideas, they're dead wrong, but they're not dead. *Spare the rod, spoil the child . . . don't pick up a crying baby or you'll spoil them . . . children should be seen and not heard.* That last one's harsh all on its own, but Mama, she went a step further."

"Okay. Can you give me an example?"

I don't have to dig too deep, though I've tried to forget it. After a few false starts, I find the words to talk about it, the day my garden seeds sprouted.

"Me and Daddy had these side-by-side gardens, his veggies and mine flowers. I'd gone all-in with the researching and sowing and tending, but I didn't really believe they'd grow, and miraculously, they broke through. I was so excited. Daddy had pulled me out of the funk that had claimed me since . . . since the basement prayer sessions." My heart's pounding, even though I've already given up this story. "Anyway, he was saying I was a flower farmer, and it was a really good moment, standing out in the light drizzle, looking at the little bits of green that had showed themselves.

"All Mama could see was that I was choosing to be out in the garden instead of inside where she was, choosing Daddy over her, and choosing to let my hair get messed up, out there in the rain. Once I came in for dinner, she was on me . . . for having no discipline with my eating and being fat, for having big boobs and a body that looked older than thirteen. And for not getting a perfect score on some fucking test or other, I remember that part, too. And then . . ." It takes me a minute to say it, nearly two-thirds of my life later. ". . . while I was talking, proudly telling about something I'd learned in the encyclopedias my dad gave me, something about trees, she . . . she turned to face me, and spoke her mind without saying a word. She just closed her eyes, and stayed like that for the rest of the dinner. I wasn't seen or heard."

"That must have been devastating," Drew Turner says quietly, "that feeling of being invalidated . . . and unwanted . . . by your mother. And of being told that you're both too little and too much."

I break down. He listens and soothes. And asks some questions about Mama, her moods, her routines and practices, her background. I try and answer, but where and what she came from? I'm at a loss. Then I get a flash of her. Crying, distressed. Anguished, really, witnessed from a wedge of doorway light. I didn't know what to do with seeing her like that, and I still don't.

"Some of her actions," he says, "along with those old-school ideas you mentioned, may be the impossible experience . . . the trauma, historical and ongoing, let's call it what it is . . . of being Black in America. And of parents groping their way through the toll of what's been done to them, and trying to figure out how to sow into their children what will maybe allow them to survive the world. That doesn't excuse it, but it may be part of what informs it. And some of it certainly has to do with her own . . . mental health issues . . . with *her* story."

"Right. Which is why it never seemed right to complain. Still, it was . . . whatever, it was hard, and it felt mighty personal. And I never knew when it was coming. I tried to be the daughter she wanted, but suddenly, I'd realize I was so, so fundamentally wrong that the woman who brought me into this world couldn't stand the sight of me and wanted me to disappear."

He pauses for a minute to acknowledge what I've shared, and then says, "Ranita. I hear you. And I see how you felt as though you were the problem, as any child would. But you weren't what was wrong. Think of the things we've been talking about, the things you know every child needs, and deserves. First and foremost, you deserved and needed to be loved as you were, for *who* you were. And a lot of grief must have come from not receiving that. And from recognizing it now."

"Yeah, add it to the grief pile."

He nods. "There is a lot to hold. A lot to work through. But I'm here to do it with you, and I believe you're stronger than you think. But what I'm saying here is that I think the problem, the causes for the ways you felt rejected and erased, they lie within your mother and the things that formed her. Geneva's behavior was about her."

I try and take it in. There's a whole fucking lot to unpack, it seems.

I've tried not to revisit the night I told about, or Mama's last year either, when so many things started coming to a head. And there's something else about that night I can feel the edges of, trying to get to the surface. But right now we're out of time.

Me and Drew Turner do our closing practice, and today my feeling is the pain of seeing. My hope is that I'm up to the task. I come out of his office blinking in the sunlight, and I feel tired and achy and stirred up as I start toward home.

And I guess it's a test I give myself, taking a route that goes past Mario's, and looking at the door as I walk past.

Today, I choose remembering.

THIRTY

1996

Tirelessly, Ranita tried to satisfy her mother, while assembling the pieces she had into a whole that would explain her. She knew many Genevas. Gifted with music. Able and together. Resourceful. Determined. Deep in faith and feeling. Seditty. Easy to take umbrage. Proud and ashamed. Unpleasable and unreachable and sometimes, cruel.

Her virtues were all on public display one Sunday, the fall before she died. And then a month later, Ranita witnessed a Geneva she barely recognized.

From July to September, she had defied her mother's authority and refused to go to church. She didn't care how long she had to spend on punishment in her room, no TV or phone time, or the carping and coldness she had to deal with, or the extra chores. She'd be 14 soon and even though she missed the singing, her mother couldn't force her to go, no matter what she thought. On a regular Sunday, Lennox couldn't be persuaded to attend either, even with Geneva's guilting. He said he had to go to work and he'd see her later, and mostly, they seemed to have a truce about church. But today was an exception for both of them. They had come to see Geneva in her full glory.

Sitting in a pew halfway back, Ranita watched the choir swaying in their powder-blue robes, clapping and fired up. Her mother had wanted them to sit in the front row, but Ranita had resisted, maintaining that they'd be able to see better, and gauge people's reactions, if the congregation wasn't behind them. In truth, she felt more at ease several rows back from the chancel.

Anchored between her father and Jessie, she let the music, the color, the warmth and excited anticipation wash over her. Until Pastor Johnson stepped up to the pulpit, and she pictured herself crossing him out with a giant Sharpie. She leaned against her father's shoulder, despite the heat wave that had everyone fanning themselves, and he turned to look at her, his eyes twinkling, and whispered, "Ranita Bonita."

Ranita imagined that her mother had come into the world singing. She sang when she was doing housework, washing clothes in the basement, cooking or vacuuming or polishing the furniture to a perfect shine, and it seemed as though her voice worked its way into every little space in the house. And she played the organ and sang with the choir, along with the teaching and private lessons.

Ranita knew she sucked at the piano, what with Geneva clapping her hands sharply and stamping her foot at her every mistake . . . allegro instead of adagio, sharp instead of flat, incorrect fingering and pedaling . . . which made her play even worse. Geneva had never suggested that Ranita join the choir, and though that gave her asylum from the relentless project to improve her, it hurt. But she knew the songs anyway, and sang them to herself when she was alone. And she had a secret, too, the good kind. She'd been singing with the middle school jazz band and the music teacher said she had a strong contralto. Geneva said the only jazz singer she could fully abide was Ella Fitzgerald, because of her perfect pitch and three-octave range, and because she was always elegant and classy. That wasn't what Ranita's voice was like. She'd been listening to her father's records and had decided that the jazz singer in whose gritty, salty voice she heard herself was Dinah Washington.

When the time for her solo arrived, Geneva stepped forward, lifting her eyes to the ceiling, and moved into it slowly, gracefully, "Precious Lord, take my hand . . ."

The whole congregation was transported by her clear, soaring voice, all of them nodding and rocking and waving their hands in affirmation while Ranita looked up at her, wondering why the private Geneva couldn't be more like the public one.

She looked and sounded like a queen. Head held high. Face glowing. And her voice also seemed to say what it had taken out of her to rule her kingdom. But the more she sang, the less she seemed to weigh, and Ranita wouldn't have been surprised if she had levitated and finished her solo hovering above the altar.

Ranita hoped her mother was pleased with the performance. If not . . . well, she didn't even want to think about it. When Geneva finished and stepped back into the choir, Ranita ached for her to see the appreciation on everyone's faces, and to look down at her and her father and see how proud they were.

Once the solo was over, the service seemed like it would never end. Ranita tried to hold on, but she was having trouble breathing and her leg was jiggling, until her father tapped her lightly to let her know it was distracting. She bit her cheek, keeping her unease on the inside, and thought about how peaceful the pine-scented air had been up in Avery's branches. When they were finally released, everyone was milling around and her mother was surrounded by people saying how beautiful her voice was. A few came over to thank Ranita and her father, as though they were responsible.

"Well, well, the Lord does work miracles. I haven't seen you here in a month of Sundays," a member of the choir told Lennox, and another said, "Hey, stranger. We've got to get Geneva to solo more often, if it'll get you up in here." He smiled and said, "Yeah, yeah, you know the shop takes up my weekends. . . . I can barely keep up with all the work." Jessie went to find her friends and as soon as they were alone, he whispered, "Come on, Bonita, let's get outside," and they moved toward the door.

Ranita smelled him before she saw him. Citrus tang and pipe tobacco. "Voice of an angel," Pastor Johnson said, pushing by without even looking at her. Then she saw him give a fifth-grade girl his special smile, and had to get outside. When her father emerged from the door and looked around for her, she was standing under the only tree in the churchyard that had survived Dutch elm disease, feeling nauseous.

And there was Geneva, looking triumphant as she came through the door. "Group hug," Ranita's father said as she joined them, and Ranita was overcome by nostalgia at the scent of her mother up close, and by the wary longing she couldn't keep herself from feeling.

A month later, she stumbled onto what seemed to be the flip side of Geneva's triumph.

After dinner, she had crawled into bed with a book, disregarding Geneva's reminder before turning in: *Pray to do better; pray to be better.*

Now she surfaced, gasping, but not from her nightmare. This time the crying was coming from outside her body. She glanced at the clock, 3:22, as she threw back the covers and got up to locate the source. Opening her door, she could tell it was coming from the only place possible, across from her room and down the hall.

She couldn't even imagine her mother's anger . . . "wrath" would be the proper word, wrath as big as Achilles', if she was caught snooping on them in their bedroom, but except for a thin triangle of light from their doorway, the hallway was dark, and she moved as quietly as possible toward the pain.

Craning her neck to peek around the doorframe, she saw them. Her mother wept raggedly, inconsolably, as though her insides were tearing, and her father whispered as he rocked her, "It's okay, baby, it's okay." Those were his words, but the look on his face said otherwise.

Transfixed, Ranita shivered. *Her* mother was a force, like gravity. This one she didn't recognize.

"It's happening," Geneva cried, her eyes wild and the hair she usually kept covered with a wig standing out from her head in clumps. "I'm unraveling again."

Unraveling? Again?

As her mother pulled away from his arms, her robe fell open, and Ranita saw her private everything. Her dark-nippled breasts bobbing, and her brown softness, and the black hair where her legs met. Only that once, opening the bathroom door, had Ranita seen her naked, and that had been a terrible mistake.

Looking now, from the darkness, Ranita had to steady herself against the wall. This mother was even more frightening than the austere and retributive one she knew.

After creeping back to her room, Ranita closed the door and got back in bed, and knowing she could never admit to the peeping or to what she'd seen, she tried on her own to fathom how this Geneva fit with all the others. *How long has she been like this? How does she hide it? Am I the root of Mama's pain?*

Eyes on the clock, Ranita listened to the crying last for 48 more minutes, dying down and then starting up again twice before tapering off. Once it was quiet across the hall she tried to get back to sleep, but she was wide awake. She said a prayer, after all.

In case God was bothering with people's troubles that night, she asked him to put her mother back together and, while he was at it, to fill her heart with motherlove.

THIRTY-ONE

I've been remembering my ass off, trying to own what all I've pulled up from the murk. The real. The raw. The pieces I need, whether or not I want them. I'm hoping they'll loosen their claim. Hoping for serenity. And I've been trying to excavate the news that got lost when I tried burying what I could not withstand.

I remember the freedom of singing. And the first time Mama took me to the little train depot library. I remember Jasper, teaching me how to set the f-stop and focus his camera, and how things looked different through that lens. I remember playing HORSE with Antoine at the hoop behind his house, before he started seeing every girl as a potential conquest. I remember stretching out on the backyard grass at dusk and listening to the crickets and birdsong and insect buzz, hoping something would see my body as welcome territory and land on me. And the feel of Avery's bark against my back. I remember making lemonade freeze pops and sitting in the back doorway with Daddy, trying to eat them before they melted in the summer heat.

Daddy. Seems like it's time to visit your grave.

303

After thinking long and hard on what I want to take with me, I go to two stores to get what I need. Then I take a bus-subway-bus trip to the cemetery, and when I get there I go into the little office and ask how to find the plot. I haven't been here since Mama's burial, and that time's blurry. They give me a map, pointing out the "address," 2020 Blossom Avenue. And as I walk the winding path through the dead and buried, I'm glad I waited until summer, with the trees thick and things blooming all around.

When I get to the plot, I stand and look at their companion headstones. He stood by her, trying to sustain and heal her. He stood by me, trying to be her counterweight. And here they are, just four feet apart. *Husband • Father • Brother*, his marker says, and I'm touched at how the aunties included what he was to me, when I was a world apart at Oak Hills.

Opening my backpack, I take out a piece of rolled 11-by-14 paper and the black oil crayon, and get down on my knees to make a rubbing of his headstone. Holding the paper as still as possible, I rub softly, evenly, patiently, and Daddy's name and life-span and roles take shape beneath my hands.

When I stand my knees are damp and my fingertips are smudged. I roll and rubber-band the paper, and then glance at Mama's marker, trying to decide if it feels wrong not to do hers, too. Looking up and around, I ask the maples and oaks and evergreens for the answer, but they seem to say the choice is mine.

Unsure about that, I take out my offerings.

I put a fishing lure, one Daddy made from cork and feathers that was in his tackle box, on top of his headstone, knowing the wind and weather will carry it elsewhere, and feeling okay with that.

I pull the packet of black-eyed Susans from my backpack, tear off the corner, and pour the little straw-like oblongs into my hand. It's hardly the ideal start for them, but who knows, maybe a few will survive. I open my hand and scatter them around his grave.

And I unzip the little pocket in my backpack and pull out the keys, one silver, one brass, and place them side by side on top of the marker, making a concrete promise to remember what all he gave me, and keep choosing love and life.

Looking back at Mama's stone, I decide to make a rubbing of it, too. Lord knows, her dying was pivotal, and her story's inseparable from Daddy's, and from mine. They both had their parts in making me the Ranitas I am and might still be.

I get on my knees again with paper and oil crayon, and just as I finish the rubbing, images of that last year with Mama parade before me. Climbing Avery and defying punishment. Meeting her in petty revenge. Refusing church and then going for her solo. The stolen glimpse of her unraveling. And the night I told Drew Turner about, when Daddy, buffer and protector, asked what I'd learned from the encyclopedias we loved and Mama closed her eyes to me.

Again, I feel the edge of the memory that I almost had ahold of in Drew Turner's office. I let it come. And another piece of that story takes shape before my eyes, like a kirigami flower. A coda, lost in all my forgetting, is returned to me.

I went back out.

After Mama tried to erase me, I went to my room to do my homework, but I was too upset. I drifted off to sleep confused, heartsick, and woke at 1:00 a.m. to the rhythm of rain. Then I opened the window, and crept downstairs in my summer nightie to unlock the back door.

Looking around, I see no bench where I can sit and fully feel my gratitude for recovering this memory, so I put down the crayon and the rubbing and get in lotus on the grass in front of Mama's stone. I feel my sit bones, focus on my breath. And I get the thing I want and need, both.

I see Daddy, sitting by the water with the morning light coming up, back in 2004. And me, strung out and desperate and cut off from the truths I know.

I breathe real deep, feel my lungs and belly fill, and hear my heart-beat, right here on this burial ground. This here's the redo I've been wishing for. The only one that's possible, the conjured kind.

Working Step 9, now and always, I try to be at peace and choose, for this moment, who I'm gonna be.

I'm at the water beside you, Daddy. It's still and quiet enough to hear birds and trees and insects in the dawning light. The water's placid, its surface smooth.

You ask me do I know what it's like to try breathing air, when water's what you know. Do I understand how that fish longed to get full-grown in the freedom of the deep? Do I know what it feels like to have a hook sunk deep in your mouth?

I do know, Daddy. I know.

In my hands I feel that tiny, slippery yellow perch I caught, thrashing while it fights to live.

I'm holding that fish.

And this time I return it to the water. I give it back.

THIRTY-TWO

1996

Ranita woke to the sound of rain that had built from early-evening drizzle to steady drumbeat.

Pulling off her sleeping scarf, she shook her hair loose and got up, enjoying the feel of the smooth, worn floorboards on her bare feet, to go to the window. Heart still aching from her mother's dinnertime cruelty, she unlocked and lifted it, and her room filled with the scents of pine and soil and rain. Leaning on the sill, she stretched out her hands to feel the wetness, and let her eyes feast on the dreamlike yard: the little brick patio she'd helped make; Avery and Devon; grass, unmown, as she preferred it; and side-by-side garden plots.

The dark's protection was nearly complete, a fingernail moon helping to keep the secret of the lush backyard miracle. And though she couldn't see them from her window, her seedlings were out there, soaking up the wetness, becoming food for the eyes and soul. Anchored by their spreading roots, and pushing above- as well as belowground. She imagined the other sentient beings that were out there, unnoticed, hidden, some too small to see.

She slipped downstairs, treading lightly. Unlocked the back door and eased it open. And stood just inside, feeling every sense wake up. She put one bare foot on the threshold and paused. What kind of craziness was this? She couldn't even imagine what punishment her mother would devise.

Stepping through the doorway, Ranita went to Avery and looked through the green that lately seemed to call her up. *Soon*, she told the tree, *I'll be with you soon.* Standing beneath the arcing branches, she watched the water drip from their tips while she stayed dry. And then she stepped from Avery's shelter into the rain.

Immersed and unfolding, coming into fullness, she began to dance.

Moving to the pulse of the water, she raised her arms, opened her hands, moved her feet and legs, stomping and hopping, prancing and dipping, winding from the waist. She swung her head, scattering raindrops from her hair. She spun, reveling in the abundance of her body, rejoicing in the elemental force that had summoned her from the confines of the house and soaked her to the skin.

What kind of dance was this? She let the question go and moved past thinking into reclamation, taking her place with all that she could see and not see, with the earth and the trees and all the other hearts beating in the dark alongside hers, with the rain, the sky, the night.

THIRTY-THREE

I've been feeling a new kind of wanting. Not a clutching, clawing, fill-the-hole drive. More of a steady *What if?* feeling.

The whole way home from work I'm thinking about Maxine. Wishing I could tell her how I went to an event for queer people of color a few weeks ago. I'd been having one of my solo dance parties, and it was feeling good to let loose and work up a sweat, when all of a sudden a song ended and I felt so lonely I could taste it. I looked up the Queer Dance Party venue on my phone and saw they were having something called the "If You Can Feel It You Can Speak It" open mike for people of color that night, and before I could back out I got myself together and headed over.

Since I'd been there to check out the dance party, I didn't feel like a complete fish out of water. This time I walked to the patio, where I could see cigarette tips burning like city fireflies, and bummed a smoke off that same bald-headed beauty as before, only this time he was looking more boy, or mixing it up different, anyhow, in tailored pants and a fedora and a full beard, along with the eye makeup and the big hoop earrings from before.

"I remember you," he said, bowing again. "You're still looking fierce." When I asked if he had a spare cigarette he teased me, "Oh, I thought you'd joined the anti-smoking brigade," and we laughed as we lit up. Then, when it was showtime, he said his name was Eduardo, introduced me to his crew, and said, "Come on, baby, let's go in and listen."

I held back for a minute, paralyzed. What if I got in there and felt wrong . . . or triggered? This little adventure was not part of my reunification plan, and maybe I should just keep to what was working. What if something went down that I couldn't handle, that put me off track? What if I saw Drew Turner in there? That would just be too many things. Or what if Ms. Barnhart saw me going in? Despite those questions making a snarl in my head, I moved toward the entrance with Eduardo. And walked through.

Felt like a major accomplishment. I was inside, after choking the first time I tried. Seemed like having somewhere to sit down, and just being called on to listen, was going to be more manageable than the whole dance party thing, even though I'd been wanting to shake my rump. I had to walk past the bar, with its glittering whiskey bottles inviting me to come closer, lit by the tiny white bulbs strung up above and the hanging 3-D stars that glowed with pinpricked light, and everyone with a drink looking more relaxed than I've felt in years. But I kept going, reminding myself I looked fierce in someone's eyes, even if I felt shaky on the inside.

The room was packed, and everything hit me . . . all the bodies milling about, the energy, the music, the smells of food from the restaurant part of the venue . . . it was a whole lot. I hung at one of the high tables with Eduardo and his friends, checking out the crowd, feeling a little bit disloyal to Maxine as I looked around at the women to see if there was anyone I could imagine maybe kissing, and then a seat opened up at the end of the back row, and I took it, relieved that I could leave if I needed to, without making anyone get up.

A youngster kicked things off with a poem calling out white feminists for being clueless about race. She was dramatic and unafraid. Seemed that way, anyhow. She looked like a born performer, too, but I think she must have studied acting, the way she used her voice and body to make her poem come alive, slowing down to build up the drama, and then slamming it home at the end. The room exploded in clapping and snapping and cheering, and I joined in.

The low light, the energy of the audience, the suspense about what I'd be hearing, all of it had me buzzing. The stories and the tellers, they were all over the map.

A sista in platform heels and a miniskirt, locs down her back like Maxine's, told a funny story about getting up the courage to ask a girl out for the first time. She acted out her knees shaking while she worked up her nerve, praying the rejection would at least be kind, and we all laughed with her, thinking on our own times of stepping out on a ledge for love.

A beauty with an inch of hair, not butch, not femme, maybe both, she talked about singing lullabies to the abuela who raised her while she fed her at the nursing home. She had me nearly crying.

I listened to a poem about the surveillance of Black men, and a nerdy guy in horn-rimmed glasses who looked like he could have been Drew Turner's cousin, he did a piece called "Stay in Your Lane," about how uncomfortable people are with bisexuals. "Straight and gay are both mad that you're not all the way on their teams," he said, "and no one feels at ease around you. People think you're just greedy, or in denial. You're the lonely B in LGBTQ." Damn, I guess that's me? A misfit within the misfits.

A long-legged beauty who was even finer than Janelle Monáe stepped onto the stage like royalty and said she was transitioning. She told a bold, funny story about her family's scorn, reminding me a little of my Mama show and the hurt underneath it, and said she's saving up the money for the surgery her health insurance refuses to cover.

I was pulling so hard for the two guys who got up to sing "Bésame Mucho" to do a good job that my whole body was tense. They were so into each other, you could just feel it. They sang, smiling and proud. Off-key, too, and it didn't matter.

And then a hairy, barrel-chested guy with a thick neck, he got up and told about how he'd stopped on his way to work to watch a bee land on a purple coneflower. Said he stood and watched while it hovered over the velvety purple petals and then touched down, dusting its spidery legs with orange pollen. "It was a small thing," he said, "too small for a story in some folks' minds," and he might have just as easily missed it, or just glimpsed it in passing, but instead he stopped and looked. He said it made him feel crazy joyful, and respectful, too.

I could not believe how brave they all were, getting up there to share their talents and what they'd been through. Keeping at it even if they stumbled or forgot what they planned to say, or if they didn't sing so good, and even if their stories were about ordinary stuff, instead of the so-called big moments. I loved sitting there with the lights low, listening to people peel back the skin to let you know what was below the surface, and it all felt important. They had stood up there to tell us so.

It wasn't a slam, or a competition. The sharing, it felt a little like a meeting, except it wasn't all about bottoming, messing up, guilt and amends, trying to believe in the future you might still have. And sitting shoulder to shoulder to listen and receive what people came to share, we felt like a congregation, in a church where everybody's welcome.

The realness was powerful, and the vibe was good and warm. (And I did see some sistas I could imagine kinda maybe wanting to know.)

Were they my people? Did I fit? I knew, while I sat there absorbing it all, that there seemed to be space for me with them, in that house. And ever since, I've been wondering do I have it in me to get up there, and if I do, what stories I've got that would be tellable, that wouldn't feel like sorrowful confessions.

Once I get home I take a long, hot shower, and the craziest thing happens. I'm not planning on it. I'm not even thinking about it. Lauryn and Nina and Minnie and Aretha, they're all running through me. The water's raining down on my bare head. And a song starts building in me until my body can't hold it in and I'm opening my mouth. Music comes out of me, rusty and creaky. I can hardly believe it. I'm singing.

And now I'm sitting here with a piece of blank paper on my blue tabletop, because it's time I reached out to Maxine. It's not loose-leaf or copier paper, and I'm trying to figure out what to say that will live up to this heavy, cream-colored stationery.

I could buy a card some real artist made with a beautiful photo and a message someone wrote much better than I could ever do, but Maxine, she'd want my own messy drawing and words. I owe her those.

I fold the paper in half. That's a start. I've made one decision: it'll be a card and not a letter. But I don't want to mess up my paper when I've only got three sheets. I'm thinking I should practice, draw it out first on scratch paper, think it all the way through before I put anything down.

I want to tell her most of what's happened, these last six months, even my glass of Hennessy. (Well, except for that tawdry little episode with Peyton . . . getting on the path to being a stalker . . . Leon and DQ haunting me . . . never mind.) I do want to say how she was not just temporary shelter, how she stays in my heart and mind. But I can't bring myself to say all that and maybe share it with the COs who screen the mail, or sign my name.

If I tell about the kids, she'll know I'm clean, on the right path, handling my business and getting it together. And she likes a puzzle, likes to read between and underneath the lines. So I'ma send her something only she will all-the-way understand. Like with our kites.

I could make a picture of an oak tree or oak leaf, and she'd get the joke: no oaks at Oak Hills, so I'm sending her one. I could send her the night sky above my building, but if I drew it true there'd only be a few dim stars. I could try and draw that spot in Franklin Park we both knew, or give her back some of the things she conjured for me. I can't decide.

Closing my eyes, I go for an imaginary walk in those unreachable woods beyond Oak Hills that I know Max can see from her puny window, picturing that red-tailed hawk and the trees that are full and leafy, after the winter bareness when I saw them last. Even though I never walked out there, I stared through my small portal to nature long enough to memorize every detail.

I conjure myself out there in a clearing, in a tall nave of trees, feeling the give of the soft, damp forest floor, smelling pine and breathing in the clear, fresh air. Bathing in the still, sacred green, I get my answer.

I start with one of Theo's red watercolor pencils, making a circle that's a little lopsided, and a wedge inside of that. And then I get inspired and take my paper to the steps out back and lay it down to make a rubbing like I did of Daddy's headstone, pushing the pencil over the step to get a rough, worn texture, everywhere but in the wedge. It's far from perfect. Coarse, even, but it'll do. A man who's leaning against the building, having a smoke, he's watching me, but I pay him no mind.

Back at my table, I go over the red rubbing with the black and brown pencils, shading it in places and giving it a scratchy look with my fingernails. Then I dip my red pencil in a little bit of water and use it to blur everything together. And now I sit for a while and think about how to make the part inside the wedge.

After cutting a strip from my counter sponge, I dip the end in the water and rub it on the tip of the red pencil, stamping it again and again in the white space, filling it up with little square red seeds. It's sketchy. Miles away from polished. But I decide it's okay, and I know Maxine will understand. And maybe moonwalk.

Inside the card I write my message:

One overnight so far. Excavation and repair work in progress. Opened my mouth tonight, more squeak than song. So rusty and raggedy I hardly recognized the voice, but it was mine. If I could I'd use all 7 of my letters to connect with yours and make GRATEFUL.

THIRTY-FOUR

Oak Hills
February 2019

Ranita got a send-off that was full of making do and freedom dreams. Everyone pitching in made it extra special, given how hard funds were to come by.

Getting through the holidays, a world away from family, daylight shrinking until it was pitch-dark at 3:30 and no Christmas spirit to be found, had taken strength and imagination. Few, if any, presents given and none received. No tree, except for the blue spruce in the far distance that Ranita and Maxine visualized themselves decorating, deciding on an ornament to add each day of Advent.

The "special holiday dinner," served at lunchtime, with cold bagged sandwiches doled out in the evening, had been dry roast beef and potatoes, steamed vegetables, and chocolate ice-cream cups. On Ranita's second Christmas inside, everyone had gotten a pint of ice cream all their own. *Mint chocolate chip, my favorite!* she'd heard the exclamations from across the chow hall, but when they opened them there wasn't a bit of chocolate to be found, just light green ice cream that tasted like toothpaste.

As they had dug into this yuletide meal, everyone tried not to picture their empty seats at the tables back home, and revisited the holiday food that was lost to them. Pineapple-studded ham, juicy turkey with corn-bread stuffing, gumbo, Cornish hens, and all the sides, savory and sweet. Pies and cakes and iced cookies. An endless supply of everyone's drink of choice.

Most had tried to latch on to a good moment, salvaged from the memories of overdrinking and overeating; the tension covered over with holiday cheer; the gulf between their lives and the holiday specials, greeting cards, and ads that were everywhere they turned. They tried to look back at the season's good news: the savior born, the light renew-ing, the kinship . . . instead of the reality of living up to the idea of the holidays and keeping the family traditions going, even if they had no resources and couldn't remember why. The display of abundance with gifts they couldn't afford. The resurgent conflicts that were too histori-cal to be put to rest. Consciously, at least, they remembered the holidays better than they'd lived them.

But they had survived, all except the one who'd followed through on her single New Year's resolution. And now Ranita was getting ready to rise up, and they were gathering to celebrate her freedom. "Come on," she'd coaxed Keisha, "get-togethers in here are few and far between, and you might as well come." Keisha turned her face to stone or so she thought, and looked away, before standing up nonchalantly and coming along to the dayroom like she was doing Ranita a favor.

Maxine walked in with chips, Twinkies, and Neapolitan ice cream, and Ranita knew what she'd had to put aside to get them. Eldora came, her family trailing behind her, shaking a baggie full of penny candy, all of Ranita's favs, along with root beer barrels and butterscotch buttons, and Naomi brought Pepsi and hot cocoa mix. Avis kicked in three bean pies, looking routinely wary and distant, and then sat on the edge of the party, crocheting the never-ending mud-colored blanket that was just like the ones Ranita had made. Maybe she unraveled it by night, Ranita thought, expecting the return of the husband she'd had to kill to save herself.

Gwen brought the ingredients to make the biggest treat of all, which they called The Chewy Good, and got busy mashing up chocolate and peanut butter cookies that she topped with caramels and Hershey's melted in the microwave, and crushed Dunkin' sticks. Despite all her practice with waiting, Ranita could hardly restrain herself from digging in while it cooled and firmed up. Once it was ready everyone had some, especially Keisha. She was shy at first, and then Gwen had to intervene before she polished off the whole container.

Some folks were at the Catholic service, though everyone knew they did as much sinning as everybody else and went to hook up with women from the other blocks. It tickled Ranita that the Catholic church brought more women together than anything else at Oak Hills.

Looking around the dayroom, Ranita saw the ones who wouldn't be leaving anytime soon. The silent youngster, forever sullen, always looking for a fight. The mouthy white girl who'd listened when Ranita was first searching for a reason to live, and the cellie she'd punched in the mouth for touching a photo of Amara, getting her first trip to the hole. One who'd taught her what all you could make from canteen food and showed her how to dye her bra pink with Gatorade, and one who'd cornered her in the shower, giving her no choice but to draw blood. Across the room was the one who'd stolen her ramen and flip-top tuna and then, two months later, offered her shoulder to cry on when Lennox died.

They were there, and so were the COs, heads swiveling like surveillance cameras as they made sure no drama kicked off at the little gathering. Williams, though, she was decent. She let them borrow a boom box, and even wished Ranita luck and told her she didn't want to see her back there.

Everybody had signed the *Birthday Wishes* canteen card, on which the first word had been crossed out, *Best* written above it and *On the First*

Day of the Rest of Your Life added underneath. When she saw the names and messages written inside, Ranita started to sniffle.

"Go 'head, baby," Eldora said, jumping at the chance to try and mother her one last time. "You earned your cry." The "Amens" followed, and then they gave Ranita the little gifts they'd made and bought and chipped in for. A pocket Bible with a bumpy green pleather cover. A sew-on Superman patch. A bouquet of peonies made from toilet tissue. Seeds, from Eldora.

Jimena, who'd taught Ranita some Spanish when she first got there, stood up and slammed a poem she'd written about Black and Latina sisterhood, and the response was so amped the COs came over and told them to calm down. And then Naomi pulled out a drawing of Ranita outside the Egyptian pyramids, sitting on the back of a sphinx. "That's you," she said. "A queen, no matter where you are." They shared stories about Ranita and gently roasted her about being a volcano that had gone dormant, and about her devotion to Atomic FireBalls, reading, Scrabble. And Maxine.

Noticed, yet unspoken, was the grief in store for her. Most of them did their time without any chosen intimacies, and some knew the pain of being left behind, if they'd been lucky enough to find any loving at Oak Hills. Though Maxine stood as upright and proud as ever, her sadness was palpable, and Ranita wished she knew what to do or say. She was laughing and enjoying herself on the outside, but her own heart was aching and uncertain.

Just two weeks before, they'd had their final rendezvous at the chapel.

Ranita was already grieving Maxine, but she'd smiled as soon as she saw her come through the door. They'd started out sitting against the wall, shoulder to shoulder, legs stretched out, and there was a rare awkward feeling between them. When Maxine asked how her reentry plan was coming together, Ranita started listing her steps for keeping to the right path. "Hope I'ma be alright," she said. "There's an opioid crisis out there, you know."

"I've heard." Maxine shook her head, and started winding up. "Soon as white folks and rich kids start dying it's a crisis, calling for compassion and holding the drug companies accountable. . . ."

Even though she'd gotten her started with their bitter joke, Ranita didn't think she could go all the way there right then. "Let's talk about something else," she said, and they both went quiet, until Maxine whispered, "Let's not talk at all," and leaned over to brush her sternum with a kiss. "Come here," Maxine said, motioning for her to sit in front and pulling a jar of hair grease from her pocket. As Maxine started massaging her scalp and hair, Ranita said, "I'll do you next, twist your locs just the way you like." And as she relaxed, she started thinking about the kite she'd left for Maxine the day before that said: *Tell me ocean.*

Ranita had put it in their hiding place behind the microwave. A last, little private thing Maxine would be able to look at, once Ranita was gone.

"So, you got some ocean for me?" she asked, and then felt Maxine laugh softly against her back.

"Which ocean you want?"

The only beaches Ranita knew were Nantasket, Carson, Revere, and she was sad to realize that she really hadn't thought about how different other oceans might be. "What are my choices?"

The Maine coast was cold and dark and rocky, Maxine told her, and on Daytona Beach the sand stretched out wide and flat enough to drive on. They decided on the Gulf of Mexico (pre-oil-drilling ruination) and Maxine conjured its salty smell and whitish traces that clung to their brown skin, its bathwater warmth and clear turquoise color. They rode the waves, feeling for shells and rocks below, and Maxine warned her that they had to watch for sudden drops and riptides, and avoid the undertow.

There were so many things Ranita wanted to know and so little time. Now was her chance. She asked when Maxine had first started talking things up.

"In my head, I guess I always did it," she said, after some thought. "When I was eleven or twelve I'd listen from the stairs to my folks . . .

their friends . . . my grandparents, talking. Grown folks' business, they used to say. And then I'd lie in bed and see myself doing all manner of things: driving a truck, slow dancing in the basement . . . with another girl. Being out at night alone, riding a motorcycle. Standing up to white folks. You'll die if you can't see yourself free."

"I know that's right."

"Well," she'd continued, "I can still see and feel those things. And you know, there's something I keep going back to lately, maybe because we're winter-locked and I'm jonesing for warmth and sunlight. Every August, when I was little, we spent precious nights on Aunt Lula's sleeping porch, and I imagine myself back to Baltimore. We'd take a road trip, eating fried chicken and ham sandwiches in the car and fighting for back seat space the whole way there, and then stuff into Lula's slice of a row house."

After switching places, Maxine talked while Ranita oiled and twisted. "It was so hot and humid, and at night they'd put mattresses out for us kids on the upstairs screened-in porch, and that way we were sort of outside, while being safe. It took us a while to calm down and stop playing and fighting, elbowing for the best spot, you know how that goes, or trying to talk someone into trading pillows, but finally . . . finally, when we were all settled down and had stopped our chattering, you could hear every single thing.

"The heavy night air came through the screens, and we could lie there and hear grown-ups playing cards and talking down below us, my dad always pointing out the shortcomings of something or other, when he spoke at all. My mother saying something so optimistic it was mythical. My aunties and uncles trading stories and laughing and arguing, and I was fighting sleep while I tried to catch each word. I could hear my cousins breathing, slow and peaceful, just before I drifted off. I guess I was listening, storing things up.

"It's a long time since I've been a girl. And I spend my nights on the inside now. But I find I can still go there, and have the outside and the roof and the porch, the night sounds, with family just below. I can choose the night air and pull it close."

"The night air in August. That's one for the free things list." Ranita wished she had Maxine's gift for conjuring, at least in her head. She hadn't told her how she'd been trying to see her ancient bowl of water in the desert, with no success so far.

"Only thing I know . . . or used to know . . . ," she said, leaning close to inhale Maxine's smell, "that's anything like the way you bring something lovely out of you and put it in the world is singing. And I don't do that anymore."

Maxine moved Ranita's hands from her hair and turned around to look at her. "I know your reasons, baby, but you're still singing inside. And you don't know what can happen, Ranita. You didn't think you'd play Scrabble. Or get your GED. Or be lovin' on a woman."

Sometimes Ranita could hardly believe the depth of where she'd gone with her, and the fullness, the pleasure, of it. But what she would do with that after she was out was another question. Maxine had said to focus on herself and the kids, release Oak Hills as it released her, and feel no weight. "Live your life, baby, whatever and what all that means." But Ranita couldn't help wondering. Would they stay in touch by mail? Would she apply to visit, once the yearlong waiting time was up? What would she do without Max's affirming presence?

"If you used to sing," Maxine said, "then it's in you."

Ranita heard Aretha's voice in her head . . . *Stand by you like a tree, dare anybody to try and move me* . . . but she asked, "What've I got to sing about?"

"What you've got to sing about is up to you."

Ranita pulled her closer and Maxine said, "You'll sing. And when you do, you let me know. Three-way postcard. Carrier pigeon. Skywriting airplane. Send word, some kind of way."

Two weeks later, celebrating and on the verge of freedom, Ranita looked at Maxine and imagined herself breaking into a serenade. If only she were woman enough to bring a song of any kind out of her right then and there, in the name of love and gratitude. She reached for the last Twinkie and stuffed it in her mouth.

Treats consumed and offerings given, the celebrants tried to stay lighthearted, hopeful, keep their emotions in check. They knew what Ranita was facing, and just how serious she had to be about her recovery. Three years and change was a damn good start, but most of them knew how shaky any amount of clean and sober was. And alongside their hope and realism was envy.

Every one of them ached for freedom. By reflex, by life-wish, every body wanted out.

"What you gon' do first?" Eldora asked.

Ranita was tempted to share her plan to honor her father by getting a pomegranate, but that felt too personal, too deep, too out there, to reveal. She reminded herself that this was not a meeting, where everyone spilled their guts. "First," she said, "I'ma take a long, hot bubble bath."

"That's right, baby," Eldora answered. "Pamper yourself."

"Then I'ma get my hair done proper."

"Amen. And put on your best outfit, thong and black lace bra, and stilettos," Naomi said.

Maxine joined in with the laughing, but Ranita knew it probably cut her to hear them talk sexy like that, vicariously enjoying the prospect of getting out. Fantasizing. Speculating. They got worked up, chiming in with what they'd choose.

"Whatever the fuck I felt like, that's what I'd do," one who'd come late to the party joined in.

Ranita wanted to say she'd sleep naked and walk around that way, too, but she knew she'd be on Jessie's living room sofa bed, and, even more so, saying that would be hurtful to everyone who was stuck for the foreseeable future at Oak Hills, where there was no such thing as privacy. Male guards watching you use the toilet and shower, and seeing you naked in the hole 24/7 when you were on eyeball, after the little paper gown they gave you tore away in the first hour or two. You never stopped feeling low about that, like a piece of something, just flesh, or a zoo animal.

"Me? I'd have no plan at all," one of them said, "open space and open time."

"I'd get me as much shrimp and lobster as I could eat."

"Ribs. I'd try and hurt myself on barbecue."

They were careful not to mention partying, but whether they were pledged to sobriety or not, Ranita knew they were all thinking of how they'd want a drink to celebrate.

"I'd walk around outside until my feet gave out, just walk around free."

"And then go home and sleep on satin sheets."

"Yes, yes, yes. And not alone. I'd damn near kill a muthafucka in the bedroom, making up for all this time without. I'd have to pick a nigga who had stamina."

"Like me," Gwen announced, getting to her feet. She'd been with so many of the women there that no one said a thing. And then her latest girlfriend staked her claim with, "Amen to that," and everyone laughed, playing it light.

"Well, I know what I'd do if I was you, first thing," Eldora said. "I'd find myself a *home*-cooked meal."

"I'd fix that meal myself, and invite all my family over to share it, too."

"I'd go to the movies and have an all-day orgy, watching one after another."

"I'd get my nails done. Manicure and pedicure, both."

"I'd ride around. Go to the beach, the park, the Esplanade. Just keep riding, all day long."

Ranita laughed. She did hope to claim some common pleasures, some privacy, a few indulgences for herself. A pomegranate. A bath. A takeout shrimp dinner. But it was hard to quiet the ache of survivor guilt when everyone around her wanted to go home, too. And as for the bigger fantasies, winning the battles with using and reunification, feeling contentment and comfort, peace and pride, she kept her hoping to herself.

The Oak Hills sistas avoided the subject of Ranita's kids, knowing she'd have to get a world of things right before she could see them, have them over, get them back. But on the question of therapy, Eldora shifted the mood to motherly realness. "You mind yourself with that couch talk they make you do; don't let them up inside your head. You been in the game, Ranita; you know how to handle yourself."

Others chimed in on the topic, and then an anxious quiet descended, until someone offered, "Things work out the way they're s'posed to. If you believe in good fortune, you'll get it." Everyone looked away, saying, *Whatever*, with their bodies, *make the story you need*. And then Avis spoke up. "You're best off expecting nothing. Then you won't be disappointed, whatever does go down."

Well, damn, Ranita thought, *what's next?* But Eldora rescued them from the gloom. "Is this a wake or a party? Let's get some music on the box and change the vibe."

Everyone except Keisha got up and danced. She sat on the outskirts, too stuffed with Chewy Good to move, Ranita thought, and taking an unopened envelope in and out of her pocket. Her face did look a little softer, showing glimpses of the youngin beneath the attitude. Ranita and Maxine danced together, close but not quite touching, and everyone began to get loose. And then Gwen started a *Soul Train* line, and even pulled Williams into the mix. She did the Whoa and then returned to the other keepers, who stood frowning.

And then it was count time, and they had to wrap it up. "I'ma miss you all," Ranita said, looking first at Maxine and then around at the others, who offered their good-byes.

"See you on the outside, baby."

"We'll get together, by and by."

"Maybe I'll see you at a meeting."

As she left, Eldora called out, "You be good now. And remember, if you can't be good, be good *at* it!" sending everyone back to their cells laughing.

Watching Maxine walk away, Ranita thought of what she'd said at that last chapel meet-up. She'd notice the free things. She'd keep going hard. And she'd see what else might be in store for her.

"Since you're part tree," Maxine had said, "let's speculate on your kin, those you'll get to know up close when you're back on the outside."

One day soon, she'd run through a warm spring shower, seeking shelter from the branches of a tree that was wide and thick with new leaves. A sugar maple. And she'd stop to catch her breath, smelling the rain and earth, the wet grass and the damp bark. And she wouldn't even really mind having gotten wet. She'd breathe in and enjoy the moment, her uncovered arms rain clean and new, and lean back against the trunk, laughing as she looked at sky that was free of pinched windows and bars and razor wire.

"That maple," Maxine had said, "it'll be there for you, Ranita, because you've got so much goodness inside."

Now that the celebration was over and she was watching Maxine disappear, back upright, locs swaying, walk unencumbered, Ranita felt a fissure of grief open up. Her freedom was imminent, but she had so many doubts, so many questions about the future, and one surged above the rest. On the other side of the walls, what would happen to the wake-up call of a woman's kiss?

She imagined Maxine reaching out with her fingertips, touching them to Ranita's chest, and answering, *It'll be right there, in the rooms of your heart.*

THIRTY-FIVE

My card's been sitting on my table for two weeks, waiting. I'm not building my patience, like Daddy was in favor of; I've been getting up the nerve to take action. But now I'm headed over to Jessie's, and if I can manage to make the words come out, I'ma be done with hiding and tell her about Maxine. Bless my card with pride and honesty before I put it in the mail.

I pack up the banana pudding I made this morning and stop at the store to get the ingredients for chicken piccata, which I watched them cook again and again at the restaurant, so I can make lunch for her. And on the way over, I catch myself humming.

Jessie answers the door and then bumps over to the kitchen with her walker, wincing and moving at a crawl, but proud and pretending she's not in pain. I offer to get her meds and fetch the Epsom salts so she can soak her feet, and she says, "Maybe later."

She sits with me while I'm cooking, nursing a cup of vanilla chai.

This recipe is all about the fresh lemon juice and capers, I tell her, like I'm some kind of expert, and then have to laugh at myself. I never had capers until three months ago.

I tell about the sleepover and my calls with the kids, touching on Miss Penny briefly with a plan to revisit that issue before school starts up. I'm entertaining Jessie with some of the things Amara's said recently and telling how she'll ask a question that just goes right to the heart of a thing and leave me speechless. "Man," I say, "our Amara, she's a lot."

"Hmmmm. She gets it honest."

"Yeah, I guess she does. I've been a handful; I know it. Anyway, hard as it is to take her scrutiny and her sass, I'm trying not to shut her down, and her kindness . . . she's letting that show more and more."

Then Jessie says, "Oh, I meant to tell you. She called before you got here. Said she tried to get you, but you didn't pick up."

My heart plummets. Here she is calling me for the first time since I got out and I'm not there for her. Did something bad happen? Is she sad, is she safe, is she stranded? Did she run into DQ?

I turn off the stove. "What happened? Tell me; I can take it."

"I have no idea, Nita, but she didn't sound upset. She was calling on Val's phone, and said she'd text you."

I go get my phone from my backpack, but I'm afraid to look. After arguing with myself for a full minute, I force myself to open the text, and my eyes fill with tears. Just three letters: *ALY.*

I feel like dancing.

Back at the stove, I ask for the news on Gil, feeling a little envious and a little anxious. Whenever he finally gets here he's coming home a hero. And I need to show him something different than what he remembers.

"Let's use a tablecloth," I say, "and candles. Make things as special as possible. Because we can."

Once we're seated and the candles are lit, she says grace and we dig in. I don't have to ask how the food is. She laps it up and raises her hand in praise. I just hope she feels like talking today, because I've got a few things I'd like to cover.

"I went to Daddy's grave."

She looks surprised and says she needs to put some flowers there. I tell her about the rubbings I made, promising to bring them over next time I come, and think of my rain dance memory that found me at the graveyard, along with some of the other gifts I've been given.

"Remember that pomegranate, Jessie, the one Daddy brought home after Mama died?"

She says *yes* with her whole body. "I'd tasted the seeds, but I'd never seen one broken open. He was trying so hard to show you something special. Like with that fishing trip he kept on pressing for until you went."

"Yeah. They've come back to me since I got out, both times he took me fishing with him, but especially the second one. . . . Let's just say the serenity was lost on me. Anyhow, as I relived it, I swore I could see the little boy in him, along with the father and man. And the kids were asking about him. I was hoping you'd tell me what he was like, growing up."

She looks off in the distance for a few minutes before speaking. "Well . . . even when he was small . . . and you know he was five years younger than me . . . he could entertain himself for hours, looking through books and magazines, studying the wooded lot out back. I remember Mama giving him a magnifying glass when he was maybe three . . . I can see it now, the black metal frame around the glass and the long handle . . . and him walking around looking at everything through it. He'd be bent over, glass to the ground, checking out grass and clover and dandelions, and watching ants and whatever else was crawling at the roots. He'd walk up to me and look up close at my knees, my hair, my freckles. So I guess he always was the quiet, taking-everything-in type.

"And he was always tinkering. Taking the wheels off my baby doll carriage and putting them on Mama's laundry basket so she wouldn't have to carry it. Making a pulley to haul things up to the second floor through his bedroom window. His first job was working on cars on the weekends with a friend of Papa's."

I'm so happy I asked for these stories. Jessie's tongue is really loose today. "What about fishing? When did he get into that?"

"Oh, Papa started taking him along when he was little . . . when he wasn't hungover, that is."

I'm wondering how this is the first I've ever heard of drinking in the family. Did I get *that* honest? I'm hoping she'll say more, but I guess she's done the most she can for now.

"I'd hear them leave before the sun was up and I was still thick with sleep. Truth is, I wanted to go, too, but my place, everyone said, was in the house, learning all those exciting things like ironing and cooking and dusting. I was real proud of your father, later on, for trying to pass that fishing stuff down to his girl.

"I think he always did love the suspense, the waiting and wondering, as much as the thrill of getting a fish on the line and bringing it in. But he was sensitive, like Theo, and when he was little, he hated that the fish died. I remember Papa telling how, at the riverbank, your father cried the first time he saw the hook in the fish's mouth and watched it gasp for breath. He hadn't realized it would have to die. 'But we're gonna eat it, Lennox,' Papa explained. 'This here's gonna be our dinner. We fish to eat.' He was heartbroken, and refused to go with Papa the rest of that summer."

"What changed?"

"I guess he started accepting the hard truth of how dying and living are tied together."

Damn. I'm back at the riverbank with Daddy, the second time around, with a whole new layer of understanding.

She looks so sad and I take her hand. "I know you miss him, too, so I don't mean to make that worse by asking about him."

"We're not a family of talkers, are we?" she says. "At least not about the harder things."

Jessie, she's stood by me. Held me accountable, too. My heart fills up with love for her. "No, we're not. But we can do different; we can stretch."

I sit here trying to figure out what and how much to say, and I don't want to tax her, but I do want to let her see me struggle. I want a woman-to-woman relationship that's real.

I tell her how a lot of stuff . . . hard and not so hard, too . . . has been surfacing since I got out. "For real," I say, "it overwhelms me sometimes . . . the . . ."

"The all of it."

"Yeah." I want to bring up Mama, but that feels too recent and too big to manage for today. "I'm trying to keep on looking at the mess," I tell Jessie, "at the whole muddle of loving and living, impossible as it feels sometimes."

She's hanging in here with me, the only sign of discomfort being the extra serving of banana pudding she reaches for. "I know that's right. Life is messy. And people are a mystery. Sometimes our choices, our tries at love, they just don't seem to make any sense. I had one husband who was the little end of nothing, and one who was true as gold."

"Well, I've been a bad chooser. Mostly."

"And I'm sure you're not done with love at thirty-six."

I feel a surge of longing. "Maybe not.

"Actually . . . ," I say, but the rest won't come out and I change course, ask about her physical therapy, about keeping up her walking, even though it hurts.

"Jesus, he gets me through most things," she says. "With him by my side I'm not alone."

I nod. Yes, I do think the Jesus I learned about, radical redeemer, would have loved my fallen, stumbling self.

"I know in the program you all have the higher power . . . the God or who you understand him to be . . . thing. But I suspect . . . maybe Jesus isn't your answer."

"Is and isn't. The church, maybe not. Jesus, maybe so."

I see all the Jessies . . . loving, tough, reluctant to know . . . flicker across her face. She gets that *Do I really need to hear this?* look, and says, "It's okay; it's your business. We don't have to go there."

I swallow the food that's in my mouth and put my fork down, my hand shaking a bit, my heart unsteady. "Jessie, along with the faith thing, which is a muddle all its own, I had another kind of help."

"I know. You had your meetings and your classes. And your books. And the visits . . . I wish could have been more often, and I wish I hadn't missed the last year, what with the stroke."

"Yeah. Those things were helpful, they were, along with the sisterhood that can sometimes happen on the inside. . . ."

After a long drink of water, I try and approach it sideways. "But . . . and . . . there's something else. . . ."

I'm floundering. And then I decide, right here and now, to take a risk. To give Jessie the chance to love me and know me, both.

"I had something else that made a big difference," I say, striving to sound upright and proud. "My last two and a half years at Oak Hills . . . I had the love of someone who inspired me. Someone who helped me start to heal."

Her eyebrows go up and I take a deep breath, making sure not to rush over the first word and sound ashamed. "She made me want to be awake, and imagine, and keep on trying to do better. I chose her and loved her. Make that present tense, even though she's still locked up. I love her; I love Maxine." My heart's beating wildly and my face is hot.

Jessie's looking at me and I'm looking away. I feel vaguely nauseous. And afraid. But I own my story and look her in the eye. And I think what she says is the biggest, deepest abrazo I've ever received.

"If you can get it," she says, "love's the thing to have."

And after I clean up and wash the dishes we sit together at the table for a long while, comfortable and quiet. The candles are still burning, and I'm watching the light come through the tight kitchen window and dance off the glasses that are drying on the counter, making them shine and spread their fragile glow around.

I've been thinking on love. All kinds. How I've felt it, given and received it. Chased after it, lost it, wrecked it, and walked away from it. I have loved and been loved. Ardently (good word). Steadily. Messily, foolishly, selfishly.

Is it a finite or boundless resource? Sustainable, like water or fish, depending on balance and care?

You can want and not get it. Feel it when you'd rather not. Want it, feel it, and not be able to choose it. And whatever folks say, it's rarely, if ever, unconditional.

Whatever kind it is . . . for your family, your lover, your friend, your people . . . there's the feeling and the talk, and then there's the showing. Love with accountability, like Baldwin wrote about. Jessie did her part to school me.

Love is a practice.

"When do you see the kids?" she asks.

"I'ma take them to the MFA this week. It's free after four on Wednesdays. It'll be my first time going there since Val took me, if you can believe that. Hope I know how to act. Hope I don't make a fool of myself. Hope Amara doesn't make a scene and we're the only Black people there, which won't surprise me. And even if she doesn't, and we aren't, I hope they don't treat us like those Black kids who went there on that school trip and got profiled." I'm thinking I'll check out what abstract art they've got there, see what sense I can make of it.

"Well," she says, "with all those things you're focused on, I hope you also enjoy looking at the artwork, since I guess that's the point of going. But you know what else, Ranita? You don't always have to take them somewhere or have a present for them."

"Yeah, I hear you. But I feel like I've got so much to make up for, so many things we've missed out on. Real outings, along with picnics in the park. The things other families do. And fishing, there's always that to aim for. But then school will be starting up in a minute, and their time won't be so flexible."

"I understand," she says, patting my hand. "But real, day-to-day life's not always full of . . . highs." She pauses to make sure I take that last part okay and then adds, "It's steadiness they need, and you they want, most of all."

Sitting here with Jessie, I'm remembering a time last summer, when I realized I felt content. That's not a feeling I'd ever been too familiar with, and I couldn't recall having had it for a good long while.

I was sitting outside, surrounded by walls and razor wire, the guard tower with its armed sentries in view, but I looked straight up and saw only sky, and I was not dazed or fiending or remorsing, not flying high or coming down, not doing anything really, except just being there.

I had that feeling with Maxine. And lying on the floor with my kids the other week, just before giving in to sleep. And even with all the shit I'm trying to keep ahold of, I've got it now. Sitting here with Jessie in the afternoon light, I've got it again.

After I fill up my water bottle and fold Jessie in a big hug, I say good-bye and start walking.

Outside there's always something new to notice, even on the routes I've walked a zillion times. Today I see a patch of thirsty marigolds someone must have planted near a plot of weeds and trash, and I empty my water bottle on them and imagine I can hear them sighing with re-lief. I see bits of city glass along the way and pocket a few colors I don't yet have. I stop to look at how a chain-link fence makes diamond shad-ows on the sidewalk, lift my eyes, and see a nest, high in the branches of a tree.

I keep on walking, marveling at the ordinary, all around. The mem-brane, holding us together.

When I come to a mailbox, I get the card from my backpack, and pulling open the handle, I say a prayer that it gets to Maxine intact and drop it in.

As I turn to head home, I feel something light and ticklish. A caterpillar's landed on my arm. Holding still, I check it out. When it turns it looks like one of those buses with the pleats in the middle. Articulated, I know from Theo's vehicle obsession, that's what it's called.

"You'll never make it over here on this path," I whisper. "You need a tree, where you can eat your fill and start on building your cocoon."

Picking it up real gently, I cup it in my hand. It panics, twisting, flipping over on its back, and then curls up and goes still, afraid, I'm sure, of my strange, enormous hand, of all the things that can and do happen in the big, wide, open world.

I choose a sturdy oak that's got full, thick branches and carry it over. And moving real slow, so as not to scare it or drop it, I lift my hand to a low branch and hold it steady while the caterpillar makes its way from hand to tree, sending it off with a silent wish that it'll know just what to do.

It might seem silly, but I feel good about this small act, and I watch it creep forward, going deeper, deeper into the green.

Focusing on my breath going in and out, I picture myself in the desert, wandering, until I notice the bowl partway submerged in sand. I pull it out. Shake it free. Sit and hold it, feeling the curve and the ridges in the warm, grainy clay. And it fills with cool, clean water, enough for a deep drink.

THIRTY-SIX

Tonight it's time for the monthly open mike again. I've been counting down the days.

Went to a session with Drew Turner this morning. Feels like I've been rubbing against a rock, trying to shed one skin after another, but at least there's been no monumental revelations in the last few weeks. Still, there's plenty left to explore.

When I started trusting him enough to open up and let him in, I thought he would sort me out and solve me. The only solution is through, not around. Just the way through.

My ghosts still rumble, but they've got less say, now that I can see and name them.

I guess it's a lifelong project, trying to be well.

After work I catch a meeting, and when I get home, I go to my little blue table and try to write out the story I'd like to tell, if I can get up the courage.

Then I fix myself some dinner, trying my hand at biscuits and greens. I'm stirring and chopping to music from the little Bluetooth speaker I splurged for, dancing around while I'm cooking. It feels okay. It feels better than okay. It feels good, and when I sit down with my place mat and cloth napkin at my little reclaimed table to feed myself, I'm smiling.

While I'm soaking in the tub, I think about the story I wrote down. And after I'm clean and dry and lotioned, I set my hair free and work my eye makeup and pick my deep-red lipstick. Then I put on all black. It's hot out, but I don't do skirts, so I choose black linen pants I got at T.J. Maxx, hand-me-down sandals from Jessie, a sleeveless top and a light jacket I found on consignment, chuckling at how I look like a wannabe ninja.

Heading back to the open mike, I feel scared and hopeful. I've gone in there once and I can do it again. I make no promises about getting onstage, but I'm ready if the spirit moves me.

When I get there this time, I don't see Eduardo out front, and my heart sinks a little. Wanting to make sure I get a seat, I go through the door and walk past the bar by myself this time, and yeah, everyone who's drinking still looks looser and more carefree. Something I'll never stop noticing. Or missing.

I take a seat, moving into the center of the row.

Tonight's MC is wearing a T-shirt with *Black Queer Lives Matter* in rainbow letters across the front. When she says, "Welcome to the Queer People of Color 'If You Can Feel It You Can Speak It' Open Mike," and she's hoping folks are fired up to share their stories tonight, it feels like she's talking to me. Her energy's so electric she's practically glowing, and she's got a lovely face, one that looks like it's seen its share of living, and she seems real comfortable in her body.

Some people already put their names on the list, and she asks them up to the little platform stage. Like last time, they're a mix.

I listen to a studly-looking sista who starts off shy but gets more and more comfortable and really builds up steam with a poem about all the things purple means to her: her nine-month sobriety chip, the color of the bearded irises her wife grows, the color of her first bicycle, her queer pride. "I always try and wear something purple," she says, pulling up the bottom of her pant leg to show a sock.

A hard, macho-looking man rhymes about the power of a really good kiss.

A trans Dominicano performs a piece on what it's like to have male privilege after a life of being talked over and sidelined.

As I'm listening, awed like last time by these fearless folks, I'm wondering what it will take for me to stand up there and open my mouth. I'm wishing I was not alone.

The next one announces their pronouns and talks about finding pleasure after your body's been someone else's playground. It's close to home. I can see how near the surface their pain is, and I'm so tense I'm not even breathing as they wrap their story up.

Maybe they're not fearless. Maybe they're just as afraid as I am and they step up anyway.

I work at getting still and calm enough to hear my breath, trying to let go of wishing for Maxine and her courage. My song, my story, it's up to me.

When MC Electric Cutie Pie says, "Last call for performers," I sit here, heart pounding, halfway hoping someone else will volunteer. And then I raise my hand. I get to my feet and say, "Excuse me," inching past the knees of all the people in my row, and once I'm on the little platform stage I want to holler, *What the fuck was I thinking?* I want to step back down and either struggle back to my seat or head for the door. But it seems like my body knows what to do until my mind catches up, and I'm still standing here, at the mike.

I look out at the room and folks look back at me, open and warm, and I decide to just receive that, and let go of how I'd look to my family, dead and living, and to all those who've asked for submission and silence in my 36-year life. Here I am. And these people in this room, they look like they want to hear me, and might even like me once they do. Their stories are thrumming through me, and mine feels like it's lit up and beating inside me, waiting to be heard. I almost shout when I see Eduardo standing at the back against the brick wall. I barely know this brotha, but for some reason, I wanted him to see me up here, telling where I've been.

"My name's Ranita, and I'm . . ." I pause, thinking of the statement that usually follows these five words, and hating the trembly sound of my voice. My heart's racing and my palms are sweating and my mouth has gone dry. I fight the urge to apologize, and begin again.

"My name's Ranita, and I have a little story to share." Being up here in front of all these people, their attention and expectations zeroed in on me, it's a whole lot. And now I'm stuck. The audience helps me out: "Take your time, baby. . . . It's all good. . . . We got you. . . ." From the back of the room, Eduardo calls out, "Go 'head, sista, tell it!"

Okay. I take a deep breath. "My story's about a pomegranate.

"My dad, he brought one home when our house was tight with grief that no one could face . . . or voice.

"He said we should wait to open it, and while the mystery was building I turned it, feeling the uneven places, the bumps and flatter spots. Working at patience, which has come to me the hard way, I've got to say, I touched the sharp little crown at the stem and tried to picture what would be inside.

"When we broke it open, it was more strange and glorious than I could have imagined.

"We spoke in whispers.

"So . . . I've been thinking about that pomegranate more than ever lately, and I can still see it, rough and scratched and not at all remarkable on the outside . . . and just beneath the skin, sinew binding it together, and chambers filled with winding layers of ruby-red jewels.

"Back then, it took me out, the wild design and beauty of it.

"My dad, he's spirit now. Gone and not gone. And that pomegranate he gifted me with, it's got a whole other meaning.

"I try and see myself as filled with ruby seeds. Everything I've lived, the things I've been and done . . . what's been done to me . . . and for me. The all of it, it's in me."

My voice catches and I pause.

"I look back, hard as that is . . . claim this now . . . imagine what might still unfold.

"And I wonder what's buried in that heart of yours."

When I step off the stage, I can't believe I did it. My legs are rickety and I feel relieved, triumphant, exposed. The applause lifts me like an ocean wave.

MC Electric Cutie Pie says, "We're done for the night, but keep coming back," just like in The Rooms, and I start making my way to the far end of the space, but people keep stopping me to say thanks for sharing and they liked my story and it really hit home. When I get to Eduardo, he bows, of course, and says, "There was nothing little about that story, Miss Ranita. It was fire. And you're looking fierce in your black."

One of his crew offers to buy me a drink to celebrate, and I say, "Wish I could go there, but I can't." From the way he's watching me answer, I think Eduardo's a fellow struggler. Standing with me under the queer umbrella, and the recovery one, too. I hang with them, enjoying the warm, playful bond they've got with each other, touched by their welcome to the fold.

When the music starts, folks take to the dance floor. Though Eduardo and his posse step right out there, I'm tempted to hug the wall, feeling shy after getting up onstage in view of everyone. Besides, no one has asked me for this dance. But I take a deep breath and leave the shoreline.

Solo, but not alone.

I move with everyone around me and feel the music pulsing through my body. In my arms and legs, torso and head and neck, waist and shoulders, blood and bones and skin. Every bit of me is here now and mine to give, to the music, to the moment, to my people, to my story.

I do a dance of declaration and defiance, until I'm drenched with sweat.

After I say my good-byes, I'm happy to be out in the late summer air, walking free. I'm noticing the trees and the night sky, smelling a hint of rain, speaking to the folks I pass. I'm playing back the stories I heard, and reliving my own moment of truth.

Here I am, alive and awake. Still going forward and backward. And brave enough to tell about it.

ACKNOWLEDGMENTS

To those of you who helped me to earn this story by sharing your experiences with me, I am immeasurably indebted: The men who were part of the Houses of Healing Therapeutic Community at the Suffolk County House of Correction at South Bay. The men at Bay State Correctional Center who were part of the Growing Together program and the PEN New England Prison Creative Writing Workshop. The women who were part of the PEN New England Prison Creative Writing Workshop at South Middlesex Correctional Center. The women at the Bristol County House of Correction and Chrysalis House. The Art and Spirituality group at the Suffolk County House of Correction at South Bay. The men and women who took part in the Prison Empowerment Program at Suffolk County House of Correction at South Bay. The men of the African American Coalition Committee at MCI Norfolk. The men at the Hampshire County House of Corrections. The men who worked on creative writing with me at Coolidge House and the Court Assisted Recovery Effort (CARE) Program. Those who worked on creative writing at the Cardinal Medeiros Transitional

Housing Program and through Cancer Support Services at the Boston Medical Center. And those on the inside whose creative work I had the opportunity to read aloud at the Through Barbed Wire Fourth Friday Series at the Community Church of Boston.

Marilyn Buck, you live on in spirit, and I'm eternally thankful for your gift of the pomegranate.

To those of you who deepened the understanding that informed this book, I am so grateful: Peter Kane; Bob David; Arnie King; Mike Myers Sr.; the Rev. Renee Wormack Keels; Robin Casarjian; Jean Fox at Aid to Incarcerated Mothers and the women who worked on creative writing there; Kate Ramsay; Sheryl Pimlott and Kris Siefert of the Substance Abuse Research Center at the University of Michigan; June Clark of Plymouth, Michigan; Buzz Alexander and Janie Paul of the Prison Creative Arts Project in Ann Arbor, Michigan; Eden Williams; Justin Steil; Vanessa Tyson; Pam Werntz; Elisabeth Houston; Jenny Phillips; Rivka Solomon; Jamie Suarez-Potts; Arthur Bembury and Richard Smith of Partakers; the City Mission Society's Public Voice Project; and my comrades from the Annual Writers Conference of the William Joiner Institute for the Study of War and Social Consequences at UMass Boston and on the PEN New England Freedom to Write Committee.

Sam Williams, my deepest gratitude for your generosity, wisdom, and example.

I am thankful to those who helped this book come into being in all kinds of ways. For the practical support that made writing possible, for the love, the interest, the listening, the knowledge shared, and the help getting heard, I appreciate you. Some of you have been showing up since I first started trying to write about the lives of prisoners, and others have helped along the way: Charles Rowell and the *Callaloo* family, Randall Kenan, Dorothy Allison, Gerald Early, Ellen Miller, Jennifer Haigh, Tayari Jones, Robin Coste Lewis, Chris Castellani, Rob Arnold, Carla Du Pree, Cristina Rathbone, Meg Kearney, Lee Hope Betcher and Bill

Betcher, Tracy Slater, Jean Trounstine, Cristina Kotz-Cornejo, Claire White, Diane Schilder, Richard Hoffman, Kathi Aguero, Deb Katz, Kaia Stern, Sandra Ruffin, Aneeka Henderson, Alexa Berton, Noel Schwerin, Kishonna Gray and Kayland Denson, Towana Wright, Cheryl Brown and the Black Women's Literary Society, Clinch and Beth Steward, Ruthie Rohde, Wyn Kelly and Dale Peterson, Joaquín Terrones, Arthur Musah, Ruth Perry and William Donaldson, Monica Weed, Sheila Coleman, Dana and Ahmed Ayad, Michel DeGraff and Elena Geretti, Paul Butler, Renée Raymond, Abha and Mriganka Sur, and Kim Vaeth.

Thanks to my MIT colleagues in Women's & Gender Studies, Comparative Media Studies/Writing, the Office of Minority Education, the Faculty Newsletter, and beyond who took an interest in this book and supported it. Special gratitude to Sophia Hasenfus, Ken Manning, Ruth Perry, Abha Sur, Michel DeGraff, Elizabeth Wood, T.L. Taylor, Lisa Parks, Jim Paradis, Ceasar McDowell, Blanche Staton, Larry Sass, Amah Edoh, Kenda Mutongi, Lee Perlman, Justin Steil, and Danielle Wood. And Moya Bailey, thank you for *misogynoir*, one word that captures a world of experience.

Thanks to my comrades in My Sister's Keeper, especially DiOnetta Jones Crayton, La-Tarri Canty, Eboney Hearn, Ayida Mthembu, Tracie Jones, and Dyan Madrey. And to the fiction writing students I have come to know over my 28 years at MIT and through the Solstice MFA program; many of you have become cherished friends, and all of you have enriched me.

Thanks to my Black Friday community, especially Ceasar and Solmaz, and Terry and Larry, for helping me to carry on, and celebrate, with joy and connection and support. And to the Women of Color in the Academy community in the Boston area.

Boundless gratitude for your help with the manuscript: Karen Wulf, I could never thank you adequately for your midwifery; Terry Sass; Lynn Roberson; Kimberly Juanita Brown; Brenda Prescott;

Misty De Berry; Renée Raymond; Justin Steil; Marcus Agard; and Em Kessler.

Thanks to my agent, Jane Dystel, force of nature, for her belief and fierce advocacy; my editor, Michelle Herrera-Mulligan, for picking up the mantle with warmth and insight; and everyone from Atria, including Alejandra Rocha, Liz Byer, and James Iacobelli for their help making this book a reality. And thanks to Daniella Wexler for seeing the way forward and backward.

Thanks to my parents, gone and not gone. To my mother, Dorothy Hicks Lee, who gave me books and stories to see by. And to my father, George Ernest Lee, whose life work as a criminal defense attorney taught me that people's stories are complicated, many of us grow up without opportunities or choices, justice is a fiction for some of us, and we all deserve to be seen.

To my brother, George Victor Lee. I have always admired your artistry and creativity. We will always be bonded. Love endures.

To my son, Jordan Sekani Lee, beautiful from the inside out. I am blessed by your radiance, your artistic talent, and your gift for reading the world.

To the ancestors who inspire me, and to all the storytellers whose words have nourished and guided me, infinite praises.